I AM JAYYN is a work of fiction. Apart from well-known actual people, events and locales that figure into the narrative, all names, characters, places, and incidents either are the product of the author's imagination or are used fictitiously. Any resemblance to actual persons, living or dead, events, or locales is entirely coincidental.

Cover photo: https://www.vecteezy.com

Library of Congress Control Number: TXu 2-406-169

Printed in the United States of America

ISBN Paperback: 979-8-9920334-0-3

ISBN eBook: 979-8-9920334-1-0

---

https://peter-d-brown.com

Contents

Part Three - Charles Town

"On my brave heart is engraved
The sorrow hidden from all eyes:
The son of a land enslaved,
Lives for it, suffers and dies."

Marti, Jose, "A Sincere Man Am I."
In *Simple Verses*, 1891

"I would permit no man,
no matter what his color might be,
to narrow and degrade my soul
by making me hate him"

Booker T. Washington

PREFACE

In late May 2023, Florida's State Board of Education went public with their proposal to control the way U.S. history is taught in Florida's classrooms. Changes to the new standards sought to prevent teachers from "indoctrinating" students.

Part and parcel of Governor Ron DeSantis' Stop Woke Act, the proposal seeks to eliminate what is known as 'critical race theory' from Florida's classrooms. Critical race theory holds that racism is far more than individual biases and prejudice. It recognizes that, through a history of chronic racism, racism has become systemically embedded within American laws, policies, and institutions.

As much as some hate to admit it, critical race theory is real; it is the truth, and it exists. Slavery and its attendant racism are irrevocably part of the cultural bedrock from which our society and its institutions grew and can't be ignored.

On July 19th, 2023, Florida's State Board of Education approved new K–12 standards for teaching African American history.

Although the changes may seem subtle, they have significant implications. For instance, previous standards asked students to *evaluate* the *contributions* of African American individuals. This has now been changed to ask students to merely *identify* African American individuals.

What's the difference? It has only recently been discovered—as late as the 1970's—that cultivation of rice in America would not have happened without expertise brought by slaves taken from the Guinea

Coast region of Africa. The European colonizers under King Charles II simply had no idea how to make rice grow in the Province of Carolina. Successful development of this crop created one of the most profitable economies in the world at the time, which in turn funded the colonization of America. This happened *because* of the *contributions* of enslaved Africans. This fact was hidden from history for over three hundred years. The colonists claimed this achievement as their own, and that's how history was written and passed down.

It wouldn't be until Peter Wood's landmark book, *Black Majority: Negroes in Colonial South Carolina from 1670 through the Stono Rebellion*, (1974), that the world would finally understand that it was Africans who brought the expertise for designing and building the major earthworks, dams, and irrigation systems that made rice cultivation possible in America, not the Europeans. Africans contributed their *sophisticated knowledge and skills* to the building of America, not just their physical labor.

Failure to credit African Americans for their contributions to America's success is complicit in forming the roots of systemic racism. Its branches and tentacles spread far and wide, creating massive conditions of inequity and disadvantage for African American citizens.

The amended teaching standards further require, when teaching the history of slavery, including "how slaves developed skills which, in some instances, could be applied for their personal benefit."

The implication here is to suggest that enslavement conveyed benefits to the enslaved, a falsehood perpetuated by our forebears for hundreds of years to justify slavery. The truth is these people were kidnapped, taken from their homes and families. They were tortured, killed, deprived of any rights whatsoever. They were worked to death in thankless service to their abductors. They were bred, bought, and sold like chattel by those with no right to own any human being.

The standards also require teaching that Blacks were complicit in perpetrating violence during Reconstruction and beyond. Examples include: the 1906 Atlanta Race Riot, 1919 Washington, D.C. Race Riot, 1920 Ocoee Massacre, 1921 Tulsa Massacre, and the 1923 Rosewood Massacre, all racially motivated incidents incited by white citizens, many in which Black citizens were blatantly massacred. Per these standards, we're to teach how the victims should share the blame.

These are all unacceptable alterations to history. Fundamental facts like these are crucial for future generations to learn the truth of history and cannot be omitted or distorted. There's nothing "indoctrinating" about the truth. We've come too far, from the Civil War up through the civil rights movement, to take such backward steps.

What you have read so far describes my motivation to write this novel. This story examines the realities of the Transatlantic Slave Trade, its injustice, and the suffering of its victims. It further acknowledges the contributions of African Americans.

The enslaved generally didn't keep many written records of their experiences. Their stories were mostly passed down through word of mouth from generation to generation. Therefore, this story recreates what such an experience might have been like by tracing the life of an enslaved African with the fictional character, Jayvyn. In doing so, I realized my characters would have to have factual and real attributes. I would need to understand as much about their circumstances as possible if I hoped to achieve even a rudimentary sense of what their experience would have been like. I have done my best to research my characters' African heritage, their journeys and experiences during the time period I chose: the early 1700's. As well, I have been as thorough as possible with regard to correctly portraying historical facts surrounding the European slave trade during this period.

I have spent much time getting to know Jayvyn, but as it must always be when one endeavors to fully assimilate another's life, I feel I have left many stones unturned. Not having had the grave misfortune to live it for myself, there's no way to truly understand the horribleness of his experience. I am thankful, however, to have taken this journey with Jayvyn. It has been educational, heartbreaking, and uplifting—maybe not in the joyous sense—but in the hopeful sense that human beings, with all of our imperfections, *can* prevail in discovering better ways to coexist in a world that continually conspires to prove otherwise.

Jayvyn has taught me many things I will carry with me for the rest of my life.

I hope, after reading this book, you will feel the same.

Part One

The Middle Passage

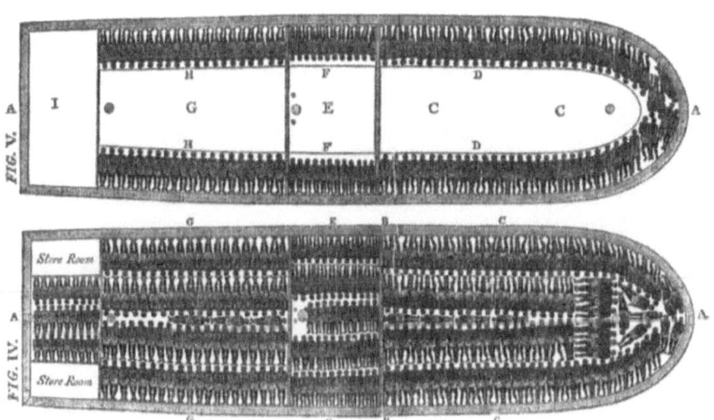

- 1 -

Taken

Foni Kansala,

Kiang West,

The Gambia, West Africa

circa 1710

Soft moonlight kissed the early dawn, its silvery glow bathing giant leaves, casting shadows across the forest floor.

Stillness reigned, but for the silhouette of a lithe African boy as he slipped quietly among the fronds.

Jayvyn inhaled the sweet morning air tinged with mist emanating from the Bitang Bolon—a narrow branch of the Gambia River teeming with fish. The moist, cool flora of the forest floor invigorated the bottoms of his feet as they lightly touched down. He never traveled far from his home, but this area was frequented by the people of his small village, and he knew it well.

Every morning, Jayvyn rose early for his morning run. He needed to be ready for the *futampaf*, the ceremonial rite of passage required of all *Ajamatau*. Upon passing this test, he'd officially transition into manhood, becoming a fully-fledged member of his tribe. He'd never witnessed the futampaf and couldn't know when it would happen. He'd only heard the stories told by his father and the elders, as it is only held when Caksusa, the village wiseman, has seen the time is right.* His father had passed his futampaf many years ago and would be very proud when Jayvyn passed his. It was important he be ready.

Birds flitted about the dense jungle flora, colorful plumage striking a vivid contrast against the dark green foliage. Avian cries resonated sharply against the morning calm. Other small creatures scuttled quickly through the undergrowth as Jayvyn ran quietly along his chosen path.

The complex forest aroma was intoxicating. Jayvyn breathed it fully into his lungs—a fragrant mix of aromatic flowers blended with sweet fruits and earthy tannins.

He relished being the only human in the forest at this enchanted hour; however, he was far from the only primate. Monkeys scampered among the high branches, wild barks from baboons occasionally broke the dawn air. The forest was alive in the morning, conferring on Jayvyn a profound sense of oneness with his world.

He awoke before anyone else, often just as dawn's first light surrendered the silhouettes of trees against the deep indigo sky. Snores emanated from the mud and grass huts as he quietly stole into the dark wall of the surrounding jungle. It was a magical time. He always looked forward to returning, refreshed and alive, to join his parents and little sister, Ifetayo, for breakfast.

Today is going to be a great day! He looked forward to helping tend

---

* *The ritual futampaf is only held every fifteen or thirty years, the time being decided by the elders*

the paddy to make sure this year's would be a good harvest. Jayvyn loved working with his father; he was a good teacher. He always took time to explain every intricacy of whatever subject they were exploring. His father was someone he very much wanted to be like.

Jayvyn's whole family, as well as most others in his village, was engaged in growing rice. The men usually tended to the preparation of the ground and the creation of new paddies, while the women took care of planting, harvesting, and processing the grain. All chipped in with the necessary weeding and other duties during the growing season.* In his village, a man's wealth was determined by his harvest, and Jayvyn was proud his father had always enjoyed good standing.

Quickening his pace, Jayvyn rounded the familiar bend signaling he'd soon be nearing his village. The sun had come up above the horizon now. Fresh dew sparkled the low-lying vegetation, refracting the sun's rays in quick flashes of colored light, like so many jewels scattered across the crisp, clean forest floor.

As he neared, Jayvyn heard what, at first, he took to be the sound of waking chatter and bustle from his village. But as he drew closer, something didn't feel right; things didn't sound normal. He heard yelling, screaming, and unusual voices. Heavy objects cracked and thumped; men of his village shouted urgently; women and children screamed. An explosion ripped the air. He smelled smoke—not the sort that came from the morning fires, but different—acrid and much thicker.

Slowing his pace, his peaceful feeling quickly became replaced with mounting fear and anxiety. *Something is terribly wrong!* Adrenaline

* *Rice cultivation is traditionally separated into gender roles in many parts of West Africa*

coursed through his veins as he crept slowly along the remaining section of trail. Indistinct shadows of men flashed and darted past open spaces in the foliage. Terrified shrieks erupted from his tranquil village.

Leaving the trail, Jayvyn hid in the bush at the edge of the clearing. Men he'd never seen before swarmed through the huts, tackling everyone—friends, mothers, fathers, uncles, elders—all of them! Fire and smoke leapt through thatched roofs. Some of the village men desperately tried to protect the others.

He looked over to his family's hut and saw his father, whom he'd never known to be a fighter, madly wield his hoe at an attacker. His father hit the man, knocking him to the ground. Suddenly, from behind, a heavy knife fell, slicing deeply into his father's shoulder.

Jayvyn knelt, paralyzed with fear as his father fell to the ground, blood running heavily from the wound. He looked on helplessly as his father tried to roll over and face his attacker, but the large blade came down, again and again, indiscriminately slashing his father until he lay still, a dark crimson ring blooming across the dirt.

His mother screamed.

She was being dragged, bruised and dirty, by her hair. His four-year-old sister, Ifetayo, cried hysterically as she, too, was pulled along by one arm. It was too much for his twelve-year-old eyes. Jayvyn couldn't move for the terror he felt. *What is happening?*

A sudden jolt knocked him on his side, a massive boot landing heavily on his neck. He hadn't heard or seen the man approach from his left. He looked up to see a pale face ringed in matted beard. It bristled with menace—teeth clenched, eyes glaring like a wild beast.

This man was a demon, like nothing Jayvyn had ever seen before. His hair was tan and his skin white, almost the shade of the moon.

The man jerked him to his feet, painfully twisting his arm behind his back. He tried to resist, but the man's grip was like iron; he was much too strong. Jayvyn fought for his footing, thorns tearing at his flesh as he was dragged roughly from the bush.

As he twisted and wrenched, the man hardened his grip, yanking Jayvyn's arm higher. Fiery pain shot through his shoulder as the powerful white ogre drove him forward across the dirt to where others from his tribe stood. Terrified, Jayvyn looked out across his now burning village. At least twenty tribal members lay dead, or very nearly, in pools of their own blood.

Strange white men were binding his people's hands together with rope. Soon Jayvyn's hands were tied as well. The group of survivors appeared to be about thirty, all as frightened as him. Men, women, children, babies—bewildered, quaking and crying—not knowing what had just occurred.

Hemp scraped roughly over Jayvyn's neck as the captors' bound him in line. Long, forked wooden poles were fastened between the necks of the men, forcing them to stay apart from one another.*

Jayvyn briefly glimpsed his mother and little sister tied some fifteen or so back. He was about to call out when the rope around his neck gave a sudden jerk, causing him to stumble. His feet reluctantly began to move as the group was pushed down a trail recently trampled by the invaders.

---

* *Long forked poles, or yokes were used to separate men in the lines, or "coffles" as they were marched from their homes*

The village crackled behind as they trudged forward; the dead and dying left where they lay. Jayvyn glanced back for a final time to see his father's unmoving form—the only home he'd ever known burning in the background. Bitter wisps of smoke briefly followed as they penetrated the thick primeval undergrowth.

They walked for hours as the day grew hotter, steam rising from the jungle floor. Any who tried to speak or call out were abruptly hit by the captors. They quickly learned they weren't to talk and should obey lest they endure further pain.

A few fell and couldn't go on, but instead of being helped, were mercilessly beat until they either got up or lay dead.

A woman from his village fell from fatigue and shock—the mother of a child Jayvyn's little sister played with often. A kind woman, always smiling, always bringing joy and laughter to those around her.

Jayvyn watched, paralyzed with fear, as a white man, wielding a thick stick, promptly descended on her. He yelled at her, hitting her several times as she tried to defend herself.

Her husband and young child screamed desperately for him to stop, but were unable to go to her. With his neck tied fast to the log and hands bound tightly in front of him, her husband could do nothing. He watched, crying helplessly, as his wife's suffering continued.

The woman, bleeding badly from her head, stumbled in a daze several times as she fought to get to her feet. But the man had hit her too hard. She sat, stunned and sobbing, as the white man untied her from the group. He then swung his stick hard, bashing her in the head several times, until she lay unmoving in the blood-tainted verdure surrounding her. Her husband and child howled with terror as they watched.

Others stood wide-eyed and helpless at the horror they'd just witnessed. Her husband and child, wracked with heaving sobs, were shoved roughly ahead, stumbling blindly down the path; the lifeless woman left where she fell.

Many hours later, they came to a clearing along the massive Gambia River, somewhere downstream of Jayvyn's village. Long wooden boats lined the shore. More white men, as well as other groups of bound, bewildered Africans, watched as Jayvyn's group emerged from the jungle. They were being loaded into the boats, which then merged with the river's swift current.

Confused and tired, Jayvyn winced as the coarse rope chafed again across the inflamed skin of his neck. Once released, a man seized him by the shoulders and pushed him toward one of the waiting boats. He was made to kneel, hands tied before him, on the hard, wooden floor of the boat amongst several other captives. White men sat at each end, weapons at the ready.

Jayvyn glanced around in a panic, trying to spot his mother and little sister, as his boat left the shore. He caught a fleeting glimpse just as they were boarding several boats behind. Jayvyn's boat then met the current, quickly increasing the distance between them.

The thick jungle canopy passed steadily over their heads, bright sun glinting through the open spaces where treetops failed to obscure the sky. A million flashes of light danced upon the moving waters.

A startled flock of guiriri stood motionless in an adjacent marsh, heads held high in frozen anticipation as the boats rounded one of the river's many sharp bends. When the boats got too close, the whole flock rose as one, emitting the shrill, whistle-like cries for which they're named.

Unperturbed, a black umbrella egret continued its stealthy march along the river's edge. Splayed wings curved mysteriously over its body to shield the light's reflection as it searched for juvenile fish.

Jayvyn absently noticed a far-off trio of hippos, slowly meandering, partially submerged, along the shallow waters inside a particularly large bend. Dense thickets of mangrove and palm choked the shore.

The sun, now starting its downward arc toward the horizon, cast growing shadows over the wide river.

The man whose wife was brutally slain knelt, head down, sobbing. His young, now motherless, child clinging at his knee—terrified, bewildered—mouth fixed in an agonized frown ringed with tearstained dirt.

After a long journey down the wide, serpentine river, they finally reached a great clearing with what seemed an unlimited expanse of water beyond. Jayvyn had never seen the ocean before. It stunned him to see water extending to the horizon and as far as he could see to either side.

After beaching their boats on the shore, the villagers were unloaded and stood looking uncertainly at their surroundings. A very large space, surrounded by a tall fence, dominated the clearing. Many white men stood outside the fence.

A large number of Blacks, none of whom Jayvyn had ever seen

before, stood inside. In fact, he'd never seen so many people in one place before. They were all tied and looked as his group did—beaten, confused, and scared.

Soon Jayvyn's group was pushed into the great fenced-in area. The ropes between them were removed, but their hands remained tied. Once inside, he saw the captors separating them into new groups. One contained men, one contained women, one had boys of similar age and size, another had girls.

Jayvyn briefly caught a glimpse of his mother and little sister as they were led into the corral. He called out once, but his view was blocked as they were separated into different groups. He hadn't even been able to speak to them since the moment they were taken. Everything had happened so fast.

Groups of white men moved through the pen, taking everyone's clothing away. With shears and razors, they cut and shaved off all their hair. Some put up a fight, but those who resisted were immediately and severely beaten with clubs. Some didn't get up but lay still where they fell.

They were defenseless against these white monsters, who would brutally kill if provoked.

Soon, they were left standing completely naked and shaved amongst each other without a shred of dignity. Jayvyn was mortified with embarrassment for himself as well as others.

Groups were being forced down a narrowing, fenced corridor toward men with hammers and tools sitting by hot fires. Their ropes were being removed, and strong iron rings hammered around their ankles. A short chain then connected one captive's ankle to another's.

The men had their hands bound together with iron bracelets; another iron ring was fixed around their necks. Sparks erupted as the hammers fell, like the sparks from new wood tossed on a roaring fire.

Then a new tool was taken from the fire—red hot—and pushed into their backs while two or more white men held them firmly against a tree trunk.* Piercing cries of pain rang out as a thin trail of smoke rose off their backs. Something was then rubbed over the spot, and the men were led to one of several large, heavily guarded stockade pens.

Jayvyn noticed others being led to open boats waiting along the shore, where they were made to sit or kneel. He saw these open boats moving across the water towards giant ships standing off in the distance. Each boat left fully loaded with captives, probably twelve or more to a boat. White men rowed and stood watch over them, brandishing weapons to ensure their obedience. The open boats returned with only white men.

He looked in awe at the ships in the distance. They looked like enormous wooden islands with large trees connected by many ropes in bizarre patterns. Instead of the usual canopy of leaves, white cloth bundles were tied here and there; smaller colored ribbons waved in the breeze from their tops. Men moved to and fro on the surface, like so many termites on a mound.

Suddenly, a strong hand pushed Jayvyn forward, down the narrowing corridor, toward the men by the fires.

**Slaves were routinely branded like cattle, often many times over the course of being transferred from one owner to the next*

He lost his rope bondage, promptly replaced by an unyielding iron ring around his ankle. The hot ring scorched his tender skin as hammer blows fell hard against his thin bones. A strong, short chain tugged on his ankle as he became attached to another boy he didn't know. He was about Jayvyn's size and looked as frightened as he was. The boy, like him, was scuffed with dirt and had scratches and bruises from the rough handling of his captors.

As a pair, they were shoved forward and held against the tree trunk by two strong white men. A third stood behind with the red-hot branding iron. The boy attached to him winced and stiffened in pain. The boy's flesh sizzled; a sickening acrid stench attacked Jayvyn's senses. Before he could think any more, the fiery iron pressed into his own back. Jayvyn instinctively recoiled, as if a thousand hornets had stung in one place. Held firmly to the tree by men on both sides, he cried out, tears welling up in his eyes. It was over in a matter of seconds. Soon after, someone rubbed oil—it was palm oil, Jayvyn realized from the familiar smell—on both of their burns.

From watching the others, Jayvyn knew they'd next be herded to one of the stockades. Once again, he turned, desperately trying to spot his mother and little sister, but couldn't pick them out among the many.* He didn't have much time to look as they were promptly shoved into a stockade.

Jayvyn, now chained to the other boy, stood amongst many others in the pen. No one was familiar. Everyone was strange and

---

**Care was taken to separate slaves from their families and other relations in order to remove them from their support, culture, heritage and to strip them of their identities.*

spoke in tongues he couldn't understand. White men stood around the enclosure, threatening to beat anyone who dared resist. It was as if they were livestock, not humans. In fact, they were packed more tightly than any prudent farmer would keep his livestock.

Jayvyn and his ankle mate eventually settled onto the dirt, exhausted and in shock. The fresh, blistering burns on their backs throbbed in pain as darkness fell around them. Minutes passed like hours.

Endless images assaulted Jayvyn's traumatized mind. Images too horrible to have imagined before—his father's terrified face as the long, heavy knife came down; his village in flames; his mother and sister being dragged and bound; the woman bludgeoned to death.

The ring on Jayvyn's ankle felt hard and cold, the skin of the boy attached hot against his own. The smell of sweat and sour breath filled the air. Metal grating on metal mixed with the groans of those around him as the long night crept slowly by. Jayvyn quietly wept until he could weep no more, his tears long since dry. He listened as others around him did the same.

In the morning, water was poured into a large bucket, which many clamored to drink from. None had anything to drink since their capture and were desperately thirsty. It was a while before Jayvyn and his mate were able to slake their parched throats somewhat. Later, a mixture of boiled rice and meal was dumped into a trough. Men and boys groveled on hands and knees, shoveling the bland mixture into their mouths. It was hardly food, but their bodies craved calories lost over their ordeal.

Indeed, it seemed they were now animals, or even less.

They sat in the enclosure through the long, hot day and into the night, only to be held again the next day and for several after. Jayvyn couldn't say how many days and nights had passed, but it seemed interminable. Time itself wasn't recognizable anymore.

When anyone spoke, white or Black, Jayvyn couldn't understand. He only saw expressions in their faces—expressions of anger and grief. They just sat and lay, chained to one another, naked and dirty, inevitably urinating and defecating wherever they could in the confined space.

Death was everywhere. Jayvyn had seen several perish, whether from injury, dehydration, or stress, whereupon they were unceremoniously removed and discarded in piles outside the stockade. The smell was unbearable: a vile mixture of sweat, feces, urine, and rotting flesh.

Every so often, captives were removed alive and new ones were added.*

The hot, sweltering days passed slowly as Jayvyn and his ankle mate sat in the large pen. Food and water were occasionally brought, but otherwise they just stood, or sat naked in the dirt, waiting... for what?

All Jayvyn knew was his once peaceful world had been inexplicably shattered, his village burned, villagers he'd known his whole life, including his father, slaughtered. He'd been separated from everything he'd ever known. Now he sat in a wooden pen, shackled to a boy he didn't know, crowded with many other strange Africans,

---

* *Slaves sometimes waited months in captivity before being loaded on ships as captains sought to maximize their loads.*

all frightened, wondering what was going to happen to them.

Eventually, Jayvyn and the boy attached to him were removed from the stockade and taken to the beach, where they were forced to sit and wait being loaded into the open boats.

Jayvyn had time, while sitting in the sand, to look around at his surroundings. He saw the process he'd just been through continuing all along the shore.

The awful stench of the stockades permeated the air. Heaping piles of bodies sat off to the side. Limbs draped over limbs in random patterns from being tossed, like so much brush, onto the growing pile. Heads lay at odd angles, eyes vacant, jaws slack, flies crawling unopposed.

Jayvyn was glad to be out of the terrible stockade but afraid of what was yet to come. Once again, he noticed the great islands of ships standing offshore.

Soon, Jayvyn and his ankle mate were put into one of the open boats, where they knelt on the floor with many others as white men rowed and stood watch over them. The boat rocked slightly as it left the shore, a few splashes of water wetting and cooling Jayvyn's skin. Gulls soared overhead, occasionally emitting loud screeches in the wind.

As the shore receded, the whole encampment where they'd been came into view. He could now see the enormous holding area where they were first held and the fires of the men with shackles and branding irons. He saw new groups of Africans, still with their hair and clothing, being marched into the clearing. It reminded him all at once that he, too, had recently and inexplicably been swept from his home.

Looking in the other direction, Jayvyn saw the immense ships drawing close. He looked back toward the receding shoreline of his home once more and wondered where his mother and sister were.

Everything became chaos again as they were loaded aboard the giant wooden ship. Jayvyn barely noticed much about the ship before being roughly herded below the surface, into a very dark, small space. He and the boy attached to him were forced onto a wooden platform suspended halfway between the ceiling and the floor. They had to lie on their backs, ankle chains fastened to the boards they were lying on.

Other boys surrounded them, packed shoulder to shoulder, for as far as he could see. The ceiling was only inches away; sitting was impossible. A mixture of breath and sweat collected in the claustrophobic space.

Moans of distress and anguished cries of pain filled the air. Jayvyn hadn't noticed for the sudden darkness but sensed they'd passed many others along the way. No words were heard in the fetid space. No air moved the stench of sweat and fear. Only suffering, bewildered sobs broke the silence.

Long, agonizing hours passed; time remained elusive. *Was it day or night? How many days had passed?** Everything melted into a never-ending nightmare.

A foul-tasting concoction of some sort of grain mixed with animal fat was fed to them once a day; ladles of stale water were occasionally brought to drink. Jayvyn noticed a boy near him who

---

* *As with the stockades, once loaded on the ships slaves could wait many weeks or more chained in the holds before the ship sailed.*

refused to eat the awful gruel.

Someone came with a strange metal tool to force the boy's mouth open.* The gruel was then poured over his open mouth. The boy choked and spit, the captors yelling and smacking him the whole time. Much went to either side of his face and down his chin, some up his nose, but he must have inevitably swallowed some as he gagged and gasped.

Jayvyn wondered how long one could survive these conditions.

Who are these strange white men, what do they want with my people? They chatter and yell in a strange tongue; they have skin and hair that is different from mine; I've never seen clothing like theirs before; and they carry unfamiliar tools.

The heat in the space was stifling—air deadly still. Jayvyn lay on the hard, unyielding planks, mind wandering in a semi-coherent state.

Low sounds of chains being lightly dragged across wood periodically broke the silence as boys shifted in their confines. Rational thought was impossible to maintain.

Long, unending hours turned into days and nights.

Jayvyn had long ago both urinated and defecated where he lay, and he knew by the smell everyone else around him had done the same. Periodically, the captors came with buckets of salty water to slosh across them where they lay, apparently in an attempt to wash the defilement away.

It was, however, only somewhat effective, serving mostly just to dilute the putrid mess. The stench was overpowering, irritating Jayvyn's nose and throat, causing his eyes to water, forcing him to hold

---

* *The tool, called a speculum orum, was standard equipment on slave ships to prevent slaves from starving themselves*

his mouth shut against the vile, noxious odor.

Sporadic sleep, mixed with shadowy darkness, added surreal dimensions to Jayvyn's concept of time. It was impossible to know how long he'd been lying there or why.

As Jayvyn's mind drifted in the stale darkness, he thought back to his village elders and the wiseman, Caksusa.

He'd seen Caksusa perform many rituals essential to the village's wellbeing and prosperity. He made mixtures of things from the earth, plants, and animals, chanted in mysterious tones, and performed sacred dances only he'd been born to know. When it was time to plant, his wisdom and blessing were sought so the crop would grow to nourish their people. Before hunts, a ceremony was performed to give their hunters good fortune and protect them during the hunt. If a member of their village was sick or injured, he healed their infirmities, sometimes preparing a juju to keep in their home or wear.

Caksusa and the other elders told stories of things beyond Jayvyn's understanding—stories of great events both before and after their time—and of other villages near or far, where the people could be either friend or foe. There were many stories of warfare between villages. Jayvyn's people took great care to remain secluded because the Ajamatau did not seek conquest or warfare.* They believed their survival was assured by knowing the land and things that came from it, and so they kept to themselves.†

The last Jayvyn had seen Caksusa, he lay near his spiritual ground,

---

* *Many tribes were hostile to other tribes, which worked to the advantage of slavers; many times enlisting a tribe to capture rival tribe members to sell to the whites as slaves*

† *The Jola were not aggressive and preferred to avoid conflict with other tribes*

head crushed almost beyond recognition; his amulet of sacred stone, wood, and feathers lay upon his blood-soaked chest.

Jayvyn had been unable to comprehend the sight. Never had he thought such a thing possible. There were no stories about this—past, present, or future. And, of these new white people, they couldn't have come from a neighboring village because no tale bore their description. Surely, giant ships such as this, people of different color, and the fires that made their bondage would have been among those stories had they been witnessed before![*] There was no reckoning the situation Jayvyn now found himself in.

As he lay in the dark, dank space, Jayvyn wondered about the boy he was attached to. He didn't know him and wondered if he was from a hostile or friendly village. He heard him weep once in a while and could feel his fear and sweat. The boy muttered words to himself occasionally. He heard the words "Allahu Akbar,"[†] or something like that, and then a string of other words with a similar sound, but had no idea what any of it meant or why he was saying it to no one in particular. Jayvyn tried to speak to him in whispers a few times but got no response.

Jayvyn turned to look at the boy on the other side of him and caught his gaze in return. It seemed they were each searching the other's face for an explanation, but all they saw in return were tears of confusion staring back.

---

* *Other tribes may have been well aware of the slavers, but the Jola, being reclusive as they were, could likely have remained oblivious*

† *Islam was a prevalent religion among many tribes of Africa and the source of much conflict between tribes as well*

Jayvyn didn't feel afraid of these boys. He couldn't believe they'd be any threat over and above the threat he already felt. After all, whatever was happening to him was happening to *all* of them together.

He decided, from then on, he'd believe—although they spoke different languages and came from different tribes— they now had everything in common. They were all the same color, bodies shaved and bruised, all trapped in the same horrible situation.

From that point forward, he decided he'd think of them as brothers.

There were no more villages.

– 2 –

Anchors Aweigh!

Jayvyn lay drifting in and out of consciousness.

Days and nights rolled into one in the dark, foreboding hold. Stale air hung, like a heavy, wet blanket, encasing his body and limbs in its sticky, viselike grip. The hot African sun beat mercilessly down upon the decks, making the hold an unbearable inferno. The smallest undertaking exacted a debilitating toll.

He had no idea how many days had passed when a new commotion abruptly broke the silence. Men shouted. Jayvyn heard the sound of metal moving against metal, such as the bonds attaching him to his companion.

Shouting mixed with the sound of clubs on flesh. The captors were moving men from the adjacent section. He heard voices, along with footsteps, as the men made their way clumsily up the steep ladder. Footsteps moved above his head, clattering to and fro over the ceiling. Loud voices combined with other sounds into an unrecognizable din.

Something is happening! The clamor persisted in the neighboring section and he thought he heard women, although it was hard to tell; they were distant and all but drowned out by the men.

The tumult in the abutting section swiftly quelled as captors struck and beat the men into silence.

Hurried footsteps continued above. A new grinding noise was added—slow, rhythmic, rough, and heavy—which could be felt as much as heard, as if large stones were being dragged up the outside of the ship. When that subsided, it was replaced with voices of men giving commands.

Loud flapping, like large mats being shaken out, followed.

The whole ship lurched—its structural members creaking against themselves—moving as one beneath Jayvyn. He heard the rippling of previously still waters—moving gently, like a river's current—along the outside of the ship.

Everyone fell silent as they listened to these new sounds, wondering what it meant. The surface they were chained to tilted slightly, head down in Jayvyn's case, giving the sense that gravity itself was suddenly betraying him.

The commotion above eased and the drone of fear and anxiety resumed. Movement could not be denied. The whole thing—the whole ship they were a part of—was moving. They were going somewhere.

A new sensation struck Jayvyn along with the movement. It was the slight sensation of an intermittent breeze. He was getting a few whiffs of new air; it was cool and clean, and it was delicious!

The hot, dank, putrid air he'd been trapped in for so many days actually seemed to contain small ribbons of relief. It was fleeting and hard to hang on to, but it came consistently, in little spurts.

Jayvyn craned his neck, trying to find the next little bit of fresh air and avoid being plunged back into the crypt. The old smells and stifling air were still there, but these small whiffs of new air gave him hope—the smallest amount of hope, but hope nonetheless.

Jayvyn's mind drifted back to what felt like a distant, bygone time—just before the mayhem began—when he was running through his beloved forest. His heart ached as he recalled the freedom of his past world. He'd left his father, mother, and little sister peacefully sleeping in their hut that morning as he snuck out for his morning routine.

Jayvyn pondered how he'd watched a salamander creeping along a mossy fallen log, thinking they were both enjoying the same world, just from slightly different perspectives. It was a feeling he had whenever he happened upon wildlife going about its business. It was, after all, their world—he was the intruder.

He and his little sister Ifetayo enjoyed countless afternoons searching for frogs, beetles, snakes, or any manner of small creature for hours on end. Each became lost in fascination as they observed the ways these animals interacted with their worlds. They were always careful not to hurt or disturb them.

He fondly thought back to his father sharing in their discoveries, pointing out how one animal might change color to blend with its environment while another's bright colors were meant to warn off predators. Or how the bicher fish, which he also called the walking fish, can 'walk' out of the water on its fins and breathe air while it hunts on land for insects and other small creatures.

Animals were fascinating. Jayvyn's father showed them how much animals and other things in the wild had to teach them if they just watched and learned the reasons they did what they did. Most of all, they learned to respect and honor the enormous variety of living things they shared the world with.

Jayvyn sadly recalled how much he'd wanted to join his family to tend the crops that day. There was so much to learn—what a healthy rice plant looked like; what types of weeds were the worst; how much water should be in the soil at which stage in the crop's growth; when the rice was ready to harvest.

His mother taught him a lot, too. She knew the right way to plant new seeds, using her heel and toes to quickly make a hole, drop the seed in, and cover it over. She was equally skilled in how to harvest, thresh, and cook the grain when it was ready, working deftly to accomplish every part of the process—all while chatting cheerfully with the other women and girls.

Tending the crops, as with all other tasks in his village, was highly communal. It involved all of the tribal members at one point or another, creating fond memories for Jayvyn.

He'd always loved working with his father; he knew so much and was such a good teacher. It always seemed to Jayvyn as if he were the most important person in his father's world. His father enthusiastically shared all he knew about anything he happened to be teaching him. Sometimes they spent whole afternoons prying open hidden nuances of whatever they were exploring. He always spent as much time as he could with his father; there was seldom anything he craved more.

And then reality rushed in, like a cruel villain, snatching the moment away.

He recalled the other-worldly sight of his father being brutally hacked to death. He remembered his blood flowing all too thickly, his upturned face, the face that had meant only pure love and kindness to Jayvyn. He shuddered as he thought about his father's vain but courageous attempts to fight. He never had a chance. He was no match for his vicious attacker.

He tried to remember his father's voice, but couldn't. The last words uttered between them had been sometime the night before. Jayvyn didn't even know what was said. Now he wanted so badly to remember. But at the time, it was insignificant—just a light, passing conversation. He couldn't have known then it would be their last.

His mind began to swim. His arms involuntarily stiffened against the boys on either side as his throat and chest constricted with the familiar feeling that comes with deep sadness. His lips trembled uncontrollably, he breathed in, short and hard, through his nose. His eyes began to water. He didn't want to cry; crying is what babies do, and he was practicing to be a man; he needed to be a man.

Thoughts of his mother and little sister entered. He recalled the image of his mother being dragged by her hair—beaten and bruised—fighting to keep her feet under her, Ifetayo dangling by one arm from the large man's grip.

Deep longing for his home and family swelled, pressing hard inside his chest. He couldn't hold back any longer. The tears came unabated, accompanied by heavy, wracking sobs. *How could it be so much had changed so quickly? How could it be that men could be so cruel?*

Jayvyn opened his eyes, realizing he must have fallen asleep. It took several moments for perplexity and confusion to give way to the reality of his horrendous circumstances. He didn't know how long he'd slept, but he felt somewhat better for it. He wished he could have stayed asleep longer—to remain asleep for as long as it took this terrifying nightmare to pass.

The ship's motion was different. It was discordant. The tilt of his platform more profound, moving back and forth, up and down, jarring him from shoulder to shoulder. Every so often, a giant thud, followed by a great splash, reverberated through the ship's timbers. It was disorientating, especially in his dim confines.

A new smell had been added to the already putrid air. He heard boys on either side coughing and retching and realized all at once what it was.

Then he, too, began feeling an uncomfortable churn in his stomach as its contents started to rise. He fought the sensation as he looked to either side, seeing only the heads of the boys next to him.

He reflexively swallowed, over and over, his swallows coming quicker and more violently by the second. Sweat poured off his brow.

Jayvyn fought as hard as he could to prevent his stomach's cargo from disgorging, but it was no use; he was no match for the hot, putrid air, the motion of the ship, and the smell of vomit all around him.

He leaned as far forward as he could and spewed the hot mess all down his chest, spattering those on either side as well.

Jayvyn glanced quickly at the boy attached to him and saw he, too, was vomiting—bubbling and spitting out of his mouth, over his face, and wherever else it went.

A new rush of nausea consumed him, and he resumed puking until there was nothing left.

However, the violent contractions continued. His sweat was cold. His arms and legs shook uncontrollably. Spasms seized his entire body in sustained rigor, preventing his breathing until they finally relented. Nothing came up but thin, viscous spittle.

At some point, Jayvyn fell back, shivering and breathing

erratically, weaker than he could ever remember. He was too stricken to wonder what was going on as cold sweat continued to pour from his body. He felt as if he could neither remain conscious nor pass out, but instead just lay in delirium, helplessly chained to the platform.

The captors came with their buckets. With a mixture of laughter and disgust, they proceeded to throw cold, salty water on their faces and bodies. Still, Jayvyn couldn't so much as raise his head.

It took a long time to splash enough water to cover everyone on his platform. He heard this repeated on other platforms, as well as in more distant sections of the ship. All around, a collective low groaning filled the air; discomfort was palpable.

Time continued to pass slowly, as it had for several weeks now. Jayvyn and the others lay helplessly chained in place, the ship rolling and bucking unpredictably over the ocean swells. Food and water were brought, but often times didn't stay down long as the terrible sickness persisted.

Jayvyn became completely disoriented. Dark brown shadows danced across the ceiling, often the only clues to his surrounds as the ship crashed relentlessly over the swells.

Sleep, as before, came and went sporadically, further deteriorating the concept of time. Yet, the ship pressed steadily onward, its timbers creaking and moaning in the darkness.

As the days melted into weeks, Jayvyn's mind tumbled through a montage of imaginations from a world he recalled with varying degrees of clarity.

One moment he'd be thinking about his mother preparing dinner with his little sister at her side. He listened to the familiar sounds of his village—men returning from the hunt victorious, carrying strings of fish or a freshly killed bush pig.

At times, his imaginations were so real he could smell the sweet breeze wafting from the jungle and the aroma of cooking rice. He heard the sounds of men's laughter mixed with snapping twigs as the evening fires were kindled.

But his visions inevitably dissolved into unwelcome memories. His mother and little sister—hair mussed, dirt streaked, hands bound and tethered—stumbling blindly through the hot, steaming jungle—eclipsed by anxiety and panic as he tried to spot them before entering the stockade.

More than once, his mind filled with chaotic images of his burning village, bodies of elders strewn where stories were told and ceremonial dances held.

How much time has passed? Jayvyn wondered as he lay in the same position he'd been in for weeks. His bones ached, flesh raw from being jostled about on the hard wooden platform.

His only sensory markers came when the small door to their section suddenly burst open, scattering light as captors came with more foul food and water. If any refused to eat, their mouths were pried open and the mix forced in, causing many to choke uncontrollably as they swallowed. Cries of protest were of no use, often met with harsh slaps of a stick.

Javyn repeatedly lost track of where he was. He often felt he was trapped in a cave, somewhere deep in the ground. Several times, he felt completely alone, forgetting he was surrounded by others. The movement of the ship confused him, he wondered why the ground shifted when it should be firm. He couldn't understand why he was unable to get up and search for a way out.

The line between consciousness and unconsciousness became indistinguishable as his mind fought its deprivation from anything familiar. He was alternately gripped by terror and profound sadness. Dissociative thoughts assailed him with things he had no chance of understanding.

Concentration was impossible. It was as if his entire existence had devolved into a mush of incoherent, unrecognizable patterns and impulses.

Long, nightmarish stretches passed with no framework for time; a second could be a day. Distinguishing dreams from reality was hopeless. Reality had been replaced.

Jayvyn tumbled aimlessly in his capsule of isolation—relentlessly cascading through an unknown universe—a universe where man had no place.

- 3 -

Daylight

Day after unending day passed as Jayvyn jostled about in the stale, dark hold, oblivious now to the occasional intrusions of the captors when they came with food or to pour water over them.

The novelty of their circumstances had long ago run its course when, at some mundane point, the captors methodically began going from pair to pair, releasing the link holding their ankle chains to the platforms.

Some, released before Jayvyn, tried to get up but were brusquely knocked back to await further instructions. When a number had been released, they were pushed—at a crouch, since that's all the room there was—towards the door they'd come in so long ago.

Those released, including Jayvyn, were brought through the low door separating their compartment from the next and came to the steep ladder they'd descended when entering this cave.

Jayvyn's bones and muscles were seized and cramped from being held immobile against the hard surface for so long; he moved stiffly. Still being connected at the ankle to the other boy made walking cumbersome.

Going up the ladder was exceptionally difficult, a captor prodded and pushed from below. Upon reaching the top, strong arms seized each pair, yanking them, two at a time, up through the open hatch.

They were met with dazzling skies so bright they couldn't hold their eyes open.

The boys stood, eyes squinted, still trying to adjust and get a glimpse of their surroundings. Strange, squeaky music was being played by one of the captors using some kind of instrument he repeatedly squeezed between his hands. Another captor clapped and danced comically to this music. Two others stood in front of the bewildered boys, prodding and hitting at their legs with sticks the boys instinctively moved to avoid.

It was all very difficult for the bedraggled boys to understand as they dodged the blows, but eventually they figured out their captors wanted them to dance as the man before them was doing. They couldn't comprehend why, but with enough prodding and shoving around, they began to move their legs in a dance-like fashion, and the hitting relented.*

One boy in their group was very weak and fell, whereupon he was swiftly kicked and beat by a captor until he struggled to his feet. But he was unable to remain standing for long, much less dance, and staggered back and fell again. The captor grabbed him and stood him up again, where he wobbled in a daze as the boy attached to him tried to balance and hold him up. The boy, however, was too weak from all he'd been through and simply collapsed where he stood.

Unexpectedly, both boys were abruptly seized by the captors and dragged to the side of the ship.

The rest of the boys were then brought to the side as well. When the captors were sure they had their full attention, they grabbed on to

---

* *Slaves were made to dance as a form of exercise when conditions permitted*

the first two boys and unceremoniously tossed them over the side into the sea. Jayvyn and the others watched in shock as the two hit the water and struggled uselessly for several moments.

Out of nowhere, something dark and lean swam swiftly through the water. The sea exploded into a white froth as the creature violently thrashed around. A few feeble screams rang out, the water turning crimson with the doomed boys' blood. Almost instantly, several more of the creatures appeared out of nowhere as the hapless pair quickly drifted toward the back of the ship.

The boys on deck watched helplessly while the unfortunate boys were mercilessly torn to pieces. No more was heard besides the violent splashing of the creatures.*

Naturally, the boys on deck were deeply traumatized. They stood dumbstruck, quaking and petrified, hardly able to take in what they'd just witnessed, a few buckling at their knees. The captors merely laughed amongst themselves.

After a short while, the dazed boys were lined up again near the place where they'd danced. There was no more music, but instead the captors gestured to another, who briefly demonstrated what the boys were to do. Before him sat a large flat stone and two buckets, one with water and the other with sand. First wetting the deck, he then sprinkled sand. Following this, he took the stone and scrubbed it vigorously over the wood. When the darkened wood had lightened its

* *Since waste was constantly thrown overboard, it was common for sharks to follow ships across the sea. The practice of throwing slaves overboard for one reason or another was also common. There are many references to slaves being devoured by schools of sharks who were always nearby*

color, he threw more water over the spot to wash the remaining sand away.

The boys were then taken to separate areas, still shackled in pairs, where they got down on their hands and knees to scrub as they were shown. The rough stone tore at the skin on Jayvyn's hands. The sand bit into his bare knees as he struggled to push the heavy stone back and forth across the deck.

The captors strolled around inspecting their work, castigating anyone failing to achieve satisfactory results.

Jayvyn sprawled across the deck when one suddenly kicked him from behind, his chest landing hard on the stone in front of him. The boy attached to him suffered a hard blow from a stick, leaving a painful stripe across his back. Similar punishments were being delivered to others as they struggled with this exceptionally hard task in their depleted condition.

They did this, all the while thinking about the terrible fate of those boys, who just a short time ago stood among them. No one talked, or even made efforts to talk, as they stayed head down and scrubbed in silence, watching carefully for their captors' next move.

Like most of his experience so far, Jayvyn lost track of how long they'd been scrubbing, but his arms, knees, and back ached with stabbing pain. Just when he was certain he could endure no more, the boys were allowed to stop.

They sat dazed and depleted as a new white man approached. The other captors stood back a little when he did. This man wore different clothing from the others and carried himself with an air of superiority.

The boys were ordered to their feet and moved to stand in a line while this new man talked and gestured unintelligibly. They had no idea what he was saying, but the sense was he was checking in and inspecting the boys.

When the man was done talking, Jayvyn chanced to look around and saw nothing but water as far as he could see in any direction. There was no more land. The trees on the ship carried huge, white sheets that billowed in the wind, with many ropes attached to them.

Looking toward the back of the ship, he saw upper levels. These were barricaded behind thick netting stretched the full width of the ship along the top of a tall, blank, wooden wall. The only access appeared to be a single, narrow ladder with a gate at its top.

Closer to him and on his level, but still towards the back, was a similar wall with closed gates on either side preventing any access.* The exhausted boys were left to look around freely for a little while longer, but stayed in the space where they were.

Soon, they were led to a large container of fresh water with a ladle hooked to its edge and instructed to drink. As one boy finished his ladle, it was taken from him and passed to the next. After they'd all drank, they were made to sit again.

A large bucket of the awful gruel they'd been eating was then brought before them. The boys shoveled the gruel into their mouths using their hands while the captors mingled nearby. It was the worst food any of them could ever remember eating, but it was the only source of nourishment they had, and so they ate it.

---

* *Care was taken to protect officers and crew from slave attacks by creating effective barriers that fully blocked off areas of the ship*

When they were through eating, their captors began making gestures accompanied by words. Some were pointing to each other and declaring, "*say-lor*," and it was easy to see they wanted to give the boys a title by which to call them. A few of the boys tried it out and were rewarded with enthusiastic nods; however, there was no kindness apparent with this instruction.

They pointed to different parts of the ship: "*deck*" was the floor, "*masts*" were the trees, "*sails*" were the large billowing sheets above, "*line*" was the term for the ropes attached, "*water*" was their drink, and "*food*" was their gruel. There were more words, some more complex than others, and it would take time and practice to learn them all.

Then they pointed to the boys and said, "*slave*."

So that was what we are. Jayvyn thought, *we're to be called slaves.*

Nothing was good, but it was a small step better than what Jayvyn had been experiencing so far. He'd been released from the platforms and let into the bright of day, allowed to breathe uncontaminated air and feed himself. Plus, he was taught a few words so he could begin to understand his captors.

The group of boys were left to rest where they were for a little while, still under the guard of a "*sailor*," but none of them had any intentions of moving or trying to run.

Run? Run where? There is nowhere to run.

So, they sat, grateful they were, at least for the time being, in a different place than below "*deck*."

As Jayvyn sat there, he watched the "*sailors*" carry a few boys and men from below who appeared not to be moving, arms and legs hanging loosely from their sides, heads lolling on their necks. As they came up, these boys and men were arranged along the sides of the ship, where they lay motionless.

Jayvyn wondered at this for a while, but his sense told him these were ones who hadn't survived what he'd barely survived himself—these "*slaves*" were dead. In fact, he didn't have to wonder; he instinctively knew this was the case and had no doubt the others with him had come to the same conclusion. It was not a surprise.

Jayvyn's thoughts once again turned to his mother and little sister. *Where are they? Are they alive or dead? Will I ever even know? And what of the others from my village?*

He recognized no one and had no way to ask. Even if he tried among the group he now saw, it was unlikely they'd understand him as every tribe spoke a different language, and he hadn't heard a single word spoken in his tribal tongue. Jayvyn glanced at his ankle partner but could read nothing from his expression except what he saw in everyone else's face—pure confusion and despair.

But at least they were given the first clues to their survival. Listen to the white man and obey his orders; be as fit as you can be; stand when told to stand; dance when told to dance; scrub when told to scrub; eat when told to eat; don't defy them and their strange requests; and maybe, just maybe, you could survive to see another day.

Jayvyn thought again of the two unfortunate boys who were thrown to the sea and the horrifying deaths they'd faced. *One boy was not even impaired and was just trying to support the one shackled to him. He did nothing wrong at all, so why was he thrown so callously to his death? Why did the "sailors" stand there laughing as the boys were devoured by—what?—what were those awful creatures that came so fast in this infinite water? Why was any of this happening? And where were they going?*

As Jayvyn contemplated these thoughts, he heard the slightly familiar sound of another group of boys, ankle irons clanking, as they were being led from below into the bright light of day. As he had earlier, they came into the light stiff, confused, unbalanced, and unable to open their eyes.

Once this new group was moved to one side, Jayvyn's group was moved nearer to the hatch.

Jayvyn looked this new group of boys over, some of them with slack jaws and dead eyes, heads swaying back, barely standing on wobbly legs. He wanted to warn them, tell them what he'd seen, let them know not to fall down, to pay attention!

He wanted to share the awful story of the two boys who were thrown overboard, but this was not possible as his group was directed to the hatch and forced below—back into the dark, foreboding dungeon that had become the place of their worst nightmares.

The smell became more and more pungent as they neared, reminding all of them of the intolerable conditions awaiting them.

One of the boys in front of Jayvyn began to panic. He screamed and fell to his knees, clawing and grasping at the sides of the hatch, crying desperately not to return.

The blow came swift and sure from a nearby sailor's club across the boy's shoulders, followed by a heavy boot to the middle of his back. But the boy clung to the hatch with his fingers, screaming and crying. The sailor tried to pry his fingers back, but they were locked in a death grip.

With a look, the sailor summoned another to help grab the boy.

They yanked him, along with the boy shackled to him, out of the hatch and roughly tossed them both on the deck. Another sailor came with a hammer and some tools and went to work releasing the shackle around the crying boy's ankle. The remaining boy, with the empty shackle dangling from his leg, now stood alone.

The group of boys who'd just come up were kept nearby as the crying boy was taken to a set of chains hung near the bottom of the largest mast. His wrists were attached to these chains, which were then raised so he was suspended with his toes barely touching the deck, his face and chest pressed into the mast. He craned his neck to look back, with terror in his eyes, towards the rest of the boys and the sailors.

One of the sailors walked off, soon to return with something in his hand. It looked like a large black spider, with its legs gathered at the top, where it was held by the sailor. The bottom of the spider's legs had roundish-looking feet. The whole thing was about as long as one of the boy's arms.*

He approached the hanging boy, looking to make sure all of the other boys were watching. When he was sure he had everyone's attention, he raised the spider high over his head, behind his back, and brought it crashing down with all his might across the boy's back.

The boy's howls of pain were hideous as the sailor repeated this action over and over, each blow landing with a resounding slap. The boy's back was instantly transformed into a crazy array of welts, but this didn't stop the sailor, who continued to thrash him with this thing.

Soon, the boy's back was bleeding and began to resemble an

---

* *Known as a cat o' nine tails. It is made up of nine knotted thongs of cotton cord, two and a half feet long, designed to lacerate the skin and cause intense pain*

animal with its hide torn off. His head dropped forward, and he became unconscious. But still, the sailor continued with several more blows. When he finally stopped, the sailor was breathing hard and covered with sweat. His face had turned red, and his eyes blazed with fire.

Another sailor came forward with a bucket of seawater and tossed it over the boy's back, dispersing the blood. For a moment, open wounds showed bits of hanging skin and flesh before fresh blood rushed to the surface.

Another bucket of seawater was thrown on him. The boy didn't move. After a few more buckets, his head sagged to the other side, and Jayvyn barely caught the sound of his quiet moan. He was alive, but by how much no one could be sure.

The sailors then took his wrists from the chains, where he fell on the spot. The sailors glared at the boys to make sure they all understood this was the price for disobedience.

The boys, standing wide-eyed and speechless, were soon directed back to the waiting hatch, where, two by two, they proceeded down into the blackness—that is, except for the lone boy, who shuffled down, dragging the empty shackle behind him.

As they descended below, their eyes adjusted, and Jayvyn saw many men lined up, shoulder to shoulder, on their backs, on two levels in the vast room at the bottom of the ladder. The upper level contained a single row of men, while the lower level, the floor, contained several rows lying head to toe.

There was little room above the heads of the men on the platforms and Jayvyn saw this was the same kind of space he'd been confined to. These men had their hands shackled in front of them as well as their ankles shackled to the man next to them. A chain was passed over and through their ankle shackles and another through the iron band around their necks so they were held in place both at their heads and feet.*

These were all men. Some younger, some older. Many lay, just staring upward; some shifted their gaze to the boys as they shuffled by. No one spoke to them, but there was a murmur of low voices mixed with groans and coughing. *How many?* Jayvyn wondered. They disappeared into the darkness, seemingly with no end.

Jayvyn noticed small open holes on the sides of the ship, almost at the level of the deck, above every tenth or so person's head. He realized this must be the source of the occasional traces of fresh air he'd perceived earlier.† They emitted a small amount of light, but not nearly enough to see well.

Then he heard the unmistakable sound of some far-off children!

Where? He couldn't see.

Soon, Jayvyn was moved, with the rest of his group, back to the platform that had held him before. This time they weren't fastened down, which allowed for limited movement. Those in the lower middle part could even sit or stand at a crouch.

In the days that followed, he noticed some boys without shackles or partners who squatted in the middle area just below his platform.

---

* *The men were typically kept in this fashion to prevent rebellions, and in many instances would be kept in place for the entire voyage*

† *Holes of about 4" in diameter were cut into the side of the hull near deck height to facilitate some ventilation as a necessary means to survival in the hot, squalid confines belowdecks*

He noticed a few sailors working to remove others' shackles.

Jayvyn's shackles were also removed, and he was freed from his companion for the first time since the day of his capture.* It was an amazingly freeing sensation to be unshackled. Now he could not only roll over, but if there was room enough on the floor, he could get off his platform. It never lasted long, though, as the center section was crowded with others wanting to change their position, too.

Gruel was brought in once a day and a ladle of water twice a day, and the slaves continued to urinate and defecate in their spaces. The sickness was also swift to return, making it very difficult to do anything besides lay in place, as the ship rolled endlessly on.

Periodically, buckets of seawater were indiscriminately thrown over them to help wash the feces, urine, and vomit away. But as before, this had relatively little effect, and they were left to sit and lay in their squalor.

Sailors came and looked in every once in a while, to see if any of them had died, whereupon the corpse would be carried above deck.

Another sailor, different from the others, occasionally came and paid closer attention to each of them individually. He picked up their arms and legs, poked them here and there, sometimes slapping their cheeks, looked into their eyes using a lamp, and forced a stick into their mouths so he could see there too. After a while, Jayvyn concluded this man must be checking to see what condition they were in.

Different groups of boys were occasionally brought to the

---

* *Typically, children and adolescents were not chained down once they could be depended on to comply*

section where the hatch was and herded up on deck, and other groups who'd been on deck were brought down.

This pattern continued, and in a week or so, Jayvyn was assembled with another group of boys and brought back on deck, where a similar routine as before was conducted.

The man with the peculiar instrument played his strange music; the sailors swatted their legs until they remembered they were to dance. Following this, the boys were shown the buckets and stones and went to work scrubbing the decks. When finished with this, they had water from the barrel, sat, and ate more of the awful gruel.

More bodies were brought up, and Jayvyn wondered what had happened to the ones he'd seen before. The answer came soon enough when he saw a few sailors pitching them over the side into the sea. This seemed to happen when they had enough bodies gathered to make the effort worthwhile. Jayvyn shuddered as he imagined their bodies being devoured by the terrifying creatures he'd seen before.*

There were a few differences on deck this time. More than one group of boys was brought on deck at the same time, along with groups of men.

Six chains ran from the hatch to the front of the ship, three per side. The outermost were set ten feet from the rail, with five feet between each row. A corridor of twenty feet ran down the middle.

The men, still shackled in pairs at the ankle, hands shackled before them, were fastened to the deck by these chains. As each pair

---

* *Because insurance would not pay for slaves lost to illness, but would cover loss from drowning, it became a common practice to throw dead slaves, or those deemed too sick to recover, overboard*

emerged, the short chain connecting their ankles was passed under the long chain. After each five pair, the long chain was fastened to a ring on the deck. When finished, each chain contained four ten-foot sections with five pairs in each, all fastened tightly enough so movement was completely restricted.*

This made it easy for Jayvyn to estimate the number of men as each chain held forty men. With six chains, he estimated two hundred forty, not counting any remaining below, too sick, injured, or dead. So, with the boys and those remaining below, he figured around three hundred surviving male slaves on the ship.

The men, too, were made to dance as well as they could in their chains, but the sailors were much rougher with them, often taunting them with pointless jabs and spitting at them. Jayvyn guessed this was pure intimidation to constantly remind them who was in charge.

He now clearly heard the sounds of women and children coming from beyond the closest barrier, which he couldn't see behind.

So that's it! The women and children are behind that wall! This is what he must have heard from his platform from time to time. He thought, *They must be kept below, beyond the men's section.*†

The sounds of the women and children made the men call out, and the women responded. This was quickly met with harsh scolds and beatings from the sailors, who made it clear this was not permitted.

---

* *Men, if lucky enough to be brought on deck, were often left chained to the deck to prevent mass reprisals*

† *Barriers were constructed across the full width of the ships to separate the men and boys from the women, girls and smallest children*

Jayvyn heard similar rebukes from sailors on the other side of the barrier, coupled with the shouts and screams of women as they, too, were hit and beaten into submission. He wondered how many women, girls, and children were on the ship.*

Jayvyn immediately thought of his mother and little sister. *Are they among them?* His heart ached as he thought of them living as he was. He couldn't bear the thought of his mother being beaten. He wondered what their condition could be, if they were even alive, or if they'd been chucked, like so much garbage, into the sea. Not able to cope with those thoughts, he resolved to think they were as strong and capable as him.

Jayvyn looked over at the group of men, most of whom were now sitting on their haunches as the sailors stood close by. He studied their faces—the faces of men, not boys—devoid of childish plumpness, much leaner, and more muscular, as if only the parts serving the purpose of manhood remained. Some had stubble as their beards began to grow back; their eyes, too, had a steady sort of seriousness to them, focused on things Jayvyn couldn't see.

Their expressions were hard, fixed, determined, proud, and unbroken despite the cruel conditions they were forced to live under.

Jayvyn didn't recognize any, but knew many of these men must be from tribes that made a regular habit of engaging in warfare. Many

---

* *Captains of slave ships typically packed as many slaves as possible belowdecks. Larger ships, such as the 297-ton Brookes, were known to carry over 600 slaves regularly, and even as much as 800; losing many to suffocation and sanitation due to extreme overcrowding. In 1788, the Slave Trade Act restricted the number to 1.67 slaves per ton, which would have reduced the capacity of the Brookes to 454 slaves, although it is doubtful how well this was enforced*

had probably seen battle before. Indeed, he saw some had old scars on their arms, legs, chests, or faces.

He thought of the stories the elders and his father had told of the futampaf—the sacred ceremony where a boy becomes a man—and he wondered what tests these men might have had to pass.

Jayvyn looked out across the endless sea. There was nothing but unbroken ocean, as far as he could see. He wondered where his home was. He didn't even know in what direction to look. The ship just sailed steadily on.

All too soon, he and the others were made to go back down the hatch—back into the abyss where souls rot and futures don't exist—where they are "*slaves*," confined and ordered by the rules of these strange and cruel white men.

The stench was indeed as bad, if not worse, and hit him like a wall.

As his eyes slowly adjusted, Jayvyn looked into the eyes and faces of his fellow captives—slaves—all mere boys such as himself, who must have parents, siblings, aunts, and uncles somewhere. They, too, must be wondering and worrying about their families and if they'd ever see them again.

Their faces were sad, confused, tired, and, in most cases, sick as well. Some looked worse than the rest, more lethargic and listless. When he met their eyes, some of the boys looked away, as if ashamed of the filth they sat in or near. But it was all they could do; there was no place else for them to go, and all anyone could do was wait for the sailors to come with buckets of sea water, which only diluted the mess.

As he scanned the hold, Jayvyn saw one boy lying prone. His

back the site of a massive wound oozing a mixture of blood and puss, rimmed with the beginnings of scab. Jayvyn realized this must be the boy who'd been so savagely beaten by the sailor with the black spider. He felt an intense pang of sorrow as he relived the cruel episode in his mind. He thought of the awful pain this boy must be in, heaped on top of the pain he was already suffering in so many ways, and knew it must be unbearable.

Another boy sat at his side with a rag and a bucket of seawater he used to dab at the wound from time to time. Jayvyn assumed this must have been provided by one of the sailors for this purpose. There was also a third boy sitting there, gently holding his hand.

As for the wounded boy, his face was expressionless and slack; his eyes looked at nothing; his mouth hung partly open, a thin line of drool running over his lower lip.

If not for his slight wincing at the dabbing rag, one would assume he was dead.

Back on his familiar platform, Jayvyn found his former ankle partner. He felt a strange kinship to this boy, yet knew nothing much about him.

Both looked at each other with what felt like mutual sympathy, and Jayvyn knew how alone they both felt. Did this boy have a family, too? Of course. He must. Everyone is born to someone in this world.

After a moment or two, Jayvyn pointed to his chest and said, "Jayvyn."

The boy's head tilted slightly as he returned Jayvyn's gaze, heightened interest showing in his eyes. After a long, thoughtful pause, he touched his own chest and softly said, "Baahir," a small tear leaving the corner of his eye.

Jayvyn felt the beginning of a tear in his own eye as he looked at this poor boy across from him. A boy whose language he couldn't speak but with whom he'd already shared so much. The feeling almost overwhelmed him. They both held the moment for what seemed like an eternity, until Jayvyn once again pointed to himself and gently said, "Ajamatau," the name of his people he so yearned to join again.

Baahir's eyes searched Jayvyn's with a mixture of confusion and curiosity, and after a prolonged silence, he gestured back at himself and said in a dry voice, "Malinké."

It was a word Jayvyn thought he'd heard before, most likely from the elders; it was another tribe of the Gambia whom he knew little of. He wondered if Baahir knew of his people.

They sat together in silence, not knowing how to continue but wanting ever so much to do so. In that moment, a bond formed between them of the same sort they felt for their missing family and friends—a bond of one human being to another in a great time of need.

There seemed to be nothing left but to savor this feeling and know they were together, not alone among strangers anymore. They each had a name other than "*slave*" and an identity tied to a heritage greater than this white man's ship.

As Jayvyn settled back on the platform, he thought about Baahir and wondered what his world was like.

Did he go for runs in the morning through a forest like mine? Did his people have a wise man like Caksusa? Was he looking forward to his futampaf? Did they see the same clouds and sunsets?

Jayvyn thought of these things in the dark, filthy void. Soon his thoughts gently carried him out beyond the stench and pain. His mind collapsed in on itself, falling into the safe darkness of sleep.

– 4 –

The Dream

Mist rose gently off the dew-soaked leaves as the first rays of sunlight shimmered softly through the thick jungle canopy. The constant, buzzing drone of a far-off cicada defined the very texture of the morning air.

Jayvyn stood, arms hanging loosely at his sides, looking out at the forest stretched before him. Idle chattering of monkeys high in the canopy told him all was ok. Quietly, he placed one foot in front of the other, slowly making his way further into the virgin wilderness.

As he moved, he felt eyes from somewhere boring into him. He glanced up to his right just in time to see a small bush baby clinging to the branches of a fig tree. It watched him curiously for a second or two before jumping back into the cover of the foliage. Jayvyn was aware of the ground passing beneath his feet as he glided silently through the bush, sun glinting through openings in the canopy to bathe his forehead and shoulders in its warm light. A river babbled close by; peace cradled his soul with the assurance he always felt when trekking through his natural world.

He passed through a landscape of faintly shifting greens and blues, tans and browns. Patches of dappled light fell white and gold at random intervals.

Sounds, too, emanated all around—birds and insects sang soothing choruses; small creatures scurried through the undergrowth, joining their rhythm to the wind as it whispered gently through the leaves. The nearby river rippled tirelessly, enswathing it all in ethereal ambience. It was a sound so gentle and pure no man-made music could ever rival it.

The smells, too, were of a freshness defying proper description. The soft breeze carried mild aromatic blends of mahogany and boswellia laced with flowering herbs and tea leaves, embedded in rich, earthy soil mixed with the musky scent of animals.

It was everything Jayvyn loved about the forest. He felt at ease as he enjoyed his timeless drift around and through its boundless beauty.

As he pushed past a bush of flowering mango, the large, complex trunk of a kapok tree came into view. Approaching through the lush jungle undergrowth, he saw a shape standing beside one of the giant, fin-like root stalks protruding from its side. Moving closer, he saw the shape was his father, naked and in perfect form. His father held out his hand and said, "Well, my son, you're here; let's get to work," as if it were the most natural thing in the world.

Unperturbed, Jayvyn continued his approach as his father came closer. They sat together on the nearby section of a long-ago fallen tree, surrounded by cassava and other low vegetation, some of which bore the flower or fruit of its species.

A rich, savory energy flowed between he and his father as they sat silently together. It vibrated softly around and within his heart, filling him with a great sense of comfort, love, and relief. They were both using sticks to scratch small lines in the circle of dirt between them for what seemed like a time with no beginning or end.

Not looking up, Jayvyn asked, "Where have you been?"

His father gently replied, "I have been right here, my son, watching you; it looks like you have been doing well,"

Jayvyn continued, "But I am not sure, father; you know many things I do not. I have done my best, but you know what is right, and I need your guidance. It is good you are back now and can show me the things I must do."

A prolonged silence followed as Jayvyn continued tracing his stick over the ground. Occasionally, he reached into a small sack to take out a handful of seeds he didn't recognize, sowing them into the lines etched in the dirt.

Without looking up, he heard his father's words once more—"You will be fine, my son." Jayvyn continued with his stick, his father's words seeming to come from a distance as he worked.

He trenched new lines in the dirt, but now it was only his hand and his stick he saw in front of him. He looked up to see his father's naked body walking away, disappearing behind a root of the kapok tree.

In a moment of panic, Jayvyn said, "Wait!" but as he stood and looked, he saw a different figure standing there.

It was a boy, tall and muscular, with tightly braided hair held by a leather band. In his right hand was a spear held above his shoulder. Jayvyn saw other weapons hanging from his waist. In his other hand, he held a shield. White paint was striped here and there on his face and body; necklaces hung from his neck. His gaze was strong and steady—a slight redness rimmed the whites of his piercing, dark eyes. His expression was serious as he held his spear, cocked and pointed directly at Jayvyn. Jayvyn froze in place, not able to make sense of this.

Then he saw the boy was Baahir.

Jayvyn pointed to his chest and said, "Jayvyn, I am Jayvyn!"

Baahir then smiled, lowered his spear, and said, "Ah! Jayvyn! It is Baahir! I am happy to see you!"

He approached a few steps, and as he did, he changed. He no longer had braided hair, but instead his head was shaved as Jayvyn knew it to be. And he brought his spear, now the size of a toy; in fact, it had become a toy.

He came and squatted before Jayvyn, and Jayvyn told him how he'd just seen his father.

Baahir said he'd just come from his village, and was on his futampaf.

As they sat and spoke, they both became children. The two got busy hiding Baahir's toy spear in the ground. It just seemed the right thing to do for some reason, coming quite naturally.

They sat there playing a game Jayvyn remembered from his childhood, one he'd played many times with his little sister; all of that seemed perfectly natural, too. It was a good feeling as the two of them sat, laughing and playing merrily.

Jayvyn then raised his gaze. Instead of Baahir, he saw his little sister, Ifetayo—smiling, sitting across from him, gleefully enjoying their game as she always did—giggling in short bursts of joy as he remembered so well.

They played like this for a while, but Jayvyn, now twelve again, grew concerned as he knew she shouldn't be here—this deep in the forest by herself—it was much too dangerous!

Picking her up, he looked for a way to bring her to safety, but was unsure which way to go.

A rustling in the bush grabbed his attention, not just from one direction, but many. He began to seize with panic.

Bringing Ifetayo to the kapok tree, he placed her as quickly as he could behind a massive fold in its roots, telling her to stay there.

He stepped away from the tree to where he could see all around.

The menacing sounds approached.

Flashes of fur dashed between the foliage, more flickered in his periphery.

A hyena sprang from the ground and disappeared back into it, right in front of his eyes! It literally came out of the ground and plunged back into solid earth as if it were nothing more than water.

Another came only partially from the ground before diving back in. They didn't move in the way hyenas move, but as if they had flexible bones, like giant snakes.

Jayvyn knew how dangerous and cunning these animals were—that they would not give up once they located their prey.

More sprouted from the earth, both in front and on each side. When he turned around, he saw more, slithering in and out of the ground.

They approached very fast, circling where he stood. But now they were just shapes—dark, foreboding shadows in the ground—zigging and zagging, closer and closer.

He screamed for Ifetayo to stay put, but his screams were

muffled and strained.

He tried to move to where she was, but his movements were awkward and slow; he couldn't move his feet. It was as if he were stuck in deep mud.

His arms and legs felt heavy and weak; he couldn't make them do what he wanted.

He tried and tried, but it seemed to take forever to take a single step.

His voice was lost as if screaming into a piece of hide wrapped tightly over his mouth.

He saw his little sister, grinning innocently as she moved from behind the root.

The lines in his face strained. He tried to tell her to hide, but could make no sound, nor could he move to protect her.

She just stood there, smiling naïvely, oblivious to the danger closing in.

His horror became unbearable. The beasts closed in. The ground beneath his feet started to heave. Jayvyn stumbled, finding it hard to keep his balance.

The canopy of trees moved wildly above his head, and he heard wind—lots and lots of wind—blowing violently through the treetops.

Trees began to crash all around, making a thundering cacophony.

He heard the river rushing madly now—a raging torrent—threatening to crest its banks.

Rain was falling close by, in a deluge—as if a monsoon.

The strange hyenas closed in faster.

His body lurched backward as if hit by an invisible force.

He hit the ground hard.

- 5 -

Storm Tossed

Jayvyn opened his eyes with a start. His world tossed and pitched erratically. It was dark, and he didn't know where he was as he fought to control the chaos.

He was still reeling from his dream, unable to comprehend the shift from where he'd been to where he was now.

People on every side were shouting and frantically moving about; water was coming from somewhere. Something crashed violently above his head, shaking the timbers holding the deck.

His mind struggled to assess his situation. He tried to sit up. He hit his head hard on the low ceiling, and was instantly knocked down.

All at once, he realized where he was—it was the ship!

Everything slammed from side to side, up and down, forcefully shifting from one direction to another. Those on the floor tumbled and tossed about as the ship's motion changed erratically.

Heavy footsteps clambered across the deck; men shouted.

As he steadied himself, he felt Baahir's hand clenched around his arm and looked to see his face wide with fright. He, too, was fighting for stability, clawing for purchase on the moving platform.

Jayvyn rolled over on his stomach, managed to swing his legs off the platform, and dropped to the floor—only a few feet away.

Hanging on to the side of the platform, he crouched, looking toward the door. Beyond was the ladder leading up to the deck.

He made his way, with great difficulty, to the door. It burst open.

Before he knew any more, a sailor grabbed his arm and pulled him through. Baahir was not far behind; the sailor grabbed him, too. Several more boys were pulled through the door.

The group of boys stood in the men's section gathered under the ladder. Several times, the ship lurched, knocking them off their feet, sending some careening into a wall or across the floor. The lucky ones grabbed onto something nearby to prevent their fall. The sailors were having difficulty, too, as they moved them to and up the ladder. Water poured down the open hatch, sometimes in great torrents, soaking anyone standing beneath.

One by one, they were pushed up the steep ladder where a sailor above grabbed hold, yanking them to the deck. Another sailor forcibly sat them down, keeping them in place until everyone was up.

Jayvyn squinted into the dark, driving wind and rain, noticing the angry, monsoon like sky. Ocean water poured over the side, washing across the deck, coursing back and forth before disappearing through small, low spaces in the rail. Shouts came from above and he saw men moving high in the rigging as the sails slapped madly about. One climbed a set of lines on the side of the ship, hanging perilously over the ocean.* He couldn't believe they weren't falling as the masts swayed chaotically over the tumultuous sea. They moved surefootedly and with purpose, bundling the wildly flapping sails into small, secure rolls along poles crossing the mast.†

A sailor came and took them two at a time, standing or not, to a

---

* *Known as a ratline*

† *Yardarms*

box near the front of the ship. A strange-looking mechanism stuck out of its middle.

The boys were made to hold on to the box until the whole group of ten were there. Jayvyn looked and saw Baahir among them.

The sound was deafening as the ship pitched wildly. Seawater crested the bow, roaring in great torrents across the deck, crashing into them as they fought to hold on.

One boy lost his grip and was swiftly washed to the side of the ship, where he smashed into the rail, preventing him from disappearing altogether into the raging sea.

A sailor fetched him and roughly brought him back to their station. Blood was smeared on one leg where he'd slammed into something as he careened across the deck.

Salt spray lashed their faces as three sailors placed the boys' hands on long handles attached to the apparatus sticking out of the box. The wide handles held five on each side.

Two of the sailors grabbed the handles with the boys. As one pushed down, the other side lifted up. Then that side was pushed down, raising the first side. The sailors did this several times while yelling unintelligibly over the noise of the storm.

They let go briefly, and the boys stood hanging on to the handles but doing nothing more, whereupon the third sailor brought his stick painfully down across their shoulders.

The two sailors, once again, repeated the action of pushing one side down while lifting the other, looking intently and hollering at the boys over the deafening maelstrom.

The sailors let go again.

Enough of the boys understood they were to push and lift as the sailors had, repeating the actions demonstrated. The rest of the boys soon followed suit. They continued like this while the sailors looked on for a few moments.

Being satisfied they knew what they were to do, the two sailors moved off across the dangerously slanting deck. The third stayed to keep a watch over the boys.

The handles were heavy, no matter which way they tried to move them, and it took the strength of all ten boys to make it happen.

At times, one or more of the boys would forget which way to go and either be lifted off the deck or pushed into it. Having the handle ripped from his grip, he instinctively grabbed the box for fear of falling across the wildly pitching deck.

When this happened, their motion slowed substantially, and the sailor standing by smashed them across their shoulders, yelling, "Pump! Pump! Slaves! Pump!" The boy regained the handle, and the rest, squinting in the hard driving rain, quickly resumed their arduous task.

Unlike scrubbing the deck, they didn't know what function they were performing or what it accomplished. They only knew the sailor standing nearby treated it as urgent.

They worked, concentrating so hard they barely had time to look around. The waves relentlessly crashed over the bow, periodically knocking them off their feet or into the wooden box. They gathered themselves together as quickly as they could before the master's stick came down, which it inevitably did, along with the command, "Pump slaves! Pump!"

Jayvyn had a position diagonally opposite Baahir and noticed he didn't often lose his balance or let go of his handle. Baahir was strong. Jayvyn saw sinewy muscles in his arms, neck, and shoulders working—his face held tight, teeth bared with effort—every part of his being engaged in the task.

Baahir was a good example. Jayvyn felt by watching him, he was able to draw strength beyond what he previously knew.

He threw himself with new zeal behind his handle. Soon other boys followed, until the whole group was shouting, baring their teeth with each rise and fall of the handles—all in unison. Theirs weren't shouts of fear, but shouts of those engaged in a common effort, like moving a giant log that would be impossible without the help of many. They "pumped" and "pumped," and the master's blows came less frequently, but this they hardly noticed.

At some point, new boys began to arrive. One by one, they were added to the levers as the boys who'd been working were taken away. Soon, a whole new group of boys worked the pump.

Jayvyn and the boys who'd been relieved sat with their backs against the wall watching the new group. The master smacked the new crew with his stick when they slowed or fell out of rhythm, yelling, "Pump! You slaves! Pump", and ultimately the new boys began to operate with the same coordination as Jayvyn's group had.

Jayvyn and his group sat, faces and bodies pounded by wind and rain, trying not to slide away as the ship pitched erratically. A tub of gruel was brought. They fed themselves with difficulty as the tub slid back and forth over the slippery wet deck.

Baahir steadied the tub so the others could get a portion without the tub sliding away with the motion of the ship. Jayvyn, following his example, held the tub for Baahir when it was his turn.

A barrel of water stood lashed to the mast where they quenched their thirst using the ladle hung from its rim. Each had to hold on to something fast as the ship furiously tossed and tumbled in the raging storm.

They were brought to the hatch where new boys were being led off, one by one, to relieve those now at the pump.

And so it must continue, thought Jayvyn as his group descended back into the hideous void below.

Going down the ladder required great care. More than one boy started that way, only to lose his footing and fall roughly down.

When he arrived at the bottom, Jayvyn saw one of the boys lying with his foot turned at a grotesque angle. It was badly broken; jagged bones pierced the skin; the boy howled and writhed in agony.

The sailors didn't move to help him but instead kicked him out of the way, making room at the bottom for the rest of the boys.

Rows of men, chained on their backs, crammed shoulder to shoulder, head to toe, disappeared into the dark reaches of the hold.

Jayvyn and the others were pushed through the small doorway to their section, which nobody bothered to close.

Looking back, he saw the sailors take the boy with the broken ankle, crying out in excruciating pain, back up the ladder. One sailor grabbed around his chest; the other took one of his legs. Using their free arms for the ladder, they climbed. The boy's shattered ankle bounced terribly off the steps as he screamed in agony, a watery trail of blood left in his path.

Although the boy was only vaguely familiar from working the pumps, his last anguished expression would live in Jayvyn's memory for a long time to come.

Back on his platform, Jayvyn lay uncomfortably as the ship continued to pound its way through the angry ocean.

The sailors continued to retrieve groups of ten to bring on deck; weary, wet boys were brought back.

Sleep was impossible as they rolled and smashed about with the motion of the ship. The debilitating sickness returned, causing most of them to lose whatever food and water they managed to get down.

The storm continued to thrash the giant ship like a hapless piece of driftwood caught in raging rapids. Many of the boys suffered cuts and bruises as they were tossed about.

In the morning, Jayvyn was brought on deck for another shift.

In the light of day, the fury of the angry sea was on full display. He watched with alarm as enormous white streaked waves towered high above the stern, tops blown into mist before collapsing and rolling under the giant ship. The wind blasted erratically, screeching through the masts and rigging—high-pitched and discordant—a cacophony like nothing he'd ever heard. The shuddering rig threatened to topple at any moment.

The boys fought against the sea as they manned the pumps, the sailors always too willing to smash their sticks across their backs at the first sign they were slowing. It was perilous, exhausting work, chilling them to the bone as rain and waves continuously raked their naked bodies.

The violent storm raged for several more days before finally blowing itself out. As the wind and seas reluctantly moderated, the ship gradually returned to its previous state. Light began to enter the hold, just enough to have a look around.

Jayvyn saw several boys who didn't appear to move much. Where most steadied themselves against the ship's motion, a few just rolled unabated, heads and limbs in unnatural positions, bodies shifting back and forth like loose sacks of grain.

Through the open door, he saw sailors bringing men up the ladder in the same way as the boy with the broken ankle. These men weren't moving. Their heads and limbs bounced off of the steps and walls as their lifeless bodies were dragged up.

The storm may have passed, but the voyage was taking its toll.

- 6 -

Work Parties The Sick and The Dead

As the day progressed, Jayvyn and most of the other boys were gradually brought up on deck where they were assigned work.

Jayvyn guessed there were about forty boys in total. Four work groups—ten on the pumps, ten on each side of the ship scrubbing decks. Jayvyn and nine others waited for instructions.

The men, too, were brought on deck. As each pair emerged, their leg shackles were passed under the chains and fastened down five pairs to a group as before.

The sun came out—the day bright, warm, and cloudless—a far cry from just a few hours ago. Gone were the towering seas. The trade winds blew steady. Salt crystals from storm driven seas sparkled thick off the masts and rigging—a silent vestige of the violent storm.

Men in uniform stood behind full-width netting on the upper-level shouting orders.

Sailors were everywhere. Many climbed rope ladders, high into the rigging, where they unfurled previously wrapped sails. Some hauled ropes to raise sails attached to the long pole extending from the front of the ship.* Others pulled on ropes at the backs of these sails

---

* *The bowsprits of large ships could extend sixty or more feet beyond the bow to carry many additional sails*

once they were up.

Several sailors stood watch over the working groups. Others kept eyes on the men, taunting them, landing hard blows if any dared oppose them.

The sea had evened out after the storm, the ship rode much easier now—rising and falling gently with the swell of the sea.

Jayvyn and his group were assigned a new task.

Positioned along the rails, five on each side of the ship, they were given buckets attached to long ropes. The other end was tied to the rail.

Demonstrating, a sailor lowered a bucket into the sea. When the bucket hit the ocean, it instantly filled with seawater. He then hauled it back up, dumping its contents into a larger bucket.

When Jayvyn first tried this, the rope painfully tore from his grip the moment the bucket touched the water. The rope paid itself out until it was stopped by its attachment to the rail.

The sailor standing near him immediately smashed a stick across Jayvyn's back. His knees buckled as he fell painfully against the rail, hitting his chin. Visions of cartwheeling over the side briefly flashed through his mind. The angry sailor gestured for him to retrieve the bucket.

Jayvyn grabbed the rope, and with great effort, pulled, hand over hand, fighting against the intense drag of the water until, finally, the bucket broke free of the ocean. He hauled the heavy load up the side of the ship, emptying its contents into the larger bucket at his feet.

Sharp slaps broke the air as others were whacked when the ropes tore from their hands.

Jayvyn lowered his bucket again, being careful to hold on tight when it hit the water. The jerk was sudden and powerful, causing a strong sting as the rough hemp bit into his palms. But this time he held the rope at all costs, pulling the laden bucket hand over hand, up the side of the ship, emptying its contents into the larger bucket.

When the larger bucket was full, a sailor pulled it away, replacing it with an empty one. The sailor then took the full bucket to the open hatch, where another sailor poked his head up and took it below.

Jayvyn continued hauling the heavy loads to fill the new bucket. As soon as it was full, a sailor took it and replaced it with an empty bucket.

The work was punishing. Harsh rebukes echoed across the deck as some failed in their task. Jayvyn was determined to keep up.

He began to anticipate the moment the bucket hit the water, taking a quick loop around his right hand, bending his elbows to take some of the shock with his arms rather than just his hands. This worked a little better, but still, the strong jerk and sudden weight were taking their toll.

As he worked, he saw the bodies of slaves being tossed over the side. These were the dead men and boys he'd seen carried up the ladder earlier.

But then Jayvyn noticed some weren't dead at all but so disabled they couldn't stand or defend themselves. He saw their eyes occasionally widen with fear. Feeble cries rang out in vain attempts to prevent being thrown over. But they were too weak. They were easily overpowered by the sailors, who threw them—still alive—into the passing sea.*

Jayvyn couldn't help but watch as the bodies hit the water. They passed quickly down the length of the ship, where they were met with great activity. It was the same as when the two boys were tossed overboard his first day on deck. Some screamed out as dark shapes swam swiftly through the water. Both dead and alive were being viciously devoured by the same creatures he'd seen before—the ocean behind red and littered with bits of flesh and body parts as the gruesome spectacle played itself out.

These creatures, he realized, were giant fish. Jayvyn now saw they had triangular fins on their backs, slicing the surface like a sharp knife, followed by a smaller wedge that lashed about as they attacked their victims. He hadn't seen fish such as this before. The fish in the rivers near his home were much smaller.

He felt a sudden wave of recognition as he remembered his nightmare from a week ago. He realized the 'hyenas' in his dream were one and the same as the monstrous creatures attacking the disposed of slaves.

Hyenas, too, will be driven into a dangerous frenzy when they come upon wounded, helpless animals. At night, in his village, Jayvyn recalled hearing eerie, frantic wailing as they ran down their quarry. The sound was otherworldly, not like any other animal, always sending chills up his spine.

He thought again of his little sister, Ifetayo, standing at the root

---

* *Slaves considered too sick or damaged to recover were commonly thrown overboard to reduce feeding and carrying costs as they could later be claimed as losses under insurance policies*

of the kapok tree in his dream. How he desperately wanted to protect her. He wondered, involuntarily, if women and children were being tossed into the sea to suffer the same death.

Instead of contemplating such thoughts, he focused solely on the task before him to avoid the boundless wrath of the sailors.

The men in chains, too, watched helplessly as sick slaves were tossed over the side. Howls of protest erupted. Several stood, only to be savagely beat down by sailors with clubs. There was nothing anyone could do but watch as this terrible thinning of slaves continued. The sailors were much more brutal with the men. One man was hit so hard he fell unconscious, blood spilling from the gash on the side of his head.

Jayvyn continued to pull on his rope, hauling the laden bucket, emptying its contents into the always-waiting bucket at his feet. The rope began to have a pinkish hue and he realized his hands were bleeding. He didn't know how many times he'd repeated the process, but knew he couldn't keep it up indefinitely.

Finally, the sailor who'd been bringing the empty buckets stopped, indicating Jayvyn's task was finished.

Setting his bucket down, he looked at his hands. His fingers quivered involuntarily, locking as he fought to open and close them. His arms, shoulders, and back screamed in agony. He staggered—exhausted—dizzy from the horrors he'd witnessed, but stood as strong as he was able, fearing if he didn't, he'd be the next one tossed into the sea.

Soon, he was led to the familiar barrier separating the men from the women—the same place he'd sat after pumping. All the boys were gathered in two sections on either side of the mast, Baahir among them. They sat, resting their backs and heads against the barrier. All exhausted and spent.

The warm sun beat down and a cool breeze swept Jayvyn's aching body. The palms of his hands burned painfully. Great patches of skin were peeled back, his tender pink flesh exposed underneath. His feelings of vulnerability and helplessness were compounded by the fact more would be demanded of him.

As he looked around, he saw other boys from the bucket assignment whose palms were raw and abraded. He thought of the boy whose flesh had been ripped from his back by the 'spider' and wondered how he was doing—if he would ever recover.

How many had gone over the side? Jayvyn recalled seeing at least six or seven. He thought of the boy with the broken ankle from the other night. He could still see his anguished face as he was carried mercilessly up the ladder. He knew without any doubt the fate this poor boy must have suffered.

He looked over at the rows of men chained to the deck before him—strong, fearless warriors mixed with gentle farmers; fathers and grandfathers; elders and uncles; brothers, and whomever they might be. Jayvyn's heart grieved for all he saw, thinking what their lives might have been before they were forcefully torn from their worlds.

Some of them looked around at others. Their eyes showed the same feelings Jayvyn had—bewilderment, hopelessness, loneliness, heartbreak, and pain—pain deeper and more profound than any man could imagine.

Tubs of gruel were brought, one for each group of boys on either side of the mast. Two were placed at the head of each chain of men.

The boys reached in and scooped the sticky substance with their hands. Small worms squirmed along here and there, but these were the least of their concerns.

Jayvyn grimaced as he dipped his throbbing hands in and brought them to his mouth. The foul lard and grain concoction stung his tender, raw hands. It was even painful to lick his palms clean of it.

The men ate the same way, passing the tub down the line as each took a handful. No one seemed too greedy for the putrid food; some ate less than others, looks of disgust evident on all of their faces.

Next came water. The boys drank from the ladle hung on the large barrel by the mast. The men were given buckets—the same ones recently used for seawater. These they passed between them, two for each row.

When they'd eaten, one of the men in uniform came and spoke to the sailors. They then made all the men stand. The sailor with the strange instrument came and played.

The men danced, chains and shackles keeping unsteady rhythm, while the uniformed man looked on approvingly. The boys were spared this detail today, as they'd already had plenty of exercise.

The rest of the afternoon was spent moving the men below. They were chained, ankles and necks, to the surfaces where they'd stay until released again. The looks on their faces were despondent as, two by two, they descended to the dungeon below.

It was near dusk by the time the boys were made to return. The light was barely enough to see the first few rows of men sweltering in their bondage.

Jayvyn couldn't tell if he'd become accustomed to the smell, but somehow it seemed slightly less revolting. The accumulated piles of feces and vomit were gone. Gone, too, were the corpses he'd seen lolling about in the morning. He knew they were among those tossed overboard.

The boy with the wounds on his back, however, lay prostrate on the platform.

Jayvyn figured the buckets of seawater he'd filled must have been used to wash down the hold. However, it was far from clean; the putrid smell remained.*

As he lay on his platform, he thought about all the events since his capture—being shackled and branded; the day the ship began to move; the dark weeks wallowing in delirium; how bright the light was when first let on deck; the filth of their feces; the crippling sickness; the lives laid to waste. All these things—all the sickening memories—swarmed his mind, right up to the horrors of today.

He figured they must have been at sea for well over a month, maybe two. *Where were they going? How long would this wretched journey last?*

Once again, he looked over at the boy, Baahir—the boy he didn't know but somehow had developed considerable respect for.

Baahir returned his gaze; the unspoken conversation of their mutual experience transpired between them.

Jayvyn looked at the palms of his hands and back at Baahir, who, in return, gave him the slightest smile.

It was a kindness Jayvyn hadn't experienced for a long time—a

---

* *Everything swabbed off the cabin sole would merely wash into the bilge below where it would wash around until being pumped overboard*

gesture of goodwill, of caring—unbidden, yet given from the heart—for no other reason than to fill another's emptiness.

Jayvyn felt moisture filling his eyes at the painful realization of their shared circumstance.

A slight smile came to his own face.

He now knew he could think of Baahir as a true friend.

- 7 -

Deterioration and Doldrums

Days and weeks dragged on as the uprooted slaves were sailed further and further from their home.

The boys, able to move around now, had adopted rudimentary stewardship for their section. In particular, an attempt was made to control filth by defecating and urinating in a common location. They chose to do this against the bulkhead on one side of the door. It was an imperfect solution, to say the least, but was all they could do given their circumstances.

The boys, as well as the rest of the slaves, were hardly doing well. Several suffered ailments they were defenseless against. Common symptoms were paralyzing cramps, so bad they lay doubled up in pain, unable to move about. This would soon be followed by explosive diarrhea, but not like any had experienced or witnessed before. The foul eruptions contained blood and mucous, leaving the afflicted so weak they just lay in their filth.*

Others, who miraculously seemed to have escaped this terrible fate, watched helplessly as their fellow captives retched and cramped in acute pain. They were unable to retain even the smallest amounts of food or water. There seemed to be nothing anyone could do for

---

* *Known as the 'bloody flux', it was one of the most lethal diseases that could break out aboard a slave ship claiming untold numbers of slaves and sailors alike*

them.

The man who periodically came to check the boys' condition—Jayvyn decided he was a doctor—administered water and some sort of medicine, but there was seldom any recovery. The afflicted soon became very thin and listless—oozing sores and lesions appearing all over their bodies. The doctor's medicines didn't work.*

They wasted away to mere skeletons of their former selves.

When it became apparent they weren't going to recover, sailors came and took them on deck, carrying them like sacks of grain instead of human beings.

Jayvyn saw at least three boys, and numerous men, afflicted the same way, dragged topside. In many instances, these boys and men weren't dead but desperately sick—reduced to a very weak state of semi-consciousness—eyes glassy, unable to focus, jaws slack, tongues black and swollen.

There was no mystery about their fates; they were never seen again.

The boy with his back badly abraded, however, was making progress. The ship's doctor had come to inspect his wounds and administered a treatment that appeared to cause great pain. It was a whitish, grainy substance rubbed directly into the wound and then covered with cloth.† After several weeks, his wounds had indeed begun to heal, leaving behind a hideous array of scars all over his back

* *Remedies could include bloodletting, ingestion of mercury or lead salts and other archaic methods that often would make things worse and even hasten death*

† *A common treatment for the wounds caused by whipping was to rub salt directly into the wound. Although painful, it was somewhat effective*

as testament to the savage beating he'd endured.

Jayvyn's hands and the hands of the other boys hauling buckets were inspected as well. The ten of them were assembled in a row, and the doctor came with a sailor to assist him.

They were made to wash their hands vigorously in a bucket of seawater. The sailor stood by to assist with this, if necessary, as it was very painful. If needed, he grabbed a boy's hands and forcefully rubbed them against each other while submersed in saltwater.

After this, they were instructed to stand with their palms held out while the doctor came and poured a small amount of the whiteish powder onto their wounds. It stung mightily.

The sailor held their arms firmly while the doctor scrubbed the grainy crystals into their skinless palms using a cloth wetted in seawater. For a time, their hands glowed bright red and throbbed with pain. The boys were spared work duty for several days, and the skin began to heal.

Routines resumed; the boys and men brought on deck every few days.

The men were assembled, as before, shackles passed under the chains and anchored in place.

The boys were assigned their now familiar tasks of cleaning, pumping, and fetching buckets of water over the side.

Some twenty men, however, had been unshackled and now participated in chores with the boys. These were men who the sailors determined posed little threat and could be effectively controlled. Some were elderly, others were slight in build and submissive in nature.

The men appearing defiant and untrustworthy remained shackled and weren't free to move about whatsoever.

There were, as expected, far fewer males in total.

Jayvyn had estimated better than fifty boys when they'd first started out, but now their number was closer to thirty.

As for the men, he'd figured about two hundred fifty in the beginning. But now, seeing only four sets of chains instead of six, he guessed their number to be closer to one eighty.

Therefore, roughly eighty or so of the total number of men and boys must have perished.*

Was it the same for the women and children? Why would I expect there to be much of a difference for them? Jayvyn wondered. *After all, they must be living with the same conditions and diseases as the men.*

Jayvyn thought of his mother and sister again. *Could they have survived this long under these conditions?*

It was still too hard to dwell on for very long. He couldn't know the answer and so had to live with uncertainty. It was truly a matter of survival for each individual trapped aboard this ship of death.

Jayvyn noticed some of the sailors now seemed to be missing, and though he couldn't know for sure, he supposed, with the onset of disease, some of them had succumbed as well.†

Many of the sailors didn't seem as robust as he'd remembered. But this certainly didn't lessen the harsh treatment inflicted upon the

---

* *Death rates for slaves onboard slave ships during the middle passage in the 1700's hovered around 25%*

† *Death rates for sailors on slave ships in 1700's hovered around 20%, not much better than the slaves*

slaves.

The men with different uniforms—the superiors—were present much of the time now to make sure the sailors were carrying out their orders. They were very harsh to the sailors as they checked on them performing their duties. If a sailor was complacent or delinquent in his task, he'd be singled out immediately by his superior, who'd often brandish a rod or some other instrument and many times use it.

One sailor was even administered the same 'spider' whipping as the boy earlier on. But it wasn't as severe. As with the other whipping, the sailors were assembled to watch the punishment, but not the slaves since it wasn't one of their own. The slaves stayed heads down in their work as the punishment was administered.

The laggard was hit maybe ten times, hands secured by the same chain as the boy. When finished, the sailor had several bright red, bloody streaks across his back and was washed with buckets of seawater. His fellow sailors helped the unsteady man through the door separating the men from the women, where his quarters must have been.*

There was rain on a few occasions, but nothing like the storm they'd been through many weeks before. Mostly, the wind blew fair and steady as the ship progressed easily across the vast, empty sea.

But there was a period of two weeks or so when no wind blew at all, nor did a single drop of rain fall from the sky.†

---

* *Crewmates during the 1700's were often taken by press gangs to be forced into service, receiving meager pay, and received punishment similar, but nowhere near as harsh as that of the slaves*

† *Slave ships coming from Africa often encountered the 'doldrums'; the area approximately 5° north or south of the equator where protracted calms persist*

During this time, the sails hung limp in the rigging while the sun beat mercilessly down on the deck. The great ship sat motionless on the flat, still ocean, the surface like silvery glass. No breeze created the slightest ripple to disturb the flat gray expanse. All was deathly quiet.

Jayvyn noticed the great, dark fish were present in numbers all around the ship, waiting to be fed the bodies of the deceased and nearly deceased slaves, as well as anything else thrown overboard.

This time, as the ship lay still, the feeding frenzy continued in full view or earshot until finished. Many of the sailors gathered at the rail to watch the grisly spectacle—laughing, pointing, treating it as great entertainment—as the terrible splashing broke the stillness.

The slaves tried to block it from their consciousness, but at this point they were either numb or too weak to give it much attention. It was no longer a novelty.

Duties, of course, were still tended to during this period. The slaves, by this time, had been put to work cleaning and scrubbing below decks. That is, to the extent of what was available to them. They still couldn't access the area toward the back of the ship where the women and children were. That area was sealed off with a solid wall spanning the full width of the ship.*

Jayvyn was able to see the entirety of the men's quarters now, which was much larger than the boys. He noticed rings fastened to the platforms as well as on the sole of the hold itself. These secured the chains passed through the ankle shackles and neck rings the men wore.

It was difficult to imagine almost three hundred full-grown men

---

* *Solid bulkheads were constructed to separate the men from the women, children, and crew quarters, keeping the men as far forward as possible*

packed into this space. Most of them remained shackled and chained the entire time. They didn't have the relative luxury of defecating and urinating in any certain location, but instead had to lie in their filth, chained on their backs, not even able to sit.*

Cleaning the area was not only physically hard, but the stench and filth in the squalid heat made it especially unbearable. The heat was worse than ever; no air moved about.

The situation for everyone was sickening, insufferable beyond anything Jayvyn had previously thought possible. But for the men who remained bound and chained since Africa, it had to be the deepest level of deprivation that could possibly be survived. In fact, if there weren't surviving men chained on deck at that moment, he wouldn't have believed it possible at all.

The ship sat lazily on the glassy sea, sun beating relentlessly down on its decks. There was no reprieve. Below decks was a sweltering oven.

Sores were breaking out on the bare skin of all the slaves from their long time spent lying naked in the hold of the ship, especially on the men who'd been forced to lie in their putrid filth day after day.

Their diets weren't helping. Some had bleeding gums; others lost teeth. It became harder and harder to move about on sore, poorly conditioned limbs. All were listless and devoid of energy, even the sailors.†

** Some captains never let their slaves out of the holds at all over the entire middle passage losing many more as a result*

† Scurvy, caused by the lack of vitamin C in their diets, was a very common disease on seagoing voyages of the time

Their food became more rancid with each passing day. More worms crawled about in the gruel. It became thicker and darker, smelling foul as the ingredients steadily rotted in the tropical heat.

The water, too, was fetid—cloudy in appearance and a thin, colored film swirled on its surface.

All of this contributed to increased gastrointestinal distress amongst both slaves and crew alike, with several more perishing from the deteriorating conditions on board the ship.

Finally, after several weeks sitting on the stagnant sea, the wind began to blow again. The sails filled, and the ship began to move. It seemed improbable at first—as if it had been forgotten the ship had ever moved at all. But soon they were scudding along as they had before the lull.

The breeze was incredibly refreshing, the sense of motion a welcome change from the nerve-racking stillness of the past few weeks. Everyone's mood lifted as the sailors once again got busy adjusting sails and tending to the ship.

The days ticked by as they steadily made their way across the vast, never-ending ocean. The weather stayed good, and the slaves were brought on deck daily to exercise and work. However, everyone moved slower, finding it increasingly difficult to attend to what was required of them.

Jayvyn figured it had been well over two months now since the ship left the shores of Africa. He lay belowdecks, listening to the water passing outside the ship, wondering if this journey would ever end.

He had to work hard just to concentrate. Accessing memories of his home became an exhausting effort in itself. *What had it been like?*

He tried to remember his village and its people, but it was becoming increasingly difficult. He wanted so much to remember what it felt like to be free—to live life as he once had.

What was it like to play with my sister and friends, to sit and listen to the elder's tales? It was all very hard to grasp, almost as if it had never been.

What was it like to rise early for my morning run? What was the fresh forest air like? How did the ground feel beneath my feet? What was the joy I experienced with my mother? The feeling of my father's strong hand on my shoulder?

Once, these things ushered forth the undeniable sensation he once knew as love. He longed to know that feeling again. The closest he could come now were feelings of sympathy and sorrow for himself and his fellow slaves.

How was it so much—nearly all of his life thus far—could be erased from his memory in such a short time?

Sleep, now, was his body's response to exhaustion and weakness, never the comforting, restful period following a fulfilling day. Dreams, if there were any at all, were fitful sensations of entrapment of one kind or another. Waking was confusion, his mind straddling the blurry space between dark fantasy and reality—as if trapped in a murky haze from which he couldn't escape.

It had been so long.

Jayvyn felt the delicate thread connecting him to his past growing thinner and thinner with each passing day.

One afternoon, as he lay stuck in a numb trance, he heard new bustling above him. Something was happening outside the void of his existence.

With difficulty, he propped himself on one elbow.

Then he heard the sailors' shouts, words yelled over and over…
"Land Ho!"

- 8 -

Land Ho!

New energy erupted as the sailors came to bring the slaves on deck.

As before, the boys were made to dance and work while the majority of men remained shackled and chained to the deck.

But the sailors were busy with different tasks as they excitedly looked off in the distance. Soon, the slaves saw it too. It was land. A sight they hadn't seen since the shores of Africa receded months ago. At first, it was just a faint mirage on the horizon, barely noticeable, like a hazy cloud refusing to fully form.

Birds, too, occasionally appeared in the skies. It dawned on Jayvyn he hadn't seen birds for a very long time. It was good to see other creatures besides the terrible fish that accompanied the ship over the whole voyage. One bird landed up in the ship's rigging. It stayed there for a long time, as if guiding them on their way.

What was the shore they were approaching? The slaves could only wonder as they'd never known anything other than their homeland. Most had no concept of any other place even existing.

The following day, routines became different. They were taken in small groups. Every inch of their bodies was, once again, shaved clean of all hair that had regrown since their capture. They were then washed and scrubbed with seawater, all of which was humiliating and made their skin raw.

The boy with freshly healed scars on his back bristled with pain as he was scrubbed. The sailor holding him repeatedly smacked the side of his head to make him stand still and take it.

Jayvyn noticed the men in shackles, too, were being stood one at a time, to be shaved and scrubbed in the same manner. Sailors stood by with clubs to quickly quell any resistance.

The doctor came again to inspect each of the slaves as before, noting the condition of each man.

All the while, the land became clearer and clearer until the colors of trees and sand could be seen.

There were hills, and for all the slaves could see, this place looked like Africa, except the coastline was much smaller. The temperature and sea felt very similar to Africa's, but something significant was different.

It was the light. It was coming from a different direction than it should be. Instinctively, all knew this couldn't be Africa. Besides, why would they have traveled so far out in the ocean only to return to the same place?

There were other differences, too, some too subtle to immediately recognize but others that couldn't be denied.

However, the biggest and most noticeable difference of all was that they weren't free Africans anymore. They couldn't return to their homes and lives, see their families or tribesmen, or honor traditions once so familiar.

No. Everything was different, strange, and cruel now. Happiness or love was nowhere to be found—not since the catastrophic day their worlds were so mercilessly torn apart and the hot irons fell upon their skin.

The marks from those irons remained in full view—deep scars, forever testifying to the day their lives changed forever.

The ship glided easily across the water toward the rapidly approaching shore. They could see other ships now—many other ships—at rest in a large, protected cove breaching the shoreline.

The sailors around them were busily engaged, making arrangements for joining the other ships as the men in uniform shouted commands. It seemed everyone was out on deck doing some important work in preparation for the end of their voyage.

What could this mean? Jayvyn wondered. It was clear things were going to change. They were coming to some new step in their journey.

Jayvyn's mind reeled through the phases of their odyssey thus far.

First, they were captured and separated from their families and tribes, then denuded, shaved, shackled, and penned. Many men and boys, and probably as many women and children, had died during this first step alone.

Next, they were shut below decks in unimaginable squalor, where many more died as they made their awful voyage across the sea.

Jayvyn had seen several slaves beaten to death. He'd seen others whipped until their flesh lay bare. He'd watched as previously healthy boys and men shit until too weak to stand, then were mercilessly jettisoned overboard to the waiting fish.

So, then, what would this next step be? Could it be any worse? Jayvyn couldn't imagine anything worse than what they'd already been through. He could only look forward to this current stage of their miserable journey to be over with.

As the ship entered the cove, the sails were collapsed and secured. Large metal hooks on long chains were lowered into the water, which stopped the ship and held it where it was. Things were indeed much different now. Just the fact that they'd come to rest and were in proximity to land was difference enough.

Sailors got busy lowering open boats into the water. Several officers got into one and were rowed off toward shore.

Jayvyn watched the small boat weave its way between the other ships, slowly making its way toward land. There seemed to be a lot of activity along the shore. Other small boats busily came and went from the other ships anchored around them.

In the middle of the cove stood a large pier with building structures surrounding it. The boat with the officers was headed to that location. On either side were open stretches of beach similar to what they'd left in Africa. Jayvyn saw many groups of Blacks standing there, with more arriving from the ships.

Palm trees bent in the breeze beyond the shore. More structures stood partially buried in the hillsides.

The hills crept up from there, covered in thick jungle foliage, broken here and there by clearings of some kind. The sky above was brilliant blue, speckled with gray and white clouds drifting lazily, casting moving shadows over the mottled green hills.

Soon, sailors came with buckets of something and began lathering it over the slaves' freshly shaved and washed skin. It was recognizable. It was palm oil, the same as had been put over their fresh burns so long ago, except this time it was spread over their entire bodies, head to toe. The slaves' skin glistened in the bright light. The palm oil didn't dry; it just stayed a wet, shiny coating on top of their skin.*

Chains were again attached to the neck rings still around each of the men's necks. Their hands remained shackled as they'd been since their capture. The boys' wrists were bound with rope.

Little by little, the slaves were brought to a series of planks arranged along the sides of the ship, where they were directed down into waiting open boats floating along the side. As before, they were made to kneel, guarded with weapons, as the sailors rowed the boats to shore.

For the first time in over two months, they were leaving the awful ship that had been their prison of death since leaving Africa.

---

* *Palm oil was used to shine up the slaves' skin to make them look as good as possible to prospective buyers*

Part Two

Seasoning

– 9 –

Welcome to Barbados

As they came to shore, Jayvyn saw many men working to unload the newly arrived slaves and put them into groups.

When they got very close, he noticed men moving between groups of recently disembarked slaves and checking them over. They lifted their arms, looked in their mouths, hit them with sticks, and inspected their genitals. Selected slaves were moved into new groupings. All were being guarded by cordons of armed men lest they wander.

Suddenly, one did, and not just wander, but fled. The slave had recently been unchained and made to stand in a new group. He took the opportunity to make a run for it, hands still shackled before him. Before, he'd been just another slave hidden within the group, but now he stood out as a lone figure, wrists bound, running desperately for the perceived safety of the not-too-distant tree line. He couldn't have had any plan in mind except to make it that far, as he knew nothing about this new land other than he'd arrived in chains.

There was a quick commotion amongst the men guarding the slaves, whereby one raised a weapon. It was something Jayvyn wasn't familiar with. A sort of a long stick but it gave a great, loud bang as smoke and fire shot from one end.

The Black man, frantically running a short distance away,

suddenly arched his back. Jayvyn saw a spray of blood belch from his side as he fell mid-stride into the sand, where he lay writhing and rolling in pain as the man with the new weapon, along with another, approached him. They grabbed onto the fallen Black man, each on an arm, and dragged him back to the group from which he'd run, his head lolling from side to side.

Jayvyn's boat made shore and ground upon the sand. They were quickly made to exit and stand on the beach with the other groups of slaves.

The wounded Black man was being held upright by his captors before the group he'd run from. Another man came to inspect him. He looked at the badly bleeding wound in his side, poking and prodding at it, while the Black man screamed in agony.

The white men conferred amongst themselves briefly, apparently reaching a decision of some sort. Following this, the wounded Black man was taken to a nearby tree. His wrists were tightly fastened to a rope, which was then tossed over a branch. He was hauled up to a point where his toes barely touched the ground, blood pouring from the hole in his side.

One of the white men, looking back to make sure all were watching, then picked a thin stick off the ground and rammed it into his open wound. The Black man howled in pain as the other man twisted and pushed the stick around, leaving it hanging from his side when finished.

Another white man, very large and muscular, stepped forward brandishing a long, thin whip made of a single strand tapered to a fine point at its end.[*] Stepping back a few paces and taking aim, he expertly brought the whip high behind his back. Its full length gracefully uncoiled in a large, continuous arch that he brought down in one sustained motion, landing it on the back of the helpless man with an air-splitting crack. A long thin stripe instantly appeared down the man's back and began running with blood.

The man screamed in agony as the whip was brought back and snapped forward again, giving off another loud report as it split his back open anew. Each wound was severe, as was clear for all to see from the blood running forth.

He was hit repeatedly until his back was laced with long, deep, crisscrossing cuts from the whip. Then, while the man was still coherent, the man with the whip took a large handful of sand and dirt and forcibly rubbed it into the fresh wounds on his back, causing him to howl out with guttural cries of intense pain.

More rope was then brought and separate strands were tied to each of his ankles. The loose ends were tossed behind and over his shoulders, one on each side of his neck. Two other strong men took the loose ends and pulled hard. His ankles came off the ground behind his back, the ropes cutting sharply into his shoulders. The men pulled until his back was completely arched inward, the backs of his ankles touching his shoulders, his chest and stomach pushed outward. The

---

* *The bullwhip is designed with several parts, the most devastating being the "fall" and "cracker". The fall is a length of thinner leather at its end, which radically increases in speed from centrifugal acceleration, exceeding the speed of sound, which gives the whip its sharp report. The cracker is a small bundle of much thinner material, e.g., horsehair, used to amplify the sound. Due to its destructive power, it is only used by cattle ranchers for its sound, but when used as a weapon it can cause catastrophic injury*

sounds he emitted hardly sounded human anymore as he swayed and spun by his wrists.

All during this shocking spectacle, men were slapping and pushing at the slaves to make sure they watched every single part of it.*

Jayvyn and the slaves in his group looked on mournfully as they watched the condemned man slowly spin.

His anguished cries broke the air, plucking at the slaves' emotional strings, spawning futile urges to somehow come to the poor man's aid. The awful fact was there was nothing anyone could do. Some of the white men laughed cruelly as they continued to poke and shove at the slaves.

The big man then laid down his whip and picked up a thick club. Yelling something back at the watching slaves, he cocked the club back and took a mighty swing, landing it squarely into the swinging man's protruding abdomen. It hit with a terrible thud, the man going silent as his breath was knocked completely from him. Blood now oozed from his mouth and nose as well as his side and back.

The Black man was left to swing from the branch, head hanging forward between his shoulders, blood dripping onto the sand.

The white men casually went back to the business of inspecting and separating the slaves.†

All of the other slaves, naturally, stood petrified and stunned by

---

* *As with most corporal punishments, slaves were made to bear witness as a deterrent*

† *Slave masters were free to design their own punishments and often sought to outdo their peers with their inventiveness. Nothing was off limits, and punishments were usually designed to be as painful and horrifying as possible*

what they'd just witnessed. It was clear now that the horrors they'd survived during their brutal passage had not been left behind on the ships.

Jayvyn's group was soon approached by one of the men inspecting the new arrivals. He was very matter of fact and routine with his movements as he lifted arms, poked here and there, instructed some to jump—using a stick for emphasis—pried open mouths, and grabbed at genitals. Women were treated indifferently.

All were then herded into this or that group at the direction of these men.

Jayvyn looked nervously around, trying to see if he spotted his mother or little sister, but it was impossible. He couldn't even be sure they were on his ship in the first place.

But the slaves had been mixed into so many diverse groups by this point that even if they were here, he wouldn't have been able to find them. He looked for Baahir, too, but he was nowhere to be seen. He, too, had been mixed in with other groups along the shore.

As the process continued, Jayvyn heard barely audible sounds coming from the man left hanging in the tree. The sound was like a high-pitched rasping. It was apparent he was somehow alive. However, no one came to his aid or paid any attention to him. He was just left there, hanging in a contorted form, blood dripping from his many wounds.

Of course, no one else ran or put up any kind of resistance And, if anyone dared utter a sound in reaction to this atrocity, they were immediately beat to the ground by whichever guard was nearest.

Jayvyn noticed the guards even included a few Black men. He

couldn't—nor did he dare try—make any sense of it.

Nothing made sense. His thoughts swirled with the same confusion as on so many other occasions since his capture. No sensation was familiar anymore—the light coming to his eyes; the ground beneath his feet; his hands in front of him; the sound of his breathing—all of it seemed surreal and unrecognizable. None of it was to be trusted. He was just a shell—there was no thought, no feeling, no meaning—just the barest impulse to survive, if only for the next moment in time.

At length, the group he was now a part of was moved. They stumbled in numbness, up the beach, past the man hanging in the tree, whose high-pitched wheezing grew fainter and fainter with each labored breath.

Finally, they arrived at a stockade. This stockade was more substantial than the one in Africa, as it had a hinged door and a roof above it.

The group was herded and pushed inside, where two large Black men wearing clothes stood equipped with sticks and clubs. It struck Jayvyn, who'd been without any sort of clothing since leaving Africa, to see Blacks in clothes. It was even more confusing to see Blacks wielding clubs, with fixed, mean-looking expressions on their faces.

He didn't doubt the obvious fact these men were not the same as the rest of them and no liberties or familiarity should be assumed just because the color of their skin matched.

The group Jayvyn was in contained some thirty slaves in all. They were a mix of age, size, and sex—all leery, scared, hungry, thirsty, and worn.

The Black guards ordered them, in small groups, to come and drink from tubs of water. Afterwards, the new arrivals were made to sit. The men in the group still had shackles on their wrists and rings around their necks so they could pose little threat. But all had witnessed enough terror by this point that none did. Besides, most were too thoroughly exhausted from their ordeal on the ships.

Sometime later, as evening descended, tubs of boiled rice mixed with other grains and lard were brought. All of the slaves were made to eat, then more water was given.

The Black guards, however, ate different food containing fruits and vegetables. No offers were made of this food, and no kindness was extended by these Black men. They were strict and acted as the white men did. It was clear to all they were in charge and shouldn't be approached.

Jayvyn, and he was sure the others, wondered at this. How was it these Black men, clearly not of the same status as their white captors, wore decent clothing, ate refined food, and held weapons against their brothers?* This wonderment, however, lodged itself as a mere footnote in Jayvyn's tired, stress-ridden mind.

His fatigue was like nothing he'd ever experienced.

Jayvyn wouldn't have believed he could feel any more depleted than he had on the ship, but the experience on the beach today—the brutal, savage mutilation of the man who'd tried to run—left Jayvyn's mind staggered beyond comprehension.

He looked around briefly at the other faces in the stockade—none he recognized—and saw a few others glancing around as well.

**Many slaves were successfully turned against their own through incentives and rewards*

All dead-eyed and slack-faced.

He laid back and closed his eyes, feeling the uncomfortable swirl of darkness surround his muddled mind as he drifted in complete emotional and physical weakness from the day's horrid events.

He now knew what to expect for the next stage in his journey.

- 10 -

Training Begins

Jayvyn was suddenly roused from his sleep by noise and commotion coming from the entrance of their stockade. He had no idea how long he'd slept, but it certainly didn't feel like enough. It was still dark, and outside the door, he saw the flicker of lanterns as men moved about.

Some of the others stirred in confusion. The guards brought new tubs of the grainy lard mixture and motioned for everyone to eat. Not all felt like eating again, especially not this. But the slightest expression of disinterest was swiftly dealt with. The guards slapped and yelled at any offending individual, one holding their face and mouth open in a firm grip while the other packed a ladle of the sickening concoction into their mouth. Seeing this, the rest did the best they could to eat some of it, lest they, too, fall victim to this harsh treatment.

The slaves in the stockade were generally in poor condition—all weak and thin from their harrowing voyage across the sea and the appalling conditions they'd survived. All were mentally exhausted and emotionally drained, confused about why they'd been so brutally ripped from their lives and separated from their families and all they'd ever known.

Soon, they were assembled outside the stockade in the barely lightening skies. A few remained inside, too weak to stand after repeated provocations.

Ropes were removed from Jayvyn's and the other boys' wrists as two Black men worked down the line of men to remove the link binding their wrists together. Another guard stood close by, with a menacing glare and a rigid stick, ready to quell any aggressive actions the men might take as their hands became free. None took any such action; they were all too weak and had seen fully there was no limit to the severity of punishment that would be delivered if they moved against the guards in the slightest way. Other white men stood nearby with weapons at the ready, watching and supervising events.

As light slowly began to take over the darkness, the slaves were led off on a short path, uphill, to a small clearing at the edge of the jungle. Some of the clearing, nearer the bottom, had had its stumps and rocks removed and the ground tilled up. Jayvyn noticed new plantings emerging in some spots.

A sad wave of nostalgia swept through him as he thought about helping his father with the crops back in Africa.

He saw the clearing was unfinished. Its furthest, uphill perimeter still laden with fresh fallen trees—stumps, rocks, and low vegetation still rooted in place. He noticed other Black men, wearing clothes more meager than the guards, coming into the clearing and moving up the hill to the perimeter. The clothes they wore were very simple and all of a tan color. These men began chopping and cutting trees not yet felled, working to gradually increase the size of the clearing.

Jayvyn and the new arrivals stood at the beginning of the clearing, naked and shaved, men and women alike, old and young. The guards began dividing them into smaller groups. The men and larger boys were split into groups of about five each. The women, girls, and smaller boys were similarly grouped. In all, there were five groups—two of the men and three of the others. Jayvyn was included with the men, along with a few other boys around his age.

Each group was then led by a guard, along with some of the Blacks in tan clothing, to a segment of the clearing. One group of men was assigned to the area being cleared, thick with freshly fallen trees. Jayvyn's group was brought to a place slightly inside of this.

Here they were shown what to do. Gathering some tools, the Blacks in tan clothing demonstrated by digging around stumps, prying rocks out of the ground, and working to remove the undergrowth. As they understood, the new arrivals were put into the mix.

Some joined the group removing stumps and such, while the rest gathered debris and carried it to the edge of the clearing where it was piled with other like debris—rocks with rocks, stumps with stumps, and so forth. Soon, all of the newcomers were working.

Several men stood nearby, white men with rifles along with some of the Black guards. Men carried felled trees to the area for debris. The trees were very large and required chopping into smaller pieces before they could be moved. Still, it took several men to move the large pieces, some stumbling and falling over the rough terrain as they struggled to get them down the hill. Guards stood nearby with sticks, flogging anyone who faltered or didn't move quickly enough.

Jayvyn saw the women, girls, and smaller boys downslope from him working in the newly tilled ground, making new plantings and tending to ones already started.

All were closely supervised by the guards as well as the established slaves in tan that had been brought to instruct them. If anyone slowed, the established slaves were quick to admonish them, with harsh words and gestures, to work hard and unceasingly.*

Jayvyn carried large bundles of brush, stumps, and rocks to the area for debris. His bare feet occasionally stumbled over sharp objects hidden on the jungle floor, causing him to fall. Each time, he was quickly noticed by a guard, who yelled and approached with his stick.

Jayvyn recovered as fast as he could, but a few times, the guard caught up to him. Jayvyn found himself lying in a fetal position, using his hands and arms to deflect the blows until he was let up to gather his load and resume his work. His body ached from the beatings as well as from the hard, unforgiving work in his depleted condition. Others suffered similarly if they failed to keep up the pace.

Soon, the sun was full in the sky, and the temperatures rose. It was very hot and humid in the jungle. There were many insects as well—stinging, biting insects that hovered around Jayvyn's eyes and ears, got into his mouth and nostrils, and crawled on his skin as he fought to keep up the work and avoid the guards' wrath.

At some point, water was brought, and the slaves were made, one at a time, to briefly stop and drink. But the break was only long enough to drink and catch their breath before being put back to work at the same unremitting pace.

Blazing hot sun and humidity caused sweat to pour into his eyes and down his face. Jayvyn felt the sting of his sweat as it passed over

---

* *It was the responsibility of those training the new slaves to instill the work ethic that would be required of them*

his freshly bruised skin, now spotted with a variety of insect bites as well.

His muscles grew numb and quivered under the weight of each new load. The rocks, varying in size, shape, and weight, were difficult to handle. They dug at his fingers and pressed into his groin as he carried them, arms fully extended. The stumps, too, were unruly in the same way, inconsistent in size and shape, and home to a variety of insects.

The dirt from the debris was constantly smeared and pressed into his body. His feet had many fine cuts from the thorns, roots, and rocks he stumbled over. The sloping ground with its uneven surface made things all the harder. It was impossible to predict where his feet would land and what the surface would be like, causing him to continuously trip.

Jayvyn's naked body became an ever-changing array of dirt, scratches, bruises, and bites—constantly streamed with sweat.

Several of the new arrivals fell unconscious, physically unable to carry on in their condition. They were revived, if possible, with shouting, slaps, and splashes of water. They were either put right back to work, or, if they were truly incapable of continuing with the same task, moved to a lighter task.

Some were taxed beyond their limitations and couldn't be roused. They were carried out, arms and legs limp, heads hanging, like the slaves thrown to the sharks. Jayvyn briefly wondered what would become of them.

Most stayed with their task throughout the day, only stopping for short intervals to drink water.

Dusk came, and still they worked. It had been at least twelve hours of constant hard labor. Men came with torches and lanterns to light the way, but eventually it became too dark to see well enough, and they stopped and marched back to the stockade.

Light flashed before Jayvyn's eyes as he walked, barely able to keep moving. He wondered how he was ever able to make it through the day. There were so many moments, from early in the day, when he was certain he wouldn't be able to last even a minute longer. Yet somehow, he'd endured far more than he ever imagined he could have. He literally felt like a walking dead person.

When they arrived back at the stockade, another tub of the same food was brought. Although it was terrible, the slaves were so depleted they had to eat anything that might give their bodies some of what was required to sustain life.

For the newly arrived slaves, the instinct to survive was all that remained. Any other of life's impulses were luxuries that simply couldn't be accessed. Luxuries like conscious thought, feelings, or sensations of any kind were simply beyond their remaining reserves.

Through the haze of his vision, Jayvyn passively noticed the guards eating nearby. He smelled the sweeter, more savory smells of their food but was unable to conjure any emotion about it; it just was.

He saw, too, some of those who'd fallen and been carried out that day. They were sitting against the sides of the stockade—slumped, nearly lifeless, faces slack, eyes vacant—much as the sick boys on the ship.

There wasn't much commotion in the stockade that night. Only occasional whimpers or groans of intense discomfort—subtle sounds of shifting—worn, depleted bodies seeking positions causing the least amount of pain—until unconsciousness mercifully overcame them. Jayvyn soon followed.

The sudden, jarring foot in his side came as a brutal intrusion to the barest beginnings of much-needed rest. Jayvyn's bloodshot eyes snapped open in the darkness. He lay bewildered by his surroundings, fighting for some kind of explanation for where he was and what he saw. Lanterns and torches flickered outside the door. Others, sleep suddenly shattered, blinked in confusion as they, too, struggled to come to terms with reality.

The guards came with more of the awful food.

It was difficult to function at all. Sleep couldn't have been more than a few hours at best.

With great difficulty, Jayvyn ate, drank some water, and got painfully to his feet. Every part of his body was sore as he rose unsteadily. He was quickly reminded of the cuts and bruises on the bottoms of his feet.

They were given a few moments to urinate or defecate, if they could, but soon they found themselves walking out the same trail they'd left only hours ago.

Jayvyn's head still buzzed with the remnants of his short sleep.

Moments later he found himself back at the same task he'd barely survived the day before. It was still dark, but the sky above the trees was beginning to show the first light of dawn.

The day became a repeat of the day before. Somewhere deep within him, Jayvyn found the barest amount of strength to carry on.

The sun rose, bringing heat and humidity with it. Insects

swarmed and bit at his naked body.

Men cried, fell, and were beat, only to rise and try again. Women and children toiled at the crops, and there, too, fell from exhaustion, only to be beat and pushed back into their work.

As they cleared the area of debris, some were put to work tilling the newly cleared ground with shovels, hoes, and rakes. Jayvyn was one.

At first, he took this as a welcome change from the work he'd been doing so far, glad to get away from the heavy rocks and insect-laden stumps—to give his feet a break from the sharp thorns and roots on the jungle floor.

But soon he found this work was as hard as the other. The ground was very firm and laden with fine roots. It took a lot of chopping and digging to loosen it.

Still, it was different, and in that respect, better. It also put him closer to the crops being tended.

Jayvyn wondered what crops were being grown.

The plants were grouped into sections. Some bore plants with large green leaves sitting atop a bulging brown root, which he recognized as yams. Another had very tall, sturdy grass growing tightly together. Still, others seemed to have short, bushy plants with orange berries or spikey green pods. Some had flowers of various colors as well.

One of the experienced workers noticed Jayvyn looking at the crops and began urgently shouting at him.

"No! No!" he repeated, shaking his head insistently. He approached quickly, taking Jayvyn firmly by the shoulders and turning him away from the crop and back to his work.

When Jayvyn lifted his head, he repeated, "NO!" and pointed to the ground where he was to till.

He uttered a few more words Jayvyn couldn't understand, insistently pointing to the ground in front of him and away from the crops. A guard looked over, but the worker waved, smiled, and resumed his work beside Jayvyn.

Jayvyn didn't know exactly what to make of this, but took it he was not to be distracted from his work and so focused on just that, not looking back at the crops again.*

The day was long and hot, just like the day before. They were allowed to drink or relieve their bladders and bowels, but that was all.

The beatings continued for anyone who faltered at their task, and as happened previously, one or two fell, could not rise, and were carried limply from the clearing.

It was well after dusk when they were marched back to the stockade. Again, Jayvyn wondered how he'd mustered the strength to continue through the day.

Sparkled light danced before his eyes as he stumbled along the narrow path, his head throbbing with each footstep. He could see pain and fatigue written on the faces of others as well.

As before, the same food was brought, and the guards ate their better food apart from the rest.

The weaker, failing new slaves lay slumped along the walls of the stockade, listless, vacant eyes staring.

---

* *The slave was dissuading Jayvyn from being too interested in the crops as they were strictly off limits for any purpose other than working them*

There was little energy among any of them, and sleep, once more, was at best a welcome relief to their pain, but too short-lived.

It seemed Jayvyn had barely closed his eyes when, once again, he was rudely awakened to eat the gruel, drink some water, and relieve himself.

He marched, with the others, through the pre-dawn darkness, back to the clearing—under the ruthless watch of the guards—for another long, hot, miserable day.

- 11 -

Graduation

The days following were much the same as the first few, although their numbers became fewer as some of the weakest slaves were removed from the stockade. Jayvyn assumed they were disposed of as the dead and dying had been back in the stockades in Africa, heaped onto a pile of rotting bodies somewhere, like so much garbage.

The surviving new slaves were becoming more familiar with their tasks, and new words began to form in their vocabularies as well. Things they heard over and over. "*Work*," for example, was the word for the tasks they were to perform. "*Go*" was another; it was the opposite of "*stop.*" But it was also the opposite of "*come.*" "*Get*" meant to retrieve, or it could also mean to do something. It was difficult because "*get shovel*" and "*get up*" meant different things. But slowly, the differences became clearer depending on the context. And there were the names of things. "*Shovel*" and "*hoe*" were tools, "*woman,*" an adult female, "*man,*" an adult male, "*boy*" if he was a young male. All in all, it was confusing, but when no one speaks your language, it becomes a necessity to learn if you are to be able to understand and communicate.

There were some among the slaves who spoke the same, or maybe variations of the same language. However, speaking one's tribal dialect was severely discouraged. When others were heard speaking in their native tongue, they were immediately reprimanded and beat. It was not to be done under any circumstances.*

Jayvyn's language was not known well beyond his tribe, and so far, he'd found no one who could converse in it or understand him. Although he might find it refreshing to easily share conversations as he once had, he ultimately became glad he couldn't since it was forbidden. In a convoluted sense, it made it easier for him to succumb to the reality he had to learn a new language.

The work remained hard, and the days were long and unforgiving. The clearing had increased in size and the garden of crops as well.

Jayvyn was learning more about what these crops were. All of it was food of some sort. The long brown tubular vegetables were called "*yams*." The shorter, pointed green pods were vegetables called "*okra*." Some of the berries were "*gooseberries*." Other fruits hung from trees, such as "*mango*" and "*banana*." There were also several varieties of groundnuts. Some of the greenery was food in and of itself.

The sturdy, tall, grass-like plants growing closely together were called "*cane*," but it wasn't clear to Jayvyn what it was used for. It was simply cut, bundled, and carried away.

But it was clear it was somehow important.

Some of the plants were recognizable to Jayvyn as being similar or the same as what grew in his homeland, such as palm trees. They were as abundant here as in Africa. His tribe used the oil and fermented it to make a potent drink the adults enjoyed and used in

---

* *Slaves were not allowed to speak in their native language like so many other things designed to separate them from their heritage and traditions*

ceremonies.*

It was strictly forbidden for anyone to take or eat anything from these crops, as was soon demonstrated. One day, while working in the clearing, there was a great commotion. One of the newly arrived Black women was working at tending the crops and had taken a yam that she began to eat. She'd been gnawing on it as she worked and was spotted by one of the other experienced slaves. This worker alerted the guards, who immediately came and seized the woman and her yam.† She was beat, removed from the garden, and brought back to the stockade.

Later, after the work day ended and everyone was marched back, they saw the woman had been put into a wooden structure called a "pillory." It stood about four feet high, had two pieces of wood with holes that could be separated, and then closed around one's wrists and neck, thereby holding them in this way—stooped over and unable to remove their hands or head.

All of the slaves were assembled before this woman, and a white man held up the partially eaten yam, pointing at the woman to demonstrate she'd taken this from the garden to eat for herself and would now be punished for her crime.

The woman was sobbing, locked in the pillory, frightened for what might happen to her. A leather strap was attached around her chin and the top of her head so it held her mouth completely shut;

---

* *Palm wine is a traditional drink among the Jolas which has been made and ritualistically consumed for many hundreds of years*

† *Stealing food as well as anything else, was considered a grave offense and would result in severe punishment*

teeth clenched tightly. One of the Black guards came with a flat metal bar he pressed between her lips, holding it firmly against her front teeth. In his other hand, he held a hammer. As the woman stared, wide-eyed and terrified, he swung the hammer at the metal bar, instantly smashing her front teeth out. Jayvyn and the others flinched as blood and broken teeth flowed from her wounded mouth. The poor woman, howling in pain, was left in the pillory overnight, through the next day, and the following night, as a reminder to all that taking or eating food from the garden would not be tolerated. The other slaves were naturally mortified by this punishment, but it was just another in the growing list of horrors they'd already witnessed.

Everyone moved past her in the morning and again when they returned that night, dried blood caked to her chin, her mouth and gums swollen and permanently damaged. All through the night she whimpered in pain. On the second morning, she was released from the pillory and immediately forced back to work. No attention whatsoever was given to her wounded mouth. At mealtimes, she was left to eat as best she could and suffer through her recovery on her own. There was nothing anyone could do for this poor woman, any more than for the weak and dying slumped along the wall. It was all anyone could do to survive themselves, and that's just the way it was.

Days and weeks began to pass, and little by little, a sort of social culture began to emerge. Jayvyn began to understand why some of the slaves who'd come before them had meager clothes, while others had better clothes and ate better food. These were people who'd learned to comply with the rules and do the bidding of the white man.

The established slaves knew what was expected of them and had been entrusted to teach the new slaves. The Black guards had, apparently, achieved a high enough level of trust that they could be relied upon to watch and discipline other slaves as the white man would.

But hadn't they, too, been captured and torn from their lives and families? Didn't they suffer the same terrible journey as the new arrivals? Had they forgotten all this? Jayvyn was greatly confused. He couldn't imagine himself rising to the level of a guard, to be complicit in the white man's diabolical scheme to torture and enslave his people.

Jayvyn also began to see there were those among the newly arrived slaves who were consistently defiant. Mostly these seemed to be men, but almost always adults. Their jaws and countenance were fixed and unyielding. He figured this was because they'd become more solid in their ways, more resistant to change. He could see it in their eyes. They stared ahead, not at someone. Like the eyes of the warriors he'd seen on the ship, their gaze was strong, fierce, wild, and independent.

There was something he both feared and admired about these people. He certainly would want them on his side in a fight, and a strong part within him yearned to be like them. But instead, he found himself afraid—not of them, but of defying the white man and suffering the consequences.

He could see these defiant Blacks lacked the humility, or maybe the cunning, to adapt well to their new circumstances. They were the ones who suffered the worst punishments.

The ones who'd learned to adjust—to adapt, to obey—were the ones with more privilege, clothing, authority, and food.

Jayvyn thought back to Baahir, the boy he'd been chained to for so long on the ship. He wondered what had happened to him and how he'd feel about this new social order.

He remembered the vivid dream he'd had on the ship. In that dream, Baahir was a warrior, he had those fierce eyes. The sudden memory of that dream stuck with him over several days as he struggled with the rules of this new "social order."

In that dream, he and Baahir had also magically returned to their childhood. It reminded Jayvyn of how happy he'd been in his village. It was what he so badly wanted; to be free and happy among his family and people again, where life was good and everything made sense.

But those thoughts didn't last for long when he realized the permanence of his situation. There was no going back. His father was dead and he had no idea what had happened to his mother and little sister.

It was moments like this he felt his fear of the white man rapidly dissolve into rage. Rage at the idea of being so unfairly swept from his life and his home; rage at being deprived of his freedom and driven to senseless work; rage at the unending pain and injustice thrust upon him and so many others.

Jayvyn could feel his countenance harden as these feelings of rage consumed him. He was reminded all at once of the defiant 'warriors.' Was he, after all, like them?

He thought again of Baahir as the warrior in his dream, remembering his fixed, fierce, uncompromising eyes—spear perched confidently above his shoulder. Again, Jayvyn wondered about himself and who he really was.

He desperately wanted to be free from all of this, to be able to return to the life he had before—the life where things made sense and people spoke his language; where he was free to run in the forest through the fresh morning air; where anger and rage had no place in his life but instead happiness and enthusiasm were the emotions that nurtured him.

But Jayvyn could see no way. He was trapped. Even if he could get away, he'd have no idea of where to go.

Hopelessness and despair were quick to return.

Work continued in the clearing, and the days remained the same—hard and unyielding—until one day when new white men arrived. They came and watched as the slaves worked, observing them throughout an entire day. They observed them back at the stockade that evening, too. The following day, when the new slaves were awakened, they weren't taken to work in the clearing.

Instead, they were washed and reoiled with palm oil as they had been when they first arrived. Then they were stood in a line in front of the stockade as these new white men came again and inspected them at will—squeezing their flesh, looking into their mouths, inspecting their genitals, poking at their limbs—the same sorts of things done on the beach that first day.*

These men then pointed to them individually, whereupon a guard took that individual and placed him in a new group for each man. A few of the sicker, weaker ones weren't pointed to at all and remained where they were.

---

* *This was very typical treatment any time slaves were to be sold or transferred to a new owner*

Jayvyn was pointed to by a man who was of medium height and somewhat round in form. His face was a ruddy, reddish shade of white, and he had balding blond hair with bushy sideburns. He wore a set of spectacles perched low on his nose and looked neither happy nor sad in his demeanor, just serious and matter of fact.

Jayvyn now stood in a group of eight selected by that man— two men, another boy near his age, two women, a girl, and a young boy about five. The white man was accompanied by three Black men, who were already his slaves. One, larger than the others, brandished a sturdy stick and looked particularly stern.

The men in Jayvyn's group were attached to each other with a chain passing through their neck rings. The slightly older boy and Jayvyn were attached to each other with ankle shackles. The women and the girl had their wrists bound and were attached to one another by a length of rope. The boy was left untied.

They were then all marched away from the stockade by the three slaves who'd accompanied the man to a waiting wagon. The wagon had a bench in the front and two horses to pull it. A white man sat near the wagon next to a hot fire.

The men were taken first, one at a time, and solidly restrained against a tree by the three slaves. The white man then took a red-hot iron from the fire and planted it in each of their shoulders, smoke pouring from the site as they writhed and screamed in pain. This was a branding iron, as had been used back in Africa, but with a different pattern on the end. After the first two were branded, palm oil was again applied to the fresh burns, as it had been in Africa. The two women and the girl were branded next and then the five-year-old boy, all of whom howled and cried.

Then came Jayvyn and the older boy's turn. Resisting was simultaneously unavoidable and ineffective, and force was needed to hold them as they anticipated the moment next to come. The older boy was burned first, clenching his teeth and crying out. Then Jayvyn was pressed, chest first, into the tree. The scorching, red-hot iron bit furiously into his shoulder as he buried his face into the tree, tears coming to his eyes.

Although it was over in an instant, the wound would hurt for many days to come. The scar would last forever.

They were then loaded into the wagon and attached to its sides by the constraints binding them together, except for the small boy, who sat in the middle, still weeping from the pain of the new burn on his shoulder. The women, too, cried softly, but were brusquely silenced by their new owner's big slave. As they sat at each end of the wagon, Jayvyn noticed the three other slaves had scars on their shoulders in the shape of the new brand.

Soon, the first white man, the one with the spectacles, came and climbed up on the seat next to the other white man, who gave a clicking command with his tongue. The horses obediently began to walk.

A renewed sickness seized Jayvyn's heart as the shores of his beloved Africa slipped further into the deep chasm of his memory.

- 12 -

Welcome to the Plantation

They traveled over dusty roads, and from time-to-time Jayvyn could see the ocean beyond the trees, its white foaming wave crests falling on the rocky shore. After a while, they left this road for another that turned inland and began to climb a hill. The road traversed the hillside for a long way and then made a sharp bend to traverse more of the hillside in the other direction. Intermittently, the ocean could be seen, much further away and downslope.

After a few more switchbacks, they turned off the road onto a more sparsely traveled, and hence rougher, track. The jungle grew thicker as the cart bounced over the rutted path, until finally reaching a great clearing in a valley, with mountains reaching high up on three sides and the ocean partially visible, far away down the remaining side.

On a hill at the top of this clearing was an immense, grand, white house with a large barn beside it. Jayvyn had never seen buildings so large before; they were even larger than the ships he'd seen. Lower down, and at a distance from the main house, were a series of much smaller, simpler houses with thatched roofs and sides arranged in rows near a large pond. On the far ridge of the hill, between the big house and the pond, was another building, more like a tower. It was wider at the base and narrower at the top. This building had a large feature extending from near its top, spanning from well above it to half way to the ground, rotating slowly, like a giant wheel.* Another long, low building sat next to it, smoke emanating from a large chimney rising from its center. Jayvyn saw people busily moving in, out, and around these buildings.

Small roads and paths led here and there between the buildings and elsewhere. People and animals scurried about. Trees, fences, rock walls, and many other developed features dotted the great clearing.

In open spaces between the hills, Jayvyn glimpsed many rows of agriculture disappearing into the distance.

Much was going on here; it was overwhelming. Even the horses and the owner's three slaves paused in awe.

Jayvyn unconsciously fingered the fresh burn on his shoulder as they entered into this lush, green valley.

The cart made a long, sweeping turn as the road curved up toward the grand house on the hill. The valley and the mountains beyond were so large and exposed they made the cart and all those in it feel insignificantly small. The road passed directly in front of the huge house.

Upon passing, Jayvyn was awed by the structure. Tall columns supported a high roof over an immense porch running the full length of the house. Large, beautiful, earthen pots with exotic plants decorated its expanse. Various types of seating were interspersed down its length. White people sitting on the porch waved. The driver and man with the spectacles waved back.

Here and there, Black people worked at one task or another.

---

* *Windmills were typical installations in sugar plantations in the 1700's used to press the sugar sap from the cane*

They wore the same clothing as the three slaves who'd come with the white men.

Behind the porch were many doors and windows indicating great, mysterious spaces beyond the facade. A wide set of steps led up the middle of the porch, with neatly tended floral gardens and manicured lawns arranged on each of its sides.

Eventually they reached the large barn beyond, and the cart came to a stop. The man with the spectacles got out and walked toward the house. His three slaves got out and untied the eight new arrivals from the wagon, indicating they should stand and wait. The driver then led the cart into the barn.

A different slave came out of the barn and got to work removing the shackles and other restraints from the newly arrived slaves. The larger Black slave stood by watching, his stick at the ready. No one made to do anything different than stand there, perfectly naked, fresh brands on their shoulders, waiting to be instructed as to what should happen next.

One of the slaves had gone into the barn and returned with some cloth items which he handed out to each of the new arrivals. They were clothes! Real clothes! Although rough and drab in color, they were something, after all these many months, to cover their naked bodies with.

Jayvyn and the men received pants and a shirt. The boy received a long shirt covering him to his knees. The women and girl were handed one-piece dresses that came to their calves. All of the cloth was of a tannish, rough sort of fabric and showed wear in places as if they'd been worn before.

For such a long time, they'd been treated worse than animals. Shame and embarrassment had long since given way to overwhelming pain and horror. Now, the ability to cloak their nakedness, to retrieve just a shred of dignity, felt surreal.*

The man with the spectacles returned from the house, holding some sort of pad and a writing instrument.† He approached the new group of slaves and looked them all over approvingly. He then pointed to himself, and in an authoritative, stern voice, announced, "Master Clark." He said it again and looked at his large slave with the stick, who went down the line and whacked the first new man on the back of his legs.

Gesturing toward the white man, he said, "Ma'sa Clark!"

When the man looked back at him, wondering what he wanted, he hit him harder on the back of his legs, gestured again at the white man, and said, louder this time, "MASTA CLARK!"

The newly arrived man was a quick study. Looking nervously from the big slave to the white man, he repeated, to the best of his ability, "m-massa clott."

The large Black man tapped him again on the leg and said, a bit slower, with strong annunciation, "Ma-sta Cl-ar-k."

The new man, mouthing this as he said it, turned and repeated, "Ma-sta K-lar-K."

The larger man nodded, saying, "again," with another tap to the leg.

---

* *Typical clothing provided to slaves at sugar plantations were made from burlap and usually made by the slaves*

† *Slave owners kept copious written records of their slaves*

The new man repeated, "Ma-sta Cl-ar-k," looking nervously at the big Black slave for his approval.

The big man, nodding slightly, said, "Good," and moved on to the next.

Having seen what was expected, the next man did the best he could, but it still took several times to come close enough for the big man's approval; however, he did eventually achieve it.

And so it went, down the line to the women and girl, and eventually to the boy standing next to Jayvyn, and then to Jayvyn himself, who all managed to come close enough, after a few tries, to satisfy the big Black man. Then the smaller boy was given the same instructions, and he also managed a good enough version to get by for the moment.

The big slave then spoke again. Not all of what he said was understood directly, but his meaning was clear enough.

"Ma'sa Clark be de boss; he be at de top o ebryting. You gotsta 'spect 'n obey Ma'sa Clark alla time, no matta what."

Then Master Clark spoke again. Looking down at the paper he held, he looked up at the first new man, pointed, and said, "Samuel."

The big Black man then looked at the new slave and repeated, "Samuel," while pointing to him.

The new man, looking confused, pointed to himself, and said, "Khalon."

The blow came swiftly from the big man's stick to his abdomen. The new man doubled over, stumbling back, the wind knocked from him.

The big slave pointed to him again and repeated, in a much

louder, harsher tone, "SAM-MUEL!"

Dazed, Khalon caught his breath, stood, looked him in the eye, and said, "I Khalon!"

Again, he was hit, only with much greater force this time, sending him reeling backward onto the dirt where he held his gut, rolling and fighting to get his breath back.

Another slave picked Khalon up and stood him back in line. His hand to his gut and face breaking with sweat, he glanced warily at the large slave.

Looking very stern this time, the big Black thumped his finger hard into Khalon's chest, and said, "SAM-MUEL! You be, SAM-MU-EL!", then raised his eyebrows in expectation.

The staggered man, realizing what he wanted, repeated quietly, "Sam-mu-ell," and pointed to himself.

The large slave said, "Good" and repeated, "Samuel."

The white man smiled, again saying, "Samuel."

Khalon looked back, lowered his head, and solemnly said, "Samuel."*

Having seen what was happening, the others understood they were being assigned new names to go by, and so the process went a bit easier from there. The next man was named "Charles."

It was bitter medicine—to first be robbed of your home and family; then your clothing; be put in chains and sailed far away; forced into cruel, unremitting labor; deprived of your native language; and now have the only thing that might still be yours—your name—taken

---

* *Slaves were renamed by their masters and forbidden to use their African names as another means to remove their identities and past*

from you as well. But, with all that had happened to this point, the most important thing for the new slaves was to get safely to the next step, and so they all complied as he continued down the line.

"Sarah" was the first woman, "Julia" the next, and the girl was to be called "Rose." All repeated their names back as best they could. No one tried to mention their real name.

He then came to the boy standing next to Jayvyn and pointed, saying, "Lewis." The boy looked down, and Jayvyn could see a tear leaking from the corner of his eye as he looked up at the big Black man, who only intensified his glare. The boy then faced the white man and meekly said, "Loo-ees," his lip trembling as he did.

Jayvyn's emotions welled up. His mind spun. Feelings assailed him from every direction.

He looked nervously at the white man, waiting to hear what name he should have instead of the one he'd been given at birth.*

Time stood still. He remembered hearing his parents talk about the meaning of names in his part of the world. His name, Jayvyn, meant 'light spirit'. His mother often reminded him of this, and it was deeply ingrained in how he felt about himself. As a small child, he would imagine his spirit dancing lightly through the forest or sitting quietly as he listened to the elders tell stories around the fire at night.

He was a gentle person by nature, always taking the time to appreciate subtle beauty wherever he found it. It could be a salamander on a mossy log, the sprouts of new rice in the spring, or his sister's radiant smile. These were the things that energized his soul,

---

* *Names had special significance among the Jola as was true with many African tribes, often decided upon through various naming ceremonies and rituals*

gave him life, and made him the person he is—'light spirit'. He loved being that person and had enjoyed his place in the world. That is, until the terrible day everything had changed.

The thought hit him hard. What had he been? What had he lost? All of the most precious things that could ever exist—a time when all was right with the present and past, and the future was everything to look forward to. These were the things that had been taken from him. Then, all had changed in an instant—the instant these sickening white monsters came, destroying everything in front of his eyes—on a beautiful morning when nothing could go wrong!

He thought again of his little sister, Ifetayo, and the meaning of her name. It meant 'one who brings happiness', *and now what had become of her?* He'd loved her so much. She was the embodiment of her name as well, for she did bring happiness, to Jayvyn and anyone else who came into her presence. *And what of her now?* He couldn't know. The last he'd known, she was tied in a line as they were marched into the holding pen on the shores of Africa—her happy world shattered—frightened beyond description.

Has she survived what I have so far? Jayvyn didn't know whether to hope for that or not. After all, she was Ifetayo and must always remain so, or she wouldn't be anything at all.

It was at this point the white man with the spectacles fixed Jayvyn with his gaze, pointed, and said, "James. You will be James."

Jayvyn looked back at the man and found himself unable to speak. His eyes became moist with tears, and he looked down at his feet. Then he felt the sharp crack of the big man's stick against his calf.

Before he could stop himself, he straightened, looked the white man directly in the eyes, and shouted, "I am Jayvyn! Jayvyn! I am Ajamatau! My name is Jayvyn, and my family..." His stream of words came so fast he didn't even notice he was speaking in *Fogni*, his native language.

His words were abruptly cut off as his world exploded into a brilliant flash of white light.

The big Black man's stick came crushing across the right side of his brow and was followed quickly by another to his cheek and nose as he stumbled backward, a sharp, metallic taste filling his mouth.

He didn't feel the other blows to his chest, as he'd already fallen unconscious.

Jayvyn lay in the dirt, unmoving, blood seeping from his nose, mouth, and face.

The big Black man's temper cooled when he realized how hard he'd hit the twelve-year-old boy. This was, after all, the boss's new property, and although he had a responsibility to bring the new slaves into line, he was also responsible to see they were productive, and for that, they must be alive and healthy.

He leaned down, gave Jayvyn a few slaps on the face, and called for water. The slave who'd brought the clothes was already on his way out of the barn with a bucket of water, which he sloshed over Jayvyn's bloody face, but Jayvyn didn't move. He bent close to listen for his breath, looked up, and nodded he was breathing. The big Black man sighed with relief.

Master Clark then spoke to his big slave, "George, have Thomas and Andrew take James down to the slaves' quarters and put him in the leg stocks outside for the night. Take his clothing, too; he can have it back when he learns his name."

"Yesuh, Ma'sa," George replied.

"This boy," Master Clark continued, referring to the five-year-old, "will be called Stephen; make him understand. That will be all." And with that, Master Clark turned and walked back towards the big, white house.

"Yesuh, Ma'sa," George said again and turned to Thomas and Andrew, the other two slaves that had ridden with them. "You hear de Ma'sa: take James to de new slabe quarter, strip 'm o hid clode, put 'm in de leg stock,

"I gotsta finish wid de rest o dese new slabe."

With that, Thomas and Andrew gathered 'James' up by the arms and ankles and proceeded down the road to the new slave quarters.

- 13 -

My Name Is James

When Jayvyn awoke, he wasn't sure where he was. It was dark; he was lying on his back on a wooden surface. He stared up and saw the sky above him, clouds drifted slowly past in the soft moonlight. He was outside. He could only see out of his left eye and could see nothing from his right. His head ached terribly. He closed his eyes for a few minutes trying to think. Nothing came to him; he had no recollection of anything for several moments, but then he felt the burn on his shoulder. Things slowly started coming back to him.

He remembered he'd been put into a new group; clothed slaves had brought him and the others to a wagon where a white man branded them again. *That is the pain on my shoulder!* They were tied into the wagon, and another white man came. *Yes, there were two white men; one drove, and the other was... he was different. He was the one who had picked me and the others to be in the new group.* He remembered horses pulling the wagon, driving for a long way, passing a shoreline where waves broke on the rocks, and then turning into the hills, climbing higher and higher, until they came to a large, green valley with a giant white house.

Yes, he remembered better; the other white man, not the driver, had spectacles, and he was the boss. *He had a name we had to learn, Missee Kuk, or something like that. Everyone had to learn this name well because he is the most important and must always be obeyed.* And now he remembered they'd been standing in clothes for the first time since his were taken in Africa.

Oh, my head hurts; he noticed he was breathing through his mouth only. He tried to inhale through his nose, but it was plugged solid. He reached to touch it, and it was sore. It felt large—very hard, and smooth on the outside—as if his skin was stretched tight. He felt around his face and could feel something crusty and dry in places. He opened his left eye again and slowly sat up on his elbows, feeling pain in his chest as he did. He tried to move his feet and looked to see they were trapped in the holes of a wooden device. He pulled, but they wouldn't come out. Looking down, he saw he was naked and there were patches of something dark and crusty on his chest and hands. He realized it was dried blood, and he could taste more blood in his mouth. He inhaled sharply through his nose, dislodging a huge glob that hit the back of his throat, causing him to choke. He instinctively coughed this up and spat it to his side. It was also blood. Then it came to him, he must have been injured somehow, but he recalled nothing more.

He laid back down and watched the sky above. Clouds drifted past the moon; a cool, gentle breeze wafted across his skin; it felt good. He felt at his right eye and realized it was swollen shut; he couldn't open it.

His head swam, and he thought about being in the stockade, the disgusting food, the hard work he'd been doing in the clearing. But his thoughts were slow and muddled, confounded by searing pain mixed with a tingling numbness that crawled across his closed eye and over his nose and lips. His mind wandered to thoughts about the ship and the terrible voyage. He thought about Baahir again.

What had I been thinking about Baahir, he wondered? There was something, but it was so foggy and seemed like it might have been in another lifetime. *Something about the new slaves—the guards. The guards had better food; they were harsh and cruel, even though they were Black and slaves too.*

It came slowly as pinpricks of light danced under his swollen eyelid. He began to remember the social order he'd seen.

Yes, that was it. It was the hierarchy of the slaves. He'd been contemplating those who were defiant compared to those who complied. That's why he was thinking of Baahir. *Baahir's a warrior*, he thought. *He'd resist the harsh and senseless demands of the white man.*

As he lay there, he remembered thinking about the meaning of his name, Jayvyn—light spirit. The thought brought peace to his mind, and he closed his one eye again.

Sucking air through his mouth, he basked in the memory of his homeland, thinking of his parents and his little sister, Ifetayo. He didn't think of their abduction, his father's death, or where his mother and sister might be, but instead latched onto the wonderful feeling of his memories before, when he'd been so happy in his former life.

His pain began to fade to the background. The breeze continued; it felt good. He heard the night creatures of the meadow chirping and nothing more. He was alone. For the first time he could remember since his capture, there was no one else around. He rested, eventually dozing back to sleep.

Jayvyn stirred as he heard voices and movement around him. He opened his one good eye and could see there was activity in the still-dark landscape. People were up and moving about, getting ready for the new day.

Someone approached and prodded him with their foot. "Get up," he said.

Jayvyn propped himself up on his elbows.

The man squatted before him. Jayvyn recognized him as one of the slaves who rode in the wagon the other day, not the big Black man.

This man held out a plate of food and said, "Eat." Jayvyn took the plate and scooped a small amount into his mouth. It was warm, and hurt his mouth to chew and swallow it. The taste wasn't as bad as the terrible food he'd been eating before.

The man looked nervously about and said very quietly, in a voice only they could hear, "My name is Andrew; I was there when you were beat. I heard you speak Fogni; this is my language, too. I am Ajamatau, like you, but you must be careful."

Jayvyn was stunned; he couldn't believe he was hearing someone speaking in his native tongue! He began to reply, but Andrew quickly put a hand over his mouth and said quietly, "No. We will speak later, but no one must know! Be quiet and eat. And your name is James; you must only use this name and never speak Fogni, do you understand?" Jayvyn nodded. Andrew said, "Good. I will help you when I can, but you must be careful or we will both be punished." Jayvyn nodded again and resumed eating.

Andrew then spoke in English, "Eat, James, yo be de stupid slabe; yo gotsta learn."

A new voice came from behind as Jayvyn was finishing his plate of food. "Andrew, how he be?"

Andrew stood and replied, "He be wake, George; he be done

eat'n. Hid eye be close, 'n he gotsde bruis'n, but I see men mo bad. I tink he be fine."

George replied, "Good. Go now; I be take oba."

Andrew then took Jayvyn's empty plate and left.

The sky was beginning to lighten now, and Jayvyn saw other slaves as they gathered and trudged off to their daily work assignments. The ones he'd arrived with were among them. Many glanced his way as he sat naked in the leg stocks, George standing before him.

George looked down at him and said, "James, you be de stupid boy, but I seed dem stupid boy afo, 'n you gotsta learn."

Jayvyn looked at him, only understanding a few of the words he spoke. He got the general meaning, though, from his facial expression and intonation. He also recognized the use of his newly given name, 'James', and decided he'd try as best as he could to pay attention to this man, George.

After the area had cleared out, George squatted down in front of him. He pointed to himself and said, "I be George; now you say." He repeated "George" with emphasis, again pointing at himself.

Jayvyn looked at him, and said, "Gorje," pointing back at him.

"Good," said George, "now say it agin…George," again pointing to himself.

Jayvyn, more confidently now, repeated, "George" perfectly while pointing back at him.

"Very good. You," he said, pointing back at Jayvyn, "you be James; do you und'stand? Say it now," and he pointed again to Jayvyn, saying, "James…James, now you say it."

Jayvyn swallowed hard, remembering Andrew's words, who'd made it very clear, in his own language, he was to adopt his new name and use it at all times. He knew what George wanted.

He looked up at him and, in his most sincere way, said, "James…I James."

George's face brightened for a moment, and he said, "Very good! Now who you be?"

Jayvyn repeated, "James, I James."

Looking relieved, George squatted down in front of Jayvyn and inspected his wounds. He looked over his eye, pulled open his lip and jaw so he could see inside, and felt his nose. Then he squeezed on his chest, where there were marks from the stick. This hurt, Jayvyn winced, but it was just from the bruising. George, looking relieved, nodded and stood.

He walked away, returning a few moments later with a bucket of water, a cup, and some rags. He asked again, "Who you be?"

Jayvyn obediently responded, "James," and George, looking very satisfied, said, "Good."

He handed Jayvyn the cup filled with water and said, "Drink, James," and Jayvyn took it from him and drank it down.

"Drink mo, James," said George, and Jayvyn refilled his cup and drank it again.

"Good," said George. "Drink mo…James."

While Jayvyn continued to fill his cup, George put the rag in the water and gently began to clean the dirt and blood from Jayvyn's face. It hurt, but George was gentle enough. Soon he was finished there and moved on to his chest and hands.

Jayvyn began to understand George differently. He was very stern and mean the other day and had firmly held him against the tree while the other white man had branded him. He didn't speak or offer the slightest bit of comfort to him or any of the other new slaves for the whole trip or while they were in front of their new master, but now he was different. He was caring for Jayvyn.

George stood again and said, "James, drink mo; I be back."

As Jayvyn sat drinking the water, he began to feel better. He thought about his brief time with Andrew earlier and was still stunned by it. His tribe was small and reclusive; they didn't interact with other tribes, but here was a man who spoke his language and called himself Ajamatau! He knew there were other tribes similar to his, but he'd never met any of them. He also knew they were few and far between because of their reclusive ways. He was enthusiastic beyond words! He never would have thought this could happen. But he remembered, too, he was to keep this a strict secret only between Andrew and himself. If he slipped and let that out, it could be the end for both of them, and he may never see or meet another of his kind ever again. So, he reminded himself he was never to speak Fogni or give anyone the slightest hint he and Andrew were anything more than fellow slaves.

George returned later that morning; the sun had fully risen, and the heat was rising with it. Jayvyn had drained the entire bucket by this time, and George filled it again for him. He asked, "What be yo name?" and Jayvyn replied, "James".

"Good," replied George. And with that, George bent to release his legs from the stocks.

After releasing Jayvyn, he stood before him. His look was stern, not particularly friendly, and he had that stick as well. Jayvyn understood this man was not his friend but his superior, and he must be careful to follow his instructions.

George handed him the rag and said, "Wash."

Jayvyn didn't immediately understand, so George pantomimed with his hands and another rag on himself.

Pointing to the water, he said again, "Wash."

Jayvyn then understood. He'd urinated where he sat and was dirty in other ways. He took the rag, dipped it in the water, and began to clean himself, which was a welcome thing in and of itself.

When he'd finished, George handed back the clothing he'd been given before, and Jayvyn put it on. George looked approvingly at him, then said, "Bettah. Now, James, we go see Ma'sa Clark."

That's it! Jayvyn realized. *He's the big boss, Master Clark.*

Looking back at George, he repeated, "Ma'sa Clark."

George looked at him and said, "Dat be right, Ma'sa Clark. He be de boss. We go 'n see 'm now, 'n you be James. Agin, who you be?"

Jayvyn pointed at his chest and said, "James," and George said, "Very good, now we go," and motioned for him to follow.

They walked up a long road, past the pond, and continued toward the chimneyed building sitting just below and next to the strange building shaped like a tower with its huge spinning apparatus. He saw a long pipe connecting the two. As they walked, George pointed to things and said what they were.

He pointed to the one with the chimney and said, "de boil'n room, fo ta cook de cane," as they passed, and "de mill, fo ta smash de cane," when they passed the strange tower. Slaves were busy at these places.

Soon they were passing the barn, and Jayvyn recollected standing in front of it when they first arrived. He remembered learning Master Clark's name there and the short speech George gave. He thought back to receiving the clothes he was now wearing and the terrible renaming process. Then he reflected on his thoughts at the time and the indignity he felt just before receiving his new name.

He noted feeling bereft as he thought about the meaning of his real name, how it defined everything about him. He recalled his thoughts about his family and previous life, of his little sister, Ifetayo. The feeling dug a large hollow pit in his stomach—a hunger which could never be satisfied—as if the very fabric of his soul had been ripped out. A biting homesickness. A deep yearning for a life he could never return to.

It occurred to him then what must have happened. He didn't comply with accepting his new name at that time, and he'd paid the consequence as a result. He couldn't remember any part of being beat, but he knew it must have been George who'd given him the beating.

As he walked with George now, he didn't feel resentment toward him for his injuries and pain, but instead a certain kind of respect. This man was trying to teach him, and for his own good, given the circumstances they were in. But he was not to be trifled with. It was serious business, and so he'd try to listen to this man and understand, in hopes he might still salvage something of his life.

They continued on their way up, passing a road that led from the clearing to the agricultural fields Jayvyn had noticed on their way in.

George pointed in that direction and said, "Cane be grow'n der." He remembered 'cane' from his time at the stockade, and saw this was the plant they'd grown and cut there; only the fields here were so much larger. He saw slaves working and carts stacked high with the giant grass-like stalks.

Soon, they were approaching the big white house. George stopped in front of the big steps. A Black woman came down to speak with him.

"Yes, George?" she asked.

"Can Ma'sa Clark come?" asked George.

"Wait here," she responded, and turned back up the big stairs into the house.

While she was gone, George looked at Jayvyn and asked, "What be yo name?"

Jayvyn, understanding well by this point, respectfully replied, "James, I be James."

Looking relieved, George again said, "Good."

Soon, Master Clark arrived on the porch and came down the steps to where they stood.

"George, I see you have brought my new boy back. This is good. How is he?" he asked as he looked over Jayvyn's closed eye and swollen nose and lips.

"He be fine, Ma'sa Clark. He sleep in de stock 'n eat in de monin'. I clean 'm up 'n work wid 'm. He learn hid less'n. He be young but kin be train."

"Ah, good, George; I had no doubt." And he looked back at Jayvyn. "So, boy, what is your name?"

And Jayvyn, although nervous, stood straight and replied, "James, I be James."

"Good, Good," said Master Clark.

"And James, who am I?" he said, pointing to himself.

"Ma'sa Clark," replied Jayvyn.

"Well then, perhaps I chose well after all!" he said.

"George, take this boy and put him to work immediately. I expect him to work hard."

"Yes, suh, Ma'sa Clark," replied George.

He turned, Jayvyn in tow, and headed back down the road.

– 14 –

Work Begins

They walked back the same way they'd come. When they reached the road that split off toward the cane fields, they followed it.

The road led past the sharp buttress of a nearby hill partially obscuring the fields. As they passed, the full expanse of the cane fields came into view. Jayvyn was shocked when he saw how huge it all was. The fields continued far in the distance and up the next hill, seemingly forever. Rows and rows of tightly packed cane reached high above the heads of people working in them. The fields were separated into sections of varying color and texture. Most were packed with swaying cane, but others were brown where the cane had already been cut to the ground. Smaller sections, containing different crops, stood out in contrasting shades of green with stripped or dotted patterns. All of it made a sort of patchwork disappearing into the distance.

Carts were scattered about, some stacked high with cane and others empty. White men were here and there, on horses or standing. They weren't working as the Blacks, but guarding and supervising as in the clearing near the stockade. Many slaves were working in the fields. Most worked at harvesting; some worked in the areas already cut; still others tended different crops. Mules stood waiting, a few hitched to loaded wagons, ready to transport the harvest to the mill.

George led Jayvyn to one of the white men and said, "Good day,

Missa Flynn. Yo need de new boy today?"

The man he called Mr. Flynn turned and said, "Ah, a new nigger, George? Why yes, I can put this boy to work. Leave him with me."

"Yessuh, Missa Flynn; hid name be James; he work hard for you."

Mr. Flynn, noticing his swollen face and closed eye, asked, "What happened to him?"

George replied, "He no want hid new name. But dat be fixt now."

"I see," said Mr. Flynn, "well, I'll show him what kind of work we expect 'round here," at which point George turned and left.

"Well, nigger James, let's get you to work! Simon! Get over here, boy," Mr. Flynn barked, motioning to a slave nearby who quickly approached.

"Take this new nigger, James, and show him how to work loading these wagons."

"Yassuh, Missa Flynn!" Simon quickly replied, turning to Jayvyn, saying, "Come on," whereby he gave a quick pull on Jayvyn's upper arm and hurried back to his work.

It was hot as Jayvyn followed Simon back to where he was working. He'd been stacking cane onto one of the carts, and had a few arm loads left to stack.

"Like dis," Simon said as he gathered up a bundle of cane and placed it onto the cart vertically as if it were still growing in the field. Another slave, standing in the cart, arranged this bundle further back so as to pack the cart tightly. He gestured for Jayvyn to do the same with the remaining armload. It seemed to him a large bundle to get his arms fully around, and the cane, dense and tall, weighed a fair amount. Jayvyn stooped, got his fingers around the bottom of the pile, and gathered it up., With some difficulty, he lifted it up to the waiting cart, which was about chest height and one-third full. The slave on the cart briskly snatched the bundle from him as another two slaves approached carrying large bundles on their shoulders. Simon had already hurried off.

He followed Simon to a nearby field where other slaves worked with machetes to cut the cane at its base and remove the leaves, leaving the stalks on the ground. Simon bent down and began gathering these stalks off of the ground, sorting them to make sure they were parallel to each other and the bases even. He worked quickly to get a full bundle together. Jayvyn fell into step beside him, picking up pieces and trying to do the same. The cane was scattered about on the ground, needing to be arranged into parallel stalks with all the bottoms lined up or else it wouldn't stack correctly on the cart. Simon looked at him, dismayed, saying, "Let's go! You gotsta be fasta!" as he threw his bundle onto his shoulder and moved off towards the cart. Jayvyn stood his bundle on end in order to put it on his shoulder, but as he went to pick it up, half the bundle sheared off and fell back to the ground. Frustrated, he quickly gathered as much as he could and threw it on his shoulder. Simon was already putting his on the cart. As they passed, Simon said, "Hurry up, James; dat no be good!" Jayvyn rushed to put his somewhat messy, thin bundle on the cart, where the other slave, looking agitated, took it, saying, "Move!"

Jayvyn turned to go back to the field and saw Simon had already gathered his next bundle and was heaving it up onto his shoulder.

Jayvyn, trying to hurry, stumbled a bit as he only had his one eye to work with and it skewed his depth perception. He was anxious about not keeping pace; his peers were showing their exasperation. The cutters glanced doubtfully at him as he tried again to put a good bundle together quickly, stalks dropping from its sides when he went to pick it up. It was clear everyone around him had more practice doing this. Additionally, he felt fatigue from his night spent in the stocks and his injuries were weighing him down. The cane, as well as the motions needed to arrange and pick it up, aggravated his chest injuries. Occasionally, the stalks hit him in the face, delivering sharp pain to his swollen nose, lips, and eye. Although he was doing the best he could, he couldn't keep up with the others, who constantly reminded him he had to work faster. He worried about being watched by Mr. Flynn and what might happen if he didn't soon measure up.

Jayvyn worked hard like this for hours straight, and thought he might be improving a little. But it was exhausting work, easily as hard as the work in the clearing had been. He saw there was water back where Mr. Flynn was, and that slaves periodically stopped to get a drink. He was parched; he'd long ago sweated out all he drank earlier that morning and needed to get some water. He approached the bucket, filled the ladle, and brought it to his mouth. He barely had time to drink when it was roughly knocked from his hand.

"What do you think you're doing, nigger? You haven't done enough work to take a break! You get your skinny Black ass back out there NOW and give me some real work, or I'll tan your hide!"

Jayvyn glanced briefly at Mr. Flynn's face and saw his rage and anger. He indeed held a whip in one hand, and Jayvyn quickly turned and hurried back to his task, desperately trying to pick up the pace and do better so as not to incur his wrath.

The day was long. And he'd started much later than the others. The carts were packed one after the other, only to be immediately replaced by a waiting empty cart. They'd worked past dusk, until the light was barely enough to see, when Simon came and finally let him know it was time to stop. Jayvyn's arms, chest, and legs ached; it felt like his bones had gone soft. And he was so thirsty; he needed to have a drink; he felt he would pass out if he didn't.

The other slaves were drinking again from the water cask, and Jayvyn timidly approached them. Some looked and snickered at him as they left to walk back to their quarters. None seemed particularly welcoming, but Jayvyn was allowed to take the ladle and drink. Exhausted, he drank several ladles full, then Simon came over and said, "Come, it be time to go," and they walked back along the road toward the clearing.

As they walked in the dim light, they passed the mill, where several carts were lined up. He could see slaves still working inside, and glimpsed machinery moving around in the shadows. They moved back past the boiling room, where other slaves still worked, and continued down the road past the pond.

When they arrived back at the slaves' quarters, George was there.

He approached Jayvyn and said, "James, dat be yo house," gesturing toward the first hut.

Jayvyn went in to find the rest of the new slaves he'd arrived with.

The room was mostly empty, with a dirt floor, a small table with a tub on it, and a candle burning softly beside it. Beside that was a cask with a ladle hanging from its side.

He stood, looking around the room. The two men and the slightly older boy were lying on mats on the dirt floor on one side of the room. The girl and the younger boy were on mats on the other side. The two women sat together on mats against a wall. It was very dim and hard to see.

One of the women, seeing Jayvyn standing there, looking tired and not knowing what to do, got up and approached him.

"Hungry?" she asked.

"Yes," Jayvyn replied. And she led him to the tub sitting on the table.

"Eat," she said, gesturing at the tub.

It was the same food Jayvyn had eaten that morning. Jayvyn reached in, scooped a handful out, and put it into his sore mouth. It was still painful to eat, but he was famished from the day's work and ate several handfuls.

The woman gestured at herself and quietly said, "Julia."

Jayvyn looked back at her and replied, "James,...I James," whereby the woman nodded and reached out, softly touching Jayvyn's wrist, then retreated back into the darkness to her mat.

Jayvyn finished eating, and drank from the nearby cask. He then found another mat remaining on the floor, spread it out near where the men were sleeping, and laid down.

Thoughts swirled in his head as he reminisced about the day's events. He thought about George and how he cleaned his wounds, freed him from the stocks, let him clean up, and brought him his clothes.

He thought about the walk up to the big house and meeting Master Clark again, and the walk to the fields where he met Mr. Flynn, who called him a nigger.

And Simon.

He thought about the work, how he failed to measure up, how the other slaves seemed to be disappointed in him. Like all of his experiences so far, it was very mixed. There were a few who seemed to look after him, and there were many who were either indifferent or outwardly hostile. It was confusing to know how, or if, he fit in anywhere.

Then he remembered Andrew from first thing this morning. How surprised he'd been when he heard him speak Fogni and told him he was Ajamatau.

It had been so many months since he'd heard his language spoken, let alone interacted with someone who was Ajamatau. Finding all this in Andrew abruptly made him realize just how alone he'd felt since his capture—loneliness and isolation masked by shock and fear from the unremitting horrors he'd witnessed.

Suddenly finding someone who shared his heritage revitalized his longing to be amongst his people once again—to sit by the fires at night listening to his father and the elders—to feel the familiar thrum of shared beliefs flowing effortlessly between members of the same tribe.

It was what he missed so badly as he struggled to understand the tribes he was now mixed in with. Although all African and Black, it didn't make them the same.

He'd been sheltered from this kind of diversity all his life because his tribe chose to be reclusive, preferring to isolate themselves from the conflicts besetting so many tribes. It was what his elders and father spoke of often—warning Jayvyn and others not to wander too far from the village lest they encounter a hostile tribe. It was why their villages were kept small, contained, and carefully situated in secluded locations—why they avoided trading with other tribes, preferring instead to subsist among themselves.

They were happy with what they had and the way they lived. It was what had worked for generations untold and how they preferred to remain.

The memories conjured all sorts of precious feelings held deeply within his soul.

Knowing now of Andrew had reawakened Jayvyn's tribal spirit; he felt a strong tug to be with others of his kind.

Andrew's caution to keep their tribal affiliation a secret made sense to him. There was a very good chance he'd never meet another member of his tribe again; plus, there was no good reason to divulge this to anyone. He wondered where Andrew was now and when he'd see him again.

It was in the middle of these reassuring thoughts that Jayvyn lost his battle with consciousness and fell, unknowingly, into a deep and dreamless sleep.

– 15 –

A New Reality

It seemed again as if Jayvyn had barely fallen asleep when George appeared at the door, yelling, "Get up! Time fo work! Get yo food 'n eat! Get up now! I no wanna habba tell ya agin!" George left a new candle burning on a small shelf beside the door and left.

The inhabitants rolled over, groaning and spent. One of the men took the food tub from the table and ambled out the door while the others stirred to something resembling life. The youngest boy sat, rubbing his eyes and looking bewildered in the darkness. The others made their way to the water cask, drank, and went outside for any personal business.

In minutes, the man with the tub returned. There wasn't much time to mingle as they gathered around the tub of food, each reaching in to take handfuls of the mixture and eat as best as they could, given the hour and how they all felt after their first full day on the plantation.

Jayvyn was particularly sore; his eye still swollen shut, his nose and lips puffed up. His chest ached, and his limbs were very sore from the half-day's work he'd done the day before. He wondered how he was going to make it through this one.

Julia was there. Gesturing towards Jayvyn, she said, "Dat be James." The others glanced at Jayvyn, recognizing the tremendous beating he'd survived only two days ago and knowing he'd spent time in leg stocks outside.

The one who'd brought the food said, "Samuel," nodding slightly.

Jayvyn remembered him as the first to receive his new name. He recalled Samuel's brief confusion and apparent reluctance to agree with his name change. It was the example for the rest that the new names weren't negotiable and they should do their best to comply. He'd mentioned his real name, but Jayvyn couldn't remember what it was, nor did it really matter. It was what earned him the reprimand he received from George, and that was what mattered.

The other woman then spoke, "I be Sarah."

Then the girl meekly introduced herself, "Rose."

Next, the boy, whom Jayvyn took to be a little older than he, shuffled a little in place and quietly said, "Lewis."

Julia then gestured to the small boy and said, "He be Stephen."

The small boy stood by Julia, staring forlornly at the ground, clinging to Julia's dress while sucking the fingers on one hand.

An awkward silence followed, and Jayvyn realized the one man remaining had just stood there, seemingly in a world of his own. He then blinked, glanced nervously about, and muttered, "Charles," but seemingly not to anyone in particular. This man was emotionless, as though not a part of the group, and just stared ahead.

Julia then broke the tension, stepped forward, and said, "James, you be bettah soon," laying a reassuring hand on his shoulder.

For the first time, Jayvyn felt something like kinship as the group introduced themselves. Something he'd not experienced since his and Baahir's exchange on the ship so many months ago. He felt they all shared something in common. Although they hadn't known each other in any significant way at the time, they'd all been at the stockade. They'd been picked and put into a new group, burned with Master Clark's brand, and stood together to receive their new names.

Jayvyn had been the only one to stand strong and defiant against giving up his identity in front of them all. That now earned him a sort of solemn respect from the others. His closed eye and bruises stood for something. They stood in testament to their sovereignty. Their lives were theirs. Lives that, although different in terms of tribe, were identical in that they were *their* lives—unique and beautiful lives, defined by *their* heritage and *their* names. Jayvyn had demonstrated to them all that their individuality was sacred. Even though they bore the thin veneer of a new name, their unique, individual souls could not be stolen. This must be kept alive in the privacy of their own beings.

A new spark awakened inside Jayvyn. The physical pain was the same, but there was something new he was confident would see him through another day.

George then announced it was time to get moving, and they shuffled outside to find their assigned work groups.

Julia and Rose, along with young Stephen, fell in with a small group of women and one older man to go to the big house and perform various duties there.

Samuel and Charles fell in with a different group of men who were destined to cut and haul wood for the boiling room fires. In this group, Jayvyn recognized Andrew from the previous morning. Their eyes met for an instant, but Andrew immediately looked away, acting as if he didn't recognize Jayvyn in any significant way. Jayvyn wanted so much to reconnect with Andrew, but he remembered Andrew's stern warning about guarding their secret.

Lewis and Jayvyn were then assigned to the largest group to resume cutting and stacking cane in carts. Sarah joined a group to tend other crops and clear the remains of cane once it was harvested. Other groups were assembled to work at the mill, boiling room, tend animals, or perform any number of tasks needed to keep the busy plantation running.

As they strode off into the predawn darkness, a song rang out from somewhere within the large group:

My time, time so long. (hah)
Look down, (hah) look down,
That long, lonesome road,
where you (hah) and I, I must go.

As the slow, mournful voice continued, their cadence began to change. The rhythm became manifest in their footsteps as they shambled up the long dirt road. Passing by the still, glassy pond, the scratchy beat broke the morning air. It was oddly comforting to Jayvyn. An expression of what they shared—a common bond—the bond of enslavement.

Stand back, (hah) stand back
All you five 'n ten cent men:
Dollar man (hah) knocking on, on my door.
Hattie Bell, (hah) Hattie Bell,

O she's my own, own true love,
*Darlin', (hah) what have, have I done?**

When they reached the boiling room, some of the group split off. At the neighboring mill, more left. Reaching the barn, others had found their destination. At the road to the cane fields, most of the remaining, including Jayvyn, carved off, leaving just the smaller group, with Julia, Rose, and young Stephen, to continue on to the big white house.

The group Jayvyn was in made their way down the road to the fields, where white men waited in the predawn light, whips in hand, ready to make sure all worked to their satisfaction.

There was no milling about as the slaves gathered their tools for harvesting and promptly headed into the fields. Again, Jayvyn found Simon and followed him to where they immediately began gathering cut cane. Another boy retrieved an empty cart, ready to receive the bundles. Jayvyn noticed Lewis was also assigned to this task. He wondered if he'd had the same difficulties as Jayvyn adapting to the work.

As the first light of dawn began to fill the sky, they were in full swing, carrying heavy bundles to the cart, heaving them up on the back where the other boy packed them in tightly. Each cart held a lot, taking many loads to fill. When it was full, a mule was harnessed, and it was driven to the mill. Empty carts were brought back.

The sun came up fully, and soon all were sweating profusely in the midday heat, which would last from before noon to early evening.

---

* *Look down that long, lonesome road—early slave song, origin unknown*

They took short breaks for water, but these were monitored by Mr. Flynn and the other bosses. If a slave was thought to be taking too many breaks or wasn't producing enough, they were roughly chased back to work. Sharp eyes were kept on everyone to make sure they stayed working hard.

Jayvyn got better at assembling and carrying the bundles, but he still fought with his injuries and adapting to the strong pace. He felt like he was being tolerated better by the other workers, or at least left alone, and Mr. Flynn didn't seem to notice when he stopped to get water. He was, however, careful to wait until he really needed a drink and be quick about it so as to attract as little attention as possible.

But Mr. Flynn had his mind on other matters. A worker cutting the harvest was not measuring up with her work and had captured his attention. Jayvyn heard him holler at the woman several times that morning. When he'd had enough, Mr. Flynn raced over to where she was cutting, whip in hand. He reached her and brought his whip brutally down across her back several times, yelling furiously while the woman cowered. It was abrupt.

When he'd finished, he turned and walked back to his area of observation. The sobbing woman resumed her work.

As this was happening, Jayvyn briefly asked Simon what was going on, to which Simon hurriedly replied, "No look! No be good; stay work!" Jayvyn didn't notice much reaction from anyone else, as if this was a common occurrence and didn't warrant any special attention. As he thought more about it, he realized it really wasn't much of a surprise to him either, remembering the punishment the woman at the stockade received just for eating a yam. He knew there was no limit to the cruelty these white men would render at the slightest provocation, and didn't wish to give any reason to bring this upon himself.

There was a brief break in the middle of the day when tubs of food were brought for the slaves. This food consisted of dried, salt fish, and corn.* Everyone stopped work long enough to take food and drink some water. The break was necessary, both for rest and to resupply their depleted bodies with nutrients needed to sustain them through the rest of the day.

During this time, Jayvyn thought briefly about Andrew again. He wondered how long he'd been on the plantation and what his work experience was like. He wondered what Samuel and Charles had learned about Andrew. Did Andrew teach them what they were to do? Did they have white task masters watching, ready to whip them? Did Andrew warn them to keep up the pace?

The scope of the plantation had become clearer to Jayvyn as the slaves were divided into groups that morning. It was much larger than he'd imagined. Some groups contained ten or so slaves, while his seemed to have at least thirty. In all, there must have been over eighty slaves on the plantation.

He wondered what Julia, Rose, and young Stephen were doing. What did they do at the big house on the hill? What would be expected of a child like Stephen? His heart broke for little Stephen. Like Jayvyn, this small, fragile boy had been separated from his village and all he

---

* *Some food, such as dried salt fish and corn, were brought in to feed the slaves, but plantation owners tried to keep this cost to a minimum by allowing slaves to grow their own food*

knew. He shuddered to think how terrifying it must be for a five-year-old to be taken from his mother and family.

And what of Ifetayo? She was even younger. His sadness increased at the thought she may have been separated from their mother. If so, she must be so frightened and bewildered! That is, if either of them were still alive.

Grief, once again, clutched at Jayvyn's heart, cold and vise-like, dragging him toward the dark chasm he knew all too well. Realizing the peril, he tore himself away before he sank too far. It was a skill he'd mastered through experience.

The shout from Mr. Flynn broke his trance. "Back to work, NOW! Move niggers! Let's go! Everybody back to work!" The slaves all got to their feet and went back to their assigned areas to resume their arduous work.

The day was long. Jayvyn tried to keep his mind numb to the task as he carried bundle after bundle, just concentrating on the steps before him. Thinking ahead any further made the job too hard, and he was afraid if he did, he might not be able to continue. It was the same method he used in the clearing at the stockade and on the ship. In fact, it was what he'd been doing since all of this began. Just make it from one moment to the next, survive each breath, don't worry about the next. It's what you do when pressed to the very edge of survival—you simply survive.

Eventually, the sun softened as it sank toward the western sky. The light began to fade, the day was nearing its end. As with every other day, work didn't stop until it became too difficult to see. Again, Jayvyn was well past where he felt he could carry on, but somehow, he did.

After quenching his thirst at the water cask, he assembled with the others for the long walk back to their compound. There was no singing this time, only the slow, blind walk of the half-dead. He noticed again the mill and boiling room were still in operation as they passed, slaves toiling away inside.

Arriving back at his quarters, Jayvyn had no energy for anything but eating what was in the tub and finding his place on the dirt floor. He was grateful for the short time he had to rest and not be under the watchful eye of some boss, but knew it wouldn't be long before the next day began. The thought this would be his life henceforth was unsettling. If that's to be the case, he'd rather not live at all.

Jayvyn suddenly realized he'd never thought of not living; the idea of ending his own life had never occurred to him before. He'd never known anyone to think such a thing, but *he* had just thought it and was shocked by it. Death was always something to be avoided. After all, living was the whole point of life.

The feeling was like being thrown from a cliff—shock and terror, tumbling through air, fighting for a purchase where none is to be had. Jayvyn imagined the boys thrown from the ship must have had a similar feeling—suddenly faced with the certainty of death as the ship sailed on, sharks closing in. What else is there to do then besides give in to reality?

Life, as Jayvyn had once known it, was something he hadn't experienced since being taken from his village. There was no joy in this life, no freedom to experience anything but misery—no way back.

He no longer had any control over his life. What kind of life is that? It is not life. It's existing in a state with no meaning. Or even worse, the meaning is you aren't free to make choices or follow your own will. It's existing in complete vulnerability and defenselessness—every moment devoted to avoiding pain—absent gratification. A life denied every single thing about yourself—your family, heritage, identity, individuality—everything and anything that makes you who you are. It's not life in the least. It's a state *worse* than death.

In the midst of this desperate parade of thoughts—relentless, morbid, looping thoughts—the curtain of unconsciousness swept seamlessly down upon him.

All thought ceased, along with any awareness of his existence, as if death itself had just descended.

Jayvyn was at peace.

- 16 -

A Break on the Horizon

The morning, like all the others, arrived in complete darkness. Jayvyn shook himself awake at the loud, abrupt calls from George, who once again put the candle on the small shelf by the door. The others in his hut ambled to life, and the tub of food was, once again, retrieved and set on the table.

As they ate, Jayvyn asked Samuel and Charles about the work they were doing.

Samuel replied, in stuttered English, "Cut wood, take de boil'n house. Take de smash cane ta dem pig."

Jayvyn asked if it was hard work, to which Samuel replied, "Yes, bery hard! Tree be hard, cut many time. Bery heby."

"Who teach you?" Jayvyn asked.

Samuel replied, "Andrew."

Jayvyn just nodded and asked, "Andrew good?"

Samuel said, "Yes, Andrew be good. Slabe, like we. He tell we de boss be look. No talk, work."

Jayvyn again nodded in understanding. "White man whip?"

Samuel said, "Yes, make bad, no work hard, some slabe be whip."

Jayvyn nodded as he remembered the woman he saw so brutally whipped in the field the other day.

A look of empathy passed between them, and it was understood this must be the case with all of the slaves, no matter where they worked, whether man, woman, or child.

As they spoke, Jayvyn noticed Charles' countenance had remained fixed and stern-looking. His eyes reminded him of the eyes of the defiant slaves at the stockade and on the ship—serious, seeming always to look off in the distance, never at anything in particular. Although Jayvyn was speaking to both of them, Charles never uttered a sound in response, as if cast in stone, his mind elsewhere.

Jayvyn's gaze then shifted to young Stephen, and again, he wondered what the boy was going through. He felt sorry this small boy was here, deprived of his life at such an early age.

Jayvyn reflected on the joy he'd once felt as a young boy in his village, with his family and the elders close by. The joy he felt when he was with his father, who laughed with him and taught him so many things. The joy he felt when playing games with the other children in his tribe, games wrought from their imaginations. The joy he always felt for Ifetayo, as he gently guided her along her path.

This poor boy had none of that, instead coldly ripped from his family and childhood to labor with strangers in a stranger's world.

Stephen slowly chewed his food, looking mostly at the dirt floor before him. Feeling Jayvyn's gaze, he briefly looked up. Jayvyn tried to smile, but was unsure how much of a smile he could really muster. The boy, looking sullen and forlorn, dropped his eyes back to the floor.

In a moment, they were all back out in front of the huts, again being assembled into their work groups. Once more, Jayvyn glimpsed Andrew through the darkness as he joined the group with Samuel and

Charles. He wished he was going with that group; he wanted to spend time with Andrew.

As his group formed up, Jayvyn saw the woman who'd been whipped by Mr. Flynn the day before. Although she didn't appear any different this morning, he knew her back must be the site of many freshly raised welts. Her tears of yesterday now dry, she quietly took her place back in line to once again labor under the unforgiving tropical sun—for the thankless man who'd beaten her. Lewis, too, again joined this group, and Sarah fell in with the group that would go to other sections of the fields.

The march began as the day before, the same sorrowful song ringing out from somewhere within the group. It started as one lone voice but was soon joined by others. The steady beat of their footsteps fell in slow, synchronized rhythm against the dirt, making a sound like so many drums being softly played against the quiet morning stillness. It felt curiously uplifting to Jayvyn, which was in stark contrast to how he felt about the upcoming day. But there was a sort of solace that came from their solidarity—a peace—as they sang the words together:

Look down, (hah) look down,
That long, lonesome road,
where you (hah) and I, I must go.

As they walked, he thought about his earlier conversation with Samuel, and wondered if he, too, harbored the same contradictory feelings. He supposed there was comfort in knowing none were alone with their burden. But at the same time, Jayvyn knew he didn't want this for the people around him any more than for himself.

Again, they gradually split off, group by group, until only Jayvyn's group remained, slowly making its way—away from the relative calm of their morning walk—back into the sweltering cane fields where unyielding white sentries stood, whips in hand.

As they approached, Jayvyn felt the peace of the morning's walk quickly fade. He realized the morning walk was one of the few times the slaves had to themselves—a fleeting moment—offering small refuge in a world otherwise filled with cruelty, hopelessness, and despair. It was one of the few moments he'd come to cherish—a brief interlude to suffering—when, like their footsteps, the slaves' hearts all beat as one.

Soon, Mr. Flynn's ugly scowl greeted them, his whip at the ready and they immediately gathered what tools they needed and went to work.

On this morning, a brief rain shower came sweeping down from the hills above. Work never stopped. They were expected to move just as quickly regardless. The ground became muddy and slick, and the wet cane more difficult to manage, but otherwise, it was cool. It didn't last very long, though. Soon enough an ephemeral rainbow burst brilliantly from the path of the departing storm, hastily retreating. The temperature, once again, began to climb.

Jayvyn noticed his right eye had begun to open a bit. It was somewhat blurry to look through, and there seemed to be a reddish haze, but it was getting better. His other bruises hurt slightly less as well, but he still had a way to go before being back to normal.

The day progressed as others had, the work arduous and

monotonous. Jayvyn gathered bundle upon bundle of the tall cane, its rough stalks grinding painfully on his chest and shoulders as he struggled to lift and carry them to the waiting carts. His sweat mixed with dust, stinging his eyes as it coursed relentlessly off his sunbaked head. All the while, sharp cane stumps pierced his bare feet, delivering painful reminders to watch his step.

Some slaves hummed as they worked. Occasionally, a song was heard—others joining in, breaking the tedium, creating a welcome distraction from their toil—time kept by the steady rhythm of machetes falling against the hard stalks of cane; leaves rusting like soft wind as they gently fluttered to the ground.

A desperately needed break came in the afternoon when dried fish and corn were brought. This time, there were some plantains as well. Jayvyn welcomed the addition of fresh fruit; it was something he hadn't had in a long time.

Jayvyn sat, hot and exhausted. Simon came to sit with him during the break, both their faces and upper bodies streaked where sweat had etched veined pathways through the dust.

Simon told Jayvyn the next day was Sunday, and it was a day they didn't have to work.* He said the slaves were allowed to use this day to rest, clean themselves, and tend to their garden.

Jayvyn was surprised to learn that they'd have a day off, and he asked him about the garden.

Simon told him there was a piece of land where slaves were allowed to grow their own food. It was where their food mostly came

---

* *From the 17th century onwards, it became customary for plantation owners to give enslaved Africans Sundays off*

from, except for things like dried salt fish and corn. Some food was brought by the white man, but the plantains they were eating today came from their garden. He said there were yams, okra, vegetables, grains, oranges, and bananas, among berries and other things. He said it was up to the slaves to take care of it.

Jayvyn's mind immediately flashed back to his homeland. He remembered the gardens of his village, with many succulent varieties of vegetables, fruits, herbs, and spices they'd use to create their meals. He'd worked with his mother, little sister, and many others from the village cultivating to ensure reliable and healthy yields. Now he understood why the food was better at their quarters. It was because the slaves had access to fresh ingredients they could prepare in the ways they knew how.

Simon mentioned that slaves who'd been on the plantation longer—those with higher standing—got the best of the yield. Jayvyn asked how higher standing was gained. Simon told him it was mostly earned by length of time and how well you got along in the group. He said George, being the boss of the slaves, was at the top. Those who earned his favor, or the favor of those close to him, enjoyed better things.

So far, Jayvyn hadn't really had the opportunity to know much about his fellow slaves since all he'd done was work and sleep. Now he saw there would be an opportunity to experience some of the social hierarchy he'd wondered about back at the stockade. It was no surprise to realize it existed here too.

However, the concept seemed foreign to Jayvyn. His village had no such ranking, where one individual was treated as better than another. In his world, everyone was an equally valuable member of the tribe, and all contributed according to their skills and abilities. Even Caksusa, the village wiseman, considered himself—and was considered by others—as equal amongst his fellow tribesmen.

Consistent with his belief, the only things having greater status were things of the natural world surrounding them—the earth, its plants and animals, the sky and weather, even the passage of time itself. Everything else was subordinate. All of it overseen by "Ata Emit," or "to whom belongs the universe."* It is the force to which everything belongs and is owned by no one. Therefore, the benevolence of the universe is for everyone, and it is only right that all should share equally in its bounty.

Caksusa had important, special abilities for the benefit of his tribe—things no one else could do. But he used his abilities just as another might use their skills to make homes, hunt for game, or make the tools they needed. By working together, they achieved whatever prosperity was needed to sustain the whole tribe. And as a whole, they shared this equally. *How could it be any different?*†

Soon, they were back at work. Jayvyn contemplated the new information Simon had given him, and it occupied his thoughts for the rest of the afternoon. He wanted to know more. Before this, he hadn't known they'd have a day to themselves. It was uplifting news. Also, they had a garden of their own where he might be able to work

---

* *The Jola typically practiced animism: the belief in a supernatural power that organizes and animates the material universe*

† *The Jola, unlike most tribes of Africa, are egalitarian, believing all tribal members are equal. All contribute and share equally in the wealth of the tribe. They do not have chiefs or any other systemized forms of hierarchy*

and actually receive benefit from it. The whole idea felt gratifying. It was something he desperately needed to feel. The afternoon, although hard, went by faster, powered by what he'd learned.

At the end of the day, he assembled, once again, with the group to walk their tired walk back to their quarters. But his spiritual energy was much greater than it had been for a long while, buoyed by the thought of a day off. He couldn't wait to learn more about the garden and his fellow slaves.

He found Lewis within the group and walked with him. He told Lewis what he'd learned from Simon about their day off, and Lewis, too, brightened with enthusiasm.

When they reached the hut, the conversation around the food was all about the coming day off. Some of the others had already learned of this, and they were just as excited as Jayvyn.

For what seemed like eternity, every single moment, waking or sleeping, had been occupied by never-ending suffering and hardship. None had a single reprieve from their ordeal since being taken so many, many months ago. The thought they'd have even an hour to themselves, let alone a whole day, just seemed inconceivable.

As they spoke amongst themselves, Julia offered up that she'd been told they could bathe at the pond and wash out their clothes. Samuel mentioned Andrew had indicated it would be an opportunity to mingle with some of the other slaves and learn who was who in their community. Jayvyn told them what he'd learned about the garden.

All of it seemed too good to be true. The thought they'd have personal time, to casually be amongst themselves, awakened a spark long ago extinguished amidst the wreckage of their lives. Now it loomed like revivification—the very embodiment of a dream—the dream of having some part of their lives back.

After they finished their food, everyone settled into their respective areas. Some conversation continued quietly, but all were exhausted from working. Soon things became quiet as one by one they drifted off.

Jayvyn lay thinking about this remarkable day. He thought about the night before—how hopeless he'd felt about everything—how he could find no meaning in life. But suddenly, here was a bright glimmer of hope, something he hadn't expected. He'd been without the smallest amount of hope for so long that it seemed he was attaining some small part of his freedom once again.

Even if it was for just one day, or even a moment, it was far more than he'd had since he could remember.

He grasped on to it like new life itself. His heart sang with the only joy he'd felt for so long.

He'd entirely forgotten that feeling, and it swaddled him in its warm glow as he gently drifted off to sleep, happy for the first time since the morning of his capture.

- 17 -

Sunday with Andrew

The morning began with shuffling sounds from those he shared the hut with. George didn't come to wake them, and light was in the sky.

Jayvyn rolled over to see some walking in and out as sunlight graced the doorway. He sat blinking as others lay sleeping on their mats. It seemed like another world to him, a world he barely recognized. It was the first morning he wasn't kicked in the side, woken in darkness, or left rotting in the stinking, dark hold of a ship.

The ship. It seemed ages ago! Like a different lifetime. But Jayvyn didn't want to lay there thinking about any of that. He wanted to get up and see what was happening around him.

He rose, and as on other mornings, someone had brought the tub of food.

He wandered outside to relieve himself, and when he did, he could see slaves moving about in the early light.

No one was assembling in groups, and there was an easy energy in the air. He returned to his hut to have some food before doing anything else.

Most everyone was up now, and conversation was taking place as they ate. It was strange for everyone to have time to themselves and the freedom to choose what they did. It left them not knowing how to handle it. But the first thing that came to Jayvyn's mind was to get outside and commune with those around him. It seemed a good way to start.

Jayvyn went outside again and looked around. Some were working on one project or another; some just sat outside talking with others. He was uncertain where to go or who to approach.

He saw Simon and decided he would go see him. When he approached, he asked about the gardens. Simon pointed to a man, whom he said was in charge, and said he should go see him.

The man was older, but not old. Jayvyn approached tentatively and the man turned to see him. He had a kindly-looking face. Jayvyn said, "I be James."

The man looked him over for a moment, and said, "A new boy. You come lats week. What you be look'n fo?"

Jayvyn said he wanted to know about the garden, and the man said, "We be go soon. You know 'bout de garden?" and Jayvyn nodded.

The man said, "Good! You kin go wid me; I be Walter."

Jayvyn mimicked "Water," because that was what it sounded like to him.

Walter, giving a quick chuckle, smiled and repeated, slower this time, "Wa-l-ter," giving emphasis to the 'l' in the middle.

Jayvyn picked up the difference and replied, "Wal-ter," and the older man smiled and nodded.

A few others came and gathered around Walter, and soon Jayvyn noticed Andrew among this group.

Jayvyn caught his eye, and this time Andrew didn't look away but instead approached Jayvyn, saying, "Hello James. How you be? You look'n betta today."

Jayvyn, who was getting better with his words, replied, "I be good."

Andrew, who realized Jayvyn had work to do on his language skills, smiled back at him and said, "Good. I be happy fo you. Yo work in de garden t'day?"

Jayvyn nodded and said, "Yes, work de garden."

Andrew said, "Good, you work wid me," and then told Walter he'd met Jayvyn and wanted to work with him, to which Walter approved.

Andrew then turned back to Jayvyn, saying, "I hep ya learn ta speak de English. 'K?"

Jayvyn looked at him, not being completely sure what he'd said, but smiled, just knowing he was finally going to be able to spend some time with Andrew.

They walked in a different direction this morning, out behind the slave quarters, where they found a foot path leading down a hill. Becoming somewhat steeper, Jayvyn soon saw plantings, in small patches, here and there. Trees and rocks spotted the ravine.

The soil wasn't the same quality as he'd seen in the cane fields. The area wasn't as open and large. The soil was thinner, sandier, with rock outcroppings here and there.* But there were, indeed, plants growing.

Tools—shovels, hoes, machetes, and buckets—were here, too. Andrew took a machete and walked deeper into the garden.

---

* *Typically, the land set aside for slave gardens wasn't the best. It was usually land that couldn't be used by the plantation owners in any other way*

As they walked, he said, "Dis be *yam*," and Jayvyn repeated, "Yam." At another leafy plot, he said, "Here be *cassava*," showing a bunch with the root hanging below. At another plot, he pointed, saying, "Dis be *gub-a-gub*." These were plants with nut-like bunches in their roots.* At another, he said, "Ova here be de *okra*," and so forth. Jayvyn knew many of the words from his time at the stockade, but there were some new ones too. He also paid attention to the words between—words he'd slowly been picking up from other conversations.

After they'd walked far down the wooded perimeter, when Andrew was sure they were out of range, he turned to Jayvyn and spoke in Fogni.

"You must understand we cannot talk like this often and must be very careful, even around the slaves. There are those among us who would betray us simply to access better conditions, either from the white man or George. It is the way it is, and you must believe me. Do you understand?"

Jayvyn responded, in Fogni, "Yes."

As they continued walking, Andrew went on, "There are many tribes represented here, and as you know, just like in Africa, they are not all friendly to each other. There is no war or aggression here; we are all slaves—surviving just as you. But there still are important differences."

Jayvyn thought about this for a moment. He wasn't sure of the causes of tribal conflict in his homeland in the first place, since the Ajamatau tried to isolate themselves. But why would conflict still

* *Ground nuts like peanuts that were named gub-a-gubs by the slaves*

persist here? After all, hadn't they all endured the same, unimaginable, conditions at the hands of the white man together? And hadn't they watched each other perish, or survive, regardless of the tribe they came from? So then, why did this not unite them as a people?

He asked Andrew, "What kinds of differences would follow us from Africa and remain to divide us in the situation we are now in together?"

Andrew stopped and looked at him intently. "This is a very hard thing for me to understand. One large source of conflict is a thing called 'religion'. It can take many forms. Sometimes the religion is called Islam, and other times it is called Christianity. There are others, too, but these are the most common. They were brought by people from outside the tribes, mostly people who are not Africans. Many tribes accept these religions over ancestral beliefs. Some for a very long time. I have picked up little bits about these religions over the years.

"You and I are Ajamatau. We live by our ancestral beliefs. Ajamatau understand Ata Emit to be the universal force that orders all else. All living things share and benefit equally from its providence."

This made empirical sense to Jayvyn; it was what he'd been taught to believe since birth. It was all he'd ever understood from the actions exhibited by the elders and the rest of the people in his tribe. There were endless stories, told by the village elders, of certain ancestral spirits who are present in animals, trees, or even the elements of earth and sky.

These spirits were good. They guarded over their people,

offering protection and help. Ceremonies were held before hunts, when planting and harvesting, when children were born, or if someone was sick, asking for their help and guidance. Sometimes the village wiseman created amulets, medicines, or performed dances to bring these spirits closer. They were an essential and present part of their everyday lives.

But he had no concept of this 'religion' Andrew was now speaking of or why it would divide people so.

Andrew continued, "These religions teach that there is some greater being over the universe itself, even Ata Emit and the spirits. They practice worship much differently than we do. They live in fear of their gods. Their gods consider them unworthy beings who must always bear guilt and beg forgiveness, even for things they have never done. They believe their gods want them to self-flagellate and make sacrifices in order to avoid their wrath. If their crops fail, sickness comes, or there is some other disaster, it is because they have failed in their worship and made their gods angry. Asking their gods for help must be done with abject supplication in ways that acknowledge their unworthiness.

"Each religion believes their god is the only god and all other gods are false. They must pay tribute to only that god, or they will lose access to all the goodness the universe provides, and they and their people will suffer for it. Their god tells them it is their duty to make all others believe in their one true god and forsake any other beliefs they have. Are you with me?"

Jayvyn was not. He couldn't comprehend all Andrew was saying. Ata Emit and the spirits of his world were there to help, teach, and nurture his people. They didn't live in fear of them.

He asked, "How could anyone be greater than the universe? Greater than the sky, sun, weather, or time itself? And why would that being believe his people to be unworthy and punish them?"

Andrew thought for a moment, taking in Jayvyn's question. It was the same question he himself had wrestled fruitlessly with over the years. "I cannot understand this myself. But it is something a great many believe. They feel strongly they must dedicate themselves to their god and religion or risk losing everything. Most importantly, they believe anyone who believes differently is a threat to them and their god. This has become a great cause of warfare and bloodshed. Do you now understand?"

Jayvyn was confused. He didn't feel the need to debate such a senseless issue, but was confounded by the notion these religions would create such division as to cause one group of human beings to hate another enough to kill them.

Andrew continued, "There is more. Many tribes have systems of social division. One man becomes richer while others are poor. The rich make the rules and control the land and wealth. They are at the top, and are chiefs, or kings. The ones below are separated into many classes. Status within tribes is based on wealth. There is competition to increase wealth and status to gain advantage over ones below.*

"Many tribes even have slaves. They raid and make war on other tribes for land, wealth, and even their people. Africans among us now would hurt or betray us if they thought it would help them."

**Many African tribes have caste systems within their social structures. The Jola are an exception.*

Jayvyn sat silent as he listened, remembering the vague stories told by his village elders about violent tribes. But these stories were related only as a caution and why the Ajamatau remained amongst themselves. The particulars weren't always discussed. Jayvyn understood not everyone could be trusted, but he found it unfathomable that one tribe of Africans would take members of another to keep in slavery!

Andrew could see confusion growing in Jayvyn's young mind, so he said, "Listen, these things I tell you are true. You must accept them as fact. It is important. It is why things will not always be the same with these Africans as it was in your village. You must be careful what you say and who you trust. But you are smart, and it is why I am telling you this."

Andrew added more. "The white man knows we are divided. This is important! He does not want the tribes to get together. He does everything he can to prevent us from becoming one. That is why we cannot speak in our own language or practice our traditional ways. No one's 'religion' or traditional beliefs are permitted. He is happy to give greater status to some over others. Keeping us divided is a way to keep control over us. Do you understand now? If we become one, we will be more powerful! And it will weaken the white man's control.*

"You and I are Ajamatau. We know our strength is in the strength of our tribe. We carry this as a means to our survival. But we are powerless in this situation. There are too many divisions. These divisions are too deeply rooted to overcome. So, you must understand,

---

* *Slave owners sought to deny tribal unity and exploit the division between tribes for their benefit since they would maintain greater control over them than if they became united*

and not try to fight this, or you will suffer many consequences!"

Jayvyn was not sure how well he understood, but nodded, saying, "So, I cannot trust my fellow Africans because of our tribal differences, because they might take advantage and use this to gain privilege?"

"As strange as it sounds, I cannot explain this any different. You do not need to fear them, but you must be wise about what you say and do, and who you trust. It is why you must understand this now."

Jayvyn looked deep into Andrew's eyes and realized he was telling him the truth. It was inconceivable that differences in beliefs could prevent his race from rising up against the obvious threat they all faced together. But Jayvyn knew Andrew had much more experience than he, and he should rely on his counsel.

"There is one more thing I would like to know."

Andrew looked at Jayvyn expectantly and asked, "Yes? What is it?"

"Where have we come to? What is this place we are now?"

"This is Barbados. It is a long, long way from Africa. It is an island; it means there is ocean on every side. It may seem large to you, but it is much, much smaller than Africa. The white man owns all of it, and there is nowhere to escape to. Do you understand?"

Jayvyn nodded and repeated, "Bar-bā-dos?" sounding the name out as he did.

Andrew nodded, adding in English, "Yes. Now, we gotsta speak no Fogni. I be hep you ta learn de English n'stead."

There were trees along the edge bearing fruits, and Andrew pointed to one, saying, "Dis be *banana*," to which Jayvyn repeated, "ba-na-na."

At another, Andrew said, "Dis be de *orange tree,*" and Jayvyn repeated that, too.

At another tree looking very much like the banana, but with larger fruit, he said, "Ova here be de *plantain.*"

Jayvyn remembered these from the day before. As with other plants, he recognized some grew in Africa, but of course the names were different.

At the plantain tree, Andrew looked for a bunch that was ready to harvest.

He showed Jayvyn the remains of a flower crusted on the tips of the fruit and rubbed it.

He said, "When dis *rub off*, de *fruit* be *ready*. You try,"

Jayvyn rubbed his finger against the dry flower, which easily came off.

"You see James? It be *ready*!" and Andrew took his machete, chopped the large bunch from the tree, and handed it to Jayvyn.

"Now, James, find de *bunch* dat be *ready*." Jayvyn looked over a few near bunches, fingering the dried flowers at the ends, until he found one as before, and said, "Dat be ready!" being mindful he was to speak English only and not Fogni.

Andrew came and showed him how to cut the bunch from the tree using the machete in careful strokes.

They each shouldered their bunches and walked back up the ravine toward the slave quarters, stopping where Walter was to report what they'd harvested. Walter approved, and they left the plantains there.

Walter then told Andrew they needed some water for the crops and Andrew said, "We get it. Come James."

He and Jayvyn went back to the area where the tools were, and Andrew said, "Take *two bucket,* James," pointing at the buckets. Jayvyn picked one up, and Andrew said, "Good, now wha dat be?"

Jayvyn, uncertain, said something like, "bakou."

Andrew laughed, saying, "buck-ket."

Jayvyn replied, "but-kit."

Andrew said, "Good, say it again, *buh-ket.*"

Jayvyn, trying hard to learn, repeated, "Buh-ket."

Andrew nodded, "Yes Yes! Very good, James! Dat be right! You learn good!"

Jayvyn, thrilled to be learning, liked Andrew very much. He was kind and reminded him of the people in his village. He even reminded him of his father, who'd taken time to teach him so much.

It was indeed an experience different from any Jayvyn had had for such a long time. It was like freedom once again, and he smiled radiantly back at Andrew for the first time since his capture. It truly felt like a miracle to him.

Andrew then looked at him and said, "You gotsta have *two bucket,* James." and took one bucket, setting it on the ground, saying, "*One*," and then grabbed another to set next to it and said, "*Two*, you see?" He then pointed at them, first taking one away and then replacing it, saying, "*One* and *two*, *one* and *two*—dat be *two bucket,* James. Do you und'stand?"

Jayvyn looked at him, mimicking, "One, two."

"Dat be right, *two bucket,* James; you gotsta hab *two bucket.*"

Slowly, the lessons became clearer to understand, and when Jayvyn saw Andrew pick up the two buckets, he retrieved another for himself and declared, "Too buk-ket."

Andrew beamed, "Very good, James! Now we get de *long stick*," and he picked one from a pile next to the buckets, handed it to Jayvyn, and took one for himself, saying, "Come, we get de *water*."

They walked up past the slave quarters and continued on to the pond, Andrew talking the whole way.

Jayvyn delighted in the sound of his voice, trying to pick out as many words as he could. He'd pass a tree and say, "*tree,*" and when he passed their quarters, he said, "*house,*" and so forth. Andrew seemed very happy to be spending time with Jayvyn, and Jayvyn's heart swelled with the sensation of enjoying some camaraderie again.

It had been so long, and he'd been so lonely he'd forgotten what it was like. Now, after being deprived of even the smallest kindness for such a long time, it was sweeter than anything he'd ever known before.

They reached the pond. Andrew showed him how to fill the buckets, placing the stick in the handles, one on each end, so they could then be balanced and carried on their shoulders. As he was doing this, Jayvyn noticed others bathing themselves nearby and more rinsing their clothing out.

Black people were all around, tending to their needs like they'd done back in his village. There were no white people, no one watching, ready to yell or whip them. It was surreal.

Andrew and he walked back to the garden with water and used it to irrigate the crops as directed by Walter.

Jayvyn was working, but it was altogether different from the work he'd been doing on the plantation in so many ways. He felt like he could do this forever. In fact, he never wanted it to end.

He could see and feel contentment in the other slaves as well, as they weeded, cultivated, and tended to the gardens.

Time had a much different feel to it today; life had returned.

Soon, someone signaled it was time to take a break, and they all gathered together for a meal.

Some yams had been boiled in a pot and mashed up with '*gub-a-gubs*,' the groundnuts he'd seen earlier. Plantains were set out as well.

The food in the pot tasted very similar to what Jayvyn had been eating in his hut. It was warm and it felt good to get something in his stomach.

As they ate and rested, Andrew introduced Jayvyn to whomever was close by. "Dis be James; today he be work wid me; he be learn de English," to which he'd be answered with a nod or an occasional smile. It was as it had been in the fields; there were limited interactions, but Jayvyn was able to at least see some of the other slaves in a new context.

While eating, Jayvyn noticed a man sitting against a tree. One of his arms was missing from just above where his elbow should be. The scar was ugly and rough.

He turned to Andrew, asking, "Where 'm arm?"

Andrew looked at him and said, "It happen at de mill. It be where de cane be press 'n de juice come out. It be bad."

Jayvyn remembered the mill—the tall building with large blades turning around. He asked, "Why bad?"

Andrew said, "Cane be press—smash—wid de big log." He used his hands to pantomime as he spoke. "Hid arm go wid de cane. De mill no stop, hid arm be cach in de log. Yes?" and looked to see if Jayvyn was following.

Jayvyn, looking rapt, asked, "How 'm arm be out?"

Andrew said, "It no be out."

Jayvyn, alarmed, asked, "What 'm do?"

Andrew sighed and said, "Dey cut it off wid de axe," making a chopping gesture at his own arm.

Looking shocked, Jayvyn asked, "Why?"

Andrew explained, "De mill be bery strong. If'n it get you, you no get out; it crush you to det. So, fo ta save 'm, dey cut 'm arm off. Yes?"*

Jayvyn nodded, wide-eyed, looking back at the man, thinking how horrible it must have been to have his arm suddenly chopped off.

He looked back at Andrew and asked, "Wha him do now?" realizing both arms were needed for most of the work he'd ever done.

Andrew told him, "Boss gib 'm work he do wid de one arm. He carry wid one arm, clean de floor, pull de cart."

After eating, Andrew said, "Come, James, dey be mo to do."

He walked over and spoke to Walter, asking if he needed anything more. Walter told him they could take a basket of food and some plantains back to the slave quarters.

Andrew shouldered a bunch of plantains, Jayvyn took the basket of other produce, and they made their way back up the short path to the huts. As they were walking, Andrew said, "We bring de food to

---

* *Many slaves lost limbs this way since the mill could not be stopped*

Lucy; she keep 'n cook de food. You und'stand?"

Jayvyn wasn't sure and said, "Hmm, no."

Andrew stopped and looked at him. "You no take de food fo yo'sef. De food be fo evry body. Lucy watch de food." Realizing this was too much English for him to understand, Andrew lowered his voice, making sure no one was near, and he repeated it in Fogni, then followed, in English, with, "Do you und'stand James?"

Jayvyn understood, answering in English, "Yes, who Lucy?"

Andrew said, "You gonna see 'er."

Soon they were at the huts, and Andrew approached one where a woman sat outside weaving something from cane leaves. "Hello Lucy, look what we got!"

She looked up from her work and said, "Very good, Andrew; leave it inside."

He and Jayvyn stepped through the door. Jayvyn saw more food stacked against the wall with a few cooking pots nearby. Two women sat inside.

"Hello ladies!" Andrew said with a smile, "Here be some plantain 'n ting from de garden. Dat be James. James, dat be Hannah 'n Mary."

Smiling, they gave a short giggle, saying, "Halo James! Tank you, Andrew."

As they left, Andrew said, "James, I be go wash at de pond. Do you wanna come?"

Jayvyn enthusiastically responded, "Yes!"

They walked to the pond, continuing to talk as they washed and rinsed their clothing. It felt good to clean up.

When they were through, the sun was beginning to get lower in the sky.

Andrew said, "I be go rest. Soon it be dark; tomorrow come fast."

Jayvyn understood most of what he said and could fill in the meaning of the rest. He responded, "Andrew, you be good."

Andrew looked at him and smiled. He said, "When someone be good, you say *Tank you*...now James, you say, *Tank you*."

Jayvyn looked appreciatively up at him and said, "Tank you, Andrew."

To which Andrew replied, "Very good, James, *you be wel come*!"

Back at the slave quarters, Jayvyn went to his hut, and Andrew continued on to his.

He had time to relax for a while, so he lay on his mat and basked in the memory of the day.

He thought back to their conversation in Fogni earlier and all Andrew had told him about tribal divisions. He remembered what he said about how the white man wanted it this way so he could maintain better control over them.

There was so much to think about. He didn't sense any outward hostility from any of the slaves, but there wasn't a lot of interaction either. Many just seemed to go about their business.

Jayvyn relished the rest he was able to take, and thought more about Andrew and the English lessons he gave him all day. He felt he'd learned a lot, and was looking forward to learning more so he could converse better with those around him. He also remembered how good it felt to have unfettered conversation in his native language, although the things they talked about were disturbing. He found the notion of other tribes engaging in slavery most disturbing.

How could that be? he wondered. There may be some among him who were quite accustomed to this who are now slaves themselves! It truly bewildered him. How could one Black man keep another in slavery? He just couldn't reconcile this.

Shifting his thoughts back to the garden, he thought how good it was to be growing food for his community again, like he had back in his village. They were growing the things they'd actually eat. It was much different to be gardening with this in mind than just toiling away in the cane fields.

He also remembered Andrew's stern warning not to take any food for himself.

Soon, other slaves joined him in his hut, and this time he took the tub to Lucy's to retrieve the food. Other slaves came and went with tubs of food as well.

Jayvyn waited while one of the women, Mary or Hannah, he wasn't sure, ladled a portion into his tub. When she handed it back to him, he said, "Tank you."

Smiling broadly at him, she said, "You be welcome."

Gratified to have used some of his new words, Jayvyn brought the food to his hut, and he and his fellow slaves ate, sharing idle conversation about their day.

Jayvyn noticed Charles was not among them and thought he must still be out doing something and would come in later. After all, this was their free day to do as they wanted.

Everyone was relaxed, but tired. Knowing the next day would soon be upon them, it wasn't long before they settled down on their mats for the night.

Jayvyn, too, settled down, content to be with his thoughts from the day. He contemplated Andrew's kindness. He treated him as he would expect any fellow tribesmen would, and he believed, *it is because he is Ajamatau.* It is how his people were.

In his mind, Jayvyn went through all the new English words he'd learned over and over. Most importantly, he practiced how to combine them into phrases to express what he wanted to say. He was surprised by how much he'd picked up just by listening, and he felt much closer to being able to carry on a conversation.

As these pleasant thoughts swirled in his head, his memories of Africa gently returned to cradle his consciousness.

His hut mates rhythmic breathing mixed with the sounds of the night.

A gentle breeze swept in, bringing with it the cool, tropical night air.

Jayvyn fell into a deep and restful sleep.

– 18 –

Escape!

The morning, as on previous days, came in darkness as George's booming voice broke the silence, bringing everyone quickly to their feet.

As he was placing the new candle by the open door, George quickly glanced around the hut.

"Somebody no here!" He exclaimed. "Who it be?" and a moment later, "Where be Charles?"

The others, still trying to focus in the dim light, looked around in total confusion.

George's voice grew louder and more urgent. "Where be dat man? Where be Charles!?" and he beamed at Samuel, "You! Come here!"

Samuel walked over to George, blinking in confusion, as he was still coming to.

George slapped him hard. "Where he be? You work wid he; you know where he be!"

Samuel, in a complete stupor, eye's watering, looked helplessly back, saying, "I not know! I not know he go! Please…"

George, with fire in his eyes, cut him off. "What d'you know? You tell me now!"

Samuel cowered, shielding his face and crying, "No. No, I - I not know! He—He…"

"Shut up! You! You! You!" George went on, pointing randomly at the rest of the slaves, "Where dat man? What d'you know? Tell me now!"

Terrified, the rest of the slaves stared back, perplexed by the outburst as well as the news Charles wasn't among them. Young Stephen stood quivering behind Julia, clinging to the side of her dress.

Julia stammered, "Please, Please Missa George. We not know a ting. We tink he here!"

"When he here? He eat here last night? He sleep here?"

They all looked bewildered at each other, trying to recall any details from the night before. Jayvyn remembered noticing Charles wasn't among them at dinner but hadn't thought much of it at the time. But, he chose not to say anything because of George's rage. No one said anything more. They just looked at George, not knowing what to say or do.

George then barked, "Go, get yo food 'n eat! Be fast! You got work to do!" and turned and stormed out the door.

They heard him going back through the huts, angrily inquiring others, saying things like, "Someone be missin! What d'you know?" and, "A man be gone! Who know some ting?"

Jayvyn, once again, took the food tub and went to Lucy's hut. As he was walking by the other huts, he saw and heard others talking and moving about nervously. Nobody spoke to him or smiled. Eyes darted back and forth; motions were quick; a serious air permeated the camp.

They, indeed, ate quickly, now acutely aware Charles wasn't among them. No one said anything as they filed outdoors to join with the others—actually impatient, on this morning, for the procession to work to begin.

George stood before them all, everyone looking his way; nobody was, in the slightest sense, at ease. "You KNOW it be BAD when someone be miss'n! He GONNA be found! You GOTSTA TELL ME if you hear ANY TING at all, if you find out ANY TING! Charles gonna be PUNISH BADLY! 'N ANYONE who KNOW or HELP HE be PUNISH BADLY TOO! Now TREE SLABE be miss'n from de camp! You KNOW what dat mean! It be BAD FO ME, 'n it be BAD FO EVERYBODY HERE 'til he be FOUND! You find out ANY TING, you tell me AT ONCE! DO YOU HEAR!? NOW, GO! And you BETTAH be work hard!"

The slaves quickly formed into their groups and started to file out. Then George stopped Andrew's group, saying, "Wait! You need de udda man!" realizing he'd need to add another to make up for Charles' absence. He quickly picked out the other man who'd ridden on the wagon with them the day the new slaves were brought. "Thomas! Go wid dat group to cut de wood today!"

Thomas quickly obliged and fell in with that group. The slaves then quietly walked up the road to work. There was no singing as they made their way up the dirt road, although quiet murmuring could be heard as they discussed the big issue of the day.

Someone had gone missing, and those who'd been through this before knew the bosses would be angry and everyone would be regarded suspiciously until the matter was resolved. What was worse was this was the third slave to go missing in the last several months.

First was a man who'd been at the plantation for some time. His name was William, and it wasn't his first time escaping. He'd been caught one time before and had suffered a severe lashing before all the others, while locked in a pillory, where he remained for a week. When he was released, he was forced to wear leg shackles connected by a short chain with weights for a period of ninety days. This made it very difficult to walk and, of course, impossible to run, but he was forced to work as usual despite this handicap. When he worked, the chain and weights slowed him down, whereupon he'd be whipped by whichever boss happened to be nearby. His back became a maze of welts and scars from the repeated beatings. He was eventually released from the shackles, and disappeared again the following month, not to be seen since.

Then, about a week before Jayvyn had arrived, a new slave had run. He hadn't been on the plantation for very long. He was a younger slave who nobody knew much about. This infuriated Master Clark, who had several of the other new slaves interrogated harshly, and he'd cut back on rations and water for the whole group for several days. They were worked extra hard as well, with longer days and shorter breaks.

Searches for these two fugitives were conducted, but so far neither had been found. And so, it was very bad news that a third slave had now escaped.

George would be under great pressure since he's the senior slave responsible for the conduct and welfare of the entire group; the rest would suffer deprivations and harsher treatment. It was in everyone's best interests to have this matter resolved as soon as possible.

When Jayvyn arrived in the cane fields, word of the missing slave hadn't yet reached the bosses, but the low mood and temperament of the slaves signaled something was amiss. Everyone grabbed their tools and went immediately to work, careful to watch their step and keep to themselves. There was no chatter or singing, only heads-down work. The bosses could definitely sense something had happened, especially since the slaves had just had their day off. They typically returned to work more refreshed and animated on Mondays.

It wasn't long before word came down. Master Clark had several of his more senior bosses pulled from the field, leaving fewer to supervise larger areas.

The remaining supervisors became doubly harsh on the slaves; they made it clear there'd be no tolerance for slacking off. The more senior slaves were acutely aware of their fellow slaves, asserting themselves on anyone who wasn't working to the highest standard.

Jayvyn, as well as every slave, felt the change; there was no mystery why this was so. Everyone worked harder; no one wanted to be singled out for anything this day.

Master Clark and his group interrogated George, who had no answers to offer. It wasn't a good morning for him. A posse was put together to search for the missing slave. The wagon was hitched up—a white man driving—two dogs and George in the back. Other white men, including Master Clark, rode on horseback, carrying arms. The party then left for a long day to search nearby woods and mountains, hoping to pick up the trail of the missing man.

Indeed, all slaves worked harder and more intensely this day, and the breaks were shorter and further between. When the meal break came, hard tack biscuits were all that was brought; the break was short as well. Tension was palpable among everyone.

Jayvyn hadn't felt trepidation like this since his first day on the island. The good feeling he had the day before was long gone. He was filled with fear and dread.

He thought back to other times he'd witnessed retribution exacted by these white men—the boys thrown to the sea, the man left hanging in the tree, the woman whose teeth were smashed out.

Now, there were slaves missing. They couldn't immediately punish the escaped, but he knew they'd have to take their rage out on someone. The remaining slaves would pay until they were found.

They worked extra-long that day, well into the evening. It was very difficult to see; work was far from efficient. But everyone did the best they could until finally the work day was called. It was well after dark when the exhausted slaves trudged back to their quarters.

When they arrived, George was waiting, along with Master Clark and two bosses, in an area lit by torches. Andrew was there as well, along with Samuel and Thomas.

Julia, Rose, and Stephen were standing in front of their hut. The other slaves were gathered outside as well. A pillory had been brought into the clearing.

Jayvyn swallowed hard. As his group approached, he, Lewis, and Sarah were singled out and told to stand with Julia, Rose, and Stephen. The others gathered with the rest of the slaves.

Master Clark then nodded to George, who stepped out in front where he could address the whole group.

He spoke in a loud, authoritative voice, "You all know dat a slabe be missin. He be one of de new slabe dat stay here," he said, gesturing to the hut on the end where Jayvyn and the rest of the new slaves stood.

"He no be find yet, but we find 'm soon. We not know when he go. Nobody in dat hut member see'n or no see'n, 'm last night."

He glanced at Jayvyn's group again, then turned his attention back to the whole assembly.

"He work wid dem men," he said as he indicated Andrew, Samuel, and Thomas.

He went on, "'n dat man," pointing only to Samuel, "he be lib'n in dat hut wid him.

"He come wid dat slabe, he work wid 'm, 'n know him de bets.

"I aks 'm, but he say he not know no ting about hid plan fo 'scape.

"We find out now if dat be true."

He then went to the pillory and instructed Andrew and Thomas to bring Samuel to it.

Samuel, wide-eyed, tears streaming down his face, pleaded, "No! No! Please! I say you trut, Missa George! I not know! Please! Please! No!"

But his pleas were no use as he was put into the device and it was closed around his neck and wrists.

Samuel hung there helplessly as George came around front.

Andrew stood behind Samuel, whip in hand.

George began.

"What Charles say to you?"

Samuel rapidly spit out, "Please! Please! Missa George! Charles no talk me!"

George nodded at Andrew, who brought the whip back, cracking it hard against Samuel's back.

Samuel jerked and cried out; his face contorted in pain.

George continued, "I aks you agin. What Charles say to you? When he go? Where he go?"

Samuel picked his head up, face streaked with tears, and said, "I not know! I not know! He no say! Please! I say trut!"

George nodded to Andrew, who again brought the whip down hard.

Samuel stiffened, crying out in anguished pain.

"Samuel, de Massa gotsta know. You gotsta tell what you know. You 'n Charles be work 'n lib togeda; you come togeda. I know you know mo! NOW! DAMN YOU, TELL ME!"

Samuel cried hysterically, looking at George.

In a much weaker voice, he said, "I not know Missa George! Please! No!"

George, again, gave Andrew the signal.

The crack of the whip made Jayvyn and the others jump.

Jayvyn knew Samuel was telling him the truth. He knew Andrew must know this too, and was astonished to see him whipping Samuel. Their eyes met briefly. He could see Andrew's eyes were wet; he had a grieved look on his face. Andrew looked away.

George continued with his fruitless line of questioning twice more. Each time Samuel gave the only response he could. He didn't know anything and could offer nothing more.

George, too, knew he was telling the truth but ordered the whip brought down two more times.

With his last response, Samuel's voice was much weaker.

He sobbed relentlessly as he sagged in the pillory—utterly

hopeless and defeated.

George finished with, "Yo gonna stay in de pillory t'night. I gonna see if yo change yo mind in de morn'n."

Master Clark nodded to the two bosses. All three turned to walk back up the long dirt road to the big white house, fading off into the darkness until all that remained was the bobbing light of their torches.

Samuel, weak and sobbing, slumped in the pillory.

George told the rest of the slaves to eat and sleep; it would be work as usual in the morning.

Food was limited to hard-tack biscuits and a few pieces of salt fish. Although depleted and hungry from the day's work, no one had much desire for anything. The events of the night left a hollow pit in everyone's stomach and a deep wound in their souls. All walked away sullenly. Samuel stayed suffering in the pillory, streaks of blood running off his back.

Jayvyn lay on his mat that night, stunned and wracked with emotion, as he thought about Samuel being mercilessly whipped—*by Andrew, no less!*—for something he had no part in. It wasn't that he hadn't seen such pain, or worse, inflicted on others during this dark chapter in his life; it was that he'd gotten to know Samuel and felt he was a good, kind, and sincere man. He knew nothing of Charles' plan or intentions to run; no one did.

And what of Andrew? How could it be the man Jayvyn had come to know as a kind and caring friend—someone who'd taken him under his wing and warned him of dangers—how could it be his heart could turn to stone against a man he knew did nothing wrong?

At the same time, Jayvyn knew Andrew had no choice. If he'd

refused to obey, he'd have been whipped right alongside Samuel.

It was an example of the divisive system Andrew tried to explain—where one man accedes to the demands of another, whether right or wrong. It was the system the whites depended on to make slavery work.

It's what keeps the slaves divided. It's why George has higher status.

– 19 –

Life and Death on the Plantation

It was hard to see Samuel still slumped in the pillory as they formed groups and trudged up the hill to work. All of the slaves seemed sullen and depressed at the sight. It was apparent to Jayvyn that none among them believed Samuel deserved his punishment. Even George seemed to lack conviction as he queried Samuel for the truth.

He could be heard saying, "I hope dat you come to yo sense," "if'n you jus say de one ting to me," or "tell me you tink him be goin." But Samuel just hung listlessly in the pillory, in a semi-conscious daze, unable to respond.

Eventually, George convinced Master Clark that Samuel didn't know anything that would help locate the missing slave, and he was released. It would be days before he was able to return to the work he'd been doing. In the meantime, he was put to work on different assignments. The first day, he performed lighter duties at the big house helping Julia, Rose, and Stephen with cleaning. Then he spent some time at the stables, assisting the man with one arm, doing chores there.

The other slaves continued to be worked extra hard; provisions remained basic. They were reminded daily to come forth with any information about the escaped slave. The search continued, but Charles wasn't found.

As weeks passed, things slowly returned to what they were before the escape. No one spoke of the slave's absence, and in the meantime, new arrivals came. Master Clark bought six new slaves. Jayvyn and his group were no longer the new arrivals. They were moved to another hut, one with slightly more in it. There were wooden platforms for their mats and a few boxes to use for seats in addition to the table. They were also accepted differently amongst the other slaves as they were now familiar with their work and surroundings.

Jayvyn continued to work in the gardens every Sunday, and Andrew continued to teach him English. He'd become much better at conversing and could now speak well enough to be understood by the other slaves.

He'd learned more about how the hierarchy was stacked within the group as well. Some slaves enjoyed meat with their meals from time to time. This always included George. There were those who ate with him, and those who didn't.

The white men occasionally slaughtered chickens and pigs, giving the parts they wouldn't eat to the slaves. This included heads, feet, and entrails. Lucy and some of the others were adept at using these parts in different ways. Some went into broths mixed with vegetables to make soups. Other parts, such as intestines, were stuffed with organ meat and roasted over the fire. When there was enough, it would be shared more broadly in the group, but the newest slaves were never included. Anyone who'd fallen out of favor would also be excluded.

Andrew continued to provide Jayvyn with valuable advice. He'd reminded him on more than one occasion no one was here by choice. It was a mixed pool of different tribes, and he should be cautious about who he formed relationships with until he understood the group well. It was better to go slow, he said, and learn over time rather than be too assertive.

Jayvyn was prudently cautious. However, he was also friendly by nature and had established good relations with Lucy and some others. Lucy shared her knowledge of making things from cane leaves. She weaved mats, baskets, and other things that could be used in a variety of ways.

A man named Hector used a machete and other tools to fashion things from wood. He made rough tables, the platforms for their mats, and the boxes they sat on. He also made a more complicated chair that used a mat made by Lucy suspended across its seat, which was much more comfortable to sit on.

Much of what they made was traded amongst them for things of equal or greater value. Some used chicken feathers, branches, rocks, and other materials to make ornamental pieces. Others sewed. But all of this had to be done in the small amount of time they had to themselves, so luxuries were sparse at best.

Jayvyn also learned more about the operations at the plantation. He found out that during harvest, which was now coming to an end, the mill and boiling house were worked round the clock, but not on Sundays. Crews worked through the night, replaced by a fresh crew in the morning. That was why he always saw slaves working at the end of the day.

He was assigned to work in the boiling house for a period, where he saw the process used to take the juice extracted from the cane and boil it down over three vats, reducing it to a syrupy slurry. Then it was put into a cooling vat, where it sat for a time to cure. After this, it was poured into barrels, called hogsheads, or clay pots, where it was cured further. The clay pots were covered with a different type of clay and kept separate from the rest. Curing in clay pots yielded a more valuable product known as white sugar. The whole process took many weeks to complete and was very complicated.

In all, four products came out of the cane. At the highest level was refined, or white sugar.* Having the greatest value, this was kept under the highest security.

Next was a less refined sugar, brown in color, called muscovado. Taken locally as currency, this was also kept under tight security.

Then there was molasses, a sticky brown syrup that drained from the sugar cured in barrels. From this, rum could be made—a potent drink similar to the palm oil liquor Jayvyn's tribe made in Africa.

All of this required special skills and had to be overseen by those who knew precisely what to do.

Jayvyn was merely a runner—a very busy and demanding job. He kept the operation going by stoking the fires, bringing supplies of lime and ash, and keeping a good supply of fresh water on hand. There was also plenty of cleaning to be done. All so the skilled workers could remain at their stations uninterrupted.

Jayvyn was able to see the mill in operation when the boiling master sent him there for one reason or another. A long tube of hollowed logs connected the mill to the boiling house.

He saw slaves feed whole bundles of cane between huge, slowly

---

* *White sugar was the product that made the sugar plantations so profitable as it was in high demand back in England and other European nations, however each product added significant value to the operations*

turning logs, or rollers, driven by the large blades outside. These massive blades, he learned, were powered by the ever-present winds that blew across the ridge where the mill was located.

Massive wooden mechanisms above the mill turned in an interlocking fashion, transferring power from the wind blades to the rollers. The heavy rollers took the cane and smashed it under incredible pressure, squeezing out any juice it contained. The juice, or sap, continuously dripped onto a pitched surface, from where it ran into the tube and down to the boiling house. After two passes through the rollers, the spent cane was heaved outside the building, where it was piled for pig feed.

The mill was impressive. Jayvyn saw why it was so dangerous to be working near. It was where the man in the garden had lost his arm. He noticed an axe kept near the rollers. It was the one used to sever the man's arm when it became trapped in the rollers. It was kept there just for that purpose.*

The harvesting had taken more than a month, and afterward, the fields had to be prepared for the next planting. This required all of the ground to be tilled with shovels and hoes and the bases of the cane plants removed, along with their roots and any weeds that had grown up. Then the turned soil was dug into squares of about four feet by four feet. These squares were banked with soil on all sides to a height of about one foot.

It was very hard work, and there were many acres of field to prepare. Jayvyn worked large sections at a time, first digging out all the

---

* *Axes were typically kept in the mills specifically for the purpose of chopping off limbs that might become trapped in the presses*

cane roots along with any weeds, then tilling the soil with a hoe, until he'd cleared and turned a patch about fifty feet by fifty feet. Then, starting at a corner, he used a four-foot stick, provided to him, to mark out a four-by-four square. He dug the soil about five inches down, pulling it to the side to create a foot tall border. Then he moved to one side to make another square, and so on, until ten four-by-four squares formed a line. Following this, he created another row of ten squares on top of the first and continued this way until there were ten rows of ten, or a hundred squares.

Each slave was instructed to work in this fashion, each in an area of similar size. Some fields had thirty or more patches this size to prepare, and there were over a dozen such fields on the plantation. At any given time, eight or ten slaves were dedicated to this task. Each was expected to finish at least half of a fifty-by-fifty patch in a day. Any less would earn him scorn from the boss and likely lashes from his whip.

Other slaves, usually the newer ones, gathered cane root and weed debris, bringing it to carts, which in turn took it to the pig pens.

When all the fields had been properly prepared and the time was right, they were planted again. Two cane plants were planted in each square then covered with manure. The manure came from piles generated year-round by horses, pigs, chickens, and other livestock on the plantation. Slaves carried baskets of manure, each weighing about eighty pounds, on their heads, from the barnyard to the fields. One basket covered about two squares.

After planting, the cane had to be watered. Buckets were carried in the way Andrew had shown Jayvyn—a stick balancing two at a time across the shoulders. Each load weighed roughly the same as the manure. The buckets were carried from the pond, up the hill, to the fields—a considerable distance. All the work was excessively difficult and hard on the body—and it was endless—six days a week, twelve hours a day.

Over the months since Jayvyn had arrived, several batches of newly purchased slaves had arrived, and many disappeared as well. Some, he knew, had died. Some from mysterious diseases, where they lost strength quickly and wasted away at the slave quarters.* More often than not, however, slaves dropped in the fields from malnourishment and overexertion.

New slaves, many already suffering severe exhaustion, dehydration, sick, or injured, were forced to work regardless of their condition. If they faltered, they were whipped until they stood and worked again. Many weren't able to resume; others staggered to their feet, feebly worked a while longer, then collapsed. They were simply worked to death.

When this happened, they were removed from the field and put into a cart until the day was done. The rest of the slaves continued working, and the cart with the body, or bodies, would be pulled to a burial ground after work.†

Shallow graves were dug, by slaves, in an area designated by the white man. Bodies were simply placed in the grave and covered with

---

* *Slaves were susceptible to many new diseases in their new environments, and other factors, such as diet*

† *As with garden plots, plantation owners would designate areas for the slaves to bury their dead. These, as garden plots, were areas that could not be used for plantation operations and were usually rocky and of poor quality*

dirt, rocks, and debris. But funeral ceremonies of any type were not allowed.

Burials would have to occur outside of the required work schedule, with the duty falling to just a few slaves at a time. It was a common enough occurrence that many regarded it simply as more work.

With so many varied tribes, a lack of strong familial or tribal relations lessened the importance of ritual ceremonies. All the slaves, however, felt burying the dead was important.

Some burial rites were common among them. In particular, the practice of burying those who died in good standing face up. This was so their spirit could escape. To be buried face down signified a life ended in disgrace. They believed a body buried this way would have its spirit trapped in the ground. In these cases, the miscreant would be buried in a location separate from the rest.*

Another reason for a slave's disappearance, Jayvyn came to find, was because they were sold. These were slaves who'd survived the rigors of the plantation and learned to work and behave well. They were 'seasoned' now and could be sold at a profit to new owners wanting a slave who was broken, trained, and could speak English.†

However, this occurred only after the harvest and sugar production cycle was complete. Following this, fewer slaves were

---

* *Slave burial sites are notoriously difficult to find by archaeologists since there were no markers and very little remained of them, however some were noted on plantation maps*

† *Seasoned slaves were found to bring a substantially higher price than those straight from Africa, or "salt water" slaves as they were called. Historical data suggests that slave owners could more than double their money after seasoning. However, many slaves would not survive the seasoning process*

needed in the daily operation. Selling some off would not only lower operating costs, but generate additional profits as well. When the time came, they were simply packed up and taken to market.

Of course, a core of slaves with specific plantation knowledge or supervisory importance, such as George, were perpetually retained to ensure the smooth continuation of operations.

Over time, Jayvyn got to know certain slaves better than others. But at the same time, some he'd gotten to know were no longer there.

One in particular was Julia. She was in their original group and had greeted Jayvyn at the cabin on his first night out of the stocks. She'd also taken young Stephen under her wing.

Stephen had grown quite fond of Julia and went to work with her every day at the big house. When they were back at the slave quarters and on their days off, Stephen would always follow her around, clinging to her dress or hand as he might his own mother.

Something had happened to Julia, however. It seems on one of her work days, she was held over late at the big house by one of the bosses. Stephen had walked back with Rose that day, whom he was also quite fond of.

The white man, it seems, was drinking rum and wanted Julia to keep him company—to bring him food, drink, and anything else he wanted. He became drunk and began to molest Julia, who fought his advances but was unable to make him stop. He raped her repeatedly and beat her badly in the process, not letting her go until late in the evening.[*]

She arrived back at the quarters, after all the other slaves had gone to sleep. Jayvyn woke to see her sobbing in the corner. Sarah, who'd woken as well, came to sit with her through the night.

The next morning, all could see she'd been beaten and was quite distraught. Her dress was torn and bloodied in spots; her face was bruised as well. She didn't explain much to anyone as she went off to work that day, but everyone could see she was severely traumatized.

In the months following, the same white man abused her several more times. Each time she returned beaten, bloodied, and sobbing uncontrollably.

Eventually, it became apparent she was pregnant. It was a devastating development in her life; her mood became sullen and depressed, but there was nothing she or anyone else could do about it. The white man left her alone when her pregnancy began to show, but she still had to go to work every day.

It was particularly confusing for poor Stephen, who'd always known her to be a bright spot in his small life. But now she was different—quiet and withdrawn. She tried best as she could to be there for him, but it just wasn't the same. All along, she felt the thing inside her growing. It was a thing—not of love—but a thing she didn't want—or want to face—a thing that would forever bring her shame.

One early morning, she was discovered missing from her quarters. George sounded the alarm, announcing a slave had gone

---

* *It was quite common for white men to rape their slaves, both male and female. In the case of females, many mixed-race children would be born, most of which would remain enslaved*

missing.

A short time later, her body was discovered floating in the pond; Julia had drowned herself.*

Jayvyn and the others in his quarters were stricken with grief. Julia, instinctively, had always been nurturing to them—all of them—providing comfort and assurance during their hardest moments. She was the first to welcome Jayvyn after his punishment and see he had something to eat. She adopted young Stephen into her heart as if her own, restoring some of what he'd so unfairly lost. And when Samuel was released from the pillory, she gently bathed his wounds, reassuring him that she and the others believed in him. She was a friend to Sarah as well when she returned, exhausted and worn from long hours in the fields. Rose and Lewis, too, had been touched by her generous caring on many occasions. She was, in many ways, the mother they'd all lost when the white man came. Now, he'd taken her as well.

Julia had taken her life sometime after work on Saturday. This availed the other slaves the opportunity to bring her body to the burial ground Sunday morning.

Jayvyn and Samuel went off to find a cart, Sarah and Rose made a small doll out of cane leaves with Lucy's help. A few other women donated beads, feathers, and shells for the hair and eyes. When Jayvyn and Samuel returned with the cart, Julia was gently laid onto it, the doll placed on her chest with her arms folded across it.

The four slaves from their original group surrounded and walked

---

* *Historically suicide rates among traditional African cultures were comparatively low as it was considered taboo in their native cultures. However, this rate increased dramatically with the onset of the European slave trade. Still, it was considered low compared to many other cultures*

with the cart as Jayvyn and Samuel pulled it up the hill to the burial ground. Andrew and many others rose to join them. It was a solemn occasion as they shuffled slowly, heads down, up the hill.

As they passed the pond where Julia had drowned herself, a lone, mournful voice began to sing:

Massa buy me he won't killa me oh,
Massa buy me he won't killa me oh,
Massa buy me he won't killa me oh,
'for he kill me he ship me regular.

The rest in the group then sang out a low chorus:

ai-a ai-a, ai-a ai-a, a
ai-a, ai-a ai-oh

The first voice continued sadly on:

'for I live with a bad man oh la,
'for I live with a bad man obudda bo,
'for I live with a bad man oh la,
'for I would go to the riverside regular.

ai-a ai-a, ai-a ai-a, a
*ai-a, ai-a ai-oh**

---

* *An African Work Song, Barbados, circa 1770s, taken down by Granville Sharp, a prominent British abolitionist and the only known manuscript of an African work song that was chanted in the sugar fields of Barbados*

- 20 -

Remembering Julia

Julia was laid to rest that morning; no white man interfered or gave notice to their song as they marched up the long, dusty road to the burial grounds.

She was buried face-up, the tiny doll resting on her chest as it had been in the cart. Rose held young Stephen's hand, his dirty face streaked with recent tears. Dirt was shoveled over Julia's body; rocks placed over her shallow grave. Nothing more was said or could be said.

The group of slaves slowly turned away and headed back to their quarters.

Jayvyn worked in the garden with Andrew that day. Most of the slaves were unusually quiet that morning, or so it seemed to Jayvyn. He supposed that, like him, they were lost in their thoughts as they pondered Julia's fate. She, too, had helped in the garden, and in her way, had contributed more than realized to the overall community.

Jayvyn reflected on how it was some people just seemed to do that—how some give in ways too numerous and small to be counted in the moment, but when they are gone, enormous holes are left in the spaces they once occupied.

Julia was one of those magical people who, by their very presence, filled the world around them with treasures unnoticed in the day-to-day thrum of life—a tree, a river, a mountain—just there until it's not.

It's only when they're gone that their importance becomes understood and their absence felt so strongly. Powerful angst and remorse consume those who failed to appreciate them when they were right there in front of them—and now realize the opportunity is lost forever.

Jayvyn thought back to the time, shortly after he'd arrived at the plantation, when the idea of ending his own life had unexpectedly occurred to him. It was a concept so completely foreign he was shocked to have even had it in his thoughts. He couldn't conceive an existence so devoid of life that death—ceasing to exist—would be a preferable choice. Now here it was, Julia—a person so full of life—had made just that choice.

It grieved him further to think how hopeless and dark her world must have become to make that choice.

As Jayvyn and Andrew weeded a patch of okra, he asked, "Andrew, how it be dat de libin' ting make to die if it kin lib? It be like de okra make not to lib, but de soil be good 'n der be water. Dat can no be."

Andrew looked at him, "James, dat be de plant. De plant gonna grow where it kin, 'n we be weed'n and car'n for de plant so dat it kin grow good. It no make de choice."

Jayvyn, feeling a bit chagrined, responded, "Yes, but it still be de libin' ting. What 'bout de bird? Or de animal in de wood? Dey be libin' ting 'n kin make dey mind."

"Dey be free, 'n it be de life dey born to lib. Dey hab de sense to surbibe, to go whereber dis be poss'ble, to find de ting dey need to lib."

Jayvyn considered this for a while, feeling he might be coming closer to the truth he was seeking, and asked, "Den, wha 'bout de pig 'n de chick'n in de barn? Dey no be free, 'n dey no go where dey want. Dey be keep in de pen 'n be kil't fo food. And de horse. Dey be whip't 'n made ta work, like we."

Andrew thought longer as he considered the new elements of Jayvyn's question and said, "I not know all ting, James, but I tink dat dey be much diff'nt den we. We be human. Dey be animal, 'n dey be keep like dat for many, many life. Dey be 'cept'n life in captiv'ty fo de reason dat we keep 'em. Dey no tink 'bout any ting else.

"We, too, be libin' in captiv'ty, yet we mostly choose ta lib. It no be de life we choose, 'n if we tink too much, we no be happy. Many o we die, but not 'cause'n we choose. Some no lib like dat 'n choose ta die. We all diff'nt."

"I be tinking 'bout Julia. She be so full o life. Eben when ting be at de worts, she find plenty o strength to give to somebody who be need it mo. How somebody so full o life choose ta die?"

Andrew looked long at Jayvyn, realizing his struggle with trying to understand the depths of Julia's despair. He had to remember this boy was only twelve, and hadn't had this type of experience with death before.

After thinking long and hard, he finally spoke. "James, we all lose many of de ting dat be mots import'nt in ah life. But, we keep de small'st 'mount o ah spirit alibe in ah soul. It may be so small dat we hab de hard time find'n it. But if we lib'n each day, it gotsta be der, 'cause'n widout it, we no lib at all.

"Julia care fo all o we in ah hard'st time. She care for de one ting we no kin lib widout. Dat be ah spirit. Dat spirit be libin' widin each one o we. We suffa caus'n de white man done take ebry ting but ah spirit, 'n dat be what we gotsta look out fo, or we gonna die.

"I tink Julia lose de last o her libin' spirit when de white man force hid seed inta her. She no bear de idea o carin' fo any part of de ting dat be take so much away from we, yet it be forc't into her like de libin' ting so she no kin git rid o it. Her body be carin' fo de bery spirit dat take ah people, ah pride, 'n eben ah name. She no kin fight ta keep her spirit alibe no more if'n de white man spirit be grow'n in her too, 'n so she choose det instead o de life widout her libin' spirit. You see? You no kin lib widout de part of de spirit what you be born wid, 'cause'n dey ain't no life der. Dat make sense?"

Jayvyn stared down at the garden patch and considered this. He thought back to the time when the idea of ending his own life had occurred to him, and remembered the feeling he'd at that time. It was what Andrew had just explained, and he agreed, "Life be no good widout de ting what make you who you be. I know dat be bad'n det."

Andrew's eyes began to water as he looked upon this unfortunate twelve-year-old boy who'd suffered—and learned—so much so fast.

He thought back to when he'd first been taken, some five years earlier at a much older age, and how hard these lessons had come to him.

"Yes, James, I tink you be understand'n, 'n so you gotsta 'member ta care fo yo spirit, ta 'member what make you who you be.

You can lib wid any ting if'n you do dat. But make sure you take care of de spirit so it kin grow agin when you be free."

"Do you tink we be free agin?"

"We all free someday, if not in de life, den when we be dead. Dat be when de spirit kin leeb ah body, 'n we be free den.

"But I b'leeb dat we may be free agin in de world, so we gotsta take care o ah spirit now so we kin lib 'til de time we be free 'n ah spirit kin grow agin."

Jayvyn's face relaxed. He felt satisfied he now understood better after talking with Andrew. Andrew was a good person. He'd always felt this, but was still bothered by seeing Andrew wield the whip against Samuel.

How could this man, this Ajamatau, who'd been so kind and helpful, be the same person who stood behind Samuel—who he knew had done nothing wrong—and whip him so mercilessly? It was impossible to reconcile this with the man he now worked in the garden with—the man who'd just explained so well the essence of one's spirit to his sustenance of life. He'd witnessed the terrible way Samuel's spirit had suffered that night as he'd flogged him into a whimpering shell of himself. How close his spirit must have come to dying that night. Julia's kindness came to mind as he remembered her quietly reassuring Samuel while nursing his wounds.

Before he could think better of it, he asked "Why you whip Samuel?"

Andrew froze in his work and stared at the ground before him. Jayvyn instantly knew he'd crossed a line. Andrew stayed still, looking down, for a long time. He knew he had to give an answer but struggled mightily with what to say.

Eventually, without looking up, he sheepishly replied, "I no got de choice."

Jayvyn remained quiet and continued weeding. He could tell Andrew was quite shaken by his question and as disturbed about what he'd done as anyone else.

After a prolonged silence, Andrew continued, "James, we be stand'n fo de ma'sa 'n de udda white boss dat night. A slabe be scap't. It be de worts ting dat kin happ'n.

"Ma'sa Clark want de ansa, but nobody got none to gib.

"George know dat too.

"To no bey de ma'sa be ta aks fo de badda punish'nt.

"Dem what be here de longest know dat de punish'nt kin be much badda den whipp'n.

"Samuel be inn'cent; we all know dat.

"If I no do it, I be punish fo dis'bedience, 'specially if I dis'bey in front o everyone.

"'N still, Samuel be whip't. He be mo whip't 'cause'n de ma'sa be madda.

"It be de ting I ain't prouda."

Jayvyn looked at Andrew and apologized. "I be sorry I aks. You be de good man; I know dat, 'n I know it gotsta be de bad ting what you do."

Andrew replied, "We all be made to do de ting we no wanna do.

"But dey be de way we kin do de good ting.

"We hep each udda when we kin. Julia do dat.

"Dem udda slabe hep me, and I be hep'n you now.

"Samuel hep we all dat night in de way dat be hard to unde'stand.

"My heart be sick wid every whip, but I know it be oba soon 'n dat Samuel be get bettah. An in a way, we all pay de price so dat one man kin be free.

"Dat man be Charles; he ain't be find, 'n I hope dat, on de small island, he kin stay free."

They both continued working in the garden until shortly after noon. Jayvyn asked no more questions, but Andrew had given him plenty to think about. He saw how it was true they all paid a price for one man's escape to freedom.

Isn't paying a price a way of helping?

It seemed strange to think of things this way, especially since no one had been asked if they'd pay this price, just as Samuel wasn't asked. However, Jayvyn did share joy in the idea one among them had escaped. Some part of him felt better if, in some backhanded way, their suffering had helped.

Once again, as was typical on these Sunday afternoons, Jayvyn and Andrew went about their own separate business. Jayvyn was in the habit of bathing and rinsing his clothes out at the pond, visiting among others in the camp, or spending some time alone. This particular afternoon, he preferred to be alone with his thoughts of Julia and the things he and Andrew had talked about.

He was unsure how Andrew spent his time since he never saw him around late on Sunday afternoons. But everyone engaged in their own activities on the one day they had to do this.

Work resumed the following day as it had week after miserable week.

Julia, although not among them anymore, was remembered in all of their hearts. Young Stephen became more attached to Rose, who seemed to fill the space Julia left. They worked together at the big house, and so it was very natural this would happen. Jayvyn was glad Stephen had someone he could attach to.

Simon, too, was gone. He was among the 'seasoned' slaves who'd been carted up and sold off. It made sense. He was very conscious of what the white man wanted from him.

Jayvyn remembered back to when he'd first been put to work in the fields and how Simon had admonished him for going too slowly or not doing the job right. Simon had also explained other rules about working on the plantation, and knew how to speak the white man's language.

He was young, too; he'd make good property for someone wanting a slave who'd been broken at an early age and would do as he was told.

Jayvyn wondered where he'd gone. He'd heard from others that ships came to carry them off, but he didn't know where they went. They simply sailed away, never to be seen or heard from again.

The new cane had been planted and was growing well. Fewer slaves were among the population now, as fewer were needed to work the plantation.

Each day, water had to be carried to the fields to water the new cane, and weeds had to be culled out.

There were the other gardens, too, which had varieties of plants that were only for the white man. These gardens were of much better quality than the slaves' garden. The soil was richer, well tilled, and the sunlight was better, so things growing there were better. But all the same, it was worked and maintained by slaves while under the strict, watchful eyes of the bosses.

At some times of the year, rain came more dependably. Mostly in the mornings, and sometimes this meant water wouldn't have to be carried to the fields.

On those days, different work would be assigned. Sometimes it meant working at the barn, where there was always plenty to do. Jayvyn learned how to groom the horses and feed the pigs. There was also plenty of manure to be shoveled out of the pens and hay and other feed brought in and stored.

Other areas needed work, too. The boiling house needed to be cleaned and repairs made after the sugar was done, and the sugar itself had to be finished and packaged for shipping. Cleaning and repairs were needed for the mill and many other areas on the plantation as well. Wood continued to be cut and stacked for the boiling room and other supplies readied for the next harvest.

In time, Jayvyn had worked in many different areas and knew pretty much everyone who was there. He became familiar with the names and faces of the white bosses He was even able to glimpse the inside of the big white house when sent there with produce from the white man's garden.

He was awe-struck by what he saw in the kitchen and beyond. It was a palace like he'd never imagined before—colorful walls, furnishings covered in fine cloth—finely sculpted cabinets, tables, and chairs. In the kitchen, there were large tables and great iron stoves for cooking.

He wasn't allowed to go any further than the kitchen and its pantry, although even in those areas the very air seemed different—cleaner, quieter—his footsteps resounded with a conspicuous echo as he walked across the hard, wooden floor.

It was as if privilege permeated the entire space, wrapping everything in a cloak of abundance.

Jayvyn certainly felt very out of place and intimidated just from being there. He was eager to come and go as unnoticed as he could. It was astonishing—the contrast between his world and the white man's.

One day, as he was working in the field, things began to feel different. Other slaves felt it too. A boss rode among the other white bosses, bringing some kind of news.

They began acting differently and called the day earlier than usual.

The slaves were all gathered together and marched to the area in front of the barn, where Master Clark and the other bosses stood before the wagon.

In it were four slaves, beaten and bound by ropes.

As they neared, Jayvyn saw one of the men was Charles, the man who'd escaped several months ago.

Then he swallowed hard.

One of the others was Andrew.

- 21 -

Crime and Punishment

Master Clark and all of the white bosses were assembled in front of the wagon containing the four bound slaves. Master Clark stood in the middle. His bosses, all bearing arms, fanned out on either. George stood in front.

Jayvyn and the other slaves' blood ran cold as they surveyed the scowls on the bosses' faces. There was no doubt as to the seriousness of the moment; no one made a sound.

George's booming voice rang out:

"In de wag'n be fo slabe. Tree dem be de run 'way, but dey be kech now."

Jayvyn looked at the slaves in the wagon. Andrew was sitting among them. He couldn't understand what had happened. George said three of them were escapees, but he knew Andrew hadn't escaped. So, he must be sitting there for another reason.

As he scanned the other faces in the wagon, he noticed the youngest boy sitting there. He wasn't anyone he recognized from the plantation, but something was very familiar about him. Jayvyn searched his mind. The only boys of that age he knew were Simon and Lewis, and he was neither of them.

He did recognize Charles, although his hair had grown considerably since he'd last seen him. But his steady stare and fixed countenance were unmistakable.

The other man was large and powerfully built. His hair was long and matted, and he had a beard as well. Jayvyn didn't recognize this man at all.

His gaze settled back on Andrew, and he felt a great pang of anxiety. Andrew had done something and was in great trouble. Their eyes met for a moment. Andrew's eyes betrayed a look of profound foreboding, unlike Jayvyn had ever seen before, further heightening his anxiety.

George continued, "You dat be here de longest know de man, William. He be de one what 'scape twice 'n be miss'n for mo den de year. De boy be Ben. He be de one 'scape rite afta he get here. De udda man be Charles, he be de last 'scape slabe."

George slowly passed his gaze over the entire group gathered before him. After a lengthy pause, he went on, "Most o you know Andrew. Andrew no 'scape. He be gibb'n dem 'scaped slabe food 'n udda ting wen dey hid'n inna cabe down de mountain.

"Andrew be miss'n on Sunday night, 'n dat be tol me. We follow 'm, 'n he led we to de cabe where de udda slabe be hid'n fo de long time. Now dey be here.

"Punish'nt be 'cided by Ma'sa Clark 'n now be gibb'n.

"Fo twice 'scap'n, 'n hid'n dem 'scape slabe, fo steal'n from Ma'sa Clark, 'n tret'n de white folk fo oba fo-teen mont, William be sentenc'ta hang 'til he be dead. Den hid head be cut off 'n stake 'n hid body be put on de gibbet ta rot til he be gone."

An audible gasp arose among the slaves. It was a punishment that had been witnessed by some before Jayvyn's time. But the severity was clear enough in its description, and horrible beyond comprehension.

Death was bad enough, but many Africans believe having one's head removed prevents their spirit from joining their ancestors after death.

The act of staking the head and gibbeting the body was to serve as a public reminder to all how severe punishment for this type of crime could be. His head would be put upon a stake, and his body hung from a high pole, or gibbet, to rot in the sun and be scavenged by birds. It would remain on display until gone.*

Willliam, upon hearing this, broke into hysterics on the cart. Struggling mightily against his ropes, he rolled off the cart and into the dirt. He continued to scream loudly until one of the bosses clubbed him into silence.

Jayvyn stood terrified at what he'd just heard, unable to comprehend the appalling entirety of it all. Images came to the surface, his mind catapulting through punishments he'd witnessed so far, from the boys devoured by sharks to the contorted man left hanging in the tree. Now more would be added to his morbid, other-worldly gallery of horrors.

George then proceeded. "Fo de crime o run'n 'way 'n no be kech fo lebben mont, de boy, Ben, be sentenc'ta fo-tee lash in de pill'ry. He be stay der fo one week. Den hid nose be cut, 'n hid face be burn, 'n he gotsta wear de iron colla fo six mont."

Another pitiful gasp emitted from the group of slaves. Again, some of those who'd been on the plantation long enough remembered the collar. It's design, with four long, heavy iron prongs extending perpendicularly from its sides, was meant to make it difficult for an

---

* *Gibbeting was a fairly common means used in the 1700's to denigrate executed criminals and deter others from repeating the crime*

escaping slave to pass through trees and thickets, and thereby easier to track and recapture. Also, the device would make him immediately identifiable to others as an escaped slave, were he not to be recaptured. In addition, the collar, heavy in itself, made it impossible to lie flat or sit against a wall and was therefore extremely uncomfortable. Nose slitting and face branding would render scars to forever identify a slave as a prior runaway. In this case, the brand left an "r" shaped scar on the forehead.*

Jayvyn still struggled with the boy's familiarity. There was something about his eyes and face—something that tugged strongly at his memory.

Suddenly, it came to him. It was Baahir! Yes! He was sure of it! His hair was much longer than when he'd last seen him on the ship. It had been a very long time ago, but once he recognized him, there was no doubt.

Jayvyn was stunned. Baahir had come to this plantation and escaped before he'd even arrived!

Swept momentarily by a rush of excitement, it was immediately quashed by the gravity of the moment—he was about to be severely punished. Jayvyn's head swam with emotion as George went on.

"Fo de crime o run'n 'way 'n no be kech fo ten mont, Charles be sentenc'ta fo-tee lash in de pill'ry. He be stay in dat fo one week. Atta, he get hid nose cut 'n face burn. He gotsta wear de colla 'n de fibe-stone weight on hid leg fo six mont. Dat so he don't run no mo."

Other sounds of woe arose from the group. This was the same

---

* *Maiming and branding runaways was a common practice so that their past transgressions would be easily recognized*

punishment "Ben" had received, but with the addition of a five-stone, or seventy-pound, weight shackled to one of his ankles by a short chain. This acted as an additional deterrent to future escape, presumably due to his size and strength. It would make it exceedingly difficult for him to walk, let alone run; however, he'd be required to work with the impediment just the same.

Finally, George came to Andrew and said, "Fo de crime o steal'n 'n gibb'n dat food 'n udda ting to dem run'way slabe, 'n known where dey be but no tell'n, Andrew be sentenc'ta be stake face down on de ground wid hid hand 'n feet 'n he be get sixty lash. He gotsta stay der fo ten day. Den he be wear de mask fo tree mont."

Another audible gasp came from the group. The iron mask was a dreaded device.* It covered the mouth, chin, and nose. It also had an iron insert that went over the tongue, which prevented the wearer from speaking, but also made it impossible to swallow. It was secured behind the head with a locking device. It would be worn day and night and only removed for short periods to eat and drink. Being staked to the ground would invite all sorts of insects and cause great irritation to his skin. He'd eat his food off the ground and urinate and defecate where he lay for ten days.

All of the punishments were designed to dehumanize and inflict as much pain and torture as Master Clark deemed suitable for the crimes. Some, such as nose slitting and face branding, were

---

* *Also known as the 'scold's bridle' which was originally used in England as a punishment for rude, gossipy women. The effect was both emotionally and physically detrimental to the wearer causing great discomfort as well as psychological harm*

recommended by law.* But slaveowners were free, even encouraged, to design punishments themselves. It was common to be imaginative and inventive and share their punishments with other slaveowners.†

George then called a slave named Isaac up to the front.

Patting Isaac on the shoulder, he continued, "Fo de inf'mation what lead to dem slabe be kech, Isaac be get mo good quarta, meat, muscovado, 'n some rum. Hid work be cut too."‡

A palpable tension moved through the group of slaves. Jayvyn looked at the man, Isaac, to see if there was any indication of regret or shame for causing their recapture or the punishments they were about to receive. But Isaac just stood, stoic and indifferent. He received his recognition and reward, then returned to the group as if nothing were different.

Jayvyn reflected, once again, on Andrew's warning to be careful about who he trusted. In the moment, Jayvyn became acutely aware of his naivety and just stared into the dirt at his feet. He dared not even look at those around him for the vulnerability he felt.

George finished, "Dem punish'nt be gibb'n now; all de slabe gotsta watch."

Upon these final words, the bosses seized William and dragged him, kicking and screaming, to a pole about twenty feet high with a

---

* *Slave codes were established as early as 1661 in Barbados and modified through 1755 in Georgia. They included prescribed punishments for slaves as well as other criteria for management. The code was titled: "An Act for the better ordering and governing of Negroes"*

† *One infamous example known as "Derby's Dose," invented by overseer Thomas Thistlewood in Jamaica, required a fellow slave to defecate into the mouth of the offending slave, who would then be gagged for several hours.*

‡ *Rewarding slaves for turning on their fellow slaves was a common means of incentive*

shorter pole crossing at its top. A rope was thrown over the cross member. William, untied, except for his wrists, was stripped naked and the rope was tied around his neck. George then selected six strong males for the job of hoisting him up. When they were in place, he stood before William. With no further ceremony, he simply ordered, "Pull!"

For a split second, William's panicked eyes glanced longingly at his fellow Africans. Then, the six slaves abruptly heaved back on the rope, pulling William off the ground. He choked, struggling and twisting, for several long minutes. Time slowed by half as he fought and kicked reflexively, eyes bulging. The rest of the slaves watched horrified, until finally his spasms slowed and his body went still.

At George's next command, William's now-lifeless body was lowered to the ground.

George then selected another slave, handed him a sharp knife and instructed him to cut off his head.

The slave starred incredulously back at George, eyes watering, both shocked and horrified at what he'd been asked to do.

George simply glared back at him, hard and unyielding.

The trembling man had no choice in the matter, lest he be the next one punished.

Steeling himself, he kneeled before the body. With great trepidation, his hands shaking badly, he proceeded to cut at the dead man's throat. Openly weeping, he realized he was cutting too lightly to even break the skin. He stopped, turned to his side, and collapsed on his forearms, bawling out, "No! I no can, I no can!"

George, using his foot, shoved the distraught slave over on his side, yelling, "Do it now! Or pay wid yo own flesh!"

The man glared hatefully back at George, then rose to his knees. With a mix of grief and rage, he threw himself back into the task.

Crazed, the man savagely attacked in a blind fury, sawing vigorously until succeeding in severing William's head from his body. Dropping the knife, he crumpled to the ground, sobbing uncontrollably.

Others watched horrified, some retching at the sight; one woman fell faint.

Here was the man, who only moments ago had been sitting alive in the wagon as his sentence was read, now lying dead, his head detached from his body.

A long stake was jammed deeply into the ground, the sharp end jutting straight up about five feet. George chose another slave to perform the next unthinkable act of spiking Willam's head atop this stake. It was done, and his head now perched ghoulishly atop the pole, dead eyes gazing back, blood running down the narrow stake.

Next, William's chest was pierced, and a chain passed through his ribcage, which was then attached to the rope he'd been hung with. His headless body was then hoisted up to the top of the pole, where it would remain gibbetted for many months to come. The location had been specifically chosen for maximum exposure. The slaves would have no choice but to view it every day on their way to and from work.

William's sentence had been carried out.

The bosses then ordered pillories brought into the clearing and turned their attention to the remaining three convicted slaves.

Charles and Ben were dragged forth, stripped, and locked into the pillories. Another male slave was selected for the first lashing.

Charles stared resolutely ahead, a determined scowl on his face. This wouldn't last long, however, as George ordered the whipping to commence.

The man standing behind Charles knew better than to go easy. It was well understood what constituted a flogging, and he brought the whip down hard.

For the first few lashes, Charles stoically bore the pain, his jaw set in rigid defiance. But by the fifth or sixth lash, the strong, resolute man began to howl. By the twentieth lash, he'd been reduced to a limp and whimpering vestige of his former self. By lash thirty-five, he passed out and hung from the pillory, blood flowing from the lines traced across his now desecrated back. Notwithstanding, five more wicked lashes were piled on top.

Ben, hanging from his pillory, had watched helplessly as the big man crumbled under the brutal punishment.

A new slave was selected by George and handed the whip. He took his place behind Ben, knowing full well what was expected of him.

Jayvyn looked at Baahir, paralyzed by what he knew was to come. Memories of first meeting him on the shores of Africa, chained together and branded, their long brutal voyage, Baahir's strength, his caring—all of it—came flooding into his consciousness.

Baahir glanced at Jayvyn, his head briefly cocking with sudden, momentary recognition. Their eyes met in mutual and instantaneous memory of the bond they shared and the unspoken communication that had passed between them over their arduous journey.

The first blow landed. Baahir's head jerked up, his eyes squinted tightly, his face grimaced in pain. The next blow came quickly, followed by another, and another. Baahir no longer saw anyone in front of him as his world dissolved in a torturous, never-ending parade of pain.

Jayvyn winced with every blow as he watched this boy—this boy who he'd adopted as his friend; this boy he shared a profound brotherhood with—receive lash after brutal lash. Blood dripped off his back, and life drained from his body. Jayvyn reflected on how they'd never been able to communicate verbally. He wondered what their first conversation might be like.

It was a bizarre thought as he watched his long-estranged friend get the life beat from him. But everything had become surreal, and Jayvyn's mind wandered in a numb sort of trance.

Finally, the whipping stopped, and Baahir slumped unconscious in the pillory next to Charles. Their backs were a matching mosaic of intersecting red cuts. Both slaves hung unconscious, but shallow breathing was noticed by almost imperceptible movements in their shoulders. Somehow Jayvyn knew they'd survive, or so he hoped, and he and Baahir would have the conversation he'd wondered about.

His trance was broken as he heard Andrew being carried forward. Andrew's voice was unmistakable as he futilely pleaded with the men he'd faithfully served for so many years. But his pleas fell on deaf ears as he was dragged into the opening and stripped naked. Jayvyn's breath caught when he saw many existing scars already laced across his muscular back.

Andrew was held face down on the ground. Stakes were driven at four corners just beyond the limits of his extremities. Ropes were attached to his wrists and ankles, tied to the stakes, and hauled tight so his arms and legs were splayed out as far and wide as they would go.

A new slave was selected by George and stood behind Andrew's naked body with the whip in hand. Nobody had any doubt this man would deliver blows as severely as his predecessors.

Andrew looked up at the group of slaves with tears in his eyes. Jayvyn caught his eye in much the same way as he had Baahir's. Tears were already in Jayvyn's eyes from what he'd seen so far. He thought he saw the hint of a compassionate smile pass over Andrew's lips just as the whip came crashing down.

Andrew buried his face in the ground while the lashes were repeated over and over again, occasionally lifting his face to scream out in agony. His back quickly turned into a crazy pattern of red, bleeding stripes laid over the raised welts of his past scars. The beating continued mercilessly as he cried and sobbed into the moist earth. It went on for a long time. Jayvyn remembered his sentence called for sixty lashes—twenty more than Charles and Baahir. He felt terrible for his friend and worried if Andrew had the stamina and willpower to endure his punishment.

Jayvyn thought back to their recent conversation about strength of spirit and privately wished for Andrew's spirit to endure. Now Andrew was on the other end of the whip. Jayvyn remembered their conversation about sacrifice for the good of the rest and wondered what possible good could come from Andrew's sacrifice.

He'd helped the slaves with their escapes; wasn't that sacrifice enough? Now they were all caught. One hung headless above them, and the other two lay unconscious in the pillories. The one who'd helped them all lay pinned to the ground before him, being flogged into a bloody mass. *What possible good could come from the price they were now paying?* It didn't, couldn't, make sense.

Finally, the last crack of the whip came.

The silence seemed unnatural.

His friend and mentor, Andrew, lay unconscious. Blood streaming off of his back, striking a vivid contrast against the green blades of grass. As with the others, Jayvyn detected the slightest movement as evidence Andrew was still breathing. He was glad he was unconscious and temporarily oblivious to the pain.

The slaves, having fulfilled their forced obligation, moved solemnly and quietly, back to their quarters, relieved, at least, to have moved past the brutal punishments they'd just witnessed.* It was indeed one of the worst days Jayvyn had experienced, notwithstanding, of course, the day he'd watched his village disintegrate before his eyes. He knew, however, for the ones still living, their sentence was far from over.

But, for the time being, the shock of what he'd seen today had sapped his mental energy far below the point where any rational thought was possible. And so, Jayvyn resigned himself to numbly going through the motions for the rest of the day.

There was no conversation, no one spoke of the things they'd

---

* *Slaves were often required to administer and participate in the punishment of their fellow slaves*

witnessed. Everyone simply moved on to their respective quarters, lost in thought.

The new day, if indeed there was to be one, would have to dawn on its own terms.

- 22 -

Serving the Sentence

The group of slaves assembled as they had on so many mornings past, dividing into their respective work groups, and began their long walk up the hill.

Jayvyn, shaken as he was by what he'd witnessed, felt like a stranger among the group of slaves as they shuffled quietly through the still morning air. No body spoke or sang, the mood was much different and subdued among them. His awakening to Isaac's treachery had rattled him. How could he be sure about the people he'd only just begun to trust?

He thought about his hut mates, the ones he'd arrived with.

Julia, of course, had been like the glue between all of them with her nurturing way. But now she was gone. Lewis was always quiet. Jayvyn had tried speaking with him on a few occasions, but Lewis preferred to keep to himself. Sarah and Rose were quiet, too, mostly just keeping company with women. Jayvyn respected this and let them be.

He wasn't afraid of Samuel. He was meek in nature and very sincere. Charles, on the other hand, was a different story. He never appeared friendly, always stern and withdrawn, and really didn't have much to do with anyone. Plus, he'd been missing for most of the time.

When it came down to it, Jayvyn realized he didn't know any of them that well.

But he, himself, was friendly and outgoing by nature, and was glad he'd gotten to know some of the others better.

Like Walter, Lucy, and several others who seemed friendly enough. Simon among them. He'd only ever tried to help Jayvyn, but now he was gone, too.

Jayvyn had grown most fond of Andrew. He was truly kind, had deep wisdom, and always appeared concerned for the greater good of all. He'd never betray anyone in a bad way. Of course not! He was out in front of the barn right now, paying for his part in helping others.

And there was Baahir, whom he'd barely reunited with.

He was surprised to realize how much he'd missed Baahir. They'd never even spoken, but somehow a bond had been forged between them, stronger than the chains that initially held them together. A yearning to know Baahir better tugged strongly at him.

Having witnessed what Isaac had done, Jayvyn felt wary of those he didn't know well. All at once he understood Lewis' reticence more.

Still being in the earlier part of the growing season, the group was about half of what it had been during harvest. This would change when the cane reached maturity, when new slaves would be brought in to replenish those who'd been sold or died off.

The group moved past the pond where Julia had drowned herself and continued on past the boiling house and the mill. Soon they reached the barn.

The sound of giant wings broke the silence as a vulture lifted to the sky. The sudden shift in weight caused William's gibbeted corpse to twist slightly on its chain, drawing Javin's attention that way. He fought to avoid the grisly sight, not wishing to relive any part of the day before. But the chilling display would remain a constant reminder for months to come.

Beside the hideous display were the live bodies of Charles and Ben, hanging in their pillories, backs caked with drying blood from the fresh wounds of their lashes. They were both conscious now but had nothing to say as the group passed slowly by; they just hung there, lithe and glassy-eyed.

Beside them, staked face down to the ground, lay Andrew, his back a mass of flesh from his even more severe whipping. His head was turned on its side. One eye vaguely watched as the group passed; a sticky line of drool connecting his mouth to the grass—the grass he'd remain part of for the next ten days.

Jayvyn and the others sheepishly gave a pitiful glance as they passed, anguished there was nothing they could do to ease their suffering. Two white men stood nearby, cradling rifles and clubs, to ensure no one attempted to interfere with or approach the men serving their sentences.

George was stationed at the barn that day, along with the man with one arm, Jayvyn, and Thomas. The rest moved on to their respective assignments.

Several slaves, engaged in the task of hauling water to the cane fields, passed by the condemned men with each carry. George ensured none stopped or tried to assist them in any way.

Jayvyn worked in and around the barn—mucking out stalls, moving hay and feed around, and helping the one-armed man.

Thomas brought a tub of food from the slaves' quarters, doling out portions for Charles, Ben, and Andrew. He held the ladle for

Charles and Ben, heads and wrists trapped in the pillory. Andrew, strapped to the ground, had more difficulty eating. The men's appetites, however, were weak. Water was brought in the same fashion, where each man did his best to drink.

The sun blazed down relentlessly, baking and hardening the thick blood crusted across each man's back, faces dripping with sweat. Water was provided in the middle of the day, but food would only be brought again at the end of the day.

As Jayvyn worked, he caught glimpses of the beleaguered men. The corpse attracted various carrion birds, which would light, peck, and tear off sizable strips of flesh. Occasionally, intense squawking would erupt as two or more birds vied for dominance over the coveted feast. In a few instances, the birds landed on the backs of the restrained and living men, pecking at their wounds, causing intense outbursts of agony. The white sentries merely pointed and laughed, taking great pleasure in the sight. The spectacle sickened Jayvyn and made his skin crawl.

His heart ached especially for Andrew and Baahir. He knew the true souls of these men. Men, like himself and so many more. Good men. Men no more deserving of this than being taken from their homes in the first place. The injustice of it all was overwhelming. Jayvyn couldn't imagine the terrible pain and suffering these poor men were enduring. He wondered how they'd ever survive it.

The week passed slowly by; each day not much better than the one before. But little by little, as time crept on, the men began to revive.

The corpse, however, was a different matter. The birds and

tropical heat had been working at it constantly. The thing hardly resembled the human being it once was. The process of decay was well underway. The smell of death both unmistakable and overpowering—a vile combination of rotting cabbage, eggs, and fish blended with a strangely sweet and pungent earthiness.

A Sunday passed, during which Jayvyn was able to observe the one named Isaac—the one who'd given the information about Andrew that had led to the escaped slaves' discovery and capture. He was idly enjoying his allotment of rum, seemingly without any feelings of guilt. No one bothered him or gave him any sort of trouble for his betrayal, least of all George, who was the only one who paid any attention to him at all.

Jayvyn thought back to some of the advice Andrew had given him about being careful who to trust. He also remembered his early confusion about the levels of status that could be achieved. He realized this was what Andrew meant about enriching one's self at the expense of others.

Isaac was one of those who'd seek to benefit from the misfortune of his fellow slaves. He was an example of the type to watch out for. Before this, Jayvyn had never really noticed Isaac much. He was just another slave going off to work each day, like all the rest. Nothing remarkable about him.

As with so many other revelations since being taken, it left him confused—with many contradictions to things he previously believed.

He felt changes taking place within him—changes to his beliefs and how he interacted with the world around him.

Jayvyn thought back to before his capture, to how innocent and trusting he'd been. It saddened him to realize how suspicious and guarded he was becoming, skeptical about the true motives of those around him. *Is this part of what it means to become a man?* he wondered. *Is it something learned during futampaf?*

Either way, he resolved it was essential for him to learn and learn well if he were to survive in the world going forward. Again, he was grateful to Andrew for helping him become acquainted with these hard truths.

Soon, Charles' and Ben's week in the stocks had passed.

On the evening of the seventh day, the slaves again assembled in front of the barn, the white men present with their weapons. A fire had been built near the stocks; a branding iron sat glowing in its coals.

Charles was first.

Strange-looking iron devices sat beside the fire. One was a massive, spherical iron weight with a short chain. An ankle shackle was attached to the other end. This was attached to one of Charles' ankles while he hung in the pillory.

George then spoke. "Charles, you be wear dat five-stone weight 'n de colla fo six mont. Den, if'n you be good, maybe Ma'sa Clark take dem off," He gestured for a man to bring the collar and attach it around Charles' neck.

The collar looked like a rimless wheel with four iron spokes protruding from its hub. When the collar was secured around Charles' neck, the four spokes stuck out perpendicularly on all sides. A thick iron pin was driven through a clasp on the collar and then peened over, thereby making removal by the wearer impossible.

George continued, "Now, you be wear de brand o de run'way

slabe."

The red-hot iron was extracted from the fire as another man firmly held Charles' chin up in the pillory. Charles' eyes widened as the burning hot iron was brought closer to his face. He fought to move his head, but the man behind him held him fast. The iron was pressed into his forehead, making a sizzling sound as it burned its way deep into his flesh. Charles let loose a guttural cry. The branding iron was removed, leaving a fresh, bright red burn in the shape of 'r' where his flesh had been burned off. The man then lathered a small amount of palm oil over the burn, and George went on.

"Now, yo nose be cut. Dem scar show you be de run'way so it no happ'n no mo."

George, himself, then approached with a sharp knife while the other slave held Charles' head in an unshakable grip. George pressed back on Charles' forehead—right over the fresh burn—with one hand. With the other, he drew the sharp knife deep and down the bridge of Charles' nose.

Wailing, Charles was released from the pillory. He fell immediately to his knees—cradling his face, blood dripping from his fingers—the prongs of his collar touching the ground before him. As he kneeled, sobbing, George turned to face Baahir, who looked back in terror.

In much the same manner, George addressed Baahir.

Jayvyn felt a large knot growing in his chest as he watched the collar being attached around Baahir's neck. Like Charles, he was told he'd have to wear this for at least six months, after which it may be removed pending Master Clark's judgment and goodwill. It was secured fast, in the same way, making it impossible to remove without the right tools and someone to use them.

Then he was approached with the scalding hot iron. Baahir's face went wild with fright as he fought, to no use, against the man's firm grip. The iron was pressed firmly into his forehead. He emitted a high-pitched scream as a hideous bloom of smoke billowed from the site. The wound was the same as it had been for Charles, excruciatingly painful.

Jayvyn looked at his friend, noticing his nose.

It was perfect.

In that moment, he became all too aware that this would be the last time he'd ever see his friend looking this way. From this point forward, he'd wear a deep, ugly scar down the center of his nose.

George approached with the sharp knife. The man behind held his head in a vice-like grip. With one quick stroke, George flayed his nose wide open. Baahir's scream intensified as blood immediately gushed over his mouth and chin.

Released, Baahir crumpled on the ground next to Charles, both holding their hands over their faces, sobbing incoherently. Their backs, clearly visible, bore large scabs from neck to waist.

How horribly these two, previously perfect, human beings had been mutilated over the last week. None of what was done would ever heal completely. There would always be deep scars from this punishment—scars they'd carry with them for the rest of their lives.

The knot in Jayvyn's gut remained, like the iron ball now attached to Charles' ankle.

Andrew, who had three more days to go before his release, stayed pinned, face-down, to the ground. His back, too, was a horrible mass of scabs interspersed with broken spots, fresh with blood, where the scabs had split from constant exposure to the sun.

The group of slaves, once again, turned to walk back to their quarters, this time supporting the two just released with their fresh wounds and new bondage. Charles made particularly slow progress as he required someone to help with the weight attached to his ankle.

When they arrived back at the quarters, some of the women fetched water and gathered cloth to begin tending their wounds. There wasn't much they could do, but they did as much as possible. It would take time for these men to heal. At the moment, they were completely helpless.

As the group settled into their respective quarters, Charles and Ben were heard softly moaning in agony.

The morning arrived early, as always, with George assembling the slaves into their respective groups.

Despite their injuries, Charles and Ben were hauled out of their quarters and assigned work. They emerged into the dim, predawn air, blood caked to their faces, moving uncertainly under the weight of their collars. Both had their clothes back, covering their mutilated backs. Each had a serious burn in the shape of "r" on his forehead where the skin was completely missing—a bright pink patch surrounded by a rim of darker, partially scabbed skin. Ben was assigned to work in the fields; Charles would work at the barn.

As they shuffled up the dirt road toward their working areas, Charles had to lift his heavy weight in order to walk. He stumbled frequently, falling on several occasions, but was quickly brought back to his feet by George's yelling and prodding. Lagging behind the rest of the group, George stayed with him, urging him roughly on. Ben was able to walk, but swayed unsteadily under the new weight of his collar with its wide prongs. No one sang or spoke this morning.

Soon, they came to the barn, where, again, they passed by the awful corpse hanging motionless from the gibbet. A lone black bird sat perched on one of its shoulders, watching the passersby like some demon sentry. The slaves moved solemnly past it.

Andrew lay not far away, still pinned face down to the ground, watching the quiet procession as it moved up the hill toward the fields.

A lone white man stood off in the dim light, cradling his rifle, keeping a watchful eye to ensure everyone kept moving to their assigned areas.

The barn crew, including Jayvyn, Thomas, and the one-armed man, split off to the barn, soon to be joined by George and Charles. When they arrived, the day commenced with Thomas, again, bringing food and water to Andrew.

Charles was put to work cleaning stalls, and Jayvyn resumed his work with the one-armed man.

Charles moved unsteadily from all of his encumbrances, clearly in pain. From time to time, the prongs of his collar hit and scraped against the stalls. The chain on his ankle rattled across the floor; the weight dragged or dropped heavily when Charles had to pick it up.

When they broke for the mid-day meal, Charles sat, staring blankly ahead, blood still oozing from the cut on his nose. Jayvyn marveled that the man could work at all and wondered how his friend Baahir, or "Ben," as he was now called, was faring.

Eventually, the day came to an end. The slaves from the house and fields came shuffling past. Tired from the day's work, Jayvyn fell in for the familiar trudge down the gently sloping hill. Charles dragged his weight behind.

As the next few days crept by, Charles' and Ben's wounds started to scab over; they began to move a bit easier, although far from lively.

On the completion of Andrew's tenth day staked to the ground, the slaves were, again, assembled in front of the barn.

This time there was no fire, but the mask Andrew was to wear was brought and laid before him.

His back was a solid mass of scab, with some areas still oozing blood and puss, as he was released from the stakes. Unable to stand unassisted, he was raised to his feet by slaves standing on each side of him. His front side was dirty and raw, with lesions from lying for ten days against the soft, moist earth, various insects feasting on him at will. His gaze appeared glassy and incoherent. He stared dimly at the group before him, a mere shadow of the vibrant man Jayvyn had known only weeks before.

George, again, resumed his place before the group and announced, "Andrew, dat maks be fix't ta yo face. You be wear dat fo tree mont, den Ma'sa Clark cide if'n it kin come off."

The group looked on with pity as his mask was brought up. A flat metal protrusion stuck out a few inches from the part that would cover his mouth. Andrew wasn't in any state to resist, softly gagging when the protuberance was inserted into his mouth, over his tongue. Small holes were bored into the regions covering his mouth and nose to allow for air. Metal straps went from each of his cheeks around the back of his head; another went over the top of his head. The straps were joined behind his head, firmly securing the mask in place.

Only his eyes and top of his head could be seen, the mask covering every part of his face below. This complete, Andrew's watery eyes stared dumbly ahead.

As with Charles and Ben, he needed one on each side to help him walk back to the quarters.

Again, it was a solemn, quiet night back at the camp as the slaves went about their day's end activities. Not much was said, but some of the women, again, gathered water and rags to do what they could for the poor men's wounds.

Andrew was quite unable to speak, but if he could, it was unlikely he had the energy or inspiration to say anything. His ordeal had sapped every ounce of strength from him.

Jayvyn imagined Andrew's spirit, the spirit they spoke of just the other day, must have been but a dying ember by then. He hoped somehow it would survive and awaken back into the light that had once been Andrew.

The punishments were now fully in place, only time remained of their sentences.

Their scars, both physical and emotional, however, would remain for life.

- 23 -

Healing Begins

Plantation operations, as always, never saw a moment's interruption. The cane, growing straight and tall, marked the calendar's ceaseless march toward harvest.

Andrew struggled with merely getting to his feet, let alone the horrible restrictions of the mask he was now saddled with. It was a handicap beyond comprehension. The worst part was the metal intrusion in his mouth, continuously pressing down on his tongue. Not only making it impossible to speak but also severely restricting his ability to swallow or produce saliva. This led to several panicky choking incidents throughout the day. His swallowing response simultaneously triggered and repressed, causing him to hunch over, desperately trying to quell the spasms preventing his next breath.

Additionally, he had no water between morning and night; the only two times the mask was briefly removed to eat and drink. The breaks were short, monitored by George and a white boss to ensure compliance. Limited to half an hour at best, they were barely enough time to swallow his food, let alone get any real relief.

Night or day, trapped in the awful contraption for up to fourteen hours, Andrew's tongue swelled from uneven moisture and pressure from the bit. The constant, frantic swallowing spasms caused excessive aches in his jaw and neck muscles. There was no escape, day in and day out.

The inability to communicate also took its toll. It was uncanny to think there was anything left for the white man to take, but he now realized there was. He'd taken his speech—his ability to express himself—to elocute. He felt relegated to a lesser class as he silently endured his pain. It was as if his mind had been locked in a prison with no visitors allowed. Yet another freedom lost; another way to be disgraced—for being Black.

The terrible wounds on his back made his suffering all the worse. He was thankful, at least, for the women who faithfully washed and tended his wounds. It would be a long time before the pain subsided. The memory and disgrace would never die.

Sunday, blessed Sunday, arrived again, and the slaves were given the day off. Baahir and Charles had been out of the pillory for a week and a half now. Although far from healed, they'd worked in the fields and recovered enough to function. The previous Sunday, they were too weak for anything but rest, so this was the first opportunity Jayvyn had to check in with his old friend.

In the morning, he found Baahir in his hut. A woman was just finishing up after gently washing his wounds. Jayvyn approached, uncertain how he'd be received. He sat and looked at Baahir while the woman gathered her things and left. It was just the two of them in the hut now.

Baahir looked over from where he lay, his head uncomfortably propped on the prongs of his collar, his nose a blood-scabbed mass, and the horrible shape of "r" burned into his forehead.

With some effort, he pushed himself up and moved so he was sitting on his mat.

He spoke softly, "You, me, ship," and gave a weak smile.

"Yes," Jayvyn smiled back. "I be Jayvyn, now I be call James."

Baahir, whose English wasn't as good as Jayvyn's, looked back at his old friend and replied, "I Ben, come first here."

Jayvyn understood well enough and studied his old friend. He understood he was at the plantation while Jayvyn was still at the stockade, that Baahir must have run soon after he'd arrived. He wondered about his experiences since they'd been separated that day on the beach.

"Ben, it be good I see you! I tink many time 'bout you. You 'n me come from Africa togeda!"

Baahir understood well enough to know what Jayvyn had said.

Nodding, he responded as best he could. "You friend. I go, be kech." He fingered his collar, casting a sad look.

Jayvyn, recognizing Baahir's speech limitations and remembering all Andrew had done for him, decided he'd try to help Baahir with his English and set to work with that in mind.

He spoke to him, saying, "Ben, I be hep you speak de English. Do you know what I be sayin'? I hep you.

"Say now: '*I-gonna-speak-English*'."

Baahir looked back at him and repeated the words as he heard them. "I gonna speeke Engish."

Jayvyn smiled broadly, saying, "Very good! Yes! Now again," and he repeated slowly, emphasizing each word, "*I gonna speak English.*"

Baahir, trying harder this time, looked back at his friend and deliberately repeated, "I gonna speak English."

Jayvyn smiled excitedly and exclaimed, "Yes! Yes, my friend! You *gonna* speak English!"

Jayvyn continued teaching Baahir throughout the morning as best he could. It was clear Baahir had picked up many of the basics, just as Jayvyn had, and needed to practice how to put words together in sentences that would be useful for communicating clearer. He knew from his experience this would be essential to Baahir's wellbeing going forward.

It gave him pleasure to know he could help him this way—in the same way Andrew had helped him so much. He remembered how Andrew had taught him, how he made it easier for him to understand, and so he tried to emulate this as he instructed Baahir.

Eventually Baahir tired.

Jayvyn spent time in the garden, as he was in the habit of doing, but reserved some time to check on Andrew as well.

He missed being able to work with Andrew the past several Sundays; it was a time he looked forward to each week. He thought many times of Andrew's wicked ordeal at the barn and was glad he was, at least, back at the compound among the slaves and that his healing could begin. After he finished tending the vegetable patches, he went to Andrew's hut.

Andrew was sitting out in front when he arrived, mask firmly affixed around his head. Jayvyn came and sat in front of him. Their eyes met. Andrew just looked back. Although the mask hid much of his expression, Jayvyn saw sorrow and pain written in his eyes. Andrew, of course, could say nothing due to the metal protrusion pressed over his tongue.

"Andrew, it be good to see you," he began. "I miss workin' in de garden wid you, but I be workin' der ebery week 'n takin' care of de crop fo you."

Painfully aware Andrew was unable to speak at all, he realized it would be up to him to do all the talking. He also realized Andrew probably appreciated hearing from him.

He continued, "Dis boy be here now. He be kech wid you. Hid name be Ben. Hid real name be Baahir. He come here fo me 'n run'd way.

"We be chain togeda in Africa 'n put on de ship. He be from de diff'nt tribe, 'n talk de diff'nt talk, 'n we no speak."

Andrew's eyes showed he was interested in what Jayvyn was telling him.

Jayvyn went on, "We be chain togeda on de ship fo many mont. It be bad. Big storm come, many slabe sick, many die.

"Baahir stay wid me. He be my friend. Afta de ship come here, we no see each udda for long time. I no tink I see 'm agin. Now he be here."

He could see Andrew was sorting through what he'd just said, so he paused for a few moments to let Andrew ponder this information.

When Andrew looked up, signaling he was ready for him to go on, he said, "I go see 'm today. He be get betta. Hid face 'n hid back be bad fo de long time, like you. De collar make ting bery hard."

Andrew nodded slightly, and Jayvyn continued, "Hid English no be good like me. I hep him ta und'stand mo, like you hep me."

Andrew's eyes brightened a bit, and he nodded.

Jayvyn could tell Andrew approved of what he'd just said. It struck Jayvyn how much he felt he could understand just by seeing the expression in Andrew's eyes and watching his movements. By this point, they'd come to know each other well enough that much could go unspoken and they'd still understand one another. It was the same as with him and Baahir. After all their time on the ship—unable to communicate verbally—enough had passed between them that spoken words seemed almost unnecessary.

He told Andrew he was going to the pond to wash now and would bring back a bucket of water and a cloth to wash Andrew's back. Andrew nodded again. Jayvyn sensed a welcoming affection in Andrew's eyes.

Jayvyn took care of his washing, returning with the water and a cloth, and helped Andrew remove his shirt. His back was a terrible mass of freshly formed scabs, still broken in many places, oozing a mixture of blood, water, and pus. Jayvyn, very gently, dabbed at his wounds with the wet cloth, Andrew occasionally wincing.

He spoke as he washed him. "Yo back be bery hurt, 'n it be bery hard to hab dat maks on yo face."

Jayvyn searched for words to reassure his friend. "You be get betta, 'n dat no be alway.

"Yo spirit be hurt bad from dat punish'nt. Dat be get betta, too.

"You do de good ting. I know dat. Udda slabe know dat, too. Everybody want you be betta. I be hep you."

Jayvyn could see Andrew's eyes watering with emotion as he listened to his words.

Andrew knew he'd taught him well. It was food for his spirit, and at that moment, he felt some of his spiritual strength returning. He wanted, more than anything, to get well just so he could continue his friendship with this remarkable twelve-year-old boy.

Then it occurred to him. How did he know he was still twelve? He must be another year older by now. *Yes!* Andrew decided, *Jayvyn must now be at least thirteen!* He'd have to hold onto this thought for when they could speak again. This boy was growing up, just as Andrew had so long ago. He felt even more affection toward Jayvyn as he thought about this.

It occurred to him Jayvyn was close to the age when he'd normally be eligible for futampaf. He must know of this from his village. All Ajamatau held this very special and sacred tradition.

Andrew became momentarily melancholy at the thought so many valuable and sacred traditions had been sacrificed when taken into slavery. Andrew knew how special it was for him to have participated in this ritual. He thought Jayvyn was ready for the experience now, especially after all he'd been through. This was another thing he'd have to remember to ask him about later.

He thought his father must have been very proud to have a boy like Jayvyn. Andrew thought if he were ever to have a son, he'd be lucky to have one as fine as Jayvyn.

It was with these thoughts in mind that they parted company that evening, Jayvyn pledging to come see Andrew when he could, once again encouraging him to stay as positive as he could and care for his spirit.

As Jayvyn lay on his mat that night, his mind, once again, cycled through all of the terrible things he'd witnessed since his abduction. He didn't know why the white man had to be so cruel to them. It was simply unfathomable that any human being would go to such lengths to inflict as much agony and suffering as possible on another human being—or anything, for that matter. *What was the point of such excess?*

He thought of William, whose body, now dismembered, hung from the gibbet for the birds to feast on daily. It wasn't enough to take his life away; they had to make certain his spirit would not be able to return to Africa—that it would remain forever under the siege of slavery. They further had to use what was left of him as a punishing reminder to the rest of the slaves—every day they passed—of what could happen if they denied the white man his self-proclaimed right over their being.

It wasn't enough to whip the slaves when caught; they had to fetter them with spiked collars and weights, and slash and burn their faces as well, leaving permanent scars.

It wasn't enough to punish Andrew with the whip; they had to leave him tied to the ground to be feasted on by insects and silence him in an iron mask.

This was Andrew—the man who accompanied Master Clark to pick up new slaves; the man who carried out whipping Samuel at his command; the man who rendered long years of loyal service as his slave.

Jayvyn saw it was nothing for Master Clark to strip everything away in an instant.

The slaves were indeed Master Clark's property. He'd do with them as he chose.

There were no limits.

- 24 -

Lessons Learned

Work resumed the following day as it would for every day into the foreseeable future—the early morning assembly into work groups, the slow shuffle up the long hill—past the terrible decomposing, gibbeted remains of what was once William.

Charles picked up the large iron ball chained to his ankle, hunched over, holding it with both hands as he struggled to work. He and Baahir were mostly assigned to the fields where they labored in the hot sun, day in, day out. Their iron collars made them easily identifiable among the rest. Every time Charles moved, he lifted the heavy iron weight, carrying it where he needed to go. The weight of the collars, too, made their work all the more difficult. There was no getting used to any of it.

Sundays came and went. Jayvyn developed a routine where he faithfully visited with both Baahir and Andrew on these days, helping Baahir with his English and talking to Andrew, who could only sit and listen. Their wounds slowly healed. Baahir's and Charles' noses were developing scar tissue where they'd been flayed open. Similarly, the oozing wounds on their backs had dried up and were forming scar tissue.

Jayvyn and Baahir's visits improved along with Baahir's English. They were able to converse and share details about themselves that previously could only be guessed at. Jayvyn remembered Baahir mentioning the name of his tribe before—it was Malinké—and Baahir explained more about his people.

Jayvyn was both shocked and fascinated to learn the practice of slavery was common within Baahir's tribe and a strong social hierarchy was strictly maintained as essential elements to their way of life. The population of Baahir's people was much larger than Jayvyn's. They were not reclusive at all and traded widely among many diverse ethnic groups. There were many divisions of sub-tribe within Baahir's tribal sector as well.

Additionally, his tribe made a regular practice of raiding and warring with other tribes. This was done, Baahir explained, in the interest of land conquest as well as religion. Captured members of tribes were typically made slaves.

He further explained, according to their tradition, one was born into a social class they could not change. Baahir's main class was known as "foro," meaning he was born to be a free man. Others were born into a class known as "jongo," or slave, and were destined to remain so along with their future generations.

Within these classifications were additional strata based on wealth and position within the tribe. Baahir's was neither a poor class nor a wealthy one, but somewhere in the middle. He explained his family were farmers, in much the same way as Jayvyn's, and they had to remain as such—and in the same wealth class—from generation to generation.*

All of this was inconceivable to Jayvyn. Baahir's tribe was typical

---

* *Many African tribes had caste systems of one type or another. The Malinké have a system where one's caste is passed on from generation to generation*

of the very people his tribe had been hiding from for generations. They were the type he and Andrew had discussed so long ago that raided their villages, took their land, and enslaved their people.

He further learned Baahir's religion was Islam and this was a key reason they made war on other tribes—to force them to adopt their religious beliefs. The words he'd heard Baahir mutter on the ship, "Allahu Akbar,"* were in the prayers he was saying to the God he worshipped.

There were so many differences between them. Everything, it seemed, except the color of their skin and their shared status as slaves, was different.

Yet, before they'd been able to share this information, they had everything in common.

As they continued learning about each other, Jayvyn began to feel less and less comfortable. He felt vulnerable now in Baahir's presence. Baahir was a warrior by tradition, and his people had made slaves of Jayvyn's people for many generations. They worshipped higher beings and had social classes that excluded others. And there was more—so much more—completely opposite to the way Jayvyn had been taught and raised.

Yet he'd previously revered Baahir for his strength and apparent integrity. In a strong sense, he still did. Baahir had never attacked him; in fact, they'd relied on each other for strength during their most difficult times. What did Baahir now think of him? Now that he knew his tribal beliefs and way of life? Did this change everything between

---

* *A phrase meaning 'God is most great', used by Muslims in prayers and as a general declaration of faith or thanksgiving*

them?

Baahir explained because he was born "foro," or free, his resistance to being enslaved was very strong. It was simply unfathomable he should ever be a slave. It was the reason he'd run from the plantation.

He explained Charles, too, was from a similar tribe—not Malinké, but one with similar practices—and he was also born foro. William had similar status. He explained it was because of their birthright as foro the idea of being a slave was completely incomprehensible to them.

Of course, nobody wants to have their freedom taken from them, but in Baahir's world, some are born into slavery and accept it as their destiny, while if you are born foro, that is your destiny. This can never be changed.

It was a difficult distinction for Jayvyn to comprehend, but he accepted it because it was such a strong part of Baahir's culture.

Over a period of weeks, Baahir's English improved to the level of Jayvyn's, and they were able to have more articulate conversations. Jayvyn shared his tribe's traditional rite of passage with Baahir, asking if his people also held futampaf. Baahir said they didn't, but had a rite of their own called *kuyangwoo*,* which marks the passage of both boys and girls into adulthood. Some elements of these traditions were similar in that they'd each spend solitary time in the forest.

**A rite of passage practiced by the Malinké which marks the passage into adulthood for their children. Between four and fourteen years of age, the youngsters are subjected to ritual circumcision and spend up to a year in the bush where they learn about rules of behavior and adult social responsibilities*

Eventually, through many discussions, Jayvyn felt his tension over their differences easing. Their conversations didn't feel adversarial, but instead were friendly in nature. Instead of feeling threatened, he found himself increasingly enthralled with desire to learn more about Baahir's tribal traditions.

The conclusion Jayvyn eventually reached was the same as he had on the ship so long ago—tribal differences had become much less important since being taken into slavery. Slavery now, in itself, was the one thing they all had in common.

Also, he and Baahir were both about the same age. They hadn't hardened in their ways as much as adults might. They needed each other as peers and survivors linked by shared tragedy. These bonds, it seemed, took precedence over any differences in their heritage. Furthermore, Jayvyn found himself respecting these differences as immutable qualities giving each of them unique strengths and perspective—like leopards and gazelles—each beautiful and gifted in its own way.

They discussed their time on the ship. Jayvyn told Baahir how he'd drawn strength and courage from him on many occasions, such as when they were manning the pumps during the storm. Baahir related the closeness he felt the night Jayvyn told him his name. He said it came at a moment when he felt more alone than ever before—he knew no one—and he missed his family and village very much. He told Jayvyn just knowing they each had names meant so much to him in that moment. He'd never forgotten it.

Jayvyn was struck by this sentiment and realized how much they had in common. They were both just boys, suddenly removed from their families and lives. Jayvyn felt, had they been born into the same tribe and village, they would have been fast friends. Despite what he'd learned about his heritage, he liked Baahir for the person he knew him to be and could tell the feeling was mutual.

They also talked about all they'd lost, up to and including their names. Jayvyn would always think of himself as Jayvyn, and he preferred to think of Baahir by the name he first knew him by. However, they both knew to call each other by those names would be unnecessarily inviting trouble. So they would use their assigned names of James and Ben when addressing each other out loud.

Jayvyn told Baahir the meaning of his name: "Light Spirit." Baahir smiled, giving a warm chuckle. "Dat be you," he said, and told Jayvyn his name meant "Dazzling and brilliant."*

Jayvyn smiled and responded, "We bote be name de right ting."

Jayvyn made a habit of faithfully visiting Andrew, as he'd pledged he would. During his visits, he always found things to talk about. Sometimes he told him about things he enjoyed back in his village, like his morning run and sitting around listening to the elders. He told him about what a good teacher his father was, how proud he was of his father's rice crop. He described his little sister, Ifetayo—told him how funny she was and how he'd loved her so. He told him about his mother as well, how she was always cheerful and bright when doing chores or playing with them.

Jayvyn also shared some of his discussions with Baahir. He told Andrew how Baahir's English was getting much better and they could talk about so many things they never could before. He related that

---

* *The meanings of the African names used in this book are authentic*

even though their worlds were so different, they'd become good friends. He explained it was because they couldn't converse and knew nothing of their tribal differences that they were able to know each other simply as people. He told him how their experiences on the ship had created strong bonds between them.

Jayvyn tried to keep their conversations upbeat and light so as to help Andrew stay positive during his otherwise bleak confinement. He also made sure to spend some of his visit cleaning Andrew's wounds, which, like the others, were healing over with a rich pattern of scar tissue.

Andrew would be alright, Jayvyn decided. He'd get through his terrible ordeal and get his voice back.

Daily, and as the weeks passed, time, in the moment, seemed to move very slowly. But as time has the habit of doing, it does pass, and when looked back on, it can take one by surprise to see how much has passed. Jayvyn knew from the height of the cane that harvest must be coming soon. It would mean he'd been on the plantation for over a year. It also reminded him Andrew's sentence would be coming to an end. Two and a half months had passed since he was put in the mask, and the sentence was for three.

Jayvyn shared this information regularly with Andrew. "In two week, you be free from dat maks, Andrew! It be oba." Then the following week, "One mo week 'n den we talk agin!"

It was a difficult line to walk, as he knew even one day in the evil contraption would be an eternity for almost anyone, but he had to give Andrew hope and remind him it was going to end soon.

As the weeks passed, the corpse hanging from the gibbet became more and more devoid of flesh. The birds had constantly been at it, along with insects and other parasites. The tropical climate made decomposition rapid as well.

By the time Andrew was freed from his mask, William's remains were practically a mere skeleton. But they'd continue to hang there until fully disintegrated.

It became hard to imagine it had been a living human being only months before. For ninety days, the slaves had passed by this macabre display twice daily.

Jayvyn, and he was sure many of the others, were haunted by the memory of William being dragged, kicking and screaming, to his death. One moment, the man had been alive in front of them all. Now his bones hung from a chain passed through his ribcage, skull perched on a stake like some otherworldly artifact.

Jayvyn wondered if it was true, since William had been decapitated, his spirit wouldn't be free to seek its ancestors. But what he saw before him now had no spirit, so it must have gone somewhere. He hoped what Andrew had said about spirits being free after death was true for William; it was what he preferred to believe.

Finally, the day arrived when George informed Andrew his mask would be removed. It was done without ceremony, but to Andrew, it was as if life itself had been restored.

Fresh air rushed in to meet his skin, so long wrapped in a cloak of iron and sweat. The bit was removed from his mouth, and his swollen tongue released from its metallic grip. It would take time to adjust to normalcy and be able to speak with ease once again, but Andrew had no desire to talk for the moment. He just relished the feeling of being free of the terrible contraption—able to drink water and swallow as he needed and not feel its weight constantly pressing down on his neck and shoulders.

The following Sunday, Jayvyn and Andrew worked in the garden together and were finally able to speak as they had before.

Jayvyn asked Andrew how he was feeling, and Andrew replied, "Betta now!"

He thanked Jayvyn for being so good about visiting him each week. He expressed how much it had meant, how he'd always looked forward to his visits.

Jayvyn said, "I be worry fo yo spirit, Andrew. I no want it be dead. I know it be de hard time fo you."

Andrew confirmed this to him. "It be bery hard—from when we be kech.

"It be bery hard ta see de way William 'n de udda slabe be punish.

"But de udda slabe. Dey be cut 'n burnt 'n suffa in de colla. 'N Charles wid de heby iron ball."

He paused for a moment, then went on. "And de one, Ben. You say dat you 'n him be chain togeda in Africa, dat you come on de ship togeda, 'n you be friend! Dat be bery good!"

Jayvyn agreed, "I no tink I ebba see him no mo."

"He be yo age?"

"I tink we be de same."

"James, you be here fo mo den de year now. You gotsta be de year olda. You gotsta be tirteen now."

Jayvyn thought for a moment: "I no tink it, but you be right."

"Did yo billage elda tell you 'bout de futampaf?"

"Yes, my fadda tell me o dat many time. It be de ting I want badly—to be de man in my billage. I tink it alla time, but it no happen fo de white man come. Now it neba happen, 'n I be bery sad."

Andrew chose his words thoughtfully: "James, you got yo futampaf. It be true dat you no do dat wid yo people, but I kin tell dat you learn de ting you gotsta wid what you do since you leeb Africa. I be hab my futampaf, 'n I be tell you dat it be so. You be de man now 'n be de full memba o yo tribe."

Jayvyn sat back and looked at Andrew. "How dat be? How you know dat?"

Andrew explained. "In de futampaf, you be gibb'n many test. Some be of brayb'ry, but brayb'ry be nuting widout de wisdom. It no be 'nuff just to brayb de sharp knife. You gotsta ta tink good, 'n no be de fool. Brayb'ry be when you take de chance for de good o everybody. You be de fool when you take de chance only fo yo'sef. You see? De brayb, wise man choose de ting what make ebrybody 'n hid whole billage safe 'n strong; de fool aks alone 'n fo hissef only. He be weak. Do you und'stand?"

Jayvyn thought about this for a long moment. He reflected back on his recent experiences, searching for an example to support what Andrew had said. When he felt he had his thoughts in order, he replied, "Yes. I tink so. De man Isaac. He be de fool. He take de chance tellin' George 'bout you so he got de reward by hissef. When hid reward be gone, he be left lone 'n weak.

"You be de brayb one. You take de chance 'n bring de food to de slabe so dey kin be free. It be de ting no slabe here ebba forget, 'n we all be stronga 'caus'n it now. It be de wise choice."

Andrew was momentarily taken aback. He hadn't expected Jayvyn to articulate his message and feed it back to him in such a fashion, especially not drawing on this most recent example. But he was right, and it could't be denied. It also touched Andrew to his very core to have it voiced that the risk he'd taken and paid so dearly for had carried forward to serve and strengthen the community of slaves in this way. Jayvyn had indeed learned his lessons well.

Andrew cleared his throat. In a most sincere tone, he continued, "Yes, James. Dat be what yo elda be teach you: what be de good choice 'n how to make de good choice. You work in de garden 'cause'n it hep everybody. You hep Ben learn de English 'cause'n it be hep him speak good to de udda people. You hep my spirit be strong 'n hep me got betta. When one o we be strong, we all be strong.

"Mots 'portant, you ain't no fool. You tink big, 'n you see de ting outside o you; you 'spect all ting. Dat be de way of ah people, 'n when you tink dat way, you be part o de tribe like de man, 'cause'n de ting you do gonna make de whole tribe stronga."

Jayvyn beamed. It was how he thought of his father, and it was how he wished to think of himself. Now here was Andrew, a man he'd come to think very highly of, proclaiming his opinion that Jayvyn had exhibited the qualities certifying his passage from boyhood to manhood in the eyes of the elders.

He felt great peace in knowing he'd developed healthy wisdom. It's what will guide his inner voice in matters of great importance as he goes through life. He'd need to trust this voice in moments when panic threatens to seize his mind, giving way to impulses that may lead him astray.

It was an art he'd have to practice at every opportunity—to slow his thinking enough to consult his inner wisdom. It is where he will find truth when confronted by sudden maelstroms of chaos and confusion that will surely lay waiting in ambush when least expected.

Jayvyn felt gratitude for the lessons his father had so gently and patiently passed on to him. He realized it's because a father teaches his son well that a father becomes an elder when his son passes into manhood. It all made sense to him now. He took great comfort knowing his father's spirit was now elevated elder status because he, his son, is prepared to face the challenges of adulthood.

Jayvyn was most grateful to Andrew, who, through his patient guidance, had taught him so much over the past year. It was he who helped Jayvyn bridge the open gaps in his logic—spaces that had been revealed through his epic experiences since capture. Jayvyn could answer more of his own questions now, and for the ones he couldn't, he possessed a better framework in which to consider them.

Jayvyn continued to visit Baahir.

He told Baahir what he'd learned from Andrew about the place they'd landed. That it is called Barbados and is a relatively small island in a great ocean. He further told him it is a very hard place to escape from because it is surrounded by the sea and there is no place to go.

Baahir expressed his hatred for the white man and how unjust it was to be taken from their homeland and heritage.

Jayvyn questioned this: "Dat no be de same ting yo tribe do when dey raid de udda billage 'n make de slabe from dey people?"

Baahir wasn't offended by this, and he explained, "It be de way o my tribe to hab slabe, but it be diff'nt from what de white man do.

In ah tribe, de slabe be de human being 'n be treat good. It be de way we lib for many life."

Jayvyn countered, "But you take de people from dey tribe 'n take dey freedom way."

Baahir responded, "Ah people make de strengt 'n size o ah tribe dat way. We be de warrior 'n take de land from dem who no kin defend it, 'n den it be ah land. When dem people no hab de billage no mo, we gib dem de home. But 'cause dey no be born in ah tribe, dey gotsta be jongo—slabe. It be de way o ah people 'n how we be lib for de long time.

"But to be de slabe in ah tribe be ta hab de place. If you be born 'jongo,' you be de slabe, 'n dat be yo place. It no be good or bad; it jus be what it be. It be de same fo dem born to any ting. I gotsta alway hab de same place. I gosta stay de farma 'n only marry in wid de udda farma, 'n my chillin gotsta do de same. It be de way we lib, 'n ebrybody like dat way o life.

"We be happy wid dat, 'n ah slabe be happy to hab dey place 'cause dey be treated good 'n it be dey life.

"It be diff'nt from what dem white men do. Here, we no slabe like de slabe in my tribe. We be like de 'ting' to de white man, 'n de 'ting' no be people 'n no hab de life. When de ting no be good no mo, it be trow way—kilt—'cause it no hab de spirit. Dat be how de white man see we; he kill 'n trow we away like de ting. He no tink dat we be people, 'n it be why I hate him.

"Dat ting on my neck—it neba be on ah slabe! Ah slabe no be burnt or hab hid face cut like me! 'N we no do like de white man do to dat man what be kech wid me! De man what hab hid head cut off 'n hang from de rope!"

Baahir's anger grew as he described this injustice. Jayvyn saw the look in his eyes change from the thoughtful boy he saw most of the time to the glare of a fierce warrior.

He put his hand gently on his friend's shoulder. "Yes, you be right, my friend; de white man no tink we be human 'n do bery bad ting. I tink dat too. I no und'stand why he gotsta do dem ting 'n be so bad, but it be de way he be. We be betta.

"We gotsta take care o de spirit; it be de only ting what keep we alibe. If it be de time what we be free again, den we gonna need dat spirit to learn de way."

Baahir calmed somewhat, seeing he had a friend who agreed and shared his distain over the senseless hatred they'd been subjected to since their capture.

"Yes, James, you be right. We gotsta be betta."

Jayvyn went on to share some of the insight Andrew had given him about why the white man wanted to keep them as divided as possible.*

"De white man bring we far from ah home and de ting we know. We be weak here, 'n he know dat. He no want we be strong. He know dat we be part 'cause all de tribe, 'n dat it make we weak. It make we easy ta control.

"Alone, we be weak 'ginst 'm, but togeda we be strong. But it be take time to be togeda.

---

* *In many ways, tribal conflict and division among African tribes assisted Europeans with developing and sustaining the transatlantic slave trade. Europeans recognized this and realized that it was in their interest to perpetuate these divisions*

"We gotsta first surbibe if we wanna find de freedom agin."

It was a hard conundrum to live with. Neither Jayvyn, Baahir, nor anyone else had any practicable idea of what could be done to achieve their freedom in the near term.

Their worlds had been so thoroughly shattered and ruined that the best they could do was try and understand how to survive and hope someday, somehow, they'd find the opportunity to have their freedom again.

- 25 -

Jaywyn's Turn

Life, if that's what it is to be called, went on. The slaves assembled each morning and trudged off to their respective work assignments, sometimes singing mournful dirges lamenting the circumstances that had been pressed upon their lives, other times in silence.

Each morning, they passed the decaying remains of what had once been their brother William, and each evening they passed by once again as it turned slowly on the gibbet.

The birds had long since picked the last scraps of meat from its bones and skull. Now all that remained were the skeletal parts—its bleached bones slowly cracking in the unrelenting tropical sun. Some of the cartilage had lost its battle, and the bones it had faithfully secured now lay scattered on the ground. Remarkably, a few patches of mangy hair could still be seen clinging to the skull, like the seaweed that dries on the rocks above the tideline—long ago dead but denying the elements for as long as it can.

Every slave who passed by the freakish spectacle harbored their own thoughts, but all in some way couldn't help to see themselves in its place—stripped of every vestige that had once been their unique, beautiful selves—now displayed as a stark reminder that nothing of their sovereignty remained. They owned nothing of themselves anymore. All had been taken by their white masters, who could do with them as they pleased.

It was this message they took to work each day as they sweat and labored in the fields, only to return with the same message to carry in their dreams.

The cane, indeed, reached high above the slaves' heads now. Harvest was fast approaching.

New slaves began to arrive as Jayvyn and his group had so long ago—bewildered and weak from the harsh ordeals suffered so far, unaware there would be no reprieve. Some were so weak they wouldn't last long, but the veteran slaves knew there wasn't much they could do to stave off the inevitable. Just as it was for all newcomers, language barriers made it difficult to communicate what would be required for their survival. Even if they could, many of the new arrivals were so depressed and depleted they might not have strength to recover. Beyond that, they may not have defenses to survive the diseases that would assault them in their new environment.

Regardless, they were put straight to work, just as Jayvyn had been. Some would drop from exhaustion and dehydration, others malnourishment.

Jayvyn saw despair reflected in the vacant stares of these new arrivals.

He was assigned to work with one of them, just as Simon did with him.

He wondered what he'd looked like on that day so long ago as he took his new protégé, John, to his task.

The boy was weak and emaciated; his mouth hung somewhat slack, and his gaze was distant, as if not comprehending his surroundings. He was slow and uncoordinated with his movements, and Jayvyn found himself far outpacing his charge.

As Simon had done with him, he scolded John harshly, telling him to hurry up; he must work harder and be faster! But the boy was simply incapable, no matter how much Jayvyn tried to help. He even stopped to assemble bundles of cane to place on the boy's shoulders, but when he hustled him off in the direction of the waiting cart, John would inevitably falter, dropping half of the bundle from his shoulder.

Mr. Flynn, again, was the boss supervising this section of the field, and it wasn't long before he noticed John dropping his bundles and moving all too slowly. He began to holler, and Jayvyn cringed as he desperately tried to bring the boy's performance up.

Soon, Mr. Flynn became outraged and stormed into the field with his whip. He caught poor John as he was fumbling with his bundle, trying to gather it up again and continue on his way to the cart, but it was too late.

Mr. Flynn's whip came down with a fury, hard and sure across the boy's back. Mr. Flynn yelled, spitting his words out with venomous hatred, bringing the whip down ever more forcefully, his rage increasing with every blow. He bludgeoned him until John was completely senseless.

When Mr. Flynn realized the boy was no longer moving, he stopped, his sweat-soaked chest heaving from the effort, madness on his beet-red face.

John lay there, unconscious, blood soaking through the rough woven fabric of his newly issued field shirt—drool running from his slack mouth.

Mr. Flynn's eyes were wild as he shifted his gaze upward to find Jayvyn.

He yelled, "You! James! You fuckin' nigger! Get your ass over here! Now! Goddammit!"

Jayvyn was terrified as he hurried to the spot.

"Yas-suh, Missa Flynn!"

"Take this fuckin' nigger up to the water and bring him 'round, you rotten little son of a bitch! It's all your fault; you no good for nothing nigger! Move!"

"Yas-suh!" Jayvyn hurriedly said as he gathered John up and carried him to the water cask.

When he got there, he laid him on the dirt.

John's head lolled back on his neck; he saw no movement whatsoever as he ladled water over his face. His eyes stared vacantly, looking past Jayvn at some indistinct point in the sky.

Jayvyn slapped at his face and shook him several times, saying, "John! John! Get up. John! Wake up!"

But the boy just lay there.

He put his head down to John's chest to listen for his breath and heartbeat, but heard only the faintest flutter, becoming weaker and weaker until finally stopping for good.

The boy was dead.

Terrified and helpless, Jayvyn looked back at Mr. Flynn, who stood with a fixed glare.

Jayvyn shook his head slowly, indicating there was nothing more he could do for this boy. Mr. Flynn's scowl deepened.

"Aw! For Chrissake! This is all your fault, you little bastard!" he hollered as he came storming over toward Jayvyn.

His foot hit Jayvyn square in the chest, knocking him backwards in the dirt as his tirade continued.

"You'll pay for this nigger! Get this piece of shit into that cart over there, and get back to work 'fore I do the same to you! And I'm gonna be watching you, so you better not fuck up again! Now move it!"

Mr. Flynn looked up to see several stunned slaves standing frozen in the field and yelled, "The rest of you niggers! Get your asses to work!" and then stomped back to his usual spot.

Jayvyn gathered the poor dead boy up in his arms and carried him to the cart, where another new slave—a woman—lay dead after collapsing earlier in the day.

He gently laid John's body beside hers, the cart shifting slightly from the new weight. They lay, arms touching, faces absently looking in different directions, their painful ordeals at an end.

Jayvyn momentarily wished for their spirits to be free, to find their way back to Africa, to be amongst their ancestors, then hurried back to the fields where he worked hard, anxious to not incur any more trouble.

When the afternoon meal break came, Mr. Flynn marched over when Jayvyn lined up for his portion.

"Oh no! Not you, nigger! Get your ass back into that field and work! You cost me enough for one day! This ain't over, you little fuck!"

Jayvyn had nothing he could say or do. It didn't matter that he'd been a good, faithful, hardworking slave all year long. He'd thought he might have earned some small amount of respect from the bosses. They seemed to trust him with a greater breadth of duty over time, such as bringing produce to the big house. But now, none of that seemed to matter.

It was the first time since his arrival that he'd met with any disciplinary action. He wondered what his fate would be as he returned to his work.

He was excessively nervous as the day went by and kept his head down, working as hard as he was able, pondering why he was being blamed for the new boy's death. There was nothing he could have done differently; the boy was simply too weak to work.

Jayvyn wondered how close he might have come to the same fate so long ago—on his first day—after being beat and left in the stocks overnight. If he'd faltered then, he thought Simon would have been judged at fault.

He wished he'd been able to eat his meal. It wasn't as if anyone really had enough to eat in the first place. He became dizzy from lack of nourishment and water as the day crept slowly into dark.

Finally, the work day was called, and Jayvyn meandered tentatively over to the water keg. Other slaves were getting a drink before their usual trudge back to the quarters.

Thankfully, Mr. Flynn didn't stop him or seem to take any notice. His mind was on the end of the day. He walked off with the other bosses, back to the big white house.

Jayvyn drank heavily from the cask, where he found Baahir, who glanced nervously over at his friend. "It be bad, yes?"

Jayvyn responded, "What I can do, Ben? I try 'n hep dat boy, but he be too weak. I not know what be happen now, but I no be ta blame."

Baahir talked quietly with Jayvyn as they made their way back to their quarters. "Der be noting you do dat be wrong, James. De white man be mad 'cause'n he beat hid new slave to det. He hasta blame dat on somebody 'sides hissef, 'n dat be you."

"Now I gotsta be punish fo someting I no do."

"Maybe dis no happen, my friend. Maybe Missa Flynn be drunk 'n forget de whole ting."

But that wasn't to be. Shortly after the slaves ate their dinner, the white men came to the slaves' quarters, and George roused everyone from their huts for an impromptu assembly.

As before, the slaves assembled in front of their huts. Master Clark, Mr. Flynn, and two other bosses stood in the light of their torches.

Jayvyn looked at the men, his heart seizing in his chest as he met Mr. Flynn's cold, cruel eyes. He just stared—unblinking—back at Jayvyn—a hard, fixed set to his face—one side of his mouth slowly turning up into a menacing sort of half grin.

Jayvyn's gaze moved to the right, where he saw George, Thomas, and Andrew. He met Andrew's eyes briefly, looking for a clue, but Andrew quickly shifted his gaze away.

Then he froze, a large lump forming in his throat. The pillory stood off to the side; the whip leaned casually against it.

George stepped to the front, addressing the group.

"Y'all know de habest be comin soon. Dat be de mots pot'nt time o de year. Ma'sa Clark be bring many new slabe fo dat, 'n it be de job o de sper'nced slabe ta teach de new slabe de work."

He paused, glancing over the group to make sure they understood.

"Today, one de new slabe die 'cause'n de sper'nced slabe no teach 'm good."

He paused again, looking over the group, finally settling his gaze on Jayvyn.

"James," Jayvyn's breathing stopped, and his mouth went dry. "it be yo job ta teach dat new slabe how ta do hid work, 'n you no do dat. 'Cause o dat, Missa Flynn got no choice but ta punish dat boy.

"Den you be told ta bring him 'round wid de wata, but you no do dat, 'n de boy be die 'caus'n it. Dis be yo fault."

Thomas and Andrew had moved into the crowd and now stood on either side of Jayvyn.

Jayvyn looked back at George, lips trembling, and uttered, "No, I try, but he be too weak; please, I try ta hep."

George then nodded to Thomas and Andrew, who took Jayvyn by the arms.

Jayvyn stiffened but offered no resistance as tears formed in the corners of his eyes.

George continued, "James, you be de good slabe 'n be show'n dat you be good; dat why Ma'sa Clark, in hid kindness, be gibb'n you de light punish'nt.

"But you gotsta und'stand dat Ma'sa Clark pay good money fo hid slabe; dey be val'ble prop'ty 'n gotsta be look't out fo.

"So dat yo learn yo less'n, yo gotsta be gibb'n ten lash in de pill'ry. You be stay der 'til de mornin'. Und'stand?"

Thomas and Andrew then brought him forward through the crowd as Jayvyn broke into tears, frightened at the thought he was soon to be locked helplessly into the pillory and whipped—for his good intentions!

He began to protest, "No! No! I no do dat ting! Please, I try 'n hep 'm!"

But he knew his words would do him no good. It was as Baahir had said—Mr. Flynn needed to blame someone and make him an example for the rest. Now it was Jayvyn's turn to pay.

Jayvyn was stripped and put into the pillory, where he hunched helplessly as he looked back at his fellow slaves, eyes wet from tears.

He resolved to be as strong as possible, since there was nothing he or anyone else could do.

George then took the whip.

Knowing full well the relationship Andrew and Jayvyn had developed over time, he handed it to Andrew.

Andrew's eyes watered up.

He said quietly, "No, George, please. I no can!"

But Jayvyn quickly interrupted.

Looking directly into Andrew's eyes, he said in a low voice, "Yes, Andrew, please, you gotsta. If you no do, dey punish you, too. Please, I no blame you."

George, still holding the whip out to Andrew, said quietly, "He be right, Andrew; you know dat be what Ma'sa Clark want; now take it."

Mr. Flynn, standing impatiently by the torches, angrily shouted out, "C'mon! What's the hold-up! We haven't got all night! Get going!"

Andrew took the whip from George.

Wiping tears from his eyes, he moved behind the pillory to face Jayvyn's smooth, as yet unscarred, back.

George, standing in front of the pillory, cast a compassionate look at Jayvyn, muttering, "You be fine."

Then he backed up two steps and announced in a loud voice, "Begin!"

Andrew steeled himself as he brought the whip high up over his head.

He grimaced, then brought it down, hard enough to satisfy the bosses but by no means having his heart in it. Still, it was enough to make Jayvyn stiffen and wince with pain, leaving a good stripe down the center of his back.

The second blow came quickly, and there really was no way to lighten the blow without raising the suspicions of the bosses.

Andrew had done this enough to know that, when done correctly, the whip did most of the work.

Another stripe appeared on Jayvyn's back, then another, and another, making the crisscross pattern Andrew knew all too well.

Jayvyn had never been whipped before and began to cry out on the fourth lash.

Soon, his wounds were bleeding.

George maintained the count. Five, crack! Six, crack! Seven.

Jayvyn's back was now cut open in several areas, blood beginning to drip over his sides.

Baahir stood silently watching his friend, involuntarily flinching with each blow.

Eight, crack! Nine, crack!

The pain was intense.

Andrew's face a mix of grief and rage as he brought the whip down for the tenth and final time.

Crack! It was over.

Jayvyn hung, slumped in the pillory, back bleeding enough to satisfy the bosses, who took their torches, turned, without any further ado, and walked off into the dark—back up the hill—to the big, white house.

The slaves dispersed back to their huts, leaving Jayvyn in the pillory.

Andrew remained, whip hanging loosely by his side, quietly weeping with grief.

Baahir lingered for a moment or two, dolefully looking at his friend. But there was nothing he could do. He, too, turned and slowly returned to his quarters.

When all had left, Andrew tossed the whip down in disgust and went to grab a pail of water and a cloth to clean Jayvyn's wounds.

Jayvyn had come around some.

In a weak voice, he told him, "No worry, Andrew, my spirit be good. You gotsta do dat. We be strong togedda; it be de good ting," whereupon, he closed his eyes and lowered his head. The cool water stung as it coursed over his fresh wounds.

Andrew stayed by his side that night, knowing time was the only cure now.

He sat by Jayvyn as he hung in the pillory, remembering how

Jayvyn had come to his aid faithfully every week and recounting all of their conversations over time.

He thought to himself, *Yes, this boy has passed his futampaf many times over; he is a man any village would be proud to have.*

He felt a deep welling in his chest as his admiration for this wonderful young man grew within him. Again, he thought, if he were ever to have a son, how fortunate he'd be if he were just a fraction of the man Jayvyn was.

With these thoughts in mind, Andrew eventually moped back to his hut knowing the morning would bring the end of Jayvyn's punishment. He'd be released from the pillory to once again resume his tortured existence as a slave.

Jayvyn hung in the pillory, the wounds on his back throbbing, drifting in and out of consciousness. Night creatures buzzed and chirped as they went about their business.

His thoughts were broken and sporadic, going from distant memories of his homeland to the events that had landed him where he now was.

He thought of the boy, John, how helpless and depleted he'd looked as Jayvyn futilely tried to teach him to work in the fields. He never had a chance; his body had simply been pushed too far from his ordeal before arriving at the plantation.

It was as Baahir had said, they weren't human beings to the white man but things, and this 'thing' was broken when the master bought it.

In his delirium, Jayvyn pictured the boy, John, as a kajundu,* one of the tools his father and he used on their rice crops back in Africa.

In his imagination, John, the kajundu, was broken. The twining that attaches the head to the shaft had become frayed, wouldn't hold the head adequately, and needed to be repaired. No matter how much he tried, Jayvyn couldn't make the tool work effectively.

In this imaginary vision, the boss, Mr. Flynn, became unreasonably outraged, seizing the kajundu and breaking it over his knee, tossing it into the dirt.

Then Jayvyn shook to his senses, remembering John wasn't a kajundu—a thing—he was a human being.

Mr. Flynn had beat him in an uncontrolled rage—beat him until John's spirit was crushed beyond repair—and his life ebbed away.

His mind continued to drift aimlessly as he teetered on the edge of consciousness.

During his more lucid moments, he wondered what John's real name was, what tribe he came from, what his life in Africa had been like before he was taken.

He thought the boy was probably younger than he was. He was certainly slighter in build and shorter than Jayvyn, but then again, he was not well nourished and in poor condition.

He wondered what had happened to his family—if he still had a family.

In his delirium, Jayvyn imagined the boy walking dazedly through his village. Some people, people he assumed to be his parents,

---

* *A tool used in traditional African rice farming, a cross between a spade and a shovel attached to a 12-foot pole*

were helping to tie him to a yoke. The boy, John, was looking back with that same uncomprehending look that was in his eyes when Jayvyn had met him.

His parents were turning around, leaving him to be led off into the jungle.

John's village hadn't been attacked, yet there he was, tied to the yoke, ready to be taken away from his home and people.

This made Jayvyn feel exceptionally sad, and he wanted to cry out to the parents to rescue their child; John didn't know what was happening and needed them.

Jayvyn, again, briefly came to his senses in the dark, realizing he was hanging in the pillory with its hard wooden grip around his neck and wrists.

He felt the stinging sensation of the fleshy wounds on his back, and then remembered—John was dead, and he was paying the price for it.

At one point during the long, fitful night, it rained—as it often did in the tropics—usually in the early morning hours before dawn.

This woke Jayvyn again. It felt cold but good against his raw back. He craned his neck so he could get some water on his face.

He saw the outlines of trees coming into view as the sky took on the first light of day.

Soon, he'd be released from the pillory.

He remembered his first night at the plantation when he awoke in the leg stocks, his face and chest beaten for not accepting his new name. He remembered how he had a difficult time figuring out what had happened, how the details came to him slowly.

He had the same feeling now.

Soon, he heard quiet footsteps approaching in the predawn light. It was Andrew.

He came with a small tub of food and some water.

George was with him and said, "I be take you outta dat ting now."

His voice was soft and low, like it had been last night when he told Jayvyn he would be fine. His touch was gentle as he released the mechanism that held him and helped him from the pillory.

He turned to Andrew and said, "Take care o him now 'n feed him; he gotsta work today."

Then George left to complete the rest of his morning routine.

Andrew sat with Jayvyn and mopped his back, while Jayvyn ate from the tub.

He spoke quietly to him in Fogni for the first time since his English lessons in the garden.

"You did well, my friend; you faced your test bravely. You are a man now."

Then quickly switching back to English, "Now eat, James, 'n drink plenty o water. You gotsta work today.

"Yo back be get bettah, 'n I be hep you." after which he handed him his clothes and went back to his own hut.

- 26 -

Seasoned

Jayvyn's back did heal over the course of several months, leaving behind telltale scars he'd carry through the rest of his life. Andrew had come every night as promised to bathe his back and tend to his wounds. Baahir, too, had stopped in to check on his friend from time to time.

Several more of the new slaves perished, both in the fields and from malnutrition and disease. One new slave ran but was caught soon after. He was given twenty lashes, with time in the pillory, and now wears a collar—the same collar Baahir was finally released from. Charles, too, had been released from his collar but still wore the massive weight attached to his ankle.

Work continued unabated throughout the harvest and sugaring, as it had the year before. This year's harvest was bigger due to additional plantings made the year before, and so the sugar yield was greater too.

This made Master Clark and his bosses happy and less agitated. Market time was coming up, too, which had most of their attention. Therefore, the slaves felt a slight reprieve from the steady pressure of harvest and sugar production.

In addition, the surviving new slaves, better conditioned for work now, could keep up with their quotas. However, the business of clearing the fields and preparing the ground for new plantings was brutal as always.

Baahir's English became as good as the rest of the slaves, and he could converse with anyone. Increasingly, he joined Jayvyn and Andrew in the garden, getting to know Andrew much better. He was as healed as he would ever be—a mass of scar where the bridge of his nose should be, 'r' forever emblazoned on his forehead.

Andrew asked about Baahir's tribe and homeland. Their spirited conversations were akin to those Jayvyn remembered. Over time, he saw the same rapport developing as he and Andrew had. It was good to know Baahir knew Andrew this way. He knew how much Andrew had helped him, and was glad to see his friend have the same dependable mentoring and guidance.

Jayvyn noticed some of the hard edges coming off Baahir's coarse exterior and knew this would help him in the long run. Like Jayvyn, he was developing a deeper appreciation for the breadth of human behavior in all its shades of good and evil. Baahir's impulsive anger was beginning to give way to a certain degree of compassion and understanding. He was still, and always would be, a warrior, but he'd be a wiser, more thoughtful warrior—the kind of warrior Jayvyn would most want to have at his side. He was happy for his friend; Andrew was a good teacher.

Stephen had grown a lot, too. He was taller, his baby-like features were more those of a young boy now. He and Rose had formed a strong bond and still worked every day at the big house. Others in the group got to know Stephen better and adopted him in much the same way as Julia had. Jayvyn felt good seeing this boy—only a year ago so lost and confused—have some semblance of family to reassure him.

He marveled at how resilient Africans were in the face of such impossible adversity. It was the strength of their spirits. Despite all of their differences, this seemed to be the one thing everyone implicitly understood. It was as if some unwritten covenant compelled all slaves to recognize and look after their fellow slave's spirit, regardless of their individual heritage.

To be sure, as with any society, there were deviants from this covenant. Isaac was a prime example. He'd so willingly and blatantly sold out Andrew, and consequently three other slaves, for better food, living, and the perceived favor of his captors.

But as Jayvyn had come to know, this was an illusion. His allotment of food and rum were soon gone; he still worked as a slave, and Jayvyn knew without any doubt the white man would do with him as any other slave.

He was simply property, with no special status over any other property. When no longer useful, he'd be disposed of as they saw fit.

But there were other consequences to breaching the unwritten covenant. The other slaves would never trust him, and he'd never enjoy the strength that comes with being a true part of a tribe. Isaac is a fool and will always remain so. When he dies, he'll be buried face down, to spend eternity with his spirit locked in the ground. He'll never return to his African ancestors. Instead, he'll remain isolated and alone. His spirit will never be free.

Over the weeks following field preparations and planting, the ranks of the slaves began to diminish. Of course, there were the usual attritions through death, but more so, as with last year at this time, groups of slaves were again being selected as "seasoned" and carted off to market.

Usually on a Sunday, George quietly came to inform whomever had been selected to come with him, and they'd disappear up the hill, never to be seen again. No provisions were ever made for these slaves to say goodbye to their fellow slaves—the people they'd sometimes spent years with. It was the same as being taken from their families and villages; they were simply loaded onto the wagon and driven to the docks.

Several Jayvyn had come to know had gone this way. Lewis, the boy who he'd arrived with, was among them. One day, he was simply gone. Lucy, the caring woman who took care of the provisions and meals and showed Jayvyn how to weave with cane, was another. Samuel was another from his group to disappear this way. They always knew this was so because there were only two ways to leave the plantation—to be sold at the docks or die, and since the slaves buried the dead, they knew who had died.

It was one such Sunday morning, before going to work in the garden, George came for Jayvyn. He simply said to come with him.

Jayvyn looked around desperately for Andrew and Baahir, but they were nowhere to be seen. George would not wait, and with a group of five others selected, Jayvyn was marched off for what would be his final walk up the long hill.

He couldn't believe it. He'd been at the plantation for over a year and a half, and suddenly it felt like he'd just arrived yesterday.

Time has a way of doing that. The time between seems interminable, but when the moment arrives and the page is turning, everything gets compressed. It feels like the blink of an eye.

The experience was surreal as he passed the pond for the last time—the pond he'd visited so many times to fill buckets for the crops; the pond where he and Andrew had spent time learning English; the pond the water came from to cleanse their wounds; the pond where sweet Julia had taken her life.

As they walked, he remembered the first time he'd heard the slaves' mournful song ring out and all the times since—the slaves footsteps falling in sync as they scuffed the dirt, breaking the quiet dawn—Charles, painfully carrying his iron ball, struggling to keep up.

They passed the boiling house, where crews had sweated and worked round the clock during sugaring; wood cut and stacked at its side.

They passed the mill that never stopped—where countless cartloads of cane were processed—where the one-armed man had lost his arm.

He heard the pigs and chickens running around the barn.

Then they passed William's remains—his lonely skull perched, unseeing, upon the stake—what remained of his skeleton slowly turning like chimes in the wind—small bones scattered like so many pearls washed upon the sand.

The wagon was already hitched up, Master Clark and two bosses stood nearby.

George took each slave and shackled his ankle to another. Their hands were tied in front of them and they were loaded into the wagon. A chain was passed through their ankle chains and secured to the wagon.

When finished, George silently turned and started walking back down the hill.

Jayvyn briefly reflected on the moment. This was the exact spot he was knocked to the ground for not saying his new name.

He watched George, the man who'd hit him, recede into the distance. Jayvyn felt a sudden pang. A part of him wanted to say something—maybe good-bye—or even thank you—at least for the times he'd cared for him.

But none of that was possible; the driver simply snapped his crop, yelling, "Ha!"

The horses began to walk.

They drove past the road that split off to the fields—the fields where he'd gone so many days to labor so hard; the fields where he'd met Simon; the fields where Baahir and Charles stood out in their collars; the fields where he met poor John, briefly, before he was brutally slain by Mr. Flynn.

They passed the big white house, where Master Clark and his bosses lived in luxury, where Jayvyn delivered the best vegetables, where little Stephen and Rose worked every day—where dear, dear Julia was raped over and over, until unable to bear her pain anymore.

Soon, they were passing out of the plantation—a journey not taken since the day Jayvyn had arrived so long ago. For the last time, he saw the plantation's giant spread from the top of the hill.

He looked down at the tiny pond in the distance, rows of slave huts beyond. He barely made out the small clearing of the garden behind. It was entirely surreal. The place he'd lived for the past year and a half, and he was leaving.

He thought about Andrew and Baahir, who were certainly

working in the garden at this very moment. He tried to see if he could spot them, but it was impossible. He noticed the occasional figure here and there, but from this distance, they were little more than ants.

They wouldn't even know he was gone yet.

What would they think and feel when they found out?

His heart ached for the chance to see them again, if only for a moment. He wanted to tell them how much they meant to him.

It wasn't the first time his heart ached this way, and it wouldn't be the last.

The cart entered the woods beyond, the plantation disappearing from his sight for good. It started its downhill journey through the switchbacks that eventually brought them out to the sea. Some of it seemed familiar to Jayvyn, although he'd only seen it once before.

Soon they were passing along the coast. White crested waves still crashed on the rocks.

The horses plodded steadily on, making their way toward the same harbor he'd arrived at almost two years prior.

The trip seemed both long and short at the same time. It was barely noon when they arrived.

This time they weren't taken to stockades, however, but to a platform in the middle of the cove.

He saw large ships anchored in the harbor beyond. To either side were the beaches where they'd landed. He remembered the man who'd run, only to be shot, tortured, and left hanging in the tree.

His mind reeled as condensed memories flooded in.

Everything had changed so quickly. Just a few hours ago, he was rising from his mat, expecting to join Andrew and Baahir in the garden. Now he was pulling up to a large pier, chained.

Many other slaves and strange white men bustled about.

When the wagon stopped, Master Clark and one of the other white men got out and shuffled off into the crowd. The third unloaded the slaves, keeping the long chain linked through their ankle chains. The slaves just stood there. None were inclined to run. After all, they were seasoned now. No one spoke either. All were too stunned and anxious about what was going to happen next.

Soon, Master Clark and the other man returned, and the three led the chained group to the platform.

In a matter of moments, the slaves were approached by new white men who looked them over as before—feeling their limbs, prying their mouths open, inspecting their eyes, and checking their genitals.

Following this, the men went to confer with Master Clark, who, after a short time, nodded, shaking hands with one of them. The negotiations were complete; the deal was done. Master Clark and his men returned to the empty cart, and departed the way they'd come.

Jayvyn and his group stood dumbfounded.

It was clear they'd been sold. But the man who sold them, the man who'd owned them for years—who they labored and died for—didn't so much as look their way.

They looked around at other groups of slaves, all looking just as bewildered.

The groups were split and led to small boats along the shore, which took them, group by group, to one ship or another. When Jayvyn and his group arrived at their ship, they were brought on deck to await further processing.

Group by group, they were released from their bondage under heavy guard. Any who resisted were severely beaten at once. Not many did.

They were made to remove their clothing, whereupon they were washed, hair cut off, and bodies shaved. Following, they were given their clothing back.

Jayvyn looked around him. The ship was much smaller than the first ship, with two masts instead of three. The total number of slaves was similarly much smaller. There were a wide variety of ages, both men and women together. Another young slave, about his size, was shackled to his ankle. As he looked around, he saw other slaves being paired and shackled as well. When finished, they stood assembled in a group, and an official-looking white man came to speak before them all.

"My name is Captain William Thompson," he began. "I am master of this ship, and you will follow my orders. Disobedience of any sort will not be tolerated. Those who disobey will be immediately and severely punished."

He paused to cast his eye over the slaves for emphasis and see that they understood.

"This is my crew." He gestured to the armed men standing around the slaves. "You will do as they say. They will feed you twice a day.

"Once we are underway, and if the weather is good, you will be allowed on deck but must remain in your chains. At night, you will sleep in the hold belowdecks.

"We will get underway immediately, during which time you will remain belowdecks.

"This passage will be much shorter than your first. We are sailing for the colony of South Carolina in America."

He then turned to his crew and commanded, "Take the slaves below and make ready to sail."

The crew immediately sprang into action, several taking slaves below, the rest going to different stations around the ship.

A shrill whistle blew from somewhere on deck as Jayvyn looked back at the island he'd just left. White sand rimmed the turquoise bay. Palm fronds swayed gently in the breeze as seabirds glided to and fro, occasionally diving into the blue-green water to catch fish. He noticed the contour of the island—its high hills painted in shades of green below silver-gray clouds speckled across a deep blue sky.

Somewhere in those hills was the plantation he'd labored and lived on with all its stories. He tried to picture what the slaves were doing right now. He imagined Andrew and Baahir, finished with their work in the garden, now washing at the pond or spending the afternoon in their usual manner. It was a world removed as he stood on the deck of this new ship waiting to depart to a new land—a land he didn't know—with people he had no knowledge of.

His trance was suddenly broken as a sailor took him by the shoulder, saying, "Let's go now, below with you niggers; you'll get your chance on deck soon. Let's go! Down below!" He and the one he was shackled to were directed to the hatch, down the ladder, into the darkness below. When all of the slaves were in, the hatch was closed and bolted from above.

Jayvyn sat with his ankle partner looking about the hold. There was a grate above their heads where dappled sunlight entered and air was allowed to circulate. The light enabled him to see that the hold was barely large enough to contain all of the slaves, who sat packed together on its sole. The ceiling was so low that standing could only be accomplished at a crouch.

Jayvyn thought back to two years before, when he'd first been put aboard the much larger ship, and wondered.

How long this time?

Part Three

Charles Town

- 27 -

The Next Leg

Heavy chains bumped and ground against the side of the ship as the anchor was hauled up. Wooden hoops clattered up the masts, sails fluttered in the wind, followed by a resounding snap as a fresh breeze filled their bellies.

The ship listed to one side, canvass coming under the press of wind; its hull sliced the blue-green bay. Other sounds abated; all that remained was the sound of rushing water and the gentle creak of the ship's timbers. They were underway.

Within an hour, the sailors came and let the slaves on deck where they were secured in groups of ten along chains arranged down the length of the deck as before on the big ship. In this case, there were only two such chains—one with four groups, the other five. A quick count told Jayvyn there was a total of ninety slaves onboard, far fewer than the first ship. The group was diverse, men, women, and children alike, all paired and shackled with another.

As they sat on deck, the boy chained to Jayvyn spoke to him. He learned his name was Jacob.

Jacob explained he'd been sold into slavery after the Asante people, another African tribe, raided his village. Jacob's tribe, known as the Fanti, had been involved in many skirmishes with the Asante tied to their quest for dominance over the Guinea Coast region.*

Jayvyn asked, "If you be tak'n by de Asante tribe, how come you be slave to de white people?"

Jacob responded, "De Asante take my people, sell dem to de Engishmun."

Jayvyn was astounded. It was shocking enough when he learned Baahir's tribe took members of vanquished tribes as slaves to *their own* people. Here was a boy whose tribe not only was attacked by another African tribe, but this tribe sold their captives to *white people* for slavery!

When he inquired further, Jacob told Jayvyn his tribe, the Fanti, did the same thing. He explained keeping captives was problematic for each of their tribes in their situation. Weapons and supplies received in trade from the English were more valuable in their quest for dominance, so both tribes enriched themselves this way.†

Jayvyn sat in stunned silence as he contemplated this new information. Since his tribe had never engaged in any such thing, he found it incomprehensible any African would sell a fellow African to these white devils knowing their brethren would be condemned to a life of pain and misery. But, after all he'd learned from Andrew about wide-ranging conflict and malignant trust among tribes, he realized how sheltered his tribe had been and how naïve he really was.

Jayvyn's train of thought was abruptly interrupted when one of the sailors barked, "On your feet, niggers! Time to dance!"

---

* *A region made up of a variety of tribal states which eventually became a British Colony in 1821 known as the Gold Coast. In 1957 it achieved its independence and is now the country of Ghana.*

† *African tribes raiding other tribes for the acquisition of slaves to sell to Europeans was a fairly common practice during the Atlantic slave trade*

The slaves got clumsily to their feet, fumbling in their chains as the deck tilted and shifted beneath them. There was no instrument played this time. The sailors simply stood before them, chanting a strange song while clapping their hands. The song was melodic and reminded Jayvyn somewhat of the songs the slaves had sung in that one sang a line, followed by a chorus sung by the others. But the sailors' song was much more upbeat in mood and tempo than the slaves' sad songs.

The sailors danced and clapped as they sang:

O were you ever in Congo River?
Blow Boys Blow!
O yes, I've been in the Congo River.
Blow me bully boys blow!

The slaves slowly fell in line, doing their best to copy the dance the sailors were demonstrating, shuffling their feet to the rhythm:

O Congo she's a mighty river,
Blow Boys Blow!
Where fever makes the white man shiver.
Blow me bully boys blow!

O yonder comes the "Arrow" packet,
Blow Boys Blow!
She fires a gun, don't you hear the racket?
Blow me bully boys blow!

O yonder comes a Creole lady,
Blow Boys Blow!
I'm sure she's a nigger baby.
Blow me bully boys blow!

A Yankee ship comes down the river,
Blow Boys Blow!
Her masts and yards they shine like silver.
Blow me bully boys blow!

And how d'ye known she's a Yankee clipper?
Blow Boys Blow!
By the stars and bars that fly above her.
Blow me bully boys blow!

And who d'ye think's the skipper of her?
Blow Boys Blow!
Why, "Holy Joe", the nigger lover.
Blow me bully boys blow!

The sailors were quite enjoying this, laughing and clapping their hands as the verses were sung.

The slaves danced, some clapping as well, unaware the lyrics depicted the voyages of the very slave ships that had come and taken them from their homes.

The shanty went on:

And who d'ye think's the chief mate of her?
Blow Boys Blow!

Why, Boss-Eyed Bill, the Bowery Runner.
Blow me bully boys blow!

And what d'ye think they've got for cargo?
Blow Boys Blow!
Why "black sheep" that have run the embargo.
Blow me bully boys blow!

And what d'ye think they get for dinner?
Blow Boys Blow!
Why, bullock's heart and donkey's liver.
Blow me bully boys blow!

O blow, my boys, and blow forever,
Blow Boys Blow!
O blow me down to the Congo River.
*Blow me bully boys blow!**

By the time the sailors were finished, everyone had danced and clapped a lot and were well-exercised.

The sailors, quite elated by the whole experience, laughed heartily as they went about their business.

So far, this journey seemed a welcome change compared to the first ocean-going experience they'd had so long ago. If not chained to the deck, many might even have enjoyed it.

But the fact was, they *were* chained to the deck and *were* slaves.

---

* *As with most shanties the exact origins aren't always clear, but most believe this shanty originated on ships engaged in the slave trade along the Guinea Coast. As is the case with shanties, stanzas are added through time*

They didn't share in the merriment of the moment.

Jayvyn was astonished by what Jacob had told him as he looked about at the other slaves. Many, like himself, had scars and welts from being whipped laced across their backs. Additionally, he saw brands scorched into their skin. Some had additional wounds or appendages missing, such as fingers, toes, or, in some instances, whole limbs, like the one-armed man. Jayvyn had no doubt all of these slaves had endured the same appalling treatment as he and the others on his plantation had.

He wondered how many of these slaves had been sold into slavery by other Africans. How many had sold their fellow Africans to white slavers? It was shocking to think these wounded, broken souls suffered at the hands of other Africans.

Jayvyn took in the ship as the island of Barbados steadily receded in its wake. No large decks sat several tiers above on this ship, and no partitions kept the men and women separated. There was, however, a slightly elevated section at the rear where a sailor stood at a great, spoked wheel.

As for its overall length, he estimated it was less than half the length of the larger ship. It was much narrower as well, probably by at least half. Two masts instead of three stood on deck, and there were fewer sails. One large sail was fixed to each mast, more or less aligned with the center of the ship as opposed to the stack of crosswise sails on the larger ship—although one such sail flew at the top of the taller mast. As on the larger ship, a long sprit extended from the bow to carry several additional sails.

This ship tilted more as it sailed along, making Jayvyn feel as if he'd slide down the deck if not careful.

The crew aboard this ship were noticeably fewer as well. So far, he'd only seen about ten or twelve sailors besides the master of the ship.*

Looking about he saw other islands in the distance, ahead and to the leeward side of the ship.

The air was cool, and the wind blew steady, which felt good compared to the often hot, stagnant air on land. Sea spray occasionally misted over the bow to wet his skin, which was cold in the cooler breeze.

Jayvyn noticed the sun setting at a different angle than it had on the previous ship. It was setting off to the left and towards the stern, whereas on the previous ship, it set slightly to the right-hand side of the bow.

Soon, the sailors came with the familiar tubs of food, set before each line to be passed from one to the next. The food was a return to the repulsive mixture of rice, grain, and lard, devoid of anything fresh. A cask of water was fastened to the mast, where, as they were released in small groups, they could drink.

When put belowdecks, they stayed fastened to their partners by their ankle shackles but were otherwise free to move about.

Jayvyn noticed a large tub, situated at the bottom of the ladder, held by pieces of wood fixed to the floor. The sailors pointed this out and said it was for "shitting and pissing." It was better than what Jayvyn had endured over the middle passage, but as he'd find out, far

---

* *Coastal schooners such as this were often used to transport smaller quantities of slaves from the Caribbean to the southern provinces of North America*

from a perfect solution.

Although there was a grating above their heads, which allowed fresh air to enter the hold, after dark it was pitch black below.

After they were closed in, Jayvyn again spoke with Jacob. He told Jacob he was Ajamatau, and Jacob said he hadn't heard of his tribe, which didn't come as a surprise. He asked Jacob about his experience on Barbados, and Jacob said he, too, had been on a sugar plantation. Jacob told him he'd arrived as a young boy, some seven or so years earlier.

Shocked to hear he'd spent seven years on Barbados, Javyn asked, "How old you be den?"

"It be long ago; I tink I be six."

Javyn looked at Jacob, realizing he'd been close to Stephen's age when taken, and asked, "Yo mudda 'n fadda be wid you?"

Jacob replied, "My fadda be kilt in de raid fo I be tak'n, 'n my mudda be sell to de diff'nt Engishmun."

Jayvyn immediately thought of both his sister and Stephen. This boy not only went through everything on Barbados alone, like Stephen, but also had made the terrible middle passage by himself as a mere six-year-old.

Jayvyn thought how horrifying his own experience on Barbados had been and couldn't imagine spending as long as seven years there, especially not seven years of his childhood. He remembered his childhood in Africa and all he'd done during that span. This boy had missed out on all of that.

He told Jacob about Ifetayo, how she was only four when taken, and how he'd worried about her. How he wondered if she and his mother had stayed together—or were even still alive.

Familiar pangs of sorrow quickly returned as he recalled his little sister, always so bright and joyful in their former life. It was unavoidable. It happened every time Jayvyn encountered another slave taken at such a young age.

They spoke a bit more about their mutual experiences, but not in any great depth. Each had a profound sense of how personal their journeys were. After all, they'd just met. So, they settled into the silence with their own thoughts as the ship sailed on.

The motion of the smaller ship was much more pronounced than the larger ship, which ultimately contributed to much sea sickness, as before. The slaves did their best to use the latrine below the hatch, but this proved exceedingly difficult with the motion of the ship, not to mention the lack of headroom and light. Additionally, liquid waste seeped out the bottom and into the bilge below them, where it mixed and sloshed around with the rest of the putrid bilge water. Despite their best efforts, the hold they were confined in soon became a stinking mixture of vomit, feces, and other pestilential substances, making all of the slaves miserable and some very irritable.

The night passed slowly. The slaves sat shoulder to shoulder, being jostled and tossed by the lively motion of the ship.

In the morning, when they came to release them, the sailors were not in good humor about what they found. They lashed out at several as they emerged from the hold.

After being brought on deck, a few pairs were released to deal with the mess below. As on the big ship, this entailed filling buckets with seawater, scrubbing with sand and stones, and letting the fetid mixture find its way to the bilge to later be pumped overboard.

Additionally, the "slop bucket," as the sailors called it, had to be brought up and emptied over the side.

Other jobs were assigned as well, such as manning the pumps and scrubbing the decks. When not working, they were confined in chains on deck, except in bad weather, when they were locked in the hold. In all cases, they remained shackled to their partners.

Being ankle partners, Jayvyn and Jacob were simultaneously released for duties, one of which was pumping the bilge. The pump on this ship was much smaller, requiring only two to operate it, which Jayvyn and Jacob could handily attend to.

Jayvyn told Jacob about the terrible storm he'd experienced on the big ship, how he and Baahir had worked with eight others pumping the bilge as wild waves swept over them.

Jacob said he only remembered his voyage as being very long. He said he'd seen many die.

When meals came, the same foul porridge was passed among the slaves. Some complained as it was a dramatic step backward from food back on the plantations, where they were able to supplement it with their own produce. The sailors were quick to address their complaints with harsh cracks from their rods, reminding the slaves they were cargo and nothing more, and so the slaves reluctantly ate the sickening gruel. But the effects of the poorer diet would soon show as their physical wellbeing deteriorated.

When conditions permitted, they were made to exercise as before—the sailors singing their shanties and clapping their hands. The slaves stood in their chains, doing their best to steady themselves against the unpredictable motion of the ship. Sometimes stumbling and falling, pulling their partner down with them.

Two slaves, irritable from being shackled to one another, lashed out after such a fall, each blaming the other. As they lay in a heap, constrained at their ankles, the man on the bottom elbowed his mate hard in the chest as he tried to get up. The man struggling to get off him responded by laying a fist into the side of the first man's head. Instantly, the two started thrashing about, toppling the pair behind while the pair in front struggled to pull the combatants apart. The sailors were quick to respond, indiscriminately bludgeoning all six with their clubs to break it up. When order was restored, the dancing continued.

Conditions varied quite a bit on the smaller ship. When the wind calmed, slaves were released in small groups to perform various tasks. But other times the wind would stiffen, making any movement above deck very difficult. When it was rough, the slaves had to remain sitting, chained to the deck, as the ship pitched and bucked across the turbulent sea.

Spray continuously came over the rails during these times, soaking the slaves as they sat cold and shivering in the wind. No one among the slaves was accustomed to this kind of cold, and many became sick from exposure to the elements. In addition, their poor diet began to have its effect.*

In just a few weeks, their condition indeed began to suffer. Some

---

* *As on the middle passage, the bloody flux as well as scurvy were prevalent due to poor sanitation and food, and on smaller ships in northern latitudes, exposure from wet and cold added to the sicknesses*

had become lethargic from constant seasickness, poor diet, and unremitting exposure to the elements—all aggravated by the growing pestilence in the hold. It was as it had been on the big ship so long ago. Some lay listless in the hold, unable to move about, shackled to another who may not be as bad off. It became an additional irritant as some became frustrated with the burden of being attached to a dying person.

One woman cried out in despair as the woman she was attached to began having uncontrolled cramps and diarrhea. She fought desperately to drag the failing woman to the tub so she could defecate there, but it was no use. The ailing woman was too weak. Her diarrhea was constant, and her foul eruptions went everywhere. No one could help; some even became angry at the spectacle and its mess, as if it were somehow the sick woman's fault. It was an indication of the despair all of them felt, for again, being helpless in their situation.

Eventually, the poor woman became so weak she couldn't move on her own. When the slaves were brought topside again, the sailors released the frail woman and carried her to the side of the ship. The other slaves watched helplessly as the sick woman was tossed mercilessly into the sea. The splash as her body hit the water was the only sound they heard. It was just one more atrocity over the course of their experience—one more nightmare to live forever in their memories. In the coming weeks, three more would follow from the sickness.

Late one morning, as the slaves sat topside, the sky began to change. An eerie calm engulfed them. A solid, platinum-gray blanket suddenly darkened their world, sun blotted from the sky. The wind direction changed abruptly, becoming much colder as it stiffened. Menacing, dark blue-black patches swept across the sea—flat, furrowed with tight, dull texture—as strong gusts plied the surface. White caps quickly formed, slapping against the hull, exploding into fine, cold spray, instantly chilling anyone in their path.

Sailors yelled, moving frantically about as they adjusted sails to the rapidly changing conditions. In a matter of minutes, the schooner began to pitch wildly about as the helmsman fought the wheel, trying to bring the ship to heel in the fast-growing tempest. Hard, unpredictable gusts began to pummel the sails, knocking the ship suddenly and dramatically on its side, the slaves sliding and tumbling across the deck, smashing into whatever was in their path.

The captain, now on deck donning foul weather gear, stood next to the helmsman, bellowing, "Get them niggers below!"

The sailors began releasing the chains holding the slaves to the deck as the ship tossed and heeled sharply. The task was much more difficult as the hobbled slaves slid helplessly about. Two by two, the sailors struggled to bring them to the open hold, where they were pushed through, many times just falling below, unable to find the ladder in time.

Jayvyn became terrified as the ship suddenly became much smaller and more vulnerable against the sea. As the sky continued to darken, the noise of the wind and the crashing seas became intense, so much so that sailors standing next to each other had to holler loudly to be heard. Rain was falling in wind-driven sheets—mixing with seawater as it came rushing over the sides in ever greater amounts—washing into and over everything in its path, including the slaves.

Jayvyn recalled the storm he'd weathered on his first passage, remembering how towering waves dwarfed the giant ship, and he became acutely aware how small this ship was in comparison. He felt certain it would never survive such conditions. A panicky feeling seized him as he looked out over the endless water.

Suddenly the schooner was knocked much farther over, so far the upper yard arm met the sea. Jayvyn and Jacob found themselves hanging from the chain by their ankles on a vertical deck—the gaping ocean at their backs. In an instant, two male slaves tumbled past them, grabbing frantically at anything to arrest their fall, but the steepness of the deck was too much. They watched as the two slammed against the gunwale, the last redoubt against the sea. But it was insufficient to stop them as the ship lay completely on its side. The unlucky pair disappeared into the frothy ocean. Nothing could be done as they briefly fought the raging torrent, quickly becoming separated from the ship, soon lost in the confused pattern of the growing seas.

The schooner lay wallowing on its side for several long minutes as the ferocious gust played itself out, sailors and slaves alike clinging for life to whatever was nearby. Slowly, the ship began to right herself as the sails slapped wildly back and forth. The captain and helmsman shouted unintelligibly against the din of the storm while sailors sprang for ropes to lower and adjust sails as seawater coursed deep and green across the deck.

As the ship came up, the sailors quickly shoved the remaining slaves below.

When Jayvyn and Jacob hit the cabin floor, they saw all of the other slaves strewn every which way along the leeward side, fighting to untangle themselves in the chaotic hold— the hatch slamming shut behind them. Jayvyn's hip and side ached from his hard landing as Jacob crashed down on top of him. It was surreal. It had all happened seemingly in the blink of an eye. Not even an hour ago, they'd been dancing to the sailors' shanties on deck.

The slaves remained locked below decks with no food or water for many days as the storm raged on. Above, sails were shortened as sailors worked round the clock to manage the stricken vessel. Several times, the small ship listed so far over the slaves tumbled clear across the hold, slamming into the other side, landing in a heaped pile of interlocking limbs. Rain and seawater cascaded through the grate, keeping them all soaked and freezing.

Jayvyn and Jacob lay uncomfortably lodged within the shifting pile of bodies—everyone kicking and elbowing, trying to sort themselves out—only to be reshuffled when the ship smashed down on the other side. Nothing was recognizable as indistinct shadows swam through the darkness. Gravity held no sway; sleep was out of the question.

When the storm finally blew itself out, three had perished from being thrown about the hold. A few had broken bones, mostly ribs, but in one case, a man broke his arm. A child lay howling in pain with a badly broken femur. An adult had crashed down on her leg when she was tossed hard against the timbers. All of the slaves were bruised, many bloodied as well.*

After allowed on deck, chained as before, they watched as the

---

* *Remaining loose in the hold of a small schooner during a violent storm, particularly while shackled together, would be especially hazardous*

three dead slaves were brought up and dumped into the sea.

Still, the child with the broken femur, a girl of about seven, lay shrieking in the hold. A sailor went below to remove the shackle holding her to another child. The sound of her wailing was unbearable as two slaves gingerly brought her up and laid her gently on the deck.

The poor thing looked so small, so terrified, as she lay screaming in excruciating pain. Her leg was grotesquely out of line, a bloody, jagged bone protruding from her skin.

All sat frozen in fear as they looked helplessly on. Jayvyn couldn't help thinking of his little sister, Ifetayo, who'd probably be about the same age now. His heart crumbled for this little girl, who lay wracked in desperate pain, unable to comprehend. This, on top of whatever else she'd been through at such a young age. He thought, *How terrible a young child should suffer so.*

His sadness soon turned to horror when the captain came to assess the little girl's condition. All knew in their gut what was about to happen. This poor, unfortunate girl was beyond the scope of any treatment that could be provided for her.

The slaves began to shout and cry in protest as one of the sailors picked her small, terrified frame up. He carried her, screaming and howling, to the side of the ship.

"Please! No! NO! NO!" some screamed as others broke into hysterical sobs. But it was no use. The sailor released his grip, dropping the poor, screaming child into the sea.

Her cries abruptly silenced when she hit the water, vanishing unseen—lost in the wake of the moving ship—leaving only images in the minds of the grief-stricken slaves.

The girl must have drowned mercifully fast.

The other child who'd been shackled to her screamed inconsolably. "Emily! Emily!" he cried, over and over, mucous and drool bubbling from his tear-streaked face.

All of the slaves sat stunned and bereaved throughout the day. The sailors left them alone to process their grief.

Some moaned from injuries. The man who'd broken his forearm suffered unattended.

The storm had taken a devastating toll.

As with the previous storm Jayvyn had been through, it became strangely calm afterward as the seas flattened out—the sailors going about the business of putting the ship back in order. Soon, the sun reemerged, and they were back under way as if nothing had ever happened—and the days drifted on.

Jayvyn counted the number of slaves who'd perished over the previous weeks. There were ten fewer among them—four died from the bloody flux; two went over the side in the storm; three died from injuries in the hold; and, of course, little Emily, tossed out alive—all now committed to the vast, infinite sea.

They'd been at sea for a little more than three weeks when they turned toward shore. The sailors, once again, became busy making preparations to land. Jayvyn heard the sailors talking about the place they were going. They called it "Charles Town."*

Soon they were passing between a large gap in the shoreline. It wasn't the same as Barbados. The water appeared much darker in

---

* *Established by King Charles II of England in 1680 as 'Charles Town', it was later renamed Charleston in 1783*

color, the air felt different, too. The land on either side of the gap went off into the distance, farther than the eye could see. Beyond, the land was very flat, devoid of any hills or mountains.

As they entered the vast bay beyond this opening, Jayvyn saw many ships, all of varying size, within. Some very large, such as the one he'd left Africa on—tall masts with many parts attached by crisscrossing lines. Others were smaller, such as the ship he was on now. Some much smaller, sailing back and forth across the massive bay.

Off in the distance, he saw rooflines of many large buildings, masts of numerous ships silhouetted against their flanks. In the harbor, other ships rested at anchor, such as in Barbados.

They made steady progress into the large harbor, moving ever closer to the buildings in the center. As they drew near, he saw that the ships along the shore were tied up to great wharves. Many people and horse-drawn carriages bustled about. Eventually, their ship rounded into the wind and dropped her sails. The sailors splashed a large, heavy anchor off the bow, bringing the ship to a halt.

A small launch was lowered, and the master, along with a few other sailors, disembarked, rowing to the wharves beyond.

The bedraggled slaves remained chained to the deck, now four groups per chain, bruised and maimed from the rough passage. The sailors then drew buckets of seawater. Group by group, the slaves were stripped and washed down once more. Afterward, they were made to eat and drink, and put back in the hold for the night.

The sensation of being still after such a harrowing voyage felt unreal to Jayvyn. He looked around the darkening hold that only a week ago had been chaos. Images of the ship lying flat on its side as the two unfortunate slaves plunged headlong into the sea flashed through his mind. At the time, he had no doubt that neither he nor the ship would survive the terrible storm. Now it seemed entirely improbable that this was the same place, sitting level—unmoving—in the placid waters of a quiet harbor.

In the morning, the master arrived back at the ship. The slaves were brought back on deck, fed, and the sailors got busy readying the ship to move. The anchor was hauled up, and the ship made its way slowly, under a single sail, toward the wharves.

After tying up, a new man boarded the ship and went through the slaves, inspecting each one, making notes as he went. When he came to the man with the broken arm, he summoned a sailor to assist him. The sailor held the slave, and the man pulled hard on his arm. The slave screamed out in pain, then the man applied a stick splint wrapped in a cloth bandage. After his inspection, the man left.

The remainder of the day was uneventful; the slaves were allowed to rest and recuperate while chained to the deck.

The evening was calm, the air still and warm. Jayvyn and Jacob watched the South Carolina sky turn from a golden hue to the rich, reddish-orange color of papaya flesh. A million crickets chirped in the marsh as silhouettes of pelicans swooped low across the twilight sky.

The slaves were again fed, given water, and put below deck for the night.

As he settled against the damp planks of the hull, Jayvyn wondered, once again, what lay ahead for this new step in his journey.

- 28 -

Welcome to Charles Town

Notices had been posted throughout Charles Town stating:

JUST ARRIVED
From Barbados
A PARCEL OF EIGHTY PRIME, <u>SEASONED</u> NEGROS
all certified free from smallpox
and of Guinea Coast Origin
consisting of:
Thirty-One Men, Fifteen Boys
Twenty-Four Women and Ten Girls
TO BE SOLD
On board the schooner Dorothy
Captain William Thompson, Master
at MIDDLE BRIDGE on Tuesday the 16th Inst.
by David Phelps
cash only

The slaves were brought back on deck early that morning and, again, secured by chain to the deck. After being fed and allowed to drink water, they were stood naked in groups while the sailors came and lathered their bodies in palm oil, making them glisten in the morning sun.

Mr. Phelps, the broker engaged for the sale of the slaves, soon arrived and inspected the lot. Following his approval, he handed each slave a loose-fitting white gown instructing them to put it on. He stood back, looking the group over, and had the sailors arrange them according to his specifications. When he was satisfied, he summoned Captain Thompson to come have a look.

"These slaves should fetch a good price, sir," he said when Captain Thompson arrived.

"Indeed, Mr. Phelps." The captain responded with some pride. "You know how to make a good presentation with your merchandise. Well done!

"Now it is essential, as I have said, to emphasize the origins of these Negros as being from the Guinea Coast. I specifically acquired this lot in Barbados based on that criteria because plantation owners here have come to prefer Guinea Coast Negros over those of different origin. This distinction will command a higher price."*

"Yes, sir, Captain Thompson. I agree and will feature this prominently in my presentation."

People soon began to arrive at the wharf. The slaves were instructed to remain standing so the prospective buyers could have a good look at them.

Jayvyn noticed white women and children among the men. It was the first time he'd seen whites other than men, and he was struck with the sense there must be families among the gathering crowd.

The atmosphere was festive as people came aboard in metered

---

* *This was recognized by the colonizers of the Carolinas after seeing how the Africans possessed much greater knowledge than they regarding the successful growing of rice*

groups to inspect the lot of slaves. Men did all of the official inspecting, the women and children sometimes providing commentary from the sidelines.

"This one looks good,"

"Here's a tall one over here,"

"She looks like the right age."

As on previous occasions, the men squeezed their arms, legs, looked into their mouths, and lifted their gowns to have a good look at their genitals. Mr. Phelps stood nearby to ensure his merchandise was handled appropriately.

Occasionally one of the prospective buyers would speak to a slave, saying something like, "Tell me about the work you can do."

To which a slave would respond, "I work in de cane field."

And the white man would sternly respond, "I work in the cane field, SIR!"

The slave would then respond accordingly.

It was confirmation the slaves were indeed seasoned, understood, and could speak English, which was very valuable to the prospective new masters.

None had the slightest idea of the harrowing journey these slaves had endured, nor did they care. They were here to buy healthy, seasoned, obedient Negro slaves that would provide the greatest service for their needs, and that was it.

As Jayvyn noticed the families of these white people, he thought of his own family. He noticed a little girl, about the same age his sister, Ifetayo, peeking shyly from behind her mother's dress. He wondered if she had an older brother who played joyful games with her and if she engaged in the same silly antics he remembered his sister for.

He looked at her mother, wondering if she was like his mother had been—understanding, gentle, and good-humored when teaching and guiding her children.

These families still had the thing most important to them—each other. Jayvyn wondered if they knew just how precious that was as he remembered his lost family. He had a difficult time imagining what it might be like for these white people if they'd been separated, tortured, taken far from their homes and families, and now stood before a strange community of Black people, to be sold off like common goods. It was impossible. It never would happen. They couldn't know the reality or extent of what he and his fellow slaves had endured up to this point, and never would.

As he stood there in the mix of surviving slaves about to be summarily sold as commodities, he remembered his time in Barbados—his long episodes of labor in the sweltering fields—where he'd witnessed so many fall dead from exhaustion and malnutrition. He thought about those he'd gotten to know—Baahir, Andrew, Stephan, Sarah, Rose, ... He wondered what had, or would, become of them and their lives henceforth. Would they make another journey as Jayvyn just had? Stand covered in palm oil, waiting to be sold? Or would they remain where they were—to work and to die on the sugar plantation?

He remembered others—Julia, William, John—whose lives were so unfairly ended by the white monsters.

It was all so unreal. He'd just been out for a morning run one day when his world was irrevocably turned upside down. A day he'd thought, *'Today is going to be a great day.'* How wrong he'd been.

Mr. Phelps began ushering people away from the slaves, saying, "Gentlemen, please, it's time for the sale to begin. Take your place over here in the buyers' gallery, and we will get started," indicating a section of the ship reserved for that purpose.

"Thank you all for coming. As you can see, Captain Thompson has brought us a fine lot of only the best, seasoned Negros, straight from the sugar plantations of Barbados, where they received the most professional and thorough conditioning by masters highly skilled in the matter. These slaves have been broken of their savagery, taught to speak the King's English, and work obediently at the direction of their master.

"Furthermore, great measures have been taken to ensure they have never come in contact with the smallpox virus and have remained healthy and vibrant, as you can see.

"Additionally, and of great importance, I should like to point out that Captain Thompson, in his negotiations with plantation owners in Barbados, especially and specifically, selected slaves originating from the Guinea Coast region of Africa."

A murmur of approval swept through the crowd of prospective buyers, eagerly anticipating the start of the sale as Mr. Phelps continued.

"Now, gentlemen," he said as he motioned toward the first few slaves in the group. "We will begin with the boys, fifteen in all, who are an excellent investment that will only get better as they grow into strong, young men! My recommended price for these prime young Negros is one hundred twenty dollars. Do I hear one hundred twenty dollars?"

A man in the group raised his hand and said, "Here!"

but was immediately outbid by a man beside him, "One hundred twenty-three!"

who was then outbid by another at one hundred twenty-five.

The price ultimately settled at the high bid of one hundred twenty-seven as Mr. Phelps said, "Sold!! To Mr. Langford in the rear! Thank you, sir!"

The boy, seven years old at best, was shuffled to the side.

Mr. Phelps had arranged the boys by age, and prices increased as the age went up. Jayvyn and Jacob were in this group, near the end, and it wasn't long before they were brought to the front. Jacob was first.

"Gentlemen, we are nearing the end of our selection of boys; what am I offered for this fine Negro?"

A hand shot up, "One hundred thirty!"

immediately outbid by another, "One hundred thirty-two!"

and another, "One hundred thirty-six!"

and so on.

When the bidding stopped, Mr. Phelps accepted the high bidder at one hundred and forty-two dollars.

Jacob was moved to the sold section. "Thank you, Mr. Turner!"

Next was Jayvyn, who stood nervously in the front now as Mr. Phelps again announced, "Gentlemen, gentlemen, this will be the last of our Negro boys today. Can I start the bidding at one hundred thirty-five?"

Hands shot up as before, soon cresting beyond one hundred and forty dollars.

"One forty-three!" one man said,

"One forty-five" said another,

"One forty-seven!" waved the next, and the bidding stopped.

Mr. Phelps barked, "One forty-seven, do I hear one forty-eight?

"One forty-seven, going once, going twice, SOLD! For one hundred and forty-seven dollars to Mr. Turner, thank you, sir!"

And just like that, Jayvyn had been sold.

The man's name was Alfred Turner.

Jayvyn was placed in the sold section with Jacob and the other boys as the auction continued. Things happened fast. How the auction worked and who bought who was not at the top of their minds, but Jayvyn and Jacob would find out later the same buyer, Mr. Turner, had bought them both. In the meantime, they stood together in the sold section, watching as the auction continued.

Next up were the ten girls, the youngest appearing to be about six, who fetched only ninety-eight dollars, followed by a nine-year-old sold for one hundred and three, on up to the oldest at fifteen, who brought one hundred and twenty-four dollars.

Mr. Turner bought two of these: the first girl, of about six, and the last one, who was reported as fifteen years old.

The older girl was a remarkable-looking young woman. She was tall with beautiful features and smooth, radiant brown skin. She carried herself with a noticeable air of dignity, reserved and quiet, yet projecting overtones of striking intellect. She was truly remarkable and stood out strongly among the field of girls.

Then came the women, twenty-four in total, with the youngest at seventeen ranging up to an estimated forty-four years old. The women in their prime, somewhere from their early twenties to thirty years of age, brought the most out of these. The older ones brought less.

Mr. Turner bought two of these as well: a woman of about twenty-three and another slightly older.

Jayvyn mused that these two were about the same age as Sarah and Julia back on Barbados. A pang of sorrow passed through him as he remembered Julia, clutching the small doll made to take with her, as they laid her in her shallow grave.

The men were now up for sale. It was clear this was the most anticipated part of the sale as buyers pressed in closer, jostling for position. Ages appeared to start around sixteen and progressed to a few older men, whom Jayvyn took to be in their early fifties.

Mr. Phelps began. "Gentlemen, gentlemen! You are fortunate to be here at this sale. This is the moment you have been waiting for!

"I now present you with the finest, and I mean *the* finest, assortment of strong, hearty, adult Negro males I have ever been so lucky to represent! Many are suitable for breeding!

"We have thirty-one of these fine creatures, all seasoned and in their prime.

"Proven, hard workers, all broken and obedient, to accomplish your most arduous tasks from morning to night.

"I will start the bidding at one hundred fifty dollars!"

"One fifty-five!"

"One fifty-seven!"

"One hundred sixty!"

"One hundred sixty-three!"

"One sixty-four!"

"Gentlemen, I have one sixty-four. Do I hear one hundred sixty-five?

"Going once, …going twice, …Sold! To the gentlemen in front, for one hundred sixty-four dollars! Mr. Carter! Thank you, sir; you have made an excellent purchase!"

and the slave stepped to the sold section.

The sale proceeded with high-spirited bidding as the slaves were sold one by one.

The high bid for the men peaked at one hundred seventy-six for a tall, burly-looking slave. Even the man with the broken arm brought over a hundred and fifty dollars.

Mr. Turner bought four of these men. Two in their twenties, one in his mid-thirties, and one around forty-five.

The sale over, the buyers all cheered, then queued to settle up with Mr. Phelps as the slaves were arranged in their sold lots.

For the time being, the sailors merely tied the lots together with rope—binding their hands, extending about two feet of rope, then binding the next slave's hands—until the slaves in each lot were connected at their wrists by a chain of rope.

Jayvyn and Jacob looked curiously at each other as they became bound with the same rope containing the ten slaves Mr. Turner had bought.

As the buyers settled up and received title to their merchandise, they took their lots and led them off the ship to their waiting wagons.

The mood was very festive, with many of the men and their

families exchanging conversation as kids scampered gleefully about.

And so it happened—in just two hours' time, the fates of eighty Africans had again been decided. Now they'd be taken by their new owners to places unknown, have revealed to them the work they'd be given, and under what conditions they'd live.

Jayvyn took one glance back to see the entirety of the ship they'd just departed. The ship that had transported them all far from Barbados, across many miles of ocean, to this new place called Charles Town. He saw Mr. Phelps settling up with Captain Thompson, both reveling in the success of their most recent venture and looking forward to the next.

Not even present in their minds were the fates of the ten unfortunate souls lost during this voyage. That was just part of the cost of doing business; it was to be expected, and besides, the profits from the sale more than made up for any losses incurred along the way.*

No thought need be given to ten human beings—ten individuals tied to unique lives and pasts—who suffered and lost their lives on the harrowing voyage.

No—sympathies were not to be expended on the likes of Negros. They were, after all, inferior to the white race in every way imaginable—unworthy and incapable of productive, meaningful lives if left to their own. It was, in fact, charitable for the superior whites to recognize their duty, as prescribed by God and King, to save these miserable, aimless creatures from a meaningless existence by showing

* *Since African slaves were considered chattel property, no human value was ever assigned to them. In fact, they were specifically considered less than human*

them a life of industry, where their salvation might be enhanced through the gifts of labour.

This irrefutable concept was, after all, reinforced weekly in sermons delivered by preachers who, in their wisdom, pointed knowledgably to abundant scripture supporting this fact.*

It was thus that the new owners and their families returned to their plantations and other enterprises, safe in the knowledge they were serving God and mankind in the most meaningful and selfless way possible—by giving these God-forsaken creatures hope and a chance at salvation they otherwise would never have.

The slaves, of course, had a much different view as they bounced down the country road, tied into the back of a horse-drawn wagon—unfamiliar scenery unfolding as they moved ever further from their homeland.

Along the way, Jayvyn and Jacob surveyed their fellow passengers, who were doing the same. The only recognition came from what they'd seen of each other during the miserable passage.

Now they were together, a new group, to become fixtures of whatever enterprise this new master had bought them for.

It was uncanny Jayvyn and Jacob had landed in the same wagon, and Jayvyn looked forward to getting to know Jacob better. He was struck by how similar this was to he and Baahir ending up together after being paired on the ship from Africa.

He continued to look around, noticing a slave in his mid-thirties

---

* *In order to justify and perpetuate the slave trade, the diocese culled and distorted passages in the Bible, combining them with popular myths about race inequality, regularly delivering this doctrine to Christian congregations*

driving the wagon for Mr. and Mrs. Turner. The three sat together on a wide bench in front.

They traveled for hours, passing several plantations along the way. Slaves toiled in the fields. Some appeared to be growing cane, but others grew strange crops they couldn't identify.*

Jacob absentmindedly murmured, "Look, it be cane. You tink dat be what we be grow'n here?"

Jayvyn responded, "Maybe. It be what we do in Barbados, maybe we be do de same work here."

He shuddered as the image of William's bones swaying from the gibbet flashed in his mind, and continued, "I hope it be betta."

Each boy then fell back into their own thoughts as they reminisced about their individual experiences on Barbados—neither wanting to repeat them.

As the light began to fade, they finally turned down a smaller road leading to a large, white house, nestled on a wide lawn surrounded by big trees with long, mossy growths hanging from their branches. Next to it was a large barn, where the wagon came to a halt.

Black servants came to greet them and tend to the horses. The slaves were unloaded and stood, uncertain and confused.

"Bartholomew, show the new slaves to their quarters, and see to it they have something to eat," said Master Turner as he climbed off the driver's seat.

The slave who'd been driving climbed down off the front bench with a noticeable limp, saying, "Yassa, Massa Tuhna," as the other

---

* *Plantation crops in South Carolina at the time included cane, cotton, indigo, tobacco, and rice*

slaves took the horses from their harnesses and returned them to the barn.

Master Turner then turned with his wife and walked off toward the large white house—children burst forth from its doors, shouting happily as they ran to greet them.

Bartholomew, limping slowly, led the new slaves down a dirt road into the darkening woods beyond.

They walked for half a mile down the long, dark, dirt road surrounded by dense forest growth, finally coming upon a series of low wooden houses in a modest clearing. These were different from what Jayvyn had remembered in Barbados. The sides and roofs were covered in wood rather than thatched cane, and they had wooden doors and open windows with shutters to close them off. There was a chimney on one end.

Inside, they looked much better than what they had on Barbados, with platforms for sleeping stacked two high around the room. In the center was a table with benches and stools. Where the chimney was, there was a fireplace with tools for cooking. The floor was wood instead of bare ground, as in Barbados.

The group was separated by sex—the men and boys going to houses for men, the women and girls to ones for women. Each house had space for eight slaves.

They were arranged in the clearing, with six on each side facing the middle.

The clearing itself was about a hundred feet long, with about seventy-five feet between the two rows of houses. In the middle was a courtyard with several open fire pits with cooking pots. Fires were lit in them, and slaves milled about.

After the new slaves were assigned to their quarters, Bartholomew brought them out and gave them bowls for some of the food prepared earlier.

This in itself was different from Barbados, where they ate from a tub using their hands. Rough-hewn wooden spoons were also handed out that they could use to scrape the food from the bowls. Bartholomew told them these were theirs to keep and they'd each be responsible for their own.

The food was meager but seemed better than what they'd had in Barbados and certainly much better than what they'd had on the ship. It was a mix of grains with other vegetables, flavored by bits of meat of some sort, and very welcome for the new slaves, who subsisted on much less over their voyage.

Bartholomew sat with them and explained they had a garden plot that was theirs to grow their own food in. They were also given remains from animal slaughters as they were available. Occasionally, they caught fish from nearby freshwater sources and trapped small animals from time to time.

However, this all had to be maintained collectively by the slaves in what little time was available outside of work, and it had to provide for all of the slaves, which numbered around a hundred. Furthermore, they had to collect all their wood and manufacture everything, such as the furniture in the houses, the bowls they were now using, and the clothing they'd wear.

As they sat, Bartholomew asked their names, but it would take time to remember them.

The girl, of about six, was named Ann. The striking tall girl was called Hannah, the two older women were Rachel and Betty. The younger two men in their twenties were Paul and Adam. The one in his thirties was Daniel, and the oldest among them was Henry.

As they'd been taught in Barbados, they weren't to use their African names, so it was pointless to learn them as such. Here they'd use the names conveyed on the title given to the owner at the time of sale.

As they sat eating, a new slave came over. Bartholomew introduced him as Victor and said he was the boss of the slaves and would tell them what work they were to do.

Victor asked their names, looking them all over as they introduced themselves again.

He explained this was a rice plantation and they were now in the harvesting and processing season.

Jayvyn brightened up when he heard him mention they grew rice.

Victor asked who had experience with this crop. Several among them acknowledged they'd grown it in their homeland. Victor responded many of the slaves had similar experience, they were mostly from regions around the Guinea coast of Africa where rice was traditionally grown.

Javyn mentioned he was from the Gambia and his father had grown rice.

Victor nodded approvingly and responded, "Den you be good hep here. Massa Tuhna aks much from hid slave; you gonna work hard wid de rest o us. You und'stand?"

All nodded, and he said, "Good, den I see y'all in de monin," to which he turned and headed off into the dark.

After eating, the slaves all went back to their assigned quarters, where they found many of their housemates already in their bunks.

Jayvyn and Jacob had been assigned to two empty bunks in one of the houses. A few glances cast their way as they entered, but nothing was said as they each settled into their bunks. It had been a long and weary trip, and nobody was up for talking or doing anything but collapsing; they were just thankful their recent ordeal was over.

Thoughts swam through Jayvyn's mind as he settled onto the hard bunk. It was difficult to reconcile all that happened over the last several weeks, let alone today. Here he was in a new place, with new slaves about to begin new work, and yet, just this morning, he'd woken in the hold of the ship that had carried him so far from Barbados.

Images, of the storm—the ship crashing crazily across the sea, water pouring through the grating—dying slaves, ravaged by sickness—poor Emily slipping, broken and terrified, from the sailor's grip—passed through his mind, interspersed with sailors dancing and clapping as they sang their shanties.

Hills of Barbados receding across a light blue-green sea mixed with dark blue waters combing the South Carolina shoreline.

The clamor of the auction—the barking of the auctioneer, high-spirited buyers outbidding one another—rang in his ears.

The long, bumpy ride through the Carolina countryside blended with visions of the once familiar sugar plantation, the slaves' quarters in the distance.

Spanish Moss dripping from trees mingled with palm trees and the long walk down the dark, wooded road.

The fog in Jayvyn's mind slowly turned, creeping closer and closer, until all that remained was darkness and quiet.

- 29 -

Rice

The bustle of slaves moving about the cabin woke Jayvyn and Jacob from their slumber. Squinting in the low morning light, they watched as others came and went, readying themselves for the ensuing day's work. A pot of porridge hung in the fireplace, simmering over a low fire.

Victor soon arrived with a small handful of clothing and gave it to Jayvyn and Jacob. "You gonna need dem. Dey be used, but dey fit you good nuff. Put 'm on, eat, 'n come outside." At which point he left again

The clothing, although dirty and worn, was suitable enough, and soon Jayvyn and Jacob came outside, where they found the other new slaves. Victor arrived again with a man and two women.

Addressing Jayvyn, Jacob, and the four men, he said, "You six go wid Hecta 'n hid group to work on de new pond."

Then, turning to Rachel, Betty and Hannah said, "You tree go to hahvest wid 'liza,"

Then to Ann, the youngest, "You gonna work in de tresn'n yard wid 'cilla."

Hector, Eliza, and Priscilla then took their new charges and directed them to follow.

The group walked down a road that led from the slaves' quarters through a short patch of trees, soon coming out into another clearing where fifteen or so women were working at various stations. This was the threshing yard where Priscilla and Ann split off to do their work.

Women were threshing newly harvested rice with long sticks that had a shorter stick attached by a loop of hide on one end.*

Thwap! Thwap! Thwap! They repeatedly hit the rice stalks, spread out on a large, wooden mat, knocking the grains free.

Other women tossed the loose grains into the air with wide, shallow baskets—called fanner baskets†—chaff gently blowing off in the breeze.

Women with long pestles thumped rhythmically into log mortars to crack the husks off the grain.

From there, the rice was tossed in fanner baskets again to remove any remaining chaff.

When finished, the rice was deposited onto another large mat for inspection and bagging.

The rest of the group progressed further along the road until they came to an enormous clearing. The massive paddy stretched into the distance on all sides.

Many slaves, mostly women, straddled long rows in calf deep mud. Sun glinted off their scythes as they swept from side to side. Others gathered the cuts, bringing them to low wooden barges floating in canals at each side. When fully loaded, these would be poled to the threshing yard.

Here, Eliza split off with Betty, Rachel, and Hannah.

In the distance, trees were being felled across a large area in

---

* *These were threshing sticks which are specifically designed for threshing the rice stalks*

† *Wide, shallow baskets typically made from woven grasses*

preparation for another paddy. Sweat soaked backs of men sparkled in the heat.

A long, earthen hill bordered the paddies. Men with various tools worked silhouetted on its top. Hector led Jayvyn, Jacob, and the four other men to this spot.

Giving them shovels, he explained the pond beyond was being excavated. Clay from its bottom was used to create the long berm which would functions as a dam. The resulting pond was really the extension of a nearby creek and the source for the irrigation system they'd devised for cultivating the rice.

Jayvyn remembered similar systems his father and other growers used on their fields in the Gambia. Tributaries of the Gambia ran nearby. They embedded hollowed-out palm trunks in their banks to flood the low swamps for planting. Once the sprouts were established, they plugged the trunks and transplanted the plants to higher ground where they'd grow thick and high.

But what he saw here was of a much larger scale. They were actually changing the flow of the creek and creating reservoirs of water to irrigate much larger areas.

Jayvyn was amazed at the scale of the work being done. Slaves labored hard as they carried large, heavy buckets of sloppy, wet clay from the man-made pond to the growing berm. From there, other slaves worked it into shape. The berm was as high as a man, as wide as two, extending hundreds of yards into the distance.*

He, Jacob, Paul, Adam, Daniel, and Henry soon found their place

---

* *Salves transformed whole landscapes by hand in South Carolina and many other parts of the south as they created rice plantations*

among the other slaves and began wading into the knee-deep water. Shoveling the clay was extremely difficult. It was stiff and unyielding, even harder to break the suction to lift the heavy shovel loads to the bucket.

Carrying the buckets was even more arduous; they weighed a considerable amount. It was more difficult than hauling in buckets of seawater or carrying buckets of manure on the sugar plantation. It was the hardest work Jayvyn had ever done, requiring all of his strength. He struggled, slipping over the clay as he carried each bucketful up the berm to dump its contents. His arms and shoulders burned with exhaustion. Clay caked his body from head to toe, baking in the hot sun.

Many insects infested the swamp. Flies and mosquitoes constantly swarmed his eyes, nose, and mouth, biting wherever they could. It was impossible to keep them away. The mosquitoes were among the worst he'd ever seen, often lining up by the dozen on his arms, face, and the backs of his legs. Swatting them away was fruitless, as the very next second they'd be replaced by more.

As on the plantation, they took a break in the afternoon for food and a brief rest. Jayvyn and the other new slaves sat together while they ate. The food was similar to what they'd eaten last night, with the addition of dried beef. Other slaves came by to meet and learn about them. A man named Joseph was among them.

"My name be Joseph. Tell me who you be 'n where you be com'n from," he asked, to which they replied they'd just come off a ship from Barbados.

He smiled, nodded thoughtfully, and repeated, "Wha' yo name

be 'n where in *Africa* you be from?"*

One of the younger men told him, "I be Paul, I come from de Congo."

The older man, responded, "My name be Henry, I be from Gabon, it be near Congo."

The other young man said, "Adam. I be from Nigeria."

To which Jacob chimed in, "I be Jacob, I come from de Mankessim Kingdom."†

Jayvyn had never heard of these places. He had no frame of reference to know how large Africa really was.

He offered, "I be James; my home be in de Gambia."

Joseph nodded and replied, "I be from Guinea-Bissau; it be near de coast, somewhere sout o' de Gambia, but far, far from Congo. I know dis from some udda at de plantation what come from lotta diff'nt place in West Africa."

Adam remarked, "In Barbados, I learn West Africa be very, very big. No one can know it all. But de slave be take from many place."

Henry, the oldest among them, added, "In my village, many story be tell of farway place in Africa. Gabon got many, many diff'nt tribe dat come from far—too many to know. Speak many diff'nt language. Dey be many war. It be how I know o dem place. Gabon be very big,

---

* *For simplicity, most of the countries and regions of Africa are referred to here in their modern form. It would be far too complicated, and beyond this text, to refer to each as it was in its development during the period that this story takes place due to shifting colonization*

† *One of the fractious tribal states that made up the latter Gold Coast, eventually becoming the modern-day country of Ghana*

but Africa be bigga den we know."*

Paul agreed saying, "Congo be like dis too. Many, many people come from many farway place wid many story."†

The others all nodded in solemn agreement.

Joseph said, "Welcome to da rice plantation. You all be meet Victah, yes? Victah know de slave here come from all de Africa, but we all lef our home 'n now be here togeda. Now we be de same, wid many diff'nt story 'n past, 'n we all work 'n live togeda. Welcome brudda.

"We hep each udda, but you gotsta work hard, and dey be much to learn. If you got de question, you kin aks me, 'n I be hep you.

"Now we gotsta git back ta work; we got lotta mo work fo de day be done."

Joseph explained they had certain goals to meet each day before their work was done. The earlier they met these goals, the earlier their day would be done. This was in stark contrast to the way things had worked in Barbados where they simply worked from dawn to dusk. For this group, they were to advance the berm to a previously marked location. When done to Victor's satisfaction, they'd be done with the day's work. Therefore, everyone had an interest in the entire group working hard.

---

* *Africa measures apx. 5,000 miles from north to south and about 4,600 miles from east to west. Its area is apx. 11.73M sq. miles vs. the U.S. at 3.8M sq. miles; more than three times the size of the U.S.*

† *These regions in particular experienced enormous tribal immigration and ethnic mixing over a protracted period known as the Bantu Expansion which has resulted in over 400 distinct ethnic groups, speaking from 440 to 680 distinct languages, throughout the broad regions of Central and Southeastern Africa*

Victor made the rounds, checking on their progress. He worked with them for a short while before moving off to another area. His job was to ensure production quotas were met in all phases of the operation.

From time to time, a slave would walk by with a load of clay saying something like, "Let go, let go! We got twenty mo feet!"

Or "You slow man! Like my ol' granmotha! If'n you don't go fasta, we no eat tonight!" to which others nearby would chuckle.

In this way, they worked together toward completing the day's goal.*

It was the same for the other groups—so many barge loads had to be delivered to the threshing yard. The threshing yard had to process it all. Ultimately this resulted in an expected yield of finished product each day. If anyone failed to keep pace, the whole group had to work longer to produce the expected results. It was the system Master Turner had worked out, and he checked daily to make sure required quotas were being met.

There were systems of reward and punishment as well, although rewards were exceedingly rare and hard to earn. For instance, if a harvest was exceptionally profitable, Master Turner might allow the slaves to expand their garden, donate some old tools for their personal use, or give them a few bolts of cloth for new clothing. Very occasionally, and if Master Turner was in a very good mood, he might go further and give something unexpected, like blankets, which he'd once done when a new field had been completed and planted ahead

---

* *Known as the 'task system' among the slave owners of the rice plantations, it was considered a novel and innovative change to slave management*

of schedule.

On the other hand, poor performance would be met with punishment of the opposite nature. Needed items would be withheld, including restricting the remains of animal slaughter or withholding the dried meat supplements he regularly provided.

Of course, out-and-out disobedience or misconduct was punishable in the way the slaves had all come to know—whippings, time in the pillory, or other painful means as deemed necessary. However, Master Turner never administered the punishments. For that he relied on his overseer, Mr. Dawson.

Mr. Dawson was a large and serious white man. He tended to most of the big picture matters at the plantation. He was not often seen during the workday, but occasionally rode his horse out to the fields to check on one thing or another. He was often busy planning the plantation's growth—meeting buyers, developing distribution channels, arranging shippers, or any number of higher-level tasks needed for the busy operation. Often times he was off-site.

Victor, on the other hand, was responsible for day-to-day production and management of the slaves. He saw a lot of Mr. Dawson, to whom he answered directly.

In the evening, the slaves returned to the compound and began making the cooking fires.

The new slaves dragged in, exhausted from their first day's labor, made much worse from the trials of their recent voyage. Recognizing this, Victor excused them from camp duties, instead gathering them together as the fires were made.

All of the new slaves sat near the fire where they'd been the night before. The men, thoroughly exhausted, were covered with streaks of dried clay. Jayvyn and Jacob, being the youngest males, were especially sore as they sat stretching and rubbing their tired muscles. The three older girls, Betty, Rachel, and Hannah, looked drawn as well. Their feet and calves scratched and muddy from walking through the paddy cutting the harvest. This in particular didn't seem to suit Hannah, who sat with a particular sort of gracious dignity, trying to hide her disgust and fatigue. Little Ann stared off in a daze from her work in the threshing yard. All had worked hard on their first day, and it showed.

As they sat, Victor spoke to them. "Y'all live troo yo first day here; dat be good. Few slave get here in good shape, 'n I know you gotsta build yo strengt back, 'n so now you gotsta rest. But you gonna make de good worka here cause'n you know how to grow de rice. Y'all bring dis wid you from Africa. I talk to dem what take you to yo work dis monin, 'n dey tell me dat y'all know how de rice be grow'n 'n fixt."

Addressing the men, he continued, "Joseph tell me he talk to you 'bout yo home. Y'all come from all ova Africa."

Then turning to the rest, "How 'bout you, Ann? Where in Africa you be from?"

Ann, a quiet girl by nature, answered meekly, "My fambly be in Liberia."

Rachel put her hand on Ann's arm and said softly, "I, too, be from Liberia!" to which Ann beamed and smiled.

"Ah, good," said Victor. "And what 'bout you, Hannah?"

Hannah responded tiredly, "I be from de Kingdom of Ashanti."*

---

* *Also referred to as the Ashanti Empire, it was one of the dominant states during the 18th and 19th centuries of what later became Ghana*

To which Jacob straightened right up, exclaiming, "It be near my village! What yo tribe be? Where yo people come from?"

Hannah, looking surprised at his reaction, responded, "We be Asante; my village be in de city of Kumassi.* Where you be from?"

An unexpected and palpable tension suddenly filled the air. It was a situation Victor in particular had wished to avoid; however, now it was too late. This didn't go unnoticed by the others, who merely sat confused.

Jacob stiffened, unsure of how to progress. He lowered his head and voice and replied, "I be Fanti; my village be near Oman kesi mu in de Mankessim Kingdom." † and after a brief pause, he added flatly, "I know what yo people be, 'n I hear o yo village."

Hannah sucked in her breath and stared, adding nothing more; however, all could see something was not right.

Victor, picking up on the uncomfortableness of the moment, quickly moved on to Betty, asking, "Betty, where be yo village?"

To which Betty answered, "I be from a village in Sierra Leone."

Victor, suddenly more animated now, said, "I be from Sierra Leone too!"

Then continued, "My people be grow'n rice fo many, many life der; de name o my tribe no be impotant. We all lef de tribe long time ago, back in Africa. Many o we be from diff'nt tribe wid diff'nt story, but here we all belong to de same tribe—de tribe o slave, yes? It not

---

* *Today's spelling of this historic village is Kumasi*

† *Currently Ghana. Mankessim became the capital city of Ghana; which was once referred to as the Mankessim Kingdom where the Fanti people reigned from the 13th to the 19th century.*

be what we like, but I no hab to tell you dis. De mots impotant ting now be dat we survive togeda. Yes?"

The slaves around him gave a solemn, tired nod as he went on, "I got to tell you my story now. I arrive here ova ten years ago. When I got here, de white man be havin' great trouble growing de rice. He not know de right way to grow de crop, and it be we, de African, dat show him de way it be grow'n."

Victor went on to explain that the whites used to try to grow the crop in the highlands using European farming methods. They tilled the ground and scattered seeds over it, hoping enough rain would fall to make the rice grow. This didn't work, and their crops turned to weeds over the growing season, yielding very little and poor-quality rice.

Victor told stories passed down to him by the slaves before him about a time when there were far fewer whites as they began to colonize the area. In those days, he said, the relationship between the slaves and their masters was sort of a partnership. They were slaves, to be sure, but it was different because all were just trying to survive as they experimented with farming this new land.

He explained that the Europeans did as they were accustomed—clearing plots in the highlands for maize and a few crops, keeping some livestock penned, just trying to grow what they needed to eat. It was hard; many crops were wiped out by droughts and winter frosts, and the livestock stayed thin, leaving mostly just maize as they struggled to survive.*

Slaves, tending both the crops and livestock, convinced their masters to allow them to do as they had in Africa. Desperate for solutions, they consented.

The slaves allowed cattle to wander throughout the land as they did in Africa. There was plenty in the region for the cattle to graze on if given the freedom to find it. This also lessened the resources needed to raise them compared with the Europeans' method of keeping livestock fenced in. The cattle thrived—the size of the herd surpassed the Europeans' wildest expectations. There ended up being enough meat not only to satisfy their needs but the entire growing population of Carolina.† In fact, there was enough left over to export large quantities to Barbados as well, where it was sorely needed.‡

Victor continued to explain that the free-range cattle often found their way into lowland swamps in search of water—places like where they were now. Over time, the slaves recognized the creeks could be

---

* *During this time, it has been reported that the whites and slaves operated more as a partnership in the interest of mutual survival, but this was not to last. As soon as the plantation enterprises became highly profitable, due entirely to the expertise of the slaves, slavery reverted to its old way with slaves again being treated as nothing more than chattel property*

† *The area started out as the colony of Carolina, originally designated as 'the lands south of 36 degrees and north of 31 degrees extending from the Atlantic to the Pacific coast of America. It was divided into the smaller territories of North and South Carolina in 1712 so that each could be overseen easier by a single governor in each colony*

‡ *This became a significant boon for the Crown by creating a lucrative subsistence relationship between Carolina and Barbados. Carolina could provide beef, wood, rice and other resources essential to alleviating land use constrictions in Barbados while Barbados provided sugar, slaves, and white plantation owners essential to economic development in Carolina*

managed and lowland swamps developed, as in Africa, to grow rice effectively.

Once seeing this, the whites moved to the lowlands, and the slaves went to work developing rice fields. They started out much smaller, but once the white man saw how well the rice grew using African agricultural methods, he started to bring in more slaves to develop larger and larger areas.

Victor continued, "De rice bidness get very big, 'n now de white man grow fa mo den he need. He be sell it to de rest o de world. He get richa 'n richa, buy mo 'n mo slave ta work de land.

"Dey know de best slave for grow'n de rice be from de Guinea Coast in Africa; dat 'cause we be grow'n rice der fo many, many life, 'n we got de xper'nce 'n know how it be grow'd good.

"Now, rice be very good here, 'n de white men, like Massa Tuhner, be very rich, 'n dey forget'n it be de slave what make dem rich.

"Like de white men in Barbados, dey be greedy fo mo 'n mo, 'n will do what dey gotsta ta be richa 'n richa, 'n den life be harda fo de slave.

"Dey got de name fo rice now; it be call 'Carolina Gold', 'n call dis place be 'De Gold Coast.'*

"But y'all be know dat it be we, de slave, what make dis hap'n."

The tired slaves took this information in, some offering commentary on how unfair it was they should enrich the white man, only to be rewarded with cruel slavery.

---

* *Not to be confused with the Gold Coast of Africa, however they are both named for the same reasons: the profitability of the trade extracted from the areas*

Victor responded that this should be nothing new to the slaves, as it was what they'd been experiencing throughout their captivity.

"Dis no matta. It be de white man what hab de big ship dat go ova de sea, tak'n what he want wherever he go. We ain't got no powa to fight dis. Maybe dis change, but fo now, we gotsta live wid it.

"Now, de food be done, 'n y'all gotsta eat 'n rest."

As they ate, Jayvyn, Jacob, and Hannah sat near each other.

Jayvyn, remembering the tension apparent during Hannah and Jacob's prior exchange asked, "How you know what be each udda village 'n tribe?"

Jacob responded, "De Fanti 'n Asante tribe be make de war for de long time."

Hannah, hearing this, immediately stiffened, eyes narrowing into glaring beacons of hate.

She heatedly spat, "*Yo* people, de *Fanti*, raid *my* village! Dey take *me* 'n *sell me* to de white man!"

As the words spilled from her mouth, tears formed in her eyes. "I no *be here* if no fo *yo people*!"

Everyone in their group was stunned, not knowing quite how to react to the sudden altercation.

Jacob then responded, "How dis be? How dat pos'ble? It be *yo* people dat raid *my* village! *I* be take by *yo people*, de *Asante*, 'n dey sell *me* to de white man! It be why *I* be de slave!"

They both stared incredulously at each other. Both knew their tribes were engaged in long-term conflict. They both knew as well the common practice of each of their tribes to take captives during raids and sell them to European slavers. They were both speechless.

The rest of the group was now doubly stunned, really at a loss for words as they considered the awkwardness of the situation.

Victor, who'd sat eating and listening, finally weighed in.

Speaking in a firm tone, he said, "Listen to me! Dis not de first time we hab de fight between tribe. It be why I say—*we done lef our tribe in Africa 'n now be in de one tribe togeda.* It be happ'n afo dat anga be follow de slave 'cross de sea, but dis done neva make fo nuttin good.

"I tell you tonight dat my tribe no be impotant. But I say to you now one ting—I, too, be take by de udda tribe in my country 'n sell'd to de white man!"*

Now Victor really had their attention.

After a lengthy pause, he continued, "People in de tribe what sell me to de white man be here now! Here at dis plantation! But what good it be fo me to hate dem now? Dey be de slave jus like me! I work with dem *every* day! We all be de slave!

"I no say my tribe 'cause den dey know, 'n I tell everybody dey betta off widout dey tribe now. Many, many tribe in Africa fight. We fight fo many reason—in Africa, but dem reason *be in Africa*!

"Now, listen to me, 'n listen good! Forget yo tribe. Forget what bring you here! You here now, 'n dat be all what matta. It no matta how dis happ'n; it be de white man what bring you here 'n he own you now, 'n dis be what we all got togeda! Do you und'stand?"

Hannah and Jacob both looked down at their feet, understanding what Victor had just said was true.

---

* *The region of Sierra Leone as well as much of Africa, had abundant tribal conflict in 1700. In this case, Victor's tribe is the Limba who were harassed by the Mande who made a regular practice of selling their foes into slavery*

The other slaves, too, had seen enough conflict in their homeland to know the truth of his words and silently nodded their understanding. Nothing more needed to be said. If Hannah and Jacob had never revealed their tribe, neither would have had a reason to form a grudge.

Jayvyn thought back to his conversations with Andrew. About the futampaf's main lesson—that wisdom made the difference with decisions affecting the whole tribe.

In that moment, his respect for Victor established itself at the highest level. Here was a man like Andrew who had the wisdom to know his tribal affiliation no longer served his situation. It didn't mean tribe and heritage weren't important; they always would be. It meant *divisions* between tribes were no longer important.

It was the very thing Jayvyn had learned from his relationship with Baahir. What once was a thing that would drive them apart instead became the thing joining them together in a different space and time. It was a lesson he'd carry with him for the rest of his life.

The slaves had their dinner and did very little else. They just crawled off to their assigned quarters to collapse for what little time they had before the next day began.

Jayvyn lay thinking about the day's events as his arms and legs pulsed with fatigue. He felt some pride in the fact it was the Africans who brought the knowledge and expertise to grow rice in this part of the world; in that regard, he could be proud of their accomplishment and thus be proud of his work.

But he also felt the injustice of being forced into slavery, of being taken from his home and family. He knew all of the slaves resented this, every day and every night, as they suffered and died from conditions thrust upon them.

Jayvyn, again, thought about the white people and their families—little children dancing with joy as their parents lined up to buy slaves. He remembered the two children running from Master Turner's house, filled with glee, to welcome their parents' home from their trip. How happy they all looked to see each other. He wondered if they knew their slaves once had happy homes and families. He couldn't understand how they could not know this.

Again, he found himself thinking about his own family—about his father—working with them in the rice fields back in the Gambia.

How different that was. He had so enjoyed working with his father as he patiently taught him the fine art of growing rice. Now, here he was, worlds away, working on a rice plantation of all things.

He missed his father. He missed his life.

- 30 -

Life on a Rice Plantation

Work was brutal for the newly arrived and depleted slaves. It took weeks to recover their strength, but eventually they managed to meet the moment—always one step beyond what they thought they could endure.

Javyn, Jacob, and Henry, the older man, continued working on the dam and new reservoir. Being stronger and in their prime, Paul, Adam, and Daniel were sent to work felling trees on the paddy under development. Hannah, Betty, and Rachel continued with the harvest, and little Ann stayed working in the threshing yard.

Days at the new reservoir were long and hot. The crew struggled, hauling heavy, wet clay, bucket by bucket, from the bottom of the pond to the slowly growing dam. The daily goal was to add about twenty feet to the berm. With thirty strong men and boys working nonstop, twelve long hours a day, it was all they could do to reach it.*

Inevitably there were obstacles. A large rock or fallen tree would be discovered buried in the clay, slowing work considerably as the crew worked to remove it.

On one such occasion, the slaves converged to free a bald cypress

---

* *These earthen dams were typically around ten feet high and twenty feet wide. A twenty-foot-long section might require up to three thousand cubic feet of clay. One cubic foot of clay weighs about 110 lbs.*

from the bottom of the pond. The giant tree had long ago fallen and was completely immersed in the soft clay. Several feet in diameter at the base, it extended an unknown distance toward the creek feeding the pond. The water deepened considerably as it neared the creek, giving them an option. They could cut it off with a large bucksaw about twenty feet from the large end, leaving the top harmlessly submerged in deeper water.

This was no easy feat, however, as it required four slaves just to work the big saw under water. Additionally, the waterlogged wood continuously bound against the blade.

It took a good part of a day to deal with this as the four slaves struggled to work in water that was better than waist deep.

Other slaves were working to remove clay from around the larger portion of the trunk when suddenly a great commotion erupted among the slaves sawing. They began hollering loudly, splashing through the water, trying to run.

All of the other slaves immediately stopped to look. It took a few moments to realize what was happening.

An alligator had been spotted swimming toward the slaves.

Several nearby slaves grabbed sticks to assist with deterring the beast, but it peeled off in a different direction, apparently frightened by all the noise. When they could see it well, it looked to be about four feet in length.

"It not be a big one," a man working near Jayvyn remarked.

Jayvyn, still shocked by what he'd seen, asked, "Der be many mo?"

To which the man replied, "Oh yes! Very many! Some dem big

'n very dang'rous. Some slave get badly hurt; one man get dead. Gaita bite 'm real bad!"

Jayvyn remembered crocodiles living along the Gambia River and its tributaries. It was a big reason why he didn't swim or wade alone in unknown waters. But here they were working every day in water where such beasts lived. And, unlike his home in the Gambia, they were surrounded by miles of swamp in these lowlands.

Leeches, too, were everywhere in the murky brown water. Jayvyn found many feasting on his legs and ankles throughout the day, which was to be expected when standing in still water for long periods. He simply picked them off as he saw them, but his legs were always dotted with red telltales marking locations where they'd been.

After the alligator threat had passed, the slaves returned to the work of sawing the tree, finally succeeding in separating the trunk from the rest.

Removing the remaining portion of the tree required the combined strength of the entire crew as they pried the waterlogged mass from the muck and used ropes to haul it to the bank. Victor came to help. He took the end of a rope, yelling "Heave!"

All the slaves pulled in unison as Victor continued to yell, "Heave! ...Heave!"

The large ropes stretched and twisted, slaves digging their feet deep in the clay, bulging muscles glistening in the sun.

Other slaves levered long logs wedged under the hulk.

"Heave! ...Heave! ...Heave!"

Finally, the massive trunk moved, giving a long, slow sucking sound as it reluctantly broke from its mucky grave. Water rushed in to fill the void as the great log inched its way to shore.

When they'd finally accomplished the task, a cheer broke out. Exhausted but triumphant, the slaves collapsed in the mud, laughing and congratulating one another on their victory.

It felt good for Jayvyn and the other new slaves to share in this sort of camaraderie. It was a feeling that had been missing from their lives for a very long time. Jayvyn's admiration for Victor swelled as he watched the others celebrating with him. It was just one more example of his natural leadership qualities in action. He seemed to always have the good of the entire group in mind as he went about his business.

That evening, as tired as they were, all the new slaves chipped in with the rest of the group to make the fires and prepare the evening meal. This being Saturday night meant they'd have the next day off, so a different energy was in the air as the slaves ate their meal. Many made special efforts to engage cheerfully with the new slaves.

"Welcome to de plantation chil,'" one older woman said tenderly to Ann, who smiled in return. "We be good people heah, take care o our own. Don't you worry yo pretty lil' head none, heah?"

Little Ann nodded her head and smiled, revealing the space where she'd recently lost a tooth.

"Lawd chil'! Where yo tooth?" She jested, "You lose dat in da rice today? What Massa Turna gonna say?" she chuckled, at which Ann giggled in return.

Seeing this, Hannah reached over and put her hand on Ann's shoulder, smiling and giving her a slight hug as she did.

Many of the men who'd worked to remove the tree from the pond that day were in good spirits as they joked about the four slaves who'd run from the alligator.

"D'ju you see Marcus run? Ha-a-a-a! He look like a duck flyin' offa de wata! Haw Haw!" one said as he ran around the fire flapping his arms comically, eliciting much laughter from the other slaves.

Another joined in, exclaiming, "Dey scare dat lil' alligata so bad I tink he climb a tree! A ha ha ha!" as he slapped his knee.

More joined in on the laughter.

Marcus retorted indignantly, "Dat alligata wad eight feet long!" which only elevated the roar.

"Shoot Marcus! Dat alligata wan't no bigga 'n a squirrel!" More uproarious laughter ensued.

Jayvyn and Jacob, who were sitting together, easily joined in laughing with the rest as the image of Marcus fighting his way through the waist deep water came to their minds.

It was infectious, and soon many others in the large group were joining in on the fun.

More wood was thrown on the fires, which became big and warm as the slaves gathered around after their meal.

At one point during a lull, a lone woman's voice rang out, strong and melodious, through the silence:

I wanter go to heav'n when I die
To hear ol' Jordan roll
O brethren

Others joined in:

Roll Jordan, roll

Roll Jordan, roll

The woman who started continued:

I wanter go to heav'n when I die
To hear ol' Jordan roll

The group, now clapping their hands, responded:

Roll Jordan, roll
Roll Jordan, roll

As the song continued, the revelry built, with more clapping to the rhythm.

The woman went on:

Oh, brothers you oughter been dere
Yes my Lord
A-sittin' in the Kingdom
To hear ol' Jordan roll

Now the group was very energized, many getting up to dance as they sang their spirited response:

Roll Jordan, roll
Roll Jordan, roll

A lone baritone rang out:

Sing it over

The clapping continued, setting a perfect rhythm for the tune, as the woman picked it up again:

Oh, sinner you oughter been dere
Yes my Lord
A-sittin' in the Kingdom
To hear ol' Jordan roll

Roll Jordan, roll
*Roll Jordan, roll**

As the group of slaves slowly broke up that evening, the song continued to ring in Jayvyn's head. It was a joyous sound made better by the rest of the group as they clapped and danced rhythmically around the fire. It reminded him of similar times he'd enjoyed back in his home in the Gambia. It was like magic; in fact, the whole evening was like magic for him.

He and Jacob sat, along with a few other stragglers, by the dying fires that night, idly engaged in quiet conversation.

"We be long way from Barbados now." Jacob mentioned.

Jayvyn thought for a moment. "Wad dem slave on yo plantation like dey be here?" he asked.

---

* *Roll Jordan Roll, spiritual song of the slaves from the 1700's*

Jacob considered his question for a while and responded, “No. We work hard, like here, but no be happy like tonight.” and after a moment, “Many bad ting alla time.” he remarked.

Jayvyn tossed a small stick he’d been playing with into the fire. “Wad dey many diff’nt tribe?”

Jacob answered, “Yes, slave come from all ova Africa.”

There was a long, welcome silence as they sat watching the fire. Occasional pops and sparks flew from the mesmerizing flames as the two dwelled on their individual thoughts, feeling no urge to disrupt the moment.

The night was cool and still; a far-off owl softly hooted from some distant tree across the swamp. It was the rare kind of night where one’s thoughts had enough space and solitude to properly form into cohesive ideas—ideas that could be slowly savored and contemplated from a variety of angles.

Finally, Jayvyn said, “Dey be dis boy I know from de plantation in Barbados. He be chain ta me in Africa, ‘n we be on de ship togeda for de very long time. Hid name be Baahir, ‘n he speak de language I not know. We no talk, but we be friend. We be togeda ‘n we stay strong.”

Another long silence ensued; shifting firelight cast shadowy forms that danced with mysterious perfection against the black night.

Jayvyn went on to tell the tale of how he and Baahir had become separated on the beach. How Baahir unexpectedly turned up much later at the plantation. He told about the terrible punishment Baahir had endured for escaping the plantation and how he’d helped him improve his English while he recovered.

Jayvyn continued, "Afta we learn de English, we speak fo de firts time," he said. "I learn 'bout hid tribe, 'n he learn 'bout mine. Dem ting we neva know b'fo, all de time we be on de ship.

"He tell me hid people make de war, take African 'n make dem de slave.

"My tribe be very small. We hide from de war. Baahir 'n me be very diff'nt. It be hid tribe what come 'n take my land 'n people."

More silence engulfed the pair as Jayvyn gathered his thoughts together.

The fire continued to snap, sending long trails of orange high above their heads and disappearing into the night.

Taking another small stick, absentmindedly scratching random patterns in the dirt, Jayvyn slowly went on, "He splain dat it be how hid tribe believe 'n dat dey do dis fo many lifetime. Everybody gotsde place where dey gotsta stay; it be de same for de slave. He say it no be like de white man do. Slave in hid tribe be people what hab de life 'n be treated good.

"De people in hid fambly be farma like me. It be dey place, 'n it be where dey gotsta stay. I learn dat from him. He teach't me dat we all gotsde diff'nces. Dey no make we good or bad; dey just make we diff'nt.

"I teach't him too. He learnt dat we be all de same in many way; dat we all gotsde special spirit what make we who we be; it be de mots impotant ting we got, 'n we gotsta take care o dat."

Jacob, having listened patiently, then asked, "But he take yo land 'n people. Dat no make him yo enemy?"

And Jayvyn replied, "No. When I meet 'm, we bote be slave. It be like Victa say. Tribe no be potant now. We no got no tribe no mo; we all be just Black slave from Africa, togeda—slave to de white man. Dat be our tribe now.

"Baahir be my friend fo I know'd what be hid tribe. He hep me stay alive on de ship, 'n I hep him. Tribe no be potant den, why it be now? Victa be right to no say hid tribe. You see?"

Jacob took all of this in, pondering it quietly for some minutes. He was thinking of his recent and unexpected exchange with Hannah and Victor's admonition about tribal rivalries having no place in their new circumstances.

Jacob had seen enough of Hannah to know she was fundamentally a good person—or at least he had no reason to think otherwise.

It was only after learning she came from the tribe that had taken him that tensions arose between them. If not for that, neither of them would have had even the smallest reason to dislike one another.

He looked back at his friend and nodded, quietly adding, "What you say be de trut. Tank you fo gibb'n yo story to me. I gonna carry it wid me fo de long time."

Jacob continued, "Today we work wid many new slave, dey come from many place in Africa. I not know dem or what be dey tribe. I only know we work good togeda on de hard ting today 'n it feel good.

"I not know 'bout de past o dem people we laugh wid tonight. But I know dat it be good to laugh, sing, 'n dance togeda. It be much diff'nt den Barbados, my friend; I be glad you be here, too."

Jayvyn smiled at him. He felt as he had after his discussions with Andrew or Baahir—or with anyone else who shared kindness when it was most needed. It was the feeling that gave him hope when there wasn't much to be found.

The fire died down and had now dwindled to a glowing bed of coals. Several of the others had quietly dispersed, while the two friends became lost in their conversation.

There was no more to say.

They, too, quietly got up and returned to their quarters for a much-needed night's sleep, comfortable in the knowledge the next day was Sunday and there would be no early call to work.

– 31 –

Sunday: A Day of Rest

Morning dawned. It was Sunday—beautiful, wonderful Sunday! A day the slaves would have to themselves for personal business and to spend with each other. There would be no work on the plantation today.

Jayvyn thought back to how much he'd relished Sundays on the plantation in Barbados. He thought about his memorable moments with Andrew.

A special kind of morning quiet enveloped the compound. Slaves quietly rattled about in their quarters, speaking in low voices, going about their morning business. Some meandered in the courtyard, readying the morning fires. There was no rush, no agenda, making the day unique among any other of the week

One of Jayvyn's housemates stirred a pot of porridge simmering in the fireplace.

"Ah, g'mornin, Africa!" Frederick cheerfully said.

Jayvyn smiled. Frederick was often whimsical in his manner and had taken to calling Jayvyn 'Africa' instead of James. He had playful nicknames for others as well. It was a pleasant trait that made him affable among the rest of the slaves. He was the de facto head of their small household, always the first to rise and make a fire to heat their porridge.

Jayvyn, wiping the sleep from his eyes, responded, "Good

mornin, Frederick!"

As they sat at the table eating, others began to stir. Jacob was in his upper bunk, head propped on one arm, looking down at the two. Another man climbed from his bunk and was stretching as he yawned in the middle of the room.

"Where be my bowl? I gotsta get some o Frederick porridge dis mornin! I can't find my bowl!" he said comically as he feigned searching for his bowl.

"Oh, here it be!" he finally said as he pulled it from his bunk and came to join them.

"Good mornin, Matty! You always be so lovely in de mornin!" Frederick said as the man sleepily sat down.

Matthew replied, "You know what be beauty, Frederick." to which Jacob chuckled as he jumped down from his bunk.

"And what 'bout me? If he be bu-t-ful, den I de one what be outta dis world!" Jacob said, batting his eyes playfully.

"You, yes, yes! You be outta dis world, Jack-o! Like de little mouse what be live in de corner!" remarked Frederick.

The others brightened with good-natured laughter.

Soon, the rest of the small cabin came to life, and more was heard outside the cabin as well. A woman called out from somewhere nearby, "Dat be Frederick I hear? How be yo lil' chick'n dis mornin, Frederick?" she giggled as she walked by.

"Ah Harriet! Dat can only be Harriet! Your lovely voice give you away every time! My chick'n be fine, Harriet; dey be eat'n now!"

More chuckles were heard, both inside and outside the cabin.

Little by little, the slaves emerged from their quarters. The day was bright and still. It would be a good day to tend the garden, gather wood, or do any number of things on their day off.

Jayvyn breathed in the clean, fresh morning air, squinting as the early sunshine beat down upon his face. He was looking forward to working in the garden and maybe walking the nearby woods to get a lay of the land.

This particular Sunday, however, would not go as planned for the new slaves.

Bartholomew arrived at the slave quarters to speak with Victor. He'd been given instructions to gather the new slaves together and bring them to the barn. Mr. Dawson had sent for them.

As Victor went around to collect the group, the levity in the air began to vanish. Jayvyn and the others didn't know what they were being assembled for and asked Victor why they had to go. Were they in trouble somehow? Everyone had been working hard, and had no reason to think there should be a problem.

"Victa, wha be happen? How come we gotsta go to de barn?" Daniel asked.

They'd only heard bits and pieces about Mr. Dawson. His image loomed larger than life in their minds, as the others had only referred to him in the starkest of terms.

Victor merely said, "Come, you no do noting bad; you no be in no trouble. It be someting all de slave gotsta do, 'n you be back here soon. But you gotsta go wid Bartolomew, now."

The now uncomfortable group followed Bartholomew out the long, dark, dirt road, Bartholomew exhibiting that peculiar hitch in his gait.

Upon arriving at the barn, the new slaves slowed and stiffened when they saw what awaited them. A large white man stood out in front, arms folded across his massive chest. His face was hard and serious as he viewed the approaching slaves. The man, in his thirties, was easily as large as the largest among the slaves. He wore a wide-brimmed hat and had a pistol strapped to his waist.

This must be the legendary Mr. Dawson, the slaves thought. Indeed it was.

Once again, a fire had been made; a red-hot branding iron rested in its coals. Unbelievably, the slaves realized they were going to be branded again.

They stood, looking terrified, as Mr. Dawson surveyed the lot.

"My name is Mista Dawson. I works for Master Turner. I runs this heah plantation and oversees you slaves." He announced in a heavy voice.

"So's you's the new niggas. Looks like Master Turner chose a fine bunch. I hears y'all comes from the Guinea Coast, where's the niggas grow rice.

"What's your name, boy?" He asked, facing Adam, the largest of the slaves.

Adam nervously answered, "A-Adam, suh."

"Ah, you a fine-lookin nigga, Adam. You work hard for Master Turner?"

"Oh, yas'suh!" he replied.

"Good, now we's gonna make you official. Step ovah heah, boy." he said, motioning to the side of the barn where two other large slaves stood.

Adam, terrified, said, "No, please, suh; I no want ta be burn, suh, please!"

Mr. Dawson looked hard at him and said, "Now boy, it ain't that bad. 'sides, every nigga heah gots to be marked. Now, make this easy on yo-sef and it be done afor ya know it. Now step on ovah heah."

Poor Adam, seeing he had no choice, slowly staggered to the barn, where the other two slaves each took a side of him. One said sympathetically, in a low voice, "Look here, brother; ain't no udda way. You just stand still, and we make dis easy as we can."

Adam looked at the two, realizing they were just following orders. He leaned into the barn and steeled himself for what was to come.

Mr. Dawson picked the red-hot iron from the fire and moved toward him. Adam closed his eyes and faced the other way. His whole body shook with fear as one side of his pants was suddenly jerked down, and the scalding hot iron was pressed into the right side of his buttock.

His skin sizzled as he cried out through clenched teeth, beads of sweat dripping from his forehead. It was over in a matter of seconds, as it had been on the two previous occasions, and once again, palm oil was rubbed over the painful burn.

He was released and hobbled off to the side, his new wound throbbing beneath his clothes. He now wore the brand of Alfred Turner—a shape combining "A" with "T" in a unique pattern heretofore identifying him as Alfred Turner's property.

The other slaves, having witnessed what they'd have to endure, cowered in anticipation.

The girls whimpered; little Ann cried hysterically.

Mr. Dawson turned to the group saying, "Let's git this little one outta the way so's she can stop cryin."

Ann hid behind Betty, clinging to her dress as the two slaves approached, her face wet with tears.

Betty pried her gently from her side saying, "It be ok, honey; dey be gentle. Now go on; you gotsta do dis."

The slaves took the wailing girl to the barn and held her, lifting her dress to expose her smooth, brown bottom. Mr. Dawson was ready and planted the scalding iron firmly in the spot he'd chosen as she shrieked out—a thin trail of smoke rising up. When it was over, she ran to Adam, who hugged her tight to his waist. She buried her face and cried.

Stroking the back of her tiny head, he said, "Der, der, it be over now, sweet chil', ain't gonna be no mo. Der, der," as she sobbed into his thigh.

The women were next, bravely stepping up in turn, trying to remain stoic as they knew there was no point in fighting. As with the others, when the moment came and the iron seared into their skin, no amount of restraint could keep them from crying out.

Then they, too, moved to the side with Adam and Ann. Little Ann, again, turned to Betty for comfort.

And so it went, each slave submitting to the inevitable as they were held fast by the other two slaves; the red-hot iron scorched into their bodies, tears forming in their eyes—soon to be coated with palm oil.

When it was all over, Mr. Dawson looked pridefully at the group and said, "Thar. Now that wan't so bad, were it? Now's yous like all the otha niggas heah. You be right back to regula in a few days an won't rememba a thing.

"Go on now, this yo day off. Go an enjoy it; you be back to work tommora."

He turned to go about the rest of his business like nothing had ever happened.

Tears still in their eyes, the wounded slaves marched slowly back to their quarters.

Jayvyn now had three separate brands burned into his skin. Each one signifying a transfer of ownership—from one hellish chapter to another. The burn would sting for days as his body fought to recover and produce yet more scar tissue to repair the wound.

When they got back to the slaves' quarters, they were greeted by some of its members with warm embraces and sympathy. The older woman, who'd sat with Ann the night before, was among them. She held out her arms, and Ann went to her, burying her little face into her dress.

The woman, Margaret, comforted her as tears came to her own eyes.

"Oh, chil', sweet lil' Annie. Precious lil' ting like you should neva hafta suffa. It gonna be okay, chil'. Miss Mahgrit, heah hep you feel betta. Now c'mon chil', we gonna find sumpin' to do," taking little Ann by the hand.

Other women were there to comfort Hannah, Betty, and Rachel, as well, and they, too, strode off to the courtyard together.

Victor was there as well. Daniel, who'd asked him before what it was all about, spoke up, saying, "Victa, how come you no tell us 'bout wha gonna happen at de barn?"

"Would dat be betta?" Victor responded. "Noting I can do to change it. We all gotsta be marked." He said as he pulled the side of his own pants down to show them his scar.

"Tellin you only make de walk harda, it no change notin'. Betta you find out der. Everybody know dat de new slave gotsta be brand'd; no one like it. Now we all de same."

The five men knew Victor was not to blame and didn't harbor ill feelings toward him. He was right. Knowing what was to come would have only served to enhance their agony with additional fear and trepidation. Besides, now it was done, and the healing could begin.

When they got to the courtyard, they found a meal had been prepared for their lunch—a hearty stew with rice, vegetables, and meat sausage. Many slaves came around offering their sincere sympathies, acknowledging the pain and lost dignity they were suffering. It was a small consolation—a sort of rite of passage to the community of slaves they were now officially part of.

After the meal, Jayvyn went to the garden to weed and help with the plants. It was where he liked to be most on Sundays. The other men went off into the woods to check traps, fish, or gather wood. Margaret began teaching Ann how to sew. The other women busied themselves in some way, whether in the garden or working on some project. It was the best way to pass time and not dwell on the pain.

As Jayvyn worked in the garden, Hannah came to work with him.

He'd been curious about Hannah and wanted to get to know her better.

Jayvyn had noticed her on the ship. She had a kind, thoughtful face, mostly kept to herself, and seemed to remain poised over the desperate journey.

She settled in beside him as they weeded a patch of yams.

After a few moments, Hannah said, "You and Jacob be chain togeda on de ship, yes?"

Jayvyn replied, "Yes."

She continued, "Did you know him well, James?"

Jayvyn thought back to the time and said, "No. We no be togeda in Barbados, only on de ship."

After a thoughtful pause, she went on, "I be tinkin 'bout de udda night, when Jacob say he be Fanti. You be der. You know our tribe be bad enemy in Africa."

Jayvyn listened patiently as Hannah continued.

"Dis not always be de way. It be said dat de Fanti be one wid de Asante five hun'red year ago; we all be Akan and live in a much diff'nt place in Africa.*

"Our past be complicated, but de Akan split into many smaller tribe a long time ago. De Fanti go first to de coast in de place where we live now, 'n we follow afta 'n be part of de much bigga Denkyira Kingdom inland.

"De Fanti stay by demsef 'n trade peacefully wid de Denkyira. But, de Denkyira be arrogant to we, 'n we hate dem.

"Our leader d'cide we gotsta make de war on dem.

---

* *The Asante and Fanti were originally part of the Akan tribe inhabiting the Sahara region in north eastern Africa. The Akan splintered into many tribes that migrated to different regions of Africa*

"De name of my tribe, Asante, mean 'because of war' in our language. It be de name we take when we rise up 'gainst de Denkyira. Our tribe got many fierce warrior who be die afore agree'n to such arrogance."

Jayvyn listened with fascination as this poised and reserved girl described her people and their violent ways.

"On de day of war, our warrior take de Denkyira king 'n kilt'm. Hid body be cut into tree part 'n sent to our tree leader, 'n dey make de Kingdom of Ashanti.*

"We join wid many udda Akan tribe 'n now be very powerful, but de Fanti remain by demsef. Dey be stubborn. Dey control many valuable and impotant trade route to de sea, 'n dey got rich deal'n wid de white man.

"We be rich wid de gold 'n got many udda valuable ting fo trade, but dey block de trade route, 'n dis be de reason we fight.

"It be true dat our way be to raid de udda village 'n take de people to sell like slave."

Hannah's voice had hardened and risen a notch. Jayvyn glanced over to see her countenance had changed as well. Her look reminded him of Baahir when he was expressing his outrage at the injustices of the white man.

Hannah continued, "My mudda be oba panin in our village. It mean she be de queen mudda. Her brudda, my uncle, be odikro, de chief.

"My mudda be de very impotant person. I 'post to be follow her.

---

* *This is a very truncated and simplified version of the otherwise fascinating and complex history of the Akan people and their migration into the region of Ghana*

"In my tribe, it be de women dat got de most impotant part.*

"When de Fanti take me, it make great trouble for my people."

Jayvn listened, but found it difficult to process everything she was telling him, much less formulate an adequate response. Many minutes passed as they continued to fidget with weeds and other matters of cultivation in the yam bed.

Jayvyn thought about all she'd said and his conversation with Jacob the other night.

Finally, Jayvn said, "You say dat de Asante 'n Fanti be de bad enemy 'n dat dey gotsta take each udda blood. It be 'bout bigga welt 'n powa.

"But you say dat each o yo tribe got mo dan dey need. It be yo pride dat keep you from join'n togeda—yet once, long time ago, you be togeda."

Hannah listened quietly as Jayvyn related his understanding of what she'd told him.

Jayvyn silently focused on the patch he was working for a few more minutes before continuing.

"Now you be find yo enemy here wid de slave, far, far from yo land. Yes?"

He glanced at Hannah and saw her eyes moist with the beginnings of tears. Her face had reverted, once again, to calm.

"Yo people be make great bad to Jacob, 'n hid people be make

---

* *In the Asante tradition, the oba panin is the "queen mother" of a village and advises the chief in all matters of importance and carries much weight in their political and social order. There are other queen mothers at higher provincial levels up to the highest that is at the head of the entire tribe.*

great bad to you. So now you gotsta take Jacob blood, 'n den everyting gonna be good. Yes?"

Hannah didn't answer but sat back on her heels, her head bowed in quiet contemplation.

Jayvyn went on, "You no aks me 'bout my people, but I gonna tell you dat you not gonna know 'bout us.

"We be de very small tribe, 'n we stay way from all de war. We no look fo power 'n be very happy wid what we got.

"In de same way, I not know 'bout yo tribe or Jacob 'fo you tell me 'bout dem.

"How I know I be chain to one so bad 'n evil like Jacob?!"

He glanced over again, raising one eyebrow in mocked concern.

Hannah looked back at him. She couldn't help herself as a sheepish grin overtook her.

"And I not know dat you be de prin-cess!

"Forgive me, prin-cess; I gonna bow to you from now on!"

At this, Hannah gave a slight giggle as she wiped the moisture from her eyes, saying, "No, James, I no be de princess; it not be like dat.

"My mudda be only de head of our village, not of all our people. Still, it be impotant."

Jayvyn, trying to preserve the right amount of respect, thought about this for a few minutes more before continuing.

"But now you be here. And dis no be Jacob fault any mo den it be yo fault dat he be here.

"Did you know dat Jacob be take to slavery mo den seben year ago?"

Hannah, looking somewhat surprised, replied, "No. Dat be long 'fo I be here! I lef my village one year ago."

"He tink he be six year old when he be take. Do you tink he know all dat you know 'bout de reason yo tribe fight?"

This got through to Hannah. She paused to consider the innocence typical of all children that age. She, too, had a little sister back in Africa—about the same age difference as Jayvyn and Ifetayo.

Her sister was five when Hannah was taken.

Hannah pondered how she and her family had taken care to spare her little sister the harsh realities she'd inevitably face in just a few short years.

She remembered how she herself was eight when her mother started to teach her the things she needed to know to one day fill her shoes, recalling how the innocence of her childhood sadly began to ebb away.

It would be the same for her little sister now. She'd be groomed for succession in Hannah's absence. She hoped her little sister would be able to savor the innocence of her remaining childhood years as Hannah had.

She also thought of little Ann—the child among them now. She wondered how young she'd been when taken into slavery—all the things she must have lost. How terrible to be suddenly taken from her family and childhood innocence—forced into the cruel world of slavery so young.

She immediately felt selfish about her recent rant—about how her dignity had suffered—about the hardship her tribe incurred when she was taken. Of course, this was true. Her mother and members of her tribe must have been very sad.

But what of Ann's mother, or Jacob's, when they discovered their children gone, forever stolen from their lives, sent off alone on the white man's ship?

When Jayvyn related how his mother and little sister had been taken—how they'd been separated on the beach, never to see one another again—she realized how much worse it could have been. To endure the terribleness of her ordeal knowing her little sister had also been taken, sent off alone to places unknown. Hannah had to admit to herself, as terrible as things were, they really could be worse.

Remembering Jayvyn's last question, Hannah finally responded, "I no tink Jacob be dat young. He be de small chil.

"He no can know such ting at dat age. He no can und'stand de reason our people fight 'n raid each udda."

They spent the rest of that afternoon in the garden together, both feeling the raw pain of the burns they received only that morning.

It was a constant reminder that the rich lives they'd once known were now a distant shimmer, their pasts receding further and further into their memories.

Now, new memories, such as Jayvyn had been collecting since his capture, stacked up in their place—changing the narrative of their lives from what they might have been.

Hannah would not become a queen mother to her people any more than Jayvyn would become an elder in his tribe.

- 32 -

Family Life on the Plantation

Time marched inexorably on, days folding into weeks. Work was measured in unending buckets as Jayvyn and the others toiled on the new reservoir. The work was slow and tedious, but progress was manifest in the results. The dam now turned to border the new paddy and two trunks, or gates had been installed, one for each paddy.

The construction of the gates fascinated Jayvyn. They functioned in the same way as the hollow palm trunks his tribe used back in Africa. Only here, a large wooden box was constructed for water to flow through. It was controlled by a gate that could be raised or lowered to allow or prevent water from flowing from one side to the other. At each gate, the earthen dam was heavily buttressed with logs to prevent its erosion. Construction was complex, but when completed, it formed an effective breech that could be controlled to flood or drain the paddies quickly.

According to what Jayvyn was told, the knowledge for this ingenious system was brought by Africans from Siera Leon who farmed large rice fields in lowlands near the coast.

Jayvyn derived a certain amount of pride just knowing this kind of expertise came from fellow Africans. That and the system of canals in the paddies is what made it possible to grow rice in the lowlands. It inspired him to learn and care about the work he was doing. It was how he'd felt working with his family back in Africa. Feelings of accomplishment like this went a long way in his circumstances.

Saturday evenings and Sundays yielded similar satisfaction as he gathered with the other members of his community. They were good people who made the best of their circumstances, carving out meaningful lives in different ways. Singing, dancing, and telling stories around the fires illuminated the personalities of those around him. Relationships grew, engendering a sense of family.

Families in the traditional sense were created as well.

Although bearing children was encouraged by Master Turner, this often proved to be difficult under the conditions in which they lived.[*] Master Turner tried to help this by giving pregnant slaves 'three quarter hand' during the final weeks of their pregnancy.[†] Still, many pregnancies ended in miscarriage; many babies were stillborn because the work was hard, nutrition was poor, and many diseases came out of the stagnating waters of the rice paddies. If they lived, many children would die before their first or second birthday from malaria or other infectious diseases. It took many pregnancies to have one or two babies grow past the age of five.[‡] To his dismay, Jayvyn further discovered any babies born to a slave would first and foremost be

---

* *Slaveowners encouraged reproduction among their slaves, chiefly in the interest of breeding new slaves, and thereby avoiding the acquisition costs. Also, if a child could be raised as a slave on a plantation, it was likely to need less in the way of training and discipline*

† *'Three quarter hand' was the practice of reducing a slave's work requirement to three quarters, many times for the purpose of bearing children*

‡ *Although fertility rates were high among slaves on rice plantations in the 1700's, it is accepted that many pregnancies ended in miscarriage or still birth. It is estimated that out of every 1,000 live births 350 infants would die, and that another 201 would die before their fifth birthday*

property of the slave's owner.*

Several children did survive to run around the quarters over the years, many of whom Jayvyn came to know. They were fun, bringing much joy, both to their parents and others, with their unlimited antics.

Two children in particular were Michael and Lydia, a brother and sister born to Silas and Clara. The two were only a year apart, and were ever the little clowns. Jayvyn and others delighted in watching them play endlessly in the courtyard; there was no end to the things they'd dream up. Jayvyn knew them since they were born. They came after several failed pregnancies, so when the two were born one right after the other, it was like a gift from heaven.

Clara and Silas were good parents. They loved their children more than anything. Clara came in from the fields three times a day to feed them while they were on the breast, then left them with Old Margaret, who stayed behind during the day to look after all of the children too young to be left alone. When Michael and Lydia got to be a bit older, their parents played with them all the time when they were off work.

As is true for most parents, Clara and Silas could think of little else. Their bonds to the children grew and deepened beyond anything they'd ever known. The children were simply their world.

Jayvyn had always enjoyed children. They reminded him of his sister and were always so fun to teach and listen to. These two kids

---

* *A legal doctrine was passed into law in 1662 called 'partus sequitur ventrem', which translated means "That which is born follows the womb". This meant that a child born to a slave inherited the legal status of their mother and was considered the chattel property of her owner*

often came to help him out in the garden. They were so curious and wanted to learn every little thing they could about plants. Jayvyn spent much time explaining what each was and the things that made them grow. Their childlike fascination with the smallest things was infectious. They conjured warm memories of him and Ifetayo sharing similar moments as their father patiently taught them.

Jayvyn enjoyed watching Michael and Lydia as they became lost in wonder, watching a worm wiggle in the soil, laughing at their shock as it suddenly disappeared into the dirt when they touched it. An anthill was the source endless amusement as they watched the ants come and go in long lines carrying leaves and things many times their size. Everything was new and enchanting; they were so inquisitive.

Jayvyn created a special section in the garden where the kids could plant a few seeds for themselves. Michael and Lydia came every day to look at the bare patch and see if anything had appeared, carefully pulling any weeds that might have found their way in. When the new sprouts finally broke through the soil, they clapped and danced with glee. Then they came every day with a little water just for their tiny plants.

Jayvyn looked on fondly as they squatted before the little patch, willing the tiny sprouts to grow before their eyes, talking quietly to the seedlings in their soft, small voices. The plants did grow over many weeks until blossoms formed, then wilted, finally yielding to emerging pods of okra. The children were so proud when they picked and brought their small harvest home for cooking. Silas and Clara gladly obliged. They created a special banquet just for them, which Michael and Lydia savored with great delight. The kids even saved a few bites for Jayvyn, which they presented with huge smiles.

Michael took great pride in helping his father gather wood. Other men chuckled as the four-year-old struggled behind Silas with a piece of wood nearly as big as he was. Lydia, too, was often seen helping the ladies around the cooking fires at night. She worked with her mother to prepare vegetables or measure rice, doing her best to look as grown up as the ladies around her.

When big enough, Michael and Lydia were brought to the fields. It wasn't so much that they wanted to go as were ordered to by Mr. Dawson, who wanted some work out of them. They were, after all, Master Turner's property.

They mostly worked in the threshing yard but also came to the fields to hoe and weed with their parents. The paddies could be dangerous for small children, however, as many hazards plagued the still water, not the least of which were poisonous snakes. Occasionally someone would run afoul of a cottonmouth or copperhead. Although seldom deadly for adults, children were a different story.

For Michael and Lydia, though, it was gratifying to join their parents and others doing the important work of adults. After all, they idolized grownups for being the good role models they were and wanted to be just like them.

One evening, when the work day was done, after the kids had gotten to be around eight and nine, Mr. Dawson came to inform Clara her children had been sold. There was no warning. Mr. Dawson was quite matter of fact about the whole thing. Just one more detail he had to attend to before his busy day was done.

Poor Clara collapsed in a fit of tears.

"No. NO! Please Missa Dawson, not my chillin'! Oh no no no!" she cried.

Mr. Dawson said coldly, "Now you knows, Clara, yo chillin belongs to Master Turner, and he can sell 'em if'n he wants.

"Now there aint't nothin you or I has to say about it. Them kids is sold an will go out to their new owner tonight, like any other nigga's been sold."

At that moment, Michael and Lydia, who'd been helping their father prep the evening meal, came walking back to their quarters. As they approached, they saw their mother was visibly upset, speaking from the doorway with Mr. Dawson.

Clara quickly ushered both kids into the cabin and stood defiantly in the doorway, pleading with Mr. Dawson not to take them.

Silas, who'd been working near the fires, looked over. Having taken notice something was amiss, he began to approach.

"Missa Dawson, wha wrong? Clara? Wha be wrong da'lin? Wha it be?" His pace quickening as his concern grew.

Mr. Dawson turned and said, "Now Silas, take it easy son. You's kids been sold by Master Turner and they's to come with me. Don't do nothin' foolish, heah?" as he placed his hand on the grip of his pistol.

"Missa Dawson! No! NO! You's can'st take 'em! Dey us babies! No-suh! NO!"

One of the other slaves, who'd followed Silas over, put his hand on his shoulders and said, "C'mon now Silas, don be makin' no truble fo yosef heah; dis de law an you can'st do nuthin' bout it."

Silas fell to his knees, sobbing and pleading to Mr. Dawson, who turned back to Clara, taking her by the shoulders to move her out of the doorway.

"C'mon you kids, you comin wid me, now, heah? Gits' what you needs 'n come out heah, I ain't waitin' round no more."

Clara tore from his grip, running to embrace her children, panic-stricken at the thought they were to be taken immediately and this would be the last she'd ever hold them.

Tears pouring down her cheeks, she took them both to her, and sobbed, "Oh Lidya, Michael! My babies!

"Dey be takin you!"

Between big heaving sobs, she continued, "Ain't nuthin I can do chil's! Oh-h-h! Lawd! Oh Lawd! Why, Why?"

Mr. Dawson, becoming impatient said, "Let's go now."

Silas, on his knees in the dirt, bawled out from his tear-streaked face as the other man held and consoled him from behind, "Missa Dawson, please! Please, suh!"

But it was no use.

Mr. Dawson said, more firmly now, "Clara, brings dem kids to me now! I ain't gonna be wastin' no mo time, heah? You know's wha's gonna happen if'n you don't! C'mon now!"

Clara and the others had seen this play out before. Children, parents, spouses, it just didn't matter. She'd seen when a mother had been sold, without notice, and taken from her home and children. She'd seen couples, deeply in love, split up for the same reason. She'd seen fathers whipped to near death in front of their families for resisting.

All the slaves knew they had no say in such matters. They were

Master Turner's property to do with as he pleased. No amount of crying or begging could change a thing.

Mustering her strength, steeling herself for what she knew she had to do, Clara said, "C'mon chillin, it be alright now. You's gotsde new massa somewhere.

"Maybe it be betta 'n heah, an' you git de betta life.

"Now, come, missa Dawson gonna take you.

"Say good bye to yo pappy now, you got to go."

Sobbing, she brought her two children to the door, where Mr. Dawson fastened a rope to their wrists.

Silas, still kneeling and sobbing in the dirt, rose unsteadily to his feet.

Mr. Dawson, placed his free hand back on his pistol, saying, "Now, Silas, keep yo head an' don't do nothin stupid, heah?"

Silas came and hugged his two children tightly.

Through his tears he said, "You be good chillin, we love you, be good an' maybe we git ta see you agin someday."

And then he slowly released them, to be led off by Mr. Dawson, back out the long, darkening dirt road.

Michael and Lydia turned back several times to snatch a last glimpse as their mother and father looked painfully on, saying, "Love you! Be good chillin! We see you agin sometime!" crying out their grief.

Soon, there was no more to see as the trio disappeared beyond a slight bend, fading off in the dusky twilight.

Clara collapsed into Silas' arms, "Oh Gawd! Oh Lawd Gawd!" she sobbed over and over, "Dey gone Silas! Our chillin be gone!"

Several of the others immediately came to console the devastated couple, but no amount of words or support could bring them comfort. Their worlds had once again been mercilessly ripped apart.

Jayvyn, having witnessed the tragic moment, felt the large, familiar lump take hold in his throat as his eyes watered up and his lips began to tremble.

How could it be, he wondered? Only moments ago, he'd made some lighthearted comment to the kids while he poured water into the pot.

Now, before the water had even come to a boil, they were gone. Just like that.

He never even had a chance to say goodbye.

Silas and Clara, after nine years loving and caring for their beloved children, were now childless, not knowing where their children were taken or what their lives would be. They'd live the rest of their lives wondering, but they'd never see their children again.

Regardless of these risks, other families formed. It was only natural for men and women to fall in love, as they always do, which inevitably resulted in children. However, it was just as common for these families to be broken up as slaves were sold to new owners.

As unlikely as it would have seemed ten or so years before, Hannah and Jacob had become good friends. They spent more and more time together until, ultimately, they fell in love.

Jayvyn marveled as their relationship bloomed over the years, considering how things had started out between them. But Hannah had discovered something new in Jacob after finding out he'd been just a small boy when taken from his village.

It awakened a special kind of sympathy within her that fostered a deep sense of caring. That caring had now blossomed into a rich and mutual love.

After the couple discovered their love for each other, it wasn't long before they moved into a family quarters as husband and wife. Soon, Hannah became pregnant for the first time. Both Jacob and Hannah were quite pleased with this new development and looked forward to meeting the child now mysteriously growing in Hannah's womb.

But, sadly, as so often happened, Hannah miscarried sometime before her ninth week from hard conditions in the paddies. The event happened without any signs, but after a while, Hannah wasn't feeling quite the same.

Slowly her intuition told her she'd lost the baby. Margaret and the other women confirmed this for her as the usual indications failed to materialize. It was devastating news to the couple, who so wanted to have a child.

However, a few months later, Hannah was pregnant again. It was obvious when Hannah began to show in her twelfth week. This time, Hannah took extra care to work carefully, rest, and get plenty of sleep.

Jacob, of course, did all he could to make sure she did. He marveled at how beautiful his wife became as the bulge in her belly grew. They were going to be parents, and neither could wait.

Jacob scoured the woods for willow shoots. Choosing whips the size of his little finger, carving them off at their base, gathering bundles in lengths from four to six feet.

Back at the compound, with guidance from some of the older

men, he set to waddling a crib for their newborn. Every evening, he sat by the fire, while Hannah rested, weaving the stalks together.

Silas, who'd long ago made one for his children, helped out.

"OK Jacob, dat be yo base, now hook dem branch in so dey stick up de side."

Jacob sat with his tongue clenched in the side of his mouth, concentrating to make sure each end was securely tucked under the base.

Jayvyn sorted the twigs, choosing the best ones for his friend.

Virgil and Henry, two of the older men, looked on.

"Henry, you tink he mak'n dem weave tight nuff?"

Henry responded, "I dunno Virg, dem lil' bugga git outta mots everyting."

"Make em tight Jacko, else he get out 'n you be try'n ta kech 'm!"

"You tink he kech 'm?" asked Henry.

"Naw, dat kid be fats as lightn'n," chuckled Virgil.

Jacob responded, "Yea, my kid be de good kid, he gonna like hid crib."

"Ya, Ya, we see 'bout dat, Jacko" the men snickered.

"We be fine out jus how fats you be," heh, heh.

All the men joined in good natured ribbing as Jacob steadily worked, the crib slowly taking shape.

Everyone was excited for the couple, and in one way or another engaged.

One day, when the crib was half finished, Hannah fell in desperate pain while out hoeing in the paddy. Several women rushed to her side and carried her to the barge so she could be floated up to the threshing yard. There, they transferred her to a cart and brought back to the quarters.

Old Margaret sat with her through the rest of the day, Hannah moaning, deep in pain with severe cramps. Jacob hardly knew what to do as he sat by her side in the evening, holding her hand as her pain persisted. She was unable to return to the fields in the morning, but Jacob was required to work as usual. Old Margaret, who'd taken up many domestic duties at the quarters, and was too old for much other work anyway, would be there to care for her.

Throughout the day, Jacob worried intensely about his wife. What, he wondered, would he do without her? It was during these moments he realized how deeply in love he was with this remarkable woman with whom he'd had such an inauspicious start. They'd already been through so much as they sorted through their complicated emotions. He'd never find another like her. He desperately didn't want to lose her.

Jayvyn reassured his friend throughout the day that Hannah was strong, Old Margaret knew how to care for a pregnant woman, and he shouldn't worry.

When the day finally came to an end, Jacob rushed back to the quarters, where he found his wife and Old Margaret.

Things hadn't changed much at that point, but Old Margaret took him aside and told him she thought Hannah might be losing the baby. She'd seen a lot of miscarriages in her time and recognized the signs. She told him there wasn't much to do besides let nature take its course and to support her through the difficult time.

By the time the week was out, Hannah had indeed lost her second baby. This time, she passed a lot of blood and tissue in the process, and it kept her from the fields for a good week more.

But in time, Hannah recovered from the traumatic and painful episode, leaving both of them heartbroken as they wondered if they'd ever be able to have children.

It wasn't easy for Hannah and Jacob, but the other slaves were there to reassure them, as theirs had been a common experience for all of them. Jacob was just glad to still have Hannah in his life.

Jacob brought the unfinished crib inside where it sat waiting, reminding the couple of their unfinished business.

The following year, Hannah and Jacob finally succeeded.

Jayvyn remembered well the day Hannah delivered a living child at last.

Old Margaret went around to announce the happy news, coming first to Jayvyn, knowing the depth of his friendship with the two.

Old Margaret was very excited. "James, James! Oh, de Lawd shine hid light on Hannah 'n Jacob today!" She exclaimed as she ran across the courtyard. "Dey got dem a new baby! Come see! Dey want me to come 'n tell you first!"

Jayvyn wasted no time to go see for himself.

When he entered their quarters, he saw Hannah, looking exhausted but happy.

In her arms, she held a bundle of cloth. Jayvyn could barely see the tip of a little, dark brown nose poking up and some tiny fingers as he approached. He watched as the fingers closed into a clumsy fist, and he heard the soft gurgling of a new voice fumbling with the notion of sound.

His heart swelled as he gazed into the blanket to see the miracle of a brand-new child, glazed eyes barely open slits, unable yet to focus on its new world.

Jayvyn's breath caught; it was as if everything else in the world stopped, leaving only the incredible beauty of this new human being. It was so small.

Several moments passed as Jayvyn felt a giant smile spread across his face. Then he realized, "It be a boy!"

Jayvyn looked at Hannah and said, "Oh! He beautiful! He be de mots beautiful ting I eva see!"

Hannah smiled back at him. "Hid name be Jacob."

Young Jacob was a delight to everyone on the plantation. He quickly ripened from the tiny, helpless infant he started out as into a robust little boy. He was filled with more energy than any of the adults could ever remember having themselves.

The other mothers who'd successfully raised a child or two laughed as they watched Hannah. One second, idly chatting while little Jacob played nearby, then suddenly taking flight, wildly chasing after her heretofore stationary son—who'd just discovered his mobility. His inquisitiveness propelled him from one curiosity to the next. No sooner did Hannah have him safely back, when he'd vanish from the spot, next seen half way up a tree. Off Hannah would go again, screaming frantically, waving her arms like a maniac.

Jacob Sr. had his new son perched on his shoulders so often it seemed as if he had two heads.

He sat around the fires talking with the other men as little Jacob buried his busy fingers in his ears, babbling incoherently, blowing spit bubbles that oozed off his chin, settling in his father's hair.

The boy was busy, simple as that! And bright! It wasn't long before his senseless gibberish evolved into words, which among his first were "no" and "stop," undoubtedly learned from his parents' frequent use.

But, as it's often said, it takes a village to raise a child, and a child among a community of slaves is no exception.

So many children died before or soon after birth that when a healthy, vibrant child like Jacob came into the world, he was cherished and looked after by most everyone. There were some, as with any community, who might lack the patience for children, but little Jacob was a very hard kid not to like. He had a way about him that charmed even the grumpiest old men. Certainly, Jayvyn, who liked children anyway, warmed quite naturally to him.

Jayvyn became like an unofficial uncle to little Jacob, who ran to see him first thing on Sunday mornings.

In fact, Jacob's parents often made the suggestion, "Go see James; he be miss'n you! He need yo help. Go find 'im." and soon Jayvyn would hear "Jame! Jame!" as little Jacob came running across the compound to find him. He didn't mind, though; he easily engaged the boy in whatever he was doing—or vice versa.

More than once, he and little Jacob set out to gather wood only to spend hours distracted by salamanders, bugs, or small, harmless snakes as they scattered from under fallen logs.

He developed a special patch in the garden, as he had for Michael and Lydia so long ago, where young Jacob could tend a few of his own plants. More than once, Jayvyn reflected on his own childhood and special memories of time spent with his father. He pondered, too, all the unfortunate children he'd seen over the years who'd missed out. So, spending quality time with little Jacob came quite naturally to him.

After four more years of failed pregnancies, Hannah and Jacob had another child. It was another baby boy they named Robert.

Like his older brother, the boy was perfect—a beautiful black bundle of new life. Jayvyn had again been third in line behind Hannah, Jacob Sr., and Old Margaret to welcome new Robert into the world, even before young Jacob, who hadn't been allowed in during birthing.

But soon after, young Jacob, now four years old, came to see his new baby brother.

He calmed immediately as he stared in awe at the miracle. This tiny, human being really did pop out of his mother's tummy, just like his parents promised.

Little Robert was the object of young Jacob's affection every day going forward. He eagerly endeavored to teach his little brother everything he'd learned so far in his abundant four-year lifetime.

The two were inseparable; young Jacob always taking Robert by the hand wherever he went. He brought him to the garden to teach him all Jayvyn had taught him about plants in the small plot Jayvyn created for them.

Jayvyn and others in the compound delighted in watching young Jacob—who, in their minds, had only just learned to talk—masterfully instruct his new protégé in the fine art of speech, as well as everything else a young boy must know.

All along, Jayvyn reminisced about times spent with his little sister, Ifetayo. It struck him deeply as he watched young Jacob take up the mantle of responsibility for his younger sibling.

Soon, little Robert was running to and fro on his own, jabbering away in full sentences to whomever he could get to listen. Jayvyn took quite a shine to little Robert as he came around to tell him of his older brother's and his latest adventures.

The boy could really talk. He brought joy everywhere with his infectious laugh and good nature.

He was the apple of his big brother's eye, following him wherever he went.

Young Jacob, too, had grown to be a fine young lad, always a good example to his younger brother.

Although further apart in age, they reminded Jayvyn of Lydia and Michael so long ago.

Not for the first time, certainly not the last, Jayvyn marveled at the abundant gifts children everywhere brought to the world—innocent, immaculate, joyful—as yet unblemished by greed, envy, or cruelty.

– 33 –

Growing Pains

Better than fifteen years had passed since Jayvyn first set foot on Turner's plantation, and he'd seen plenty. He arrived when fifty or more acres had been nothing more than wooded swampland. Now, new paddies stretched across these acres for as far as the eye could see in several directions. The yield from harvests had more than tripled.

In fact, plantations all throughout South Carolina had seen explosive growth as their products were shipped far and wide to satisfy the world's demand. Business was booming.

Demand for slaves had increased so much that seasoned slaves were no longer available. Great numbers were coming directly from Africa now, with no seasoning whatsoever. Known as 'saltwater slaves,' they spoke little to no English. They were taken directly from the ship to the plantation and put straight to work. Brute force was the only training these new slaves got. Work could be attained at the end of the whip, with or without verbal communication—that could come later.

The slave population in general had increased substantially throughout South Carolina to the point there were now more Blacks than whites.* Because of this, laws were changing with ever greater frequency. New laws now required one white boss for every ten slaves on a plantation. When Jayvyn had first arrived, Victor supervised all of the slaves, and things had worked well. But the slaves were a much tighter group then. Everyone spoke English and cooperated well. Now there were fifteen white bosses in the fields managing over a hundred and fifty slaves, many who didn't speak a lick of English. Measures for discipline had become much stricter and harsher as a result. Bosses roamed the fields, whips in hand, much as they had in Barbados. Although Victor was still the foreman of the slaves, he had no say in matters of discipline. Whippings used to be an exception at Turner's plantation, now they happened multiple times a day.

Conversations around the fires at night began to take a noticeably more somber turn. Information about potential routes to freedom began to circulate as new slaves arrived from other plantations.

A slave named Amos from the Wick plantation mentioned, "Las yea, nigga lef fo Saint Ahg'st'n. It be sum place down sout. Dey say dey gib'n de slave dey freedom if'n dey kin make it. He ain't come back."

Nathan, a recent acquisition from Eben Hattersley's loomworks, agreed, "Yeah man. Udda folk be talkin dat too. Sez dey be Span'sh folk. I hea dat from sum nigga what bring'n de cott'n. Mo den a few be goin, ain't none com'n back."

Jayvyn, Jacob, and the other men listened with fascination. So did many younger slaves.

---

* *By 1715, South Carolina had the highest ratio of blacks to whites in all of colonial America, exceeding 60%*

If they went south to a place called St. Augustine, they'd be given their freedom.* The story created a lot of intrigue among the slaves, although details of how to get there were sketchy. Even so, many would try. However, the consequences if caught were severe.

Silas remarked, "Some dem get'n kech."

"Yea, dem nigga ketcha gitcha, it sho be bad," said Virgil.

Jacob added, "Das wha I hea. Dem what be kech git'n mest up pretty bad."

"Dat right Jacko," Virgil continued, "dey be com'n in de plantat'n sumtime too. De boss ain't got nuth'n ta say bout it neitha, dey jus come."

The other men nodded in agreement.

Jayvyn recalled a time when a slave patrol rode into their quarters. "Memba when dey find dat book in Abe's cab'n? Dey hurt dat man bad."

"Yea man! Tie'm to de tree 'n cut hid back op'n right den 'n der, fron o ebrybody," Jacob added.

"Lef 'm hang'n 'n bleed'n, den jus rode off, dey did," remarked Virgil.

Amos shook his head, "All dat fo a book he no kin eb'n read."

A slave patrol had ridden onto Turner's plantation one weekend to search the quarters and found a book in one of the slave's bunks.†

---

* *In 1693, King Charles II of Spain ordered his Florida colonists to give runaway slaves from British colonies freedom and protection if they converted to Catholicism and agreed to serve Spain*

† *Beginning in 1704, monitoring and punishing slaves became compulsory duty for all white citizens whether slave owners or not. Many communities passed laws that required most white males to serve as members of armed patrols*

Taking matters into their own hands, they had severely whipped the man on the spot.*

Victor, who'd been sitting in the shadows remarked, "Missa Daws'n none to happy bout dat. Took ol' Abe outta work. Had ta git de docta ta come fix'm up."

He went on, "Massa Tuhna be some mad when he find out. Ol' Abe so wreck't he hadda sell'm."

The Turners had been at their summer retreat in Rhode Island at the time.† When he learned about the incident, Master Turner became infuriated.‡ After all, the slaves were his property, and this was his plantation. He lodged a firm complaint in Charles Town, and the patrols hadn't been back since.

All the men sat solemnly shaking their heads at the memory.

"Dem patrol eb'n be break'n up de slaves gett'n togeda like we be now," Silas said.

"Yea man, dey no wan us be sing'n, danc'n, 'n be hab'n no fun, o nutt'n," lamented Jacob.

Master Turner vehemently objected to this since he wanted his slaves to be happy with their lives on his plantation. He didn't mind their singing and dancing on the weekend; it had never caused the least

---

* *Regulatory guidance for these patrols might suggest things like restricting lashing to no more than 20 lashes, but was seldomly enforced*

† *This became typical among plantation owners, who would head north to cooler climates during the summer due to the increase in malaria brought by the large influx of slaves imported directly from Africa*

‡ *Many slave owners resented the slave patrols for overstepping their authority by coming onto their land to inspect and discipline their slaves according to <u>their</u> standard instead of the master's*

amount of trouble. Besides, he was in control of his slaves.*

"Yea, well you jus min yo bidness 'n don be mak'n no ruckus 'n de massa leeb we alone," said Victor.

"Das right," added Virgil, "long's we don make no truble dem patrol no be com'n round hea," he said raising his gaze to some of younger men.

"hm-m-m," "yassa," a few mumbled in response.

By this time, little Robert had surpassed the age young Jacob had been when his little brother was born.

Young Jacob, now nine, had been required to work in the fields for several years now and had grown much taller of late. His arms and legs seemed to jump ahead of the rest of his body, creating a certain clumsiness characteristic of most children that age. He was constantly knocking things over, stubbing his toes, and banging his head.

During the first few years after Jacob was put to work, little Robert missed his older brother during the day, so his parents allowed him to go and watch his older brother work as long as he behaved. When he followed his older brother into the paddies, his parents made sure they were always close by to help keep an eye on little Robert.

Soon enough, though, at the age of five, little Robert was made to work, starting at the threshing yard.

Robert was a good worker, always taking his job seriously. He was proud to be following in his big brother's footsteps. It wasn't long

---

* *As the slave population exploded, many whites became afraid that any slave gatherings could lead to uprising and revolt, and therefore sought to break them up, even on plantations. Permissive owners were seen as weak and posing a threat to the other white residents of the surrounding community*

before he was allowed to help take newly cut stalks of rice off the barge during harvest and load them on carts to bring to the threshing yard.

He prided himself on being able to keep up with the rest. Soon, others in the compound were referring to little Robert as 'little man' when he sat and ate with the other men at the fires. They treated him like a little man, so he acted the part, puffing his chest out and putting on a character far beyond his years. He elicited many smiles and much laughter from those around him. Everybody loved little Robert and adopted him as their own.

Soon, after turning six, Robert was allowed to work in the paddies. He worked near his brother, helping to carry bundles of weeds to the barges, later to be transported for burning.

One sunny afternoon, when he was out working in the paddies, little Robert suddenly gave a loud shriek from a corner near the canals. Young Jacob, hearing his younger brother cry out, dropped his hoe and sprinted down the irrigation ditch, where Robert sat crying, holding his ankle. Others, too, dropped what they were doing and came running.

When he got to him, young Jacob peeled little Robert's hand away to see two bleeding puncture wounds, side by side, about an inch apart. Suddenly, a man beside them yelled, "Snake! Snake!" pointing at a large cottonmouth coiled in the grass. Without any hesitation, another man took his hoe and smashed the viper into a twitching mass of dying serpent no longer posing a threat.

Turning his attention back to Robert, young Jacob swept up his little brother, screaming in agony, and rushed him to their quarters.

Several other men and women followed.

They immediately began cleaning his wound, squeezing around it to express as much blood and venom out as possible. Someone in the rice paddy had run to find his parents, who soon arrived at the quarters. Old Margaret was there as well.

Several gave suggestions for what to do in the event of a snake bite. It had happened before, as snakes were ubiquitous on the plantation, but everyone knew there was no single effective method of treatment. It would be a matter of trying to keep the wound clean and hope most of the venom hadn't made it in.

The bite, however, was bad. Before night, Robert's leg had swollen into a grotesque yellow-green mass as the venom began to eat away his flesh. The pain was agonizing. His family sat with him through the long night.

Someone brought horehound from the forest to use as a poultice because they'd heard Native Americans used it as an effective treatment for snake bites.*

But the swelling around the wound continued. The bites expanded, exposing large open sections of putrid, blackening flesh.

Robert vomited several times through the night and, by morning, was very dehydrated. He lay pale and listless, unable to keep water or anything else down. The infection had progressed to an angry, festering wound that continued to bleed unabated.

Robert's breathing steadily became more rapid and shallow.

---

* *This was a traditional remedy practiced by Cherokee and other American Native tribes for the treatment of snakebite*

Realizing Robert was in real danger, Victor tried to locate Mr. Dawson. But he was off the plantation that day and couldn't be reached. Master Turner was at his summer residence in Rhode Island.

Hannah, Jacob Sr., and young Jacob sat stunned and helpless as they watched Robert become less and less responsive. There was nothing anyone could do.

Eventually the small boy's eyes became glassy and unfocused.

Turning his head, he gave one long, final exhale.

Little Robert was dead.

Young Jacob ran screaming and crying across the courtyard, not knowing where to run or what to do. His brother, his one and only brother, the boy he'd loved and cherished so much, was gone!

Just yesterday, everything had been normal as they headed to the fields. It was just another routine day, but now, suddenly, everything had changed! How could this happen so quickly and with no warning?

Jacob's ten-year-old brain wrestled the mirage that threatened his world as Jayvyn came and held him in his arms.

Jacob fought to get away as his mother and father's bawling permeated the air around them. Others ran to the cabin to try and console the devastated parents as they stared incredulously at their young son's now-lifeless form.

Hannah's guttural screams and cries echoed throughout the compound that morning as she fought the terrible truth.

Her cherished six-year-old son had passed before her very eyes.

Jacob Sr. stayed by her side and wept as well.

It was the worst misery he'd ever known—a tragedy his mind couldn't accept. Every so often he stole a glance at his motionless son, only to collapse again in a fit of anguished tears. Hours passed before he was finally able to summon the strength he knew his family would need.

"He be gone, my love. Dey be nutin' mo we can do. De Lawd call our li'l Robert home, 'n he got to go." He said, fighting back his tears.

Hannah fell into his embrace and shook as she cried and cried.

Jayvyn had managed to calm young Jacob as much as possible. He tried to explain the inexplicable as young Jacob stood shaking and sobbing.

"Tings happen, Jacob, tings we no can control. Your brudda not know dat de snake be der, but dis kin happ'n to anybody.

"You seen udda die; we no tink it eva happen to we, but it do.

"Now, yo parent need you de mots. Dey need you ta hep 'em, 'n it be someting you gotsta do," tears in his own eyes as he rubbed young Jacob's back and shoulders.

"Soon you be de man, 'n you gonna know death in many way.

"Dis be hard, but you no gotsta to do it alone.

"I be here, yo fadda be here, 'n dey be many udda dat hep you, too."

Jayvyn held young Jacob's trembling body in a loving embrace, hot tears burning into his shoulder.

"Now, come, you gotsta be wid yo parent. Dey need you now."

Jayvyn stood and wiped his eyes. Young Jacob, straightened. They walked hand in hand to his parents' quarters, where they'd all begin a new journey through life without Robert.

As in Barbados, Master Turner had set aside some land in the forest that the slaves could use to bury their dead. It wasn't good land, it was swampy and hard to dig, but at least they had a place to lay their loved ones to rest.

Little Robert's body was wrapped in sections of old cloth and carried by torchlight out to a small grave that had been prepared earlier for him. Lights flickered and danced as the sad procession moved slowly through the trees. Hannah, Jacob, and young Jacob wept softly as his body was placed gently in the ground.

Between sobs, Hannah offered some parting words. "We sees you agin baby, somewheah fah fah from heah, you be free now my chil, you be free."

It was the saddest of days. Jayvyn took it pretty hard when little Robert died. Tears filled his eyes as he thought about how much Hannah and Jacob had lost—so, so unfairly.

And poor, young Jacob. Lost his only brother, whom he adored so much.

How terrible it must be for a boy, at the tender age of only ten, to lose someone so important in a world where there's so little to begin with.

Jayvyn's heart ached badly for young Jacob. All he could think about was how he and little Robert were always together, inseparable from the start.

Jayvyn's feelings for his lost sister surfaced, remembering how badly he'd grieved for her over the years. He'd wondered countless times, and still did, if she'd survived and what her life had become.

It was a question he'd never be able to answer, any more than young Jacob would be able to answer why it was his dear little brother who'd been bitten by the snake that day.

– 34 –

Law and Disorder

In the years following Robert's death, young Jacob changed. He became much harder in his demeanor, focusing only on the work he had to do on the plantation.

Now thirteen, it was difficult for Jayvyn, or his parents, for that matter, to draw him out. He'd lost something he'd never be able to recover, and with it went the innocence and joy of childhood. Instead of spending his free time with his parents or in the garden with Jayvyn, he'd go off somewhere by himself, often appearing quiet, sullen, and angry.

As populations increased and the laws became ever more restrictive, levels of defiance among slaves grew in step. The unruliest among them were the saltwater slaves, but rancor was quickly spreading throughout the community. Many of the younger renegades were more militant and prone to impulsive acts of rebellion. They were also the ones to pay the stiffest penalties.

Both Jayvyn and Jacob Sr. had noticed young Jacob keeping company with other militant young men, and both were worried about him. His countenance was becoming more like a warrior and less like the jubilant young man they'd once known. Jayvyn missed the old Jacob, and both he and his father had spoken about it.

One day after work, Jacob mentioned, "James, I feel de anger grow'n in de slave today."

Jayvyn replied, "It be true, Jacob; I feel it too."

Jacob asked, "You tink it is cause dey be so many new slave come straight from Africa now?"

Jayvyn pondered the question for a while before responding.

After considering his answer, he replied, "I tink de one what be com'n from Africa be mo angry.

"Dey be com'n straight from de homeland 'n not be broken by de white man whip.

"But it be mo dan dat. Tings be diff'nt here now den when me 'n you come. You know?"

To which Jacob responded, "Yes. Hannah say dis too. Many mo white men wid de whip alla time. We seed 'em whippin, sometime many time a day. Spec'ly dem new slave who no speak English. But no one be safe."

He went on, "I worry 'bout my son, James. He be change afta Robert die. He angry alla time.

"Hannah 'n me, we try talk'n wid'm, but it ain't de same. He don' wanna listen ta us.

"I see 'm sittin 'n talk'n wid some dem angry new slave from Africa, 'n it worry me. Dem de one what be whip'd alla time, 'n dey be de one what run from de plantation, 'n we seed wha happen when dey be caught."

Recently, three slaves who'd escaped with a larger group of seven were caught. When they were delivered back to Master Turner, they'd already been beaten and bruised by their captors.

Similar to Barbados, Mr. Dawson brought the captured slaves to the slave compound for punishment so all could bear witness to the consequences for running. As in Barbados, Victor was tasked with reading out their punishments. Anyone who knew Victor knew it was a duty he detested.

The punishment had been forty lashes, followed by being chained in the barn until fitted with iron collars. And, as in Barbados, slaves were selected to administer the lashes, further fueling the growing resentment among them.

They didn't have their noses slit or faces burned, but the lashes were severe and the collars were just as burdensome.

Jayvyn remembered the punishment well. The slaves' backs had been transformed into a skinless, bloody pulp, and although it had been well over a month, they were still in their collars and would be for some time.

Jayvyn said, "I gotsde same worry.

"He be like de son to me, too. I try talk'n to 'm, but it be de same fo me. He got de strong mind.

"You no want ta see him whip'd or ta gotsta wear de colla like dem udda slave. I no want dat too.

"But if you only kin give one ting to yo son, would it no be hid freedom?"

Jacob was taken aback. He hadn't thought about the issue in these terms.

He'd already lost one son, and it almost destroyed both he and Hannah. He didn't think he could ever go through pain like that again.

As he considered what Jayvyn had said, his eyes moistened, and he replied, "It be de one ting I want fo him de mots."

The tears forming in Jacob's eyes spilled from his lids. Beginning to choke, he continued, "But dat mean Hannah and me neva see 'm agin."

Jayvyn felt heartsick for Jacob as he listened. Of course, the thing any of them wanted most for a loved one was for them to have their freedom, but like everything else in their lives, it would have to come at a cost.

Pressure was being felt all over South Carolina, on every plantation, in every household where slaves were kept as whites attempted to maintain absolute control over them. But there were so many slaves in South Carolina by this point it was impossible to keep them isolated from each other.

Africans certainly weren't strangers to the art of communication. It was quite common among many tribes to send and receive messages by drum in their homeland. It was why drums and horns had long been prohibited by the white man; they wanted to prevent such communication.

Although slaves were closely watched and had to have written passes when off the master's property, they gathered and carried information wherever they went. Bartholomew was a prime example. He always had his ear to the ground. When off the plantation with Master Turner, he picked up information in countless ways. Human beings are nothing if not innovative; slaves were no exception. Communication of necessary information was as unstoppable as water; it inevitably flowed to every corner of the slave population; it was just a matter of time.

The grapevine was abuzz with significant changes being made to slave laws. These laws, or codes, originally modeled after the ones in

Barbados, were embellished by South Carolina's legislation to clarify and fix all Negros as absolute property—in body and soul—of whomever should own them.

There was no such thing as a free Negro. All Blacks were permanent slaves with no rights or freedoms whatsoever, either now or in the future; any offspring inherited the same status. The law literally came to specify slaves as "things" rather than persons.* Negros were not human beings at all, but goods at the white man's disposal. One legal opinion argued: *"As goods, therefore, they may be used, while, like other goods, they perish with the using."*† More fundamentally stated—slaves could be used up as the owner wished, until fully destroyed—like any other tool or possession. They could be used for the payment of debts, taken in the same way as all other goods and chattels—Negros were purely assets of the master white class to use as he chose.

In the interests of public safety, the laws required and empowered all white citizens to exact punishments on Blacks, up to and including death, without impunity, for reasonable suspicion of misconduct. The worst penalty a white could incur if found guilty of murdering a Black *out of sheer "wantonness or bloddymindedness"* would be three months in prison and restitution to the owner of fifty shillings.‡

The more this type of news got out, the more radically minded slaves became. Slaves who, to this point, had worked hard for Master Turner now seemed to be drawing from some deep inner well—a

---

* *The original legal document stated "the cardinal principle of slavery—that the slave is to be regarded as a thing—is an article of property—a chattel personal..."*

† *William Goodell, The American Slave Code, 1853, p. 77, referred to as "The Law of the Relation"*

‡ *Statutes of South Carolina 1712*

place deep within their soul that was, and would always remain, anchored to their proud African heritage.

Jayvyn saw it in their eyes and heard it in their silence; the pressures from the ever-tightening rules and laws were crowding their spirits into a dangerous corner, one from which no peaceful avenue of escape existed. Tensions were rising among his fellow slaves in ways he'd never felt before.

The more emboldened slaves became, the harsher the white man's restrictions got. The South Carolina legislature passed the Security Act, requiring all white males to carry firearms at all times when outside their homes, even to church on Sundays.* Aware of the tenuous situation that existed with their Black majority, the white community was beginning to panic.

All of the increased security measures were well known to the slave population, only amplifying their resentment. It was just a matter of time before tensions reached the breaking point. All that was needed were the right set of circumstances to spark the bulging powder keg.

In late summer of 1739, just such conditions converged.

Most plantation owners and their families were off at their summer retreats in the north. The remaining whites were mostly concentrated in Charles Town, where they were particularly vulnerable to diseases. Yellow fever and other diseases came directly off the slave ships arriving from Africa. Further, cholera was prone to break out in the area due to poor sanitation. Inadequate drainage in the low, swampy community had given Charles Town the reputation

---

* *Known as the Security Act of 1739*

as one of the unhealthiest cities in the American colonies.

In 1738, one slave ship in particular made things much worse.

The *London Frigate* landed in Charles Town after a long voyage from Africa, bringing with it an outbreak of small pox that ravaged the entire city. During that year and the next, most of Charles Town's residents were perpetually sick; hundreds would die.*

At the same time, war between Spain and England was fast approaching.†

The combination of a swelling Black population, a third of its white citizens sick, and war on the doorstep stretched the colony's government thin. Controlling the slaves was becoming ever more difficult and ineffective.

Coincidentally, Charles Town was also engaged in a project to improve its roads and fix the sanitation problem.‡ To accomplish this, slave labor was commandeered from several local plantations. In the interest of completing the project quickly, slaves were put to work from sun up to sun down, and much to their dislike, Sundays as well.

One such Sunday, September 9, 1739, a group of twenty or so slaves working on the roads were left unsupervised as Charleston's white people went to church.

Seeing an opportunity, a slave by the name of Jemmy planned to

---

* *In 1738, the slave ship London Frigate brought a case of smallpox that would infect over two thousand of the city's six thousand residents, of whom over three hundred would die*

† *Tensions arising from shipping disputes, Britian's recent colonization of Georgia, and other imperial conflicts, strained an already fragile peace between England and Spain, which finally culminated in the 'War of Jenkin's Ear' in 1739, which would involve the colonial dispute over the border between Georgia and Florida*

‡ *Known as the "Act for Cutting and Making a Path" 1739*

take advantage of the situation.

He fabricated white banners that read "Liberty" and inspired other slaves to join him. They marched south toward Florida, beating drums and recruiting others along the way.

When they reached the Stono River Bridge, they came upon Hutchinson's store, which was well stocked with guns and ammunition. Here, they overwhelmed and killed its two storekeepers, cutting their heads off and setting them on the steps outside the store. They took all the provisions they wanted—including liquor—and armed themselves well. From there, they continued south, killing plantation owners, their families, and burning their houses along the way. As they went, slaves from these plantations joined them. The mob swelled to some eighty slaves.

In an unlikely twist of fate, they haphazardly ran into a group of white South Carolina officials on horseback returning from a trip. Among them was South Carolina's Lieutenant Governor, William Bull. The officials evaded the mob and sped back to Charles Town, where they quickly assembled a militia to go after the escaped slaves.

The militia caught up to them in a large field. A firefight ensued. The Blacks, several who'd been drinking the stolen liquor, were disorganized and no match for the experienced whites. Nearly half of the rebels were killed. The ones who'd escaped were soon caught. Many were executed, their heads put on stakes along the road as a deterrent to other would-be escapees.*

The white community tried to suppress news of the rebellion

---

* *Famously known as the Stono Rebellion, it was the largest slave rebellion to date at that time*

from spreading throughout the slave community, but word traveled fast. Jayvyn and his fellow slaves at Turner's heard the whole story. The energy among renegades increased to a fever pitch. The event inspired many, strengthening their resolve and fortifying their courage from knowing a large group of slaves had finally risen up to fight for their freedom. The slaves of Stono were heroes among the slave community. Even though they were martyrs, their brave action caused many to decide it would be better to run—even die trying—than die a slave.

Many of the fiery young rebels on Turner's plantation became more emboldened. Several ran off, but one in particular took his aggression out another way.

The young African, whose name was Mose, was known for resisting authority. He worked indolently—at a slow pace, intentionally doing poor-quality work.

Not long after the rebellion, while the slaves were weeding a nearly finished crop, he deliberately ruined half a row of rice, about three hundred feet, before a boss noticed what he was doing. Instead of carefully weeding with his hoe, as the slaves had been trained to do, Mose was just knocking the mature rice plants into the watery trench and leaving the weeds where they were.

Upon seeing this, the boss became predictably enraged, catching the attention of all of the slaves as he stormed into the paddy, whip in hand. When he caught up to the young man, he raised his whip high, but to everyone's astonishment, Mose shot his hand out, snatched the whip from the boss's grip, and brought it hard across his face.

The boss staggered back, falling in the wet paddy. The young

African was on him in an instant, repeatedly bludgeoning his face with the whip. He got four or five good blows in before anyone could react.

Suddenly, a shot rang out. Mose stumbled back and fell.

The white boss had managed to pull his sidearm and shot Mose in the chest, killing him instantly.

The silence in the paddy was deafening. Both slaves and bosses stood in disbelief over what they'd just witnessed.

Soon, another boss came to the assistance of the one who'd been beat. His face and side of his head were gashed and bleeding heavily from the vicious blows.

Mose lay nearby, head down in the water, chest soaked in blood.

As the injured boss was helped out of the paddy, the other bosses brought their whips and guns. They ordered the rest of the slaves back to work with loud, angry shouts. At first, no one moved. Several of the more aggressive slaves appeared poised to attack. Jayvyn wasn't sure what would happen next.

But some of the cooler-headed slaves implored the others to stand down and get back to work. The crisis didn't escalate. However, work for the remainder of the day was far from productive as the slaves stewed and fumed over what had taken place.

Predictably, the bosses on Turner's plantation increased their vigilance and arms as well.

In the evenings, talk around the fires was low and serious. Updates arrived regularly about happenings on other plantations. The older men, who kept well informed by the grapevine, shared information with the rest of the group.

Virgil reported, "Y'all hea bout dem trunk what broke ova at

Wick's? Empty de whole pond 'n ruin all de rice!"

Amos remarked, "Yeah. How dat happ'n? Dey no break on dey own."

Virgil chuckled, "No suh-ree, no suh! Ain't no way. Dey slave do dat!"

"Serv'm right," remarked Silas.

"Wha bout dat bacca bahn up ta Boone? Burnt ta de groun, lost all dey baccy fo de whole yea!" Matthew said.

Fredrick replied, "Hoo-wee! Dey sho hab dem a good smoke dat night!"

"Yeah, too bad de wind don't blow dis way," Silas jibed.

Other men chortled their agreement.

"All dat fine baccy! Wadda shame!" lamented Virgil.

"Wan't no lightn'n," remarked Jayvyn.

"No suh," said Virgil, "dey nigga no be happy."

Low snickers circled the fire as men exchanged knowing glances.

"Yeah boy, eva sin dem nigga in Stono git up dey be lots o truble." Silas noted.

The following spring, public officials in Charles Town enacted new legislation in response to the Stono Rebellion by passing the Negro Act of 1740. It further stiffened already restrictive conditions imposed on the slaves and codified many already accepted norms into law, such as making it illegal to teach any Negro to read or write, assigning stiff penalties for anyone who did.

But other new elements were added as well. Whites were rewarded for the retrieval of any escaped slave, dead or alive. A white could expect to receive compensation for remitting the scalp of an escaped slave, provided both ears were still attached. If an escapee was taken alive, they were instructed to deliver the slave directly to a workhouse.*

Furthermore, whites were given greater latitude to 'put to immediate death' any Negro they found to be grossly disobedient and non-submissive—provided they weren't just being willfully cruel and barbaric—because, as it was written in the Act, "*cruelty is not only highly unbecoming those who profess themselves Christians, but is odious in the eyes of all men who have any sense of virtue of humanity.*"†

The law further prohibited gatherings of more than five slaves at a time on Saturday evenings or Sundays, even on the owner's plantation. It also mandated slaves' clothing couldn't be comparable to any white person's, specifying it had to be made from "*Negro cloth.*"‡

New laws were designed to further degrade and deprive Blacks of any semblance of freedom or personage whatsoever, but Jayvyn had a hard time comprehending one rule in particular—Negros were no longer permitted to grow their own food. He couldn't understand the purpose of this. *Wasn't it in the slave owner's interest to have his slaves grow their own food?*§ *How had this ever created a problem for the white*

---

* *Workhouses developed around 1738 in Charles Town as a place where runaway slaves could be taken to for holding. In 1768 the workhouse became exclusively a place of correction, where for a fee, slaves could receive the most up to date methods for ensuring effective discipline. These workhouses would be equipped with all of the latest devices and implements of torture along with experts in their use*

† *Taken verbatim from section XXXVII of the Negro Act of 1740*

‡ *Negro cloth was specified as: duffels, kerseys, osnabrigs, blue linen, check linen or coarse garlix, or calicoes, checked cottons, or Scotch plaids*

§ *This was most likely to deprive the slaves of any potential income streams they might realize from selling excess food stocks they might be able to grow*

community?

However, it was the law now. The gardens he'd so carefully tended over the years were destroyed, removing one of Jayvyn's only sources of contentment.

And since they weren't allowed to congregate as before, they took their meals in their quarters. Curfew was enforced by the bosses and slave patrols.

Not only was their status relegated to mere property and "*things,*" they were now regarded as *"disobedient and evil-minded Negroes"**—not worthy of the slightest agency over their lives.

* *Text from section XLVII of the Negro Act of 1740*

- 35 -

Resistance and Subterfuge

The memory of the Stono Rebellion lived on for slaves and whites alike, taking on mythic proportions as the story passed from generation to generation.

For whites, it confirmed their worst fears and suspicions. The slaves could and would revolt, and there were many more of them than whites. Some whites even began leaving the South out of fear for themselves and their families. In response, the legislature enacted a series of restrictive levies on the importation of new slaves directly from Africa, hoping to bring about a better balance.

However, as it turns out, most of these restrictions became less than effective in the face of plantations' burgeoning success. Plantation owners needed slaves to keep their plantations productive and profitable, and the Crown was on their side. So, in time, and to the dismay of many of Charles Town's white citizens, the slave trade returned to business as usual.

For slaves, the legacy of the Stono Rebellion continued to strengthen and bolster their courage to resist and overcome their bondage.

Resistance took many forms as slaves figured out how to circumvent and bypass one restriction after another. Many snuck off the plantations at night without passes to attend secret late-night gatherings or visit slaves from neighboring plantations. Routes through the woods were established to avoid, and if necessary, out maneuver, slave patrols.

As slaves shared their knowledge and ideas, varying methods were developed to thwart and sabotage production on plantations in very cunning and insidious ways. One of the favorites capitalized on the reputation whites had given Negros for being stupid, lazy, and "evil-minded."

For a long time, whites had been referring to the Black race in disparaging and derogatory language. It was reflected in all of their documents and even in the sermons regularly delivered to congregations. It was accepted in the manner of their spoken language whenever referring to the Negro race. Not surprisingly, it had also been a source of much pain and irritation among Africans over the years.

Fine! They thought. *If that's what they think, then let's give it to them!* Slaves cleverly developed the subtle art of feigning the attributes whites had ascribed to them. In doing so, they'd find out just how dumb and gullible the master race could be.

Equipment might break, or a load of finished rice might fall over into the dirt—by accident, of course. The pig might get out of his pen and take half a day to catch while causing its own mayhem. Or a slave might "sprain dis heah ankle, Massa!" or "tinks I's gots de fever!"

With a little imagination and some daring, there were plenty of ways to keep the white man guessing.

Gender was taken into consideration as well. Women were better equipped to play the 'sick card' and men were better at incurring 'equipment failures'.

However, common sense ruled the day. Slaves could still be severely punished if they weren't convincing enough.

Slowing production in these subtle ways was but one act of passive resistance. However, when done on a large scale, it became an effective way to sabotage the white man's design of high profits through free labor.

Another method, one partially compensating for losing the right to grow their own food, was to avail themselves of the white man's food and other supplies where they could do so without being noticed. A chicken here or there, some eggs, or a few onions or turnips now and again could easily be written off to attrition. Just don't get caught!

This was easily validated among the slaves as justifiable sharing as opposed to theft. After all, how much had the white man helped himself to what belonged to the slaves?

Since slaves had been banned from growing their own food, feeding them had become a bigger burden for plantation owners. Out of necessity, Master Turner had taken to providing extra allotments of dried beef, corn meal, lard, and other food stocks.

But the slaves had more than this. Master Turner had long allowed the slaves to take the 'broken' rice, the grains failing to pass muster as whole grains. In fact, the slaves preferred it for its enhanced ability to soak up broth and sauce. Around the plantation, the slaves called these broken grains "middlins,"* and they went particularly well with some of the critters they caught or pulled out of the swamps, like catfish, crawfish, squirrels, and numerous other small game prevalent

---

* *Midllins are commonly known today as grits*

in the area. Additionally, they still received the refuse from animal slaughters.

Furthermore, the slaves found many indigenous plants to be good food—even weeds such as dandelion and pokeweed.

Over time, many plants had made their way from Africa as well—foods the slaves were very familiar with—such as sorghum, benne, atidua beans, and gub-a-gubs.* Several of these plants had now become naturalized throughout the lowlands and were readily available in the wild.

The slaves also made good use of Indian corn as well as corn meal, ingredients whites used only for animal feed.†

So really, combined with their skills and resourcefulness, the slaves had a pretty good pantry at their disposal.‡

The only problem was time. It took time to gather these ingredients and prep them for use, and time is one thing slaves never had enough of.

In contrast to myriad new rules stiffening penalties and restricting the behavior of slaves, bland measures had also been legislated to inhibit cruel treatment by whites that might agitate and provoke another rebellion.

Acts of out-and-out murder could result in large fines and other penal actions. However, if death or maiming resulted merely from

---

* *Benne is now known as sesame, atidua is the original Akan name for black eyed peas. Gub-a gubs, as previously mentioned, was the popular name among slaves for peanuts, which may have been brought to North America by Africans, although they are believed to have their origins in South America*

† *Often used to make 'pone bread'*

‡ *This is the origin of the popular Gullah Geechee cuisine of today*

excessive or "undue correction," then just a fine of a much lesser amount would apply.* But to plantation owners, who had no real desire to harm their property in the first place, the additional cost for such behavior did function as a deterrent.

This carried little assurance among the slaves, but it did make Jayvyn wonder about Mose. If the white boss, who fatally shot Mose that day had moderated his response, maybe Mose would be alive today.

In any case, the message to the white bosses was to use more discretion when meting out punishments. In response, Master Turner issued new guidance to his men.

The change was noticeable. The bosses seemed less apt to beat a slave on the spot. Instead, they took the offending slave, along with their complaint, to Mr. Dawson, who then decided what should be done about it. Of course, bothering Mr. Dawson with trivial matters would demonstrate poor judgment on the part of the bosses. So, although they might get angry, spit, and yell at impertinent behavior, the slaves usually got some amount of warning before being hauled in for punishment.

This made it a little easier to put into effect the "stupid, lazy" routine. And they did.

They enjoyed watching and learning how far they could safely take the act as the white bosses turned red with frustration at the

---

* *Section XXXVII of the Negro Act of 1740 specified a fine of £350 for accidental death from correction, or £100 for intentional maiming including: blinding, taking a limb, cutting out the tongue, castrating, burning, and more*

"stupid, lazy niggers."

It became a subtle way to fight back and restored just a little bit of agency in their lives. It felt good. When they played the white man like that, it made them feel they had the upper hand in some small way. It also revealed some of the white man's vulnerabilities for a change.

More and more, Jayvyn came to appreciate the older, more thoughtful rebels. They were smart. They knew how to craft subterfuge in ways the white man couldn't quite put his finger on. It also made for a lot of entertainment in the fields and around the fires at night.

"Hey Martin! Dat wad pretty slick da way you bust yo hoe today! Got ol' Pinky's trousers in a big ol' knot! Ah-ha-ha!"

The slaves called one of the bosses Pinky because it was the color he turned when he got mad.

"Yeah man! He sho did turn pink! Jus like one dem fat ol pigs in da barn!" Martin replied with a laugh.

"Betty couldn't a move slowa out der in dat mud, ain dat right Betty?" remarked Adam.

"Shut yo mouth, Adam! You know how sick I be git'n!" Betty retorted with a sly giggle.

"Yeah Betty, you be sick alright! Jus look atchu, can hardly stand, po ting!" Adam said as he hobbled around mocking her.

Jayvyn, Jacob, and the other slaves laughed heartily as Betty placed the back of her hand on her forehead, saying, in a high, frail voice, "But, I be jus a woman, an you know how delicate we be!"

Lucas, Betty's husband, spit a spray of water as he retorted, "In a pig's eye woman! You ain't dat delicate wid me!" to which everyone laughed.

"Shoot Lucas, you so dumb you lucky she don't club you one!" Frederick chimed in.

"Oh, she do! She do! Dat what I mean!" Lucas replied.

The others laughed and slapped their knees as Betty leaned into Lucas, giving him an affectionate hug.

Remarkably, Jayvyn thought, despite their circumstances and all the mean-spirited things the white man did, his people could still find joy and stuff to laugh about. It was just one of the traits he loved so much about his race.

After everyone settled down a bit, Jayvyn and Jacob sat by the fire, listening while some of the other men quietly repeated news they'd recently heard.

"You know, I heah'd dem nigga down in Flo'da got dem a fort an be fight'n da Brits wid de Spanish army. Got dem fancy uniform, guns an ebryting!" said Silas, who frequently had a good line on gossip.

"Yeah, dat right, Silas. I heah'd dey be fight'n de good fight down der. Served up a pile o lead on some dem soldier from round heah. Kilt a lot of 'em, sent de rest packin. Dat wha I heah."* remarked a man named Ceasar.

"Dey be a bunch o nigga left de Boone place 'bout a mont ago, no one seen em since. I heah dey wad seben o 'em. Dey say dey be

---

** Known as the Battle of Bloody Mose, General Oglethorpe and the Brits initially seized Ft. Mose in St. Augustine, but it was later reclaimed in a successful and brutal counterattack by the Spanish, its black militia, and the Yamasee, a Native American Tribe causing the British to retreat from Florida* goin ta join de fight." Virgil said.

"Yeah, I heah dat too. I sho hope dey make it." Replied Silas.

As they listened, young Jacob came over to join his father and Jayvyn.

Now fourteen, Jacob was getting to be a young man. He'd sprung up quite a bit in height and was filling out from hard work in the fields.

His father, Jacob Sr., knew young Jacob listened intently to the discussions of the older men, and he'd come to the conclusion he was old enough now and should know what was happening around. Besides, he'd rather he heard things in his presence and from the men with more discretion than the younger, more impulsive rebels. He still worried his son might be inspired by the hasty younger men to do something foolish.

Picking up on the discussion, young Jacob said, "I heah dey be some Injun be hep'n 'm so dey make it."

Giving a quick glance to Jacob Sr., Virgil said, "Dat be true, but donchu be git'n no idea, boy. Dey be catch'n plenty o nigga too, 'n when dey do, dey ain't always comin back alive, y'heah?"

The other men grunted in solemn agreement.

A moment later, Silas spoke, "Sum tol me dem slave catcha com'n back wid just de scalp, an dey be git'n paid for dat. Dey don't even hafta hab da body."

"Man! Dat be bad alright! I sho hope dem nigga from Boone be ok." Virgil lamented, shaking his head slowly.

Jacob Sr. stiffened as he listened, thinking about his own son, unconsciously placing his hand on young Jacob's knee.

He knew how his son was thinking. He knew how all the young

men were thinking. They'd seen and had enough of the white man's injustice. All of them had romanticized about the Stono Rebellion and imagined how, if only *they* had been there, it surely would have succeeded—*they* would have beaten the white man right then and there.

The young bucks talked amongst themselves and acted their courage out in their minds with fine detail. When they heard about Boone's slaves escaping, they were right there with them, making their way stealthily through the wilderness, night and day.

When they heard the stories about the Spanish Black militia, it was *them* their minds eye saw, proudly adorned in handsome, dark blue uniforms, grasping long, military muskets—shining bayonets fixed at the ready. *They* watched *their* white bosses approach across the still, benign battlefield, unaware of the total annihilation awaiting them just a few short steps away.

There was no doubt about the outcome. The white man would have no chance when he engaged *them* on the battlefield—a level battlefield—where each man was equal.

Jacob really couldn't blame his son. It was the same when he'd been his age. Every boy fantasizes about proving himself in some way. Every man wants his son to be strong, brave, and make something good of himself.

But when the moment approaches, reality weighs in—the matter becomes more serious. All a father really wants is for his son to grow up, to survive and become a man, and to live a better life than him.

Jacob did want all of that for his son. He just couldn't stomach the idea of losing another son—his only remaining son—especially not that way.

Likewise, he couldn't bear the thought of Hannah, again, going through what she had when they lost Robert. She was a strong woman, but everyone has a limit as to how much they can take. She'd already been through more than most could handle. He wasn't sure she could endure another tragedy of that magnitude, and he was certain he could never survive without her.

Jayvyn felt the depth of Jacob's emotions, noticing his hand on his son's knee. Although he had no children of his own, he could imagine the intense feelings a parent must have for their child.

Once more, thoughts of his own family entered his mind as he watched his friend's endless love pour out for his son. He remembered the day young Jacob was born, watching his small, alien fingers fumble their way into a tiny fist while Hannah held him swaddled in cloth. Likewise, he recalled the joy on their faces as they gazed in wonder at their newly born child.

He thought of little Robert, too, remembering how easily young Jacob filled his older brother role—how inseparable the two were. Little Robert's death had devastated them all, and he wondered what Robert might be like now, had he lived. Would they both aspire to join the escaped slaves? To journey to Florida and fight the Brits? Probably so, he thought. After all, boys will be boys.

In the year following, reports trickled in about rebellions that were planned but failed. One incident in particular resulted in the public hanging of over fifty slaves. It was rumored that a fellow slave reported details of a planned rebellion to his master, who then intercepted the rebels on the day of the uprising. It was further reported that the snitch was compensated with clothes and a little money.

When Jayvyn heard of this, he was immediately reminded of Isaac back on Barbados, the slave who informed George about Andrew taking food to the escapees. He remembered the abhorrent punishments the slaves received and the price Isaac would ultimately pay with the loss of his spirit for all eternity.

How bad would the consequences be for the slave who caused over fifty slaves to be hanged? Hanged for nothing more than seeking their freedom?

Why did he do it? Jayvyn wondered.

From what he'd heard, he was rewarded with only a few clothes and a little money.

He remembered Isaac had been rewarded with better rations, lighter duty, and some rum.

But at what cost?

The cost was measured in lives and freedom—both for the ones they turned in, as well them.

The snitches would live the rest of their lives, in this world, bearing unfathomable shame.

But they'd endure eternal torment in the afterlife.

No amount of reward could justify the cost.

Jayvyn felt both loathing and pity for them.

- 36 -

Initiation into Manhood

The slaves on Turner's plantation continued to receive valuable information through the grapevine.

More and more slaves were risking escape, however seldom was ever heard about their individual success. News of failed attempts, on the other hand, always got around.

Vigilance had increased to prevent and catch those attempting to flee. Patrols and plantation bosses constantly surveilled roads at night on the lookout for slaves who happened to be in the wrong place at the wrong time. If caught out without a pass, consequences could be severe.

The new province of Georgia had been established some time ago, and over time, the slaves learned bits and pieces about this territory through the grapevine. Most relevantly, they had to cross it if they wanted to reach Florida.

Surprisingly, although Georgia was a British colony, slavery was prohibited there. But this didn't mean it was a safe haven for escaped slaves. Far from it. Slave catchers were more than welcome to patrol there. Further, citizens of Georgia were quite willing to return captured slaves themselves and reap the rewards.

In fact, there was great pressure from Georgians to adopt slavery; however, the proprietors and military lobbied hard against this. This was because England was at war with Spain, and since Spanish Florida granted slaves freedom with compulsory military service, it was considered risky to have a large pool of recruits close by.

Their case had been proven by the Battle of Bloody Mose, when the Spanish, with the help of the Black militia, successfully defeated the British.

However, things changed rapidly in 1742, when the emboldened Spanish made an attack on Georgia. This time, the British successfully repelled the Spanish and its Black militia in an engagement known as the Battle of Bloody Marsh.

Following the Spanish defeat, attitudes regarding the Negro threat changed, and soon Georgia's citizens were flaunting official policy and bringing in their own slaves.*

Also, Fort Mose had been ruined in the Battle of Bloody Mose and Florida's Black citizens were relocated deeper into St. Augustine.

After that, stories of active fighting in the Black militia abated, dampening enthusiasm among young Blacks.† However, the promise of freedom was still strong incentive to get to Florida.

Acts of resistance still persisted among the slaves—work slowdowns were a normal, even expected activity; equipment regularly broke; sickness was faked; things were taken.

But the incident of the slave who snitched, causing fifty hangings two years ago, along with similar snitching episodes since, had put a

---

* *Importation of slaves into Georgia was illicit at first, but by 1751 the practice of slavery was officially permitted in the colony*

† *Fort Mose would be rebuilt by the Spanish in 1752, however its free black citizens remained in St. Augustine per the governor's order. In 1763, Spain ceded Florida, and thus Fort Mose, to Great Britian*

check on mass rebellion. The idea there could be an informant among them had become a regular concern.

To some degree, this relieved Jacob Sr. as open talk of rebellion from young agitators had quelled. His son wasn't getting as stirred up as before. However, young Jacob, now sixteen, was far from settled.

Even so, He'd found more common ground with his son lately. He seemed inclined to listen to the older folks and take information from the grapevine more thoughtfully. Jacob Sr. had no problem with his son developing a healthy level of resistance to slavery; he just wanted him to practice it in smart ways. He dreamed he'd someday earn his freedom for good and live a full and happy life.

But, unfortunately, one day midway through his sixteenth year, young Jacob was caught by Mr. Dawson with one of Master Turner's chickens.

It was one evening, after dark, when he had no business being out. He was caught red-handed in the coop as the other chickens squawked in protest. He'd already wrung the neck of the chicken he was holding to keep it quiet, so there was no question about what he'd done.

Mr. Dawson was finishing up work at the barn when he heard the ruckus in the chicken coop. Seeing a shadowy black form inside, he hollered, "Stop right theah, nigga!"

Jacob froze in his tracks, dropping the dead chicken where he stood. He didn't know what to do. He thought about making a run for it, but he was surrounded by fencing, and Mr. Dawson was approaching the only door out. He'd never make it.

"Uh, I seed a chicken outside, suh, an went to put it back!" he said, thinking as quickly as he could.

"You put the chicken back, zat right, nigga? You mean this heah dead chicken at yo feet?"

Jacob fumbled as he searched his rattled mind for what to say.

"Maybe dat 'cause o de fox, suh!" he barked out desperately, but Mr. Dawson was having none of that.

"Fox takes the chicken wid him, boy," and he cuffed Jacob hard on the back of the head, sending him sprawling in the dirt.

Mr. Dawson then yanked him up by the scruff of his neck and marched him directly over to Master Turner's front porch, where he knocked loudly on the door.

When Master Turner answered, Mr. Dawson said, "Cots this'un nigga stealin' from the chicken coop, boss," holding Jacob firmly by the back of his neck. "Wha's you wan me to do wit him?"

Master Turner scowled at Jacob in the dim light.

"Is that right, boy? You stealin' from my chicken coop? After all I do for you here at my fine plantation?" and went on angrily, "Is that how you repay me? What business do you have takin' my chickens, boy?"

Jacob, shaking, looked up at Master Turner, terrified to realize what he'd just been caught doing.

He stammered, "I-I-I don know Massa Turna, I-I went der causa mistake, I-I tink it be for de slaves, Massa Turna, maybe dat why I be der, causin I tink you..."

Mr. Dawson cuffed him hard on the back of his head, knocking young Jacob to the ground again. "Don you lie ta the Masta, you mangy nigga! You in nuff truble as is, heah?"

"S-s-sorry suh!" He said, dazedly getting to his feet.

"Wha we gonna do Master Turner? You wan me to whip him good?"

Master Turner considered the situation and said, "No, Mr. Dawson, it's late and you have other business. Chain him up in the barn for the night; he'll keep fine there.

"But stealing's become a bit of problem around here lately. This isn't the first thing to go missing. I think it's time we deliver a message to the rest of the slaves about stealing.

"Tomorrow's Sunday. In the morning, you and the other men can take him to the slaves' quarters to make an example of him."

"Yes, sir," Mr. Dawson said, and turned with Jacob's neck in his vise-like grip.

"Come wid me, boy, you's sleepin heah."

Jacob was put in shackles and chained to one of the large rings used to hold slaves for whipping. He lay scared and alone through the night, helpless to move anywhere. He wondered what the master meant by 'make an example of him'. He'd find out soon enough.

That night, Hannah and Jacob Sr. worried late into the evening as their son hadn't returned. They had no idea what happened to him.

Jacob Sr. privately worried his son might have run off. Even though he seemed a little more settled these days, they both still worried continuously about him.

Both had witnessed the drastic change in their son's behavior after Robert died, but six years had passed since then.

Both had done all they could to help young Jacob understand and accept the loss of his brother. They knew it had been a defining moment in his young life and would set the tone for his transition into adulthood. They just had to hope he made it through his adolescent years.

In the morning, when he still hadn't returned, Hannah and Jacob Sr.'s worry deepened, but neither dared to say anything to anyone else. If he'd run, they'd certainly be interrogated and most likely whipped for any information they might have.

As they were having their porridge in the morning, Victor came and told them he'd spoken with Mr. Dawson that morning. He told them Jacob had been caught stealing one of Master Turner's chickens and had spent the night chained in the barn.

Hannah put her hand to her mouth, exclaiming, "Oh No! Not our Jacob!" as tears immediately filled her eyes.

Jacob Sr. placed his arm around her shoulders and turned to Victor, asking, "Victa, wha dey gonna do? Wha gonna happen?"

Victor looked sympathetically at the pair. Everyone had felt sorry for Jacob and Hannah since the loss of Robert. It had been an event that shook the entire community. All the slaves loved the two little boys who brought so much joy to the group; all collectively worried for the family as they recovered. Many were aware of the change in young Jacob's disposition and had made efforts to help him too.

Victor responded, "I'm sorry. Jus hafta wait 'n see."

At that moment, the clip-clopping of hoofbeats was heard approaching from the road leading to the master's house—a murmur grew among the slaves outside.

Hannah started to shake as the three of them turned and headed out the door.

They looked out to see several shapes on horseback emerge from the dark woods, followed by the wagon driven by Bartholomew. Connected to the back, chained by his wrists, walked their son, Jacob—dirty and scared. Clear lines from recent tears streaked his dust-covered face.

Hannah froze in her tracks, not knowing what to do. Before she could think much more about it, she broke from her husband's embrace and burst into a run.

"Jacob! Jacob!" she cried as she ran toward him.

Mr. Dawson reached out and caught her with the back of his hand, knocking her to the dirt.

"Best you stay away, Hannah!" he bellowed. "This boy o yo's done some things he gotsta ansa fo now."

Hannah lay crying, "No! No! Please, not my Jacob!" as Jacob Sr. ran up, lifting her from the dirt.

Jacob Sr., trying to reason, said, "Please, Missa Dawson, he just a boy! We talk to him! He won't make no mo trouble! I promise!"

Mr. Dawson, without a shred of sympathy, looked back and said, "He just as much a man as you now, Jacob, an has ta learn his lesson like any udda nigga.

"Now stand back an don make no trouble fo yo sef, heah?"

Jacob, knowing there wasn't anything he could do, took Hannah gently by her shoulders as she shook with tears.

"C'mon Hannah," he said, "maybe dey go easy on im."

Still crying, he took her to the edge of the growing throng of slaves, who gathered in a large semicircle before the bosses.

Mr. Dawson, who was out in front, motioned for Bartholomew

to bring the wagon to the forefront, young Jacob securely attached to its back.

When everything was in place and the assembly of slaves had become reasonably quiet, he stepped forward to address the group.

"You all knows you's gots it pretty good heah at Masta Turner's plantation," he started.

"He a good man, an treats you niggas bettah 'n most any otha owna round heah. All he evah ask is dat his niggas work hard fo him.

"He gives you a good place to live, clothes on yo back, food, a day off, an mostly lets you live in peace.

"Any a yous thinks diffn't, you speak up right now."

He paused, gazing over the group to see who'd dare to disagree with what he'd said.

No one did.

"Das wha I thought. You knows how good yas got it.

"Now, las night, I see's dis heah nigga in Masta Turner's chicken coop stealin his chickens! He in theah after dark when nobody gots no bidness theah at all. Caught'm red-handed wid dis heah chicken wid its neck already wrung!" he said as he flung the chicken down onto the back of the wagon.

"Could'a shot 'm right then an theah.

"But Masta Turner a fair man an don wants ta hurts his nigga's if'n he can heps it, so's I takes him to the Masta an he showed him mo mercy 'n he deserves.

"He let 'm sleep in da barn whiles he thinks what to do 'bout it. Das mo dan I'da done, you can bet!

"Now you all knows it ain't right to steal from de Masta, an dis heah nigga gots ta be punished.

"But, since Masta Turner de fair man dat he is, he only gots to have twenty lashes to learn hid lesson.

"We ain't gonna cut no finga's of'n him, not dis time, but if'n dis stealin happens agin, den things gonna get worse.

"Am I makin mysef cleah?" He barked.

The slaves all feared Mr. Dawson and took him completely at his word. They shuffled, heads down, nodding and mumbling their understanding.

"Good! Now takes dis nigga ova tha tree theah an fix'm in place." He said, indicating a nearby sycamore.

One of the bosses went to young Jacob and removed his shirt. Taking him by the chain, he said, "C'mon nigga, time to pays fo dat chick'n," as the other bosses nodded their agreement.

The chain holding Jacob's wrists was passed high around the trunk of the sycamore so his arms were above his head, his chest pressed tightly against the bark.

Mr. Dawson handed the boss the cat-o-nine tails he'd brought.

The man stood behind young Jacob as Hannah buried her face against Jacob Sr.'s chest and sobbed.

It wasn't long before she heard the first crack as the sinister whip fell upon her son's previously unblemished back. She stiffened, crying out as she tried to block the thought of her baby, whom she'd cared so gently for since birth, being mercilessly flogged. She'd seen too many whippings and knew well the damage it caused.

At the second crack, she heard her son cry out, his cries intensifying on the third and fourth. She couldn't bear it as she buried her face deeper into her husband's chest, his embrace abruptly constricting with each fall of the whip.

Five, six, seven, and still her baby cried out. In her mind, he was still a boy. He'd been hurt so badly already it made her soul break. She sobbed uncontrollably, unable to look up and see her tender-hearted son being thrashed so viciously. It was a nightmare beyond comprehension as the whip crashed down over and over again. Soon, she didn't hear Jacob's cries anymore and knew he must have mercifully passed out, but still the beating continued.

Finally, the awful noise came to an end and Hannah tentatively looked up. Her son hung limp and ruined—his back a bleeding mass, blood running down his legs, collecting on the dirt below. The white man stood panting, shaking out the bloody ends of the whip, having finished his deed to the satisfaction of the other white bosses.

Bartholomew sat head-down in the wagon as the bosses climbed up on their mounts and turned. Clip clop, clip clop, back up the long, dark road to the master's big house. Soon, the clip-clopping faded away. They were gone.

All was quiet again as Hannah and Jacob went to their son; Jayvyn and others came with water to clean poor young Jacob's back.

They gently took him from the tree and brought him to their quarters, where they laid his body face down on a low bunk.

Hannah wept as she sat by his side for the rest of the day, gently mopping his wounds with a wet cloth. Jacob Sr. sat with her, and others brought herbs they knew to be soothing aides to healing. Some made teas from elderberry leaves; others brought aloe and horehound weed.*

Jacob woke in agony later that morning, feeling the deep bruises and open wounds laced across his now excoriated back. Hearing his moans, his mother gently stroked the back of his head, consoling him with her soft voice.

Her cooing sounds were soothing and reassuring to Jacob; it was the sound he remembered so often as a young boy during those times when only the comfort of a mother's love would do. He turned his head, looking from one eye, to see her face. He saw she'd been crying as he brought one arm up to rest on her lap. She just looked back, softly saying, "Sh-h-h-h now, chil, yo need yo rest," and he closed his eyes again, happy to be in his mother's care.

Later that day, Victor came to check on him. "How he be?" he inquired.

Jacob Sr. quietly said, "He strong; he be fine. But it gonna take time."

He sadly shook his head. "You see dat hid back be bad. Dey whip him hard, Victa."

Victor responded, "Yes, Jacob. Yo son be strong, like you. Tomorrow he can rest; I be tell de boss.

"Margaret be here, 'n she look afta him."

"Tank you, Victa," Jacob responded, and Victor left the family to nurture their son.

Several more slaves stopped in to see how young Jacob was doing that evening, Jayvyn among them. Everyone was deeply impacted by

---

* *Many slaves brought deep knowledge of the medicinal qualities of many plants and herbs from Africa*

the episode, especially those who knew young Jacob's past and how much he'd been struggling.

Later that evening, Jayvyn, once again, reflected on the day young Jacob was born.

He reminisced about the absolute beauty and perfectness he saw when he looked upon his newborn body.

He'd watched the boy take his first steps and learn the words he'd use to speak his mind.

His chest had swelled with pride when he saw how lovingly he adopted his younger brother.

He agonized over how beautiful and bright this wonderful human being had once been and the excessive hardships he'd had to face so early in life.

It brought him to tears now, as he recalled the savagery of the punishment inflicted on him—his once tender, unbroken skin now doomed to wear the vulgar scars of slavery for the rest of his life.

- 37 -

Every day shall be Sunday, Hallelujah

As was true for every slave who suffered the ravages of the whip, it would be months before young Jacob's wounds healed. However, he was given only two day's rest before being ordered back to work.

The long, hot days in the sweltering fields were unbearable. The rough kersey fabric rubbed against the raw, fresh wounds on his back. Working without a shirt was not an option. The punishing rays of the sun were far too harsh for his skinless back. However, the roughness of the fabric was quick to remove the first membrane of scab.

Renewed bleeding soaked through, sticking his tender wounds to the fabric. Removing his shirt had to be done slowly as the blood-caked cloth was pulled from his back. His mother continued to bathe his back every night with lotions and salves, and over time they began to work their healing powers.

Not surprisingly, Jacob's mood had regressed back to sullen brooding. His manner, once again, became quiet and dark as he bore his indignance alone. Not one to talk openly about his pain and suffering, young Jacob withdrew into himself, putting up protective barriers to shield him from the world's cruelty.

He stuck to his work in the fields, eyes shifting suspiciously about, face devoid of the smiles and animation he'd been known for as a small child. His parents and others were saddened to see him this way, but everyone understood, given what he'd been through.

As before, many went out of their way to engage cheerfully with him in hopes of bringing him out of his funk, but it was to no avail.

He'd barely begun to come around after the tragedy of his brother's death when he was harshly knocked off his feet again. Hopelessness and despair rushed in to fill the deep rut gouged from his youthful soul.

It was a heartrending setback for his father as he thought about the closeness he and his son were just starting to achieve. Instead of father and child, they were beginning to broach the realm of man to man all fathers dream of—where father and son can share mature thoughts on the level of equals. He lamented now that it would probably be years before they reached that place again.

Young Jacob's wounds had barely begun to form permanent scars when Hannah and Jacob Sr. woke one morning to find him missing again. Their hearts sank as they remembered his debacle over the chicken incident, and they hoped there was some reasonable explanation for his absence. Later that morning, after the slaves had all reported to work, Victor came to inquire his whereabouts.

"Where be Jacob?" he asked Jacob Sr. as they were gathering their tools for the day.

Jacob Sr. hesitated uncomfortably as he thought of what he would say. Putting his hand on Victor's shoulder, he steered him away from the ears of those nearby. In a nervous voice, he quietly said, "He not be in hid bed when we wake up Victa, we don't know where he be."

Victor, whose responsibility it was to account for all the slaves, shot him a concerned look, asking, "Jacob, did he go to bed in your quarters?"

Jacob Sr. responded, "Yes, Victa, he be der wid me 'n Hannah. She clean hid back an he go to sleep. We no see he gone 'til de morn'n. We be worry."

Victor sighed. "Dat no be good. Go to work, Jacob, 'n don't say nuting. Maybe he show up."

With that, Jacob Sr. went to work trying not to behave any differently than he would any other day, but his mind was on his son.

Hannah and he sat together during their mid-day break, worrying between them while trying not to betray the knowledge of their missing son. However, since young Jacob usually joined them for lunch, it was hard for others not to notice. Both of them grew progressively more nervous as their son's absence became more obvious.

Finally, Victor came and said, "Hannah, Jacob, yo son be miss'n. De boss aks me 'bout 'm, 'n I gotsta say I no seen him.

"Missa Dawson want to see you bote. He tell me to get you; you gotsta come wid me now."

It was a moment they dreaded as they rose to follow Victor back to the barn where Mr. Dawson waited.

They walked slowly out of the fields, through the compound, and proceeded uncomfortably up the long dirt road to the barn.

Along the way, Jacob Sr. asked Victor what he should say.

Victor responded, "You gotsta tell 'm all dat you know."

Jacob Sr. complained, "But we don't know nuting! He jus be gone!"

Victor said, "Den tell 'm dat. Dat be all you know."

Jacob Sr. and Hannah's nervousness increased as they approached the barn. When it came into view, they saw Mr. Dawson standing in the doorway, glaring unhappily.

"Wheah yo son, Jacob?" he demanded when they got close.

Jacob Sr.'s mouth instantly went dry as he responded, "I not know, Missa Dawson. He jus be gone when Hannah an I wake up in de morn'n."

"Hannah, what you gots ta say?" he barked.

Hannah stammered, "Dat be wha happen Missa Dawson. He be in hid bed las night, jus like alway, an we go ta sleep. He jus be gone in de morn'n, dat all we know.

"We be worry 'bout 'm!"

Mr. Dawson eyed both of them up and down. "That's all you know, eh? You ain't hidin him somewheah is you?"

Jacob Sr. said, "No, No, Missa Dawson! We not know where he be!"

Appraising them cooly, Mr. Dawson finally said, "Well, we see bout dat.

"Dat boy o yo's been some truble, and I hopes fo yo sake an his dat he ain't done sump'n stupid.

"Go back to work, we be lookin fo him, an if'n we don find'm, you's gots some splainin to do, heah?"

"Yassuh, Missa Dawson, suh!" Jacob Sr. replied as sincerely as he could.

Then he and Hannah followed Victor back out to the fields.

As they walked along, Hannah kept repeating, "Oh, Lawd! Whea he gone, Jacob? Victa, wha gonna happen?"

Her mind ran wild with fear and apprehension at the realization her son had disappeared, probably run. Jacob Sr., too, had reached the same conclusion.

There wasn't much Victor could say. They all knew the consequences of slaves running away.

Jacob Sr.'s mind swirled as he thought about the three slaves who were caught a few years back. They'd been severely whipped and forced to wear collars around their necks for six months. He didn't want that for his son.

Worse yet, he remembered the grisly news Silas had delivered about slave catchers only having to bring a scalp for a reward. He couldn't bear the thought as he wondered where his son was and what he was doing.

His gut churned with anxiety.

All through the day and into the night, he and Hannah remained perplexed, dreading the days to come.

By this time, it had become widespread knowledge that young Jacob had disappeared. Some of their neighbors came by to express their concern and lend their support, but everyone shared Hannah and Jacob's trepidation.

The best any of them could hope for was they never saw or heard from young Jacob again. At least that way, they could comfort themselves with the notion he'd made it to freedom somewhere. After all, there had been many such stories of success.

Not very assured, Hannah and Jacob slept fitfully and rose to work as usual the following day, somewhat comfortable in the knowledge their son at least hadn't been found.

That evening, young Jacob still hadn't returned, and they inquired with Victor to see if he had any news. Victor didn't, but all of them knew full well that vigorous efforts were being made to find him before too many days passed.

The morning dawned, and still young Jacob hadn't been found. At this point, each passing day brought a small amount of hope.

By evening, the news of young Jacob's absence had made the grapevine.

As was the case with every escape, slaves from neighboring plantations began rooting for his success. If any happened to see him, it was likely they'd help him as much as they could—whether by hiding him, giving him food and supplies, or pointing him in the right direction. In any case, news picked up about him was sure to make it back to the slaves at Turner's plantation.

Chatter within the plantation teemed as the slaves discretely weighed their optimism. With every passing hour, their hopes grew. By the fourth night, the talk around the evening meal was encouraging.

Silas and the usual group sat opining among themselves.

"You know, four dem otha nigga be scaped from heah 'bout four yeah back 'n neva be found." Silas remarked.

"Dat right, Silas! Dey neva catched dem otha seben from Boone neitha!" Virgil weighed in.

"Whole lotta dem make it somewheah. I bet dey be libin da good life whea-evah dey end up," chimed Ceasar.

"You know Jacob, dat boy o yo got hissef a head on hid shoulda. He know how ta keep quiet an stay outta sight," encouraged Silas.

"Yeah, 'side he a man now, ain't dat right? What he be now? Sebenteen?" asked Virgil.

Jacob Sr. nodded but kept silent. While he found their optimism encouraging, he missed his son immensely. All he could think about was somehow reuniting with him somewhere else, far away from the plantation and anything to do with slavery. It was the stuff of his dreams, where he and Hannah would somehow be reunited with both of their children and enjoy a different life—the life they all deserved.

Silas looked over at him thoughtfully, "Cheer up, Jacob, we all keep'n im in our praya; you can bet on dat.

"You gotsta hab hope, an if'n anybody can make it, yo son hab de betta chance den most, ain't dat right, fellas?"

"Yeah, dat right." The rest of the men added their sincere agreement with thoughtful looks of encouragement.

Jayvyn nodded supportively to his friend, saying, "Jacob, de one ting you want de mots fo Jacob be hid freedom, yes?

"Now he be gone to take it. Miss'n 'm be de price we gotsta pay fo hid freedom, but it be de fair price."

Jacob Sr. couldn't help the tears in his eyes, but he was thankful for the kind words of support and encouragement from those around him.

He appreciated Jayvyn's words immensely. It was not too high a price if his son attained his freedom. He was right. It was the thing he wanted more than anything for his son. He'd rather miss him than have him remain here as a slave.

However, the following evening, word began to circulate that a slave had been caught the night before. There could be no doubt it was young Jacob since there were no other reports of a slave escaping recently.

The mood of the slaves was solemn and quiet that evening, as everyone anticipated young Jacob's return and the punishment awaiting him.

Hannah was especially distraught and fretted continuously as the women of the group tried to console her the best they could. No one, however, was offering the hope that maybe it wasn't young Jacob who'd been caught. This wasn't a time for false hopes.

As it had been with so much in their lives, reality would have to be confronted and lived with, no matter what it was. Both Jacob Sr. and Hannah were crushed as they awaited further news.

The reality of the news was far worse than anyone knew, however.

Bartholomew, being the closest to Master Turner, learned before anyone else.

Young Jacob had indeed been caught the previous evening. He'd made it about twenty miles or so from the plantation and was caught stealing food from another plantation to the south.

As had happened before, he was caught by the plantation's overseer, who wasn't as understanding as Mr. Dawson had been. Instead of taking him to his plantation's owner, he alerted a few of the lower bosses.

For whatever reason, they weren't going to let young Jacob get away with whatever he'd done and took it upon themselves to deliver justice in the way they thought he deserved.

He was found in the morning hanging by his neck from a tree about two miles down the road from this plantation. Someone notified the night watchman, who recognized Alfred Turner's brand on young Jacob's hip, and a rider was sent to Turner's plantation.

Master Turner had Bartholomew hitch the team to his wagon, and the two of them followed the horseman back out to the spot where young Jacob was found.

There they were met by the night watchman, who'd been questioning some of the citizens in the area to see if they knew anything. He'd been to some nearby plantations as well, but nobody had anything to offer that would help reveal who'd done this.

When he arrived, Master Turner was shocked by what he saw. Young Jacob's body, still hanging from the tree, showed signs of severe beating. His face was severely bruised, both of his eyes were swollen shut, and both hands had been cut off.

Master Turner, justifiably outraged to find that his slave had not only been hung but tortured and mutilated as well, notified the night watchman he intended to lodge his grievance with the magistrate's office in Charles Town.

After cutting young Jacob down, he and Bartholomew loaded his body onto the buckboard and proceeded back to the plantation.

Upon arrival, Master Turner informed Mr. Dawson of the matter.

After a brief discussion, it was decided, due to the extreme desecration of young Jacob's body, it would be better if Mr. Dawson had his men bury it somewhere off-site and keep the details from the slaves so as not to rile them.

They both agreed it was a delicate situation, and Mr. Dawson thought it would be best to think of some other cause of death. He also advised notifying Hannah and Jacob Sr. of their son's death as soon as possible in order to get ahead of the news. Master Turner agreed.

Mr. Dawson set out to assign two of his field bosses the task of getting rid of young Jacob's body and then find Victor and tell him to fetch Hannah and Jacob Sr. and bring them to Master Turner.

Sometime later that afternoon, Victor came for Hannah and Jacob Sr. in the field. They assumed young Jacob had been found, but were confused as to why Master Turner wanted to see them. Neither of them had ever been asked to go see Master Turner directly before. But Victor had no other news. He only said they were to go with him right then, right in the middle of work.

Both of them looked nervously at each other as they walked out with Victor, wondering why *Master Turner* would call them in from the fields.

When they arrived at the big house, Master Turner came out onto the grand porch to speak with them. He told them young Jacob had been found alive by the slave patrol. Then he went on to say an unfortunate accident had happened while they were keeping him overnight and young Jacob had died.

Hannah stood dumbfounded for a moment before fainting dead away as Victor reached out to catch her in his arms.

"Wha yo mean he die, Massa Turna?" Jacob Sr. asked incredulously, unable to comprehend the news he'd just heard.

Looking down at his feet, Master Turner replied, "Uh, they weren't, uh, sure what happened; they think, uh, they think it might have been his heart gave out. That's all I know."

Jacob Sr., becoming visibly upset, said, "He a healthy boy, Massa Turna. Boy, don jus up 'n die like dat!

"I wansta know wha happen to my boy! Where he be? Where my boy?" as tears formed in his eyes.

Master Turner, clearly not having his explanation thoroughly worked out, became exasperated. He didn't need to elaborate on his reason for any nigger dying. It was his property, after all!

Not in the habit of having to answer to any slave, he flippantly responded, "Look, Jacob, he's dead! They buried him there. Now that's all I can tell you!

"I lost a good nigger; it cost me plenty, and I'm not happy about it either!" as if that was end of the matter.

Jacob Sr. couldn't believe what he was hearing. His mind snapped in that instant.

Without another thought, he took a hard swing at Master Turner, hitting him squarely in the face.

Master Turner staggered back, blood flowing heavily from his nose and lip. But before he could begin to regain himself, Jacob Sr. leapt on top of him and began bashing his head off of the floor.

Victor sprang into action as fast as he could, setting Hannah down and grabbing Jacob Sr. from behind, yelling, "Jacob! Jacob! Get off!" as he pulled him off of Master Turner.

Master Turner lay dazed on the porch as Mr. Dawson sprinted from the barn.

He couldn't believe his eyes.

"Wha's happen heah?" he yelled.

"Masta Turner, sir! You alright?"

Then, turning to Bartholomew, who'd emerged from the house, he yelled, "Git some whatta an a towel, nigga! Hurry!"

Bartholomew turned in a panic, saying, "Oh Yassa!" and ran back to the house, soon returning with a towel and a pitcher of water.

Master Turner had sat up by that time, took the towel, and dabbed it at his face and the back of his head.

"I'm alright, Mr. Dawson," he proclaimed. "That there nigger attacked me."

Mr. Dawson turned in astonishment toward Jacob Sr. and Victor, his face a mixture of disbelief and rage.

"Dat true? You mad, nigga? You hits yo masta? Victah, take dis nigga an chain him up in da barn!"

"Yassuh, Missa Dawson," Victor said quickly, and struggled backward with Jacob Sr.

Two other slaves emerged from the barn as they heard the commotion and helped to restrain Jacob Sr. with chains, while Mr. Dawson turned his attention to his boss.

Victor then returned to Hannah, who was sitting, dazed and confused after fainting on the porch.

"Wha happen? Whea be Jacob?" she asked as she looked over the surreal scene.

"Nevah you mind, nigga," barked Mr. Dawson.

He continued, "Victor, git this nigga outta heah, and git back ta work!

"You otha nigga's git back to work," he shouted to the two standing by the barn door.

His first priority was to get Master Turner inside and settled into a chair.

Victor took Hannah, his arm around her, as she staggered, unsure of what had just happened.

She looked over at Jacob Sr., who stood in shackles, chained to the door, bursting out, "Jacob! Jacob! Wha happen?! Victa, why Jacob be der? What dey gonna do to Jacob?!" she cried in her confusion.

Victor just tightened his arm around her and said, "C'mon Hannah, you gotsta come wid me now; jus take it easy; ebryting be ok; jus walk wid me," as gently as he could, but Hannah continued to sob hysterically as she tried to wrest from his grip.

"Victa! Victa! Wha happen, Victa?" she sobbed as they made their way unsteadily back to the quarters.

"Wha my Jacob do Victa? Oh Lawd, Massa Turna say my boy dead! Victa! Wha happen?" she uttered between sobs, and Victor just continued to console her as well as he could as they walked down the long, wooded road.

By the time they'd reached the quarters, Hannah had quieted her mind enough to be able to speak a little clearer, but naturally she was still extremely upset.

She straightened, took Victor by the shoulders, looked him straight in the eye, and said, "Victa, you gotsta tell me now. Please, Victa, I gotsta know wha happen."

Victor looked back at her, knowing he had to explain what had just happened.

He hesitated, thinking, *How kin I do dis? How kin I tell dis po woman, who jus find out her son be dead, dat her huband 'tacked hid masta? A sho deat sent'nce!*

Then he steeled himself, digging deep, and said, "Hannah, it be bad. Jacob no be 'cept'n Massa Tuhna reason yo son be dead. He be real mad 'n hit Massa Tuhna 'n tack'm, knock'm to de groun'. Missa Dawson chain'm to de barn, ain nutin nobody can do now."

Hannah looked back at him, her eyes wide, lips trembling. "Oh Lawd! Oh Gawd! Dey gonna kill'm fo sho!! 'N my baby be dead! Oh Victa!" and went back to bawling irrepressibly.

Victor, not being sure what to do, stayed with Hannah until the slaves came back from the fields. Victor had Hannah in her quarters, where he tried over and over to console her, but it was no use.

He lied, "Maybe dey go easy on Jacob, on 'count yo son die."

But both of them knew that was unlikely. The worst thing a slave could do was hit a white man, let alone attack his master! It was simply unheard of.

But Victor said, "Hannah, you jus hafta wait 'n see. Dey be nutin else you can do."

Coming in from the fields, Jayvyn went to see why Jacob Sr. and Hannah had disappeared from work that day and check if there was any news about young Jacob.

When he entered, it was obvious something was terribly wrong. Soon he heard the whole unbelievable truth of what had happened that afternoon.

He did the best he could to pick up where Victor left off, but there wasn't much he could do to console Hannah.

Soon the family she and Jacob Sr. shared the quarters with arrived, and the lady of the house, who knew Hannah well, took over for Jayvyn, who went to the courtyard to find Victor.

News spread fast, and it wasn't long before everyone at the quarters knew about what had happened.

Jayvyn asked Victor if young Jacob had really died from complications with his heart, and Victor only replied it was what Master Turner had said.

Poor Hannah was in hysterics through the night, wracked with confusion about what had happened to her son and what the fate of her husband, the only one she had left in the world, would be. Her misery knew no bounds. All anyone could do was to sit with her.

In the morning, Bartholomew came to the slaves' quarters, as he often did, to bring news from the big house.

The slaves were all milling about, getting ready for the day's work and having their breakfast. He told Victor Master Turner was going to be alright and that they were leaving for Charles Town soon with Jacob Sr.

He also told Victor, privately, that he knew young Jacob hadn't died from heart failure but had been mutilated and hung.

Both Victor and Bartholomew knew he had no business changing Master Turner's story and he'd be severely reprimanded should anyone find out. But under the circumstances, Victor understood the slaves, and especially Hannah, had a right to know what really happened. But the sordid details could wait. Her world was destroyed enough for one day.

Victor appealed to Mr. Dawson to allow Hannah the day off. He explained her level of distress and said she wouldn't be able to concentrate on any sort of task.

Mr. Dawson hesitated, but knowing the fate awaiting Jacob Sr. that day, he reluctantly acquiesced.

Margaret stayed with Hannah throughout the long day, doing her best to comfort her in her grief over young Jacob, trying to keep her from jumping to conclusions about her husband's fate. But she knew in her heart of hearts there was no hope for him.

It was later that evening when the slaves were informed that Jacob Sr. was taken to Charles Town to be publicly hanged.

The news was brought by Mr. Dawson, who rode in on horseback.

He summarily announced, in the presence of all the slaves, "fo da crime o 'tacking and injur'n Masta Turna, Jacob was brought ta Charles Town t'day an hang'd in public 'til he dead."

His business finished; he simply turned and rode away—back out the long, dark, dirt road.

Hannah broke down, immediately falling to the ground in desperate sobs. "Oh no! No! NO! Wa I gonna do? My whole family be gone!!" as the other women rushed to her side.

She was carried off to her quarters, crying hysterically, where they did the best they could to console and support her in her grief. But Hannah was devastated beyond repair.

She cried through the night and into the next day until her voice was completely gone. Everyone tried to help, but nothing seemed to work.

Poor, sweet Hannah was left all alone in the world, crushed and bereaved over the loss of her entire family.

All the slaves felt terrible for her; the women gathered around, trying to give their support, the men took up the chores of Jacob Sr., trying to help.

She was forced back into the fields, but she just stood over her hoe, rocking back and forth, oblivious to the shouts and taunts of the white bosses who tried to intimidate her into action.

She was unresponsive to their threats. Some of the other slaves angrily shouted at the bosses to leave her alone.

Knowing how fragile the situation was, they grudgingly relented.

She was lost in a world no one could break into and one she couldn't break out of. Her entire world had been utterly destroyed—shattered—obliterated beyond recognition; not a single scrap left standing that could be redeemed.

There was nothing anyone could do to console the dear, sweet thing, and one day, she, like Julia so long ago, took her own life.

She was found one morning, hanging from one of the big live oak trees out by the big white house, moss dripping from its branches.

Master Turner found her in the morning and brought her body to the slaves so they could bury her—out in the swamp with the rest of the slaves—which they did.

Jayvyn figured she was about forty or so years old.

The slaves gathered around her body that evening.

One of the carpenters had made her a coffin from some old wood scraps and blackened it with charcoal.

They laid her gently into it while most wept. It was the saddest day the slaves had seen in a long, long while.

Torches sparkled through the dark woods that night as she was carried off by a large, slow-moving procession to the grave dug earlier for her.

As she was lowered into her watery grave, a song broke out from somewhere in the group. The rest of the slaves mournfully joined in:

No more rain fall for wet you, Hallelu, hallelu,
No more rain fall for wet you, Hallelujah

No more sun shine for burn you, Hallelu, hallelu,
No more sun shine for burn you, Hallelujah

No more parting in de kingdom, Hallelu, hallelu,
No more parting in de kingdom, Hallelujah

No more backbiting in de kingdom, Hallelu, hallelu,
No more backbiting in de kingdom, Hallelujah

Every day shall be Sunday, Hallelu, hallelu,
*Every day shall be Sunday, Hallelujah**

After the burial, the slaves solemnly turned, torches in hand, and walked slowly back to their quarters.

Jayvyn was especially devastated that night as he remembered his long history with the family, starting so long ago when he was chained to Jacob Sr. on the schooner, *Dorothy.*

His tears flowed freely as he thought about poor Jacob Sr., whom he'd come to know not only as a friend, but as an exceptional human being.

Jacob Sr. had never harmed anyone in this world. His love for his sons and family was pure and knew no bounds. He'd fathered two of the sweetest children Jayvyn had ever known, and now all of them were gone.

The final tragedy that had beset Hannah was cruel beyond comparison. She was such a wonderful woman.

Through a river of tears, he thought back to his early discussions with Hannah, when she first told him about her tribe and homeland.

He thought to himself—*A true queen mother has left our midst.*

* *No more rain fall for wet you—early slave song. Like most, the true origin is unknown*

- 38 -

Tributes and Tempests

Jayvyn carried the sadness of Jacob Sr. and Hannah's tragic lives with him for the rest of his years.

Neither Hannah nor Jacob Sr. ever found out the full truth about what happened to young Jacob. Jayvyn was thankful for that. He couldn't imagine increasing their already unbearable burden with the horrible realization of what had occurred.

But the full story came out after Hannah's death, both from Victor and Bartholomew. The truth was further corroborated as it made its way through the grapevine. A number of people had seen young Jacob's mutilated body that morning, including some slaves.

No one ever came to discover precisely who was responsible for the awful deed, but enough leaked out about young Jacob's theft to determine which plantation he was caught at. The overseer there did admit to catching him red-handed but denied any knowledge about what happened after.

But it didn't really matter. It never went any further.

The owner of that plantation, however, did, out of professional courtesy, pay Master Turner, the fifty shillings stipulated by law for the loss of his slave—even though he wasn't really responsible for it.*

---

* *50s = £2 10s was specified restitution for wantonly causing the death of another's slave*

After all, it was just common decency and the gentlemanly thing to do.

Besides, Master Turner managed a successful appeal to the magistrate in Charles Town for an additional twenty pounds for the loss of young Jacob. He cited, since his death resulted from legitimate punishment for theft, he was owed restitution because a danger to the larger community had been removed.

He'd negotiated this arrangement at the same time he petitioned the court for Jacob Sr.'s public hanging.

He effectively argued it was in the interest of public safety to have Jacob Sr. executed, since he clearly posed a deadly threat, as evidenced by the assault made on Master Turner.*

Since the law provided restitution for the loss of a slave due to lawful discipline, he sought a public execution. That way, he had proof positive he lost his slave as a result of measures taken in the interest of public safety. He received seventy pounds for his noble sacrifice.†

The details of Master Turner receiving compensation for his dead slaves reached the slave community via Bartholomew.

As he often did, Bartholomew ambled into the slaves' compound one Sunday to visit.

"It sho be de shame wha happen to dat fadda 'n hid boy, yassa," he began.

"Massa Tuhna take ol' Jacob right to de maji-state where he gots

---

* *In 1712, revisions to South Carolina law stipulated the death penalty for a Black injuring a white man*

† *All jurisdictions provided for restitution to owners who suffered losses of their property due to discipline as an incentive for slave owners to take such disciplinary action rather than sell their 'dangerous' slave to another jurisdiction*

hissef a hang'n'.

"Dey din't waste no time, dey' clare 'm guilty right on de spot, an afta dey got de crowd togeda, din't take no time, dey strung poor ol' Jacob up right den 'n der, dey did… yassa, dey did." he related as he shook his head in sorrow.

"Den, Massa Tuhna, he went wid de maji-state back to da cote house, ana dey gib 'm money fo Jacob 'n hid boy causin' dey gotsta be punish fo wha dey do so dey don be hurt'n no mo white folk.

"Dat wha dey do, cause Massa Tuhna, he pay good money fo hid nigga, yassa."

The other slaves listened, but knowing how badly the law was stacked against them, it really wasn't a big surprise.

However, every little bit they heard only served to increase their resentment. Everyone had liked Jacob Sr. and his family; he was a good man, and everybody knew it. It made them all sad and angry to know this good family had been taken so unfairly.

They felt especially bad for Hannah. She had no part in any of it, the poor woman. All she wanted was to make the best of her situation. She was so happy to have her wonderful family to look forward to in her otherwise bleak existence.

Life went on at Turner's plantation, albeit with an uneasy air for a time.

For a while, it seemed the white bosses had eased up somewhat in their harshness. They didn't seem so quick to snap and yell at the slaves for minor offenses. They were well aware the slaves had been deeply affected by the traumatic ordeal.

The episode simmered and replayed itself over and over in the slaves' minds. In fact, the story affected slaves for miles around as the heartrending tale made its way across the grapevine.

It was the topic of discussion around the evening fires for a long time as the slaves lamented the profound injustice of Jacob Sr. and his family's fate.

But the slaves, being the resilient people they were, honored their memory by recounting the virtues that made this family so special.

One evening, Jayvyn related, for the first time, his discussion with Hannah so long ago, where she'd revealed to him her family's high status. He related how she'd been next in line to follow her mother as oba panin, or queen mother, in her village.

The slaves sat captivated as he went on to explain what that meant. Most thought such positions of authority, wisdom, and influence were held only by men. Never had it occurred to them a woman could hold such a position. However, as they remembered Hannah, it was easy to imagine her in such a role.

She'd always exhibited fine qualities indicative of good grooming. They realized now that she possessed just the type of temperament strong leaders possess. It had been evident in the strength of character she brought to her family.

Jayvyn went on to explain how he and Jacob had been chained together on the schooner so long ago. How Jacob Sr. had been only six years old when taken from his tribe.

He went on to tell the story of how Jacob Sr. and Hannah discovered they'd both been sold into slavery by the other's tribe. How this had sparked initial hatred between them.

The slaves listened in wonder as they considered this

extraordinary revelation.

Knowing the depth of love between them, no one would've ever guessed this to be the case.

Their respect and admiration for these lost members only deepened in their hearts. Hannah and her family had indeed been wrought from the purest love.

Aware of his slaves' despair, Master Turner decided to return the garden plot as a small concession to help ease tensions.

It was inevitable anyway, seeing as no real attention had been paid to this by the white community. It certainly was a practical way to provide food for the slaves. Besides, many of the plants had naturalized and resurfaced in and around the plot.

Still, it was received as a benevolent gesture by the slaves.

Jayvyn, among the most committed and enthusiastic, went to work right away.

Many remembered Jayvyn being among their best gardeners and took great satisfaction seeing him enjoy his craft once more.

As he worked, he fondly reminisced about the children who'd helped him in the past. He remembered the joy in their faces as they tended their own little plots.

Almost without thought, he developed such a section again, deciding he'd dedicate it to Jacob and Robert. And Michael and Lydia, the children so abruptly torn from Silas and Clara years ago.

He determined to nurture this space in honor of all slaves born to this world with such bright lights in their souls, only to leave downtrodden and brokenhearted.

It wasn't long before the garden was orderly and cleared of

weeds. New plantings flourished in its beds.

Jayvyn became lost in the meditative art of gardening, his soul stoked with peace and tranquility.

The okra he planted in Michael and Lydia's honor grew extra full and bushy. Abundant, cream-colored flowers with rich burgundy centers bloomed brightly. The lush foliage reminding him of the joyous, energetic young pair.

He wondered what their lives had become and hoped, as their mother, Clara, had, that they'd landed in a better place. He mused they must be adults by now, probably even in their thirties. Jayvyn had difficulty imagining them as anything but kids and wondered if he'd recognize them today.

Probably not, he guessed.

He remembered young Jacob and Robert in much the same way—beautiful white-pink blossoms dancing gleefully up tall stalks of benne.

He imagined Hannah and Jacob Sr., reunited with their happy family, off in some other world where they were free and would forever remain so. Jacob and Robert, running hand in hand, from one happy moment to the next—parents looking adoringly on—as they discovered the wonders of their new world.

In moments like this, he thought of his life's path—colliding and intersecting with the paths of others—leaving indelible marks on his soul. It seemed miraculous, or was it?

Maybe instead it was fate—prearranged and orchestrated by the mysterious magic of the universe—what his people referred to as the hand of Ata Emit.

He'd never know.

As the seasons came and went, Jayvyn and the rest of the slaves labored as usual to cultivate the rice. Master Turner's fortunes soared to levels he never imagined possible.

The plantation thrived and grew as slaves cleared more acres to convert into paddies. New reservoirs were created, channeling massive volumes of water to flood the new fields as needed.

The work, as always, was hard, with hot summers and sometimes bitterly cold winters. But never was there a summer so hot as one in particular.

It was a year Jayvyn and the others would never forget. Temperatures soared so high many slaves dropped in the fields from heat exhaustion. Many animals, too, perished in the unbearable heat. It was the hottest any of them could remember, and it took its toll.

Evenings brought little relief as the slaves did what they could to stay hydrated and rest, but everyone and everything moved slowly out of necessity. Even the bosses had a hard time, just sitting on their horses in the blazing, hot sun while the slaves labored. It was truly unbearable, for both man and beast alike.

South Carolina had seen its share of storms over the years. Some summertime storms could bring torrential rain, and, on a few occasions, hurricanes swept in from the Atlantic. However, the year of the worst heat wave in memory brought a storm more powerful and devastating than anyone could have imagined.*

One day in September, as the crops were nearing harvest, turned

---

* *This was the great Carolina hurricane of 1752 occurring over Sept. 14-16 which practically destroyed Charles Town and much of its surrounding communities*

into the most unusual day Jayvyn could ever remember. Unusual in two very notable ways.

The first, which he never came to fully understand, was that he went to bed on a Monday, expecting, as always, the following day would be Tuesday. But on this particular Monday, the white man, for whatever reason, decided the following day would be Thursday.

Although the slaves puzzled with the reasoning behind this, it was a bit of welcome news because it meant they'd enjoy a one-time-only four-day work week as opposed to the standard six. No one argued.

Coincidentally, the date also changed from September 2nd to September 14th—just like that. It was no big deal to the slaves; the white man had done lots of unexplainable things over the years.*

However, the thing making September 14th truly exceptional was a drastic change in the weather.

The day started out normal enough. It was hot and miserable. The slaves suffered as they had all of that stifling summer.

Except, an eerie, peculiar stillness permeated the long, hot afternoon as it dragged into evening. The air seemed to hang—hot and silvery—casting otherworldly shimmers on everything it engulfed.

After the evening meal, the weather began to change. At first, a slight breeze, accompanied by rain showers was welcome relief from the insufferable heat.

** Sept. 2, 1752 was the day that the British latently decided to change from the Julian calendar system, established by Julius Ceasar in 45 BC to the Gregorian calendar, which had been established by Pope Gregory XIII in the 1580s. In order to synchronize to this change, eleven days would be instantly chopped out of the year with the new system changing Tues. Sept. 2nd to Thur. Sept. 14th at midnight*

But in the wee hours, the wind increased by many times. Rain was falling in great, dense sheets across the compound.

As the day dawned, the sky lightened, but no sun would show as the vicious storm gathered momentum.

Jayvyn and the others hunkered down in their quarters. The walls shuddered and shook. Violent blasts of wind and rain threatened to blow the hut apart at any moment.

No fires were kindled that morning. The fireplaces were sodden. Rain cascaded freely down the chimney. Wet soot and ash flowed across the cabin floor.

It felt, at times, the whole cabin would be hurled across the compound.

The door nearly ripped from Jayvyn's hand as he opened it to take a look outside.

Branches cartwheeled across the courtyard. Sheets of rain swept tempestuously over the already puddled ground. Tops of nearby cypress and pine bent sharply. Furious gusts pummeled the lowlands.

The sky was angry. Fast-moving clouds streaked overhead, driven by wind so strong Jayvyn could hardly keep his eyes open. No one was out in the courtyard. If they were, he doubted they'd stay standing for long.

There would be no work in the fields today. Jayvyn struggled to pull the door closed against the tremendous force of the wind.

All through the morning, wind and rain howled as the storm continued to strengthen. Conversation was not possible against the deafening roar of the storm.

The slaves huddled together on one of the lowest bunks. Walls bent and bowed wildly, threatening to crumble with every blast. Jayvyn doubted he'd ever witnessed a storm like this, recalling the violent tempests at sea. The impulse to run, somehow get away, was overwhelming—panic ensuing with the realization there was nowhere to go.

A large tree nearby splintered with an ear-shattering crack, followed by a deep thud, felt as much as heard.

The slaves watched disconcertedly as water rose until it began slopping over the lower bunk—a foot off of the floor. They climbed onto the second level. Water continued to rise. There had never been anything like it before.

By afternoon, the wind and rain mercifully began to taper off. Soon it had abated to the point where the slaves dared get off of the bunk and walk out into the knee-deep water.

Jayvyn and his hut mates emerged stunned at what they saw.

Trees were down everywhere. The one they'd heard fall close by was a large sycamore. It had smashed down across one of the cabins and now lay smothering it under large, broken branches. Other slaves were busily trying to help anyone trapped inside.

Jayvyn and the others ran to help.

A woman, hauled out of the wreckage—bloody, broken, but alive—was carried to a nearby cabin. Two others were recovered with lesser injuries. Two more miraculously emerged, shaken but relatively unscathed. They were lucky to have been shielded by a part of the roof that hadn't completely collapsed.

Three more were still inside as the slaves frantically pulled and sorted through the heavy, tangled debris. When they finally reached the inhabitants, they found them dead, pinned under water by debris. It was unclear whether they'd drowned or died from blunt trauma, but it really didn't matter.

The rain and wind died down against the fading crimson sky. A calm settled in as the skies cleared, making the surrounding ruin seem even more surreal. The slaves looked at each other, bewildered by what had happened to their world. Water coursed through the compound, around their legs, slowly finding its way back to the swamps.

It would take days to recede completely. Several shacks had all or part of their roofs torn away. Some were missing doors, window shutters, and parts of walls.

Victor arrived, making his way among the slaves to get a head count and a sense for the wounded. He reported that part of the roof had been torn from the barn and several outbuildings destroyed. No one could make it to the rice paddies. They were under five feet of water. It was total devastation.

The death toll climbed as the slaves discovered four small children drowned and five others killed either by debris or drowning.

Several animals perished as floodwaters overcame everything around. Even Master Turner's house suffered damage when the branch of a giant live oak sliced through the eave. He and his family weren't there, however, as they hadn't returned from their summer retreat in Rhode Island.

Jayvyn stood, shaking his head in disbelief at the utter shambles. Every part of the plantation he'd worked on for the past forty years was destroyed. The shacks skewed this way and that. The grounds strewn with debris. Mud streaked across the courtyard, filling the firepits and coating the floors of the huts. The rough chairs around the fires were relocated throughout the compound or in the swamps.

Jayvyn and his neighbors instinctively assumed a triage mentality, addressing the most pressing needs first.

The three occupants injured in the smashed hut were being attended to. The doctors in the group, all women, gathered in the cabin serving as the ad hoc hospital to begin tending the wounds as well as they could.

The first woman retrieved had a badly broken leg, several broken ribs, and multiple lacerations to her head and body. She was dazed and in rough shape.

The other two were better but still had injuries needing attention. One had a mangled shoulder, elbow, and several scrapes and bruises down one side of her body. The other had been hit in the back with heavy debris, leaving deep gouges and abrasions.

It was mayhem as the slaves tried to get their heads around the situation. Men wandered through the quarters looking for survivors. Several more injured emerged from the debris.

Soon, nightfall overtook them; it became too dark to work anymore. Slaves doubled and tripled up in huts still sound enough to house them.

Jayvyn's hut had survived comparatively well. Close to twenty slaves crowded the tiny shack—two to a bunk with more laid out on the mud caked floor. Dry things were simply not available. Nor was food.

Morning dawned sunny and bright. The slaves got busy sorting out the overwhelming mess before them.

Natural leaders rose from the ranks out of necessity.

Betty organized a group to look for anything useful—regardless of who it belonged to—setting things out to dry, taking stock of what they had.

Silas, Virgil, and a few others brought the dead to the edge of the woods for later burial. Some of the women consoled the families of the dead as best they could.

Frederick organized a group of men to work on damaged huts, retrieving boards, shutters and whatever they could find to stabilize walls.

Victor organized a few work parties to go to the barn and Master Turner's house, some recovered tools from outbuildings. Another group of men began tackling the enormous sycamore that had fallen across the courtyard.

Jayvyn joined others looking for items swept into the swamps. Shutters, doors, and planks ripped from walls and roofs were scattered far and wide. He slogged blindly through the muddy water, occasionally coming across a blanket, dress, or some personal item tangled in branches and rubble.

Jayvyn tugged repeatedly on a piece of fabric stubbornly lodged in the flotsam. A few boards and branches drifted lazily to the side. Suddenly, a foot popped out of the quagmire. Momentarily staggered, Jayvyn realized he'd been tugging on the pants of a dead man. Turning the body over, he saw it was Joseph. Jayvyn briefly reflected on how welcoming Joseph had been on his first day so long ago—now Jayvyn was here to bid him farewell. The body of one of his hut mates was found close by. Evidently, the two had left the shelter of their cabin during the storm—probably looking for a safer place, or perhaps their cabin was destroyed—no one would ever know for sure. They were taken to the edge of the woods to rest with the other dead.

All the surrounding fresh water sources had been contaminated by overflowing swamps and floating debris. Every crop on the plantation, including the slaves' garden, was thoroughly wiped out.

Limited food was salvaged from stores of rice and feed corn. A few dead animals were butchered for what meat could be salvaged before it rancidified. But that was it. Food and water were seriously deficient.

Mr. Dawson and his crew quickly took stock of all food, giving Victor strict instructions for rationing. Sustaining one hundred fifty hardworking slaves, along with Mr. Dawson's crew, wouldn't be easy with what they had.

Reports trickled in from surrounding townships. Charles Town was hit the hardest. Most of its buildings were decimated. Hundreds had died, and all but one of the ships in its harbor lay wrecked upon the shore.

Whole ships had been tossed against buildings like battering rams, reducing both ship and building to rubble. Other ships had been swept through bridges, crushing and eliminating them entirely. Hulls lay smashed and broken over the city's streets. Every dock ripped from its pilings and flung upon the battered city. All of it was a mad tangle of hulls, bricks, masts, rigging, carriages, roofs, steeples, and everything else in or around the point of land that had once been Charles Town.

The water had risen more than ten feet above its highest mark. Every sort of good or produce, either in storehouses or on the ships, had been ruined or flushed out to sea.

This was the state of widespread destruction afflicting every part of the coastal lowlands. Thousands of trees littered every road and byway, hindering any sort of relief effort. It was truly a scene of annihilation beyond the bounds of anyone's wildest nightmare.

News of the devastation traveled up the east coast. Communities far and wide began to respond as best they could, sending needed food and supplies. Of course, the first priority was getting food to the white folks.

The slaves went hungry—many perishing—before the first meager supplies of corn reached them.

Everyone who lived in the storm-ravaged area began the monstrous task of cleaning up and rebuilding. It was all anyone did—slaves and whites alike.

But no sooner had they begun—only *just* begun—to get their feet under them, when they were hit with a second hurricane—a mere two weeks after the first![*]

It was unbelievable!

The slaves had barely repaired a few of the roofs on the buildings still standing when they were deluged again.

Once again, they hunkered down in what was left of their quarters as wind and rain battered and shook their fragile huts. Jayvyn and those with him cringed with anticipation, wondering if this storm

---

[*] *On Sept. 30, 1752 the area would be hit by a second hurricane of lesser strength that would last over 2 days*

would reach the intensity of the last. The rain fell in torrents for two full days, water quickly rising to the same level as before.

The trees bent and the cabins shook. However, to their great relief, the storm proved far less destructive than the first.

Although no one on Turner's plantation died directly from this second storm, it was insult added to injury. The fields and grounds were flooded anew, and the stores they'd managed to collect largely ruined.

After both storms passed, the slaves went back to work, repairing all that had been lost over the terrible month.

In the months to follow, more slaves were lost to injury, starvation, and disease. They worked harder than ever with inadequate food and other provisions. Of the hundred and fifty or so slaves on Turner's plantation before disaster struck, thirty-seven would perish from events related to the two storms. Sadly, among them was the first woman who'd been rescued from under the fallen sycamore. Infection had set in; her injuries beyond the ability of the slaves to treat.

Eventually, the swamps retreated to normal levels, and the burial grounds dried out enough to bury the dead. Funerals were kept small and brief. The priority was to get the bodies in the ground where they could safely decompose without further contaminating living areas and spreading disease.

The slaves worked longer hours and under harder conditions than any remembered. The plantation and Charles Town were slowly rebuilt, and rice crops staggered back to life.

As testament to their hard work, the year following the disaster, slaves managed to bring rice yields back to half their pre-storm levels.

By the year following, 1754, South Carolina's rice production had remarkably been restored to pre-hurricane levels, although it would take many more years before all of the damage would be fully overcome.

However, the complete restoration of Charles Town and its colony would be hampered by forces not readily apparent to the slaves, forces that would unleash a groundswell of change yet to come.

– 39 –

Going Home

In the years following the disastrous hurricane of 1752, a growing chain of events sparked significant changes that would ultimately transform the colony of South Carolina as well as the rest of colonial America.

Although fast afoot, these changes weren't immediately apparent to the slaves, who were doing all they could just to stay alive while serving the increased demands placed upon them by the white community.

Besides rebuilding the plantations and restoring rice production, the slaves were also pressed into service restoring the community infrastructure—roads, bridges, buildings—both in the countryside and Charles Town itself. Work was much harder than usual, with longer days, higher demands, less food, and harsher treatment. Jayvyn and his fellow slaves all agreed these were some of the hardest times they could ever remember, made even harder by the fact their living quarters remained in desperate need of repairs as well.

As with all things, the slaves' needs were last to get attention and would have to be attended to in what little time they had to themselves. Evenings and Sundays were consumed with this task as the tired and worn slaves restored their living areas piece by piece. Some of it never did get back to its former state. Half-trees stood rooted in the ground—slip-shod repairs and deeply eroded ground remained as permanent testimony to the terrible storm.

In time, however, repairs to plantations and the community were accomplished, and the slaves' quarters restored well enough that life around the campfires resumed its place. As before, this was where the slaves caught up with the news around them.

From the grapevine, they learned many new Europeans had been migrating to South Carolina—not just British, but people from many European countries. The British had been attracting more Caucasians in order to increase the ratio of whites to Native Americans and Blacks.*

"Y'all heah bout dem white folk been comin on da ship?" asked Silas, who always seemed to be the one to bring up new and interesting news.

"Yeah man, I head dey be lotta em," replied Lucas

"I heah dey talkin all kinda diffn't word we nebba heah a'fo. Dat what I heah from sum brudda what be trav'ln wid dey massa to a place call Melia.†

"Say dey talk sumpin call'd German. Say dey don know a word dey sayin," said Virgil shaking his head.

"Dey say ain't many nigga out dat way," chimed Martin.

** Governor Robert Johnson established the Township Act of 1730 in an effort to attract "hardy, fighting men" from Europe as protection from Native Americans, Spanish, and French forces as well as to balance out the large population of Africans. Populations of Welsh, Scotch, Irish, German, and Swiss significantly increased. Total population in South Carolina tripled from 1730 – 1775, mostly after 1750*

† Amelia was an early township settled by Swiss and German speaking Europeans, known today as St. Matthews, SC

"Dat caus'n dem white folk is po. Dey ain't like de white folk round heah," added Virgil.

"Yeah, well dey got a lotta injun out dat way dey be fightn' alla time," remarked Silas.

"French too, dey help'n dem injun. Lotta kill'n be goin on."

These were stories Jayvyn had been hearing for a while about what everyone was calling the Cherokee War.[*]

The British pushed to expand territory to the west in order to accommodate all of the new European immigrants. In doing so, they came up against fierce resistance from the Cherokee Indians, backed by French colonists who occupied territories to the west and north.

"Mo nigga be comin from Africa too. Dey be lotta mo folk round heah n' ebba a'fo.

"Georgia got dem slave now, lot o em[†]. An de plantation round heah be gitt'n bigga n' ebba." Martin quipped.

"Yeah, sho be diffn't," remarked Silas as he chucked another log onto the fire, sending a trail of sparks high into the night sky.

"Heah dem rich folk in Chas-ton none too happy wid de Brit deese day. Seem dem Eng'sh ain't hep none wid de fixn up afta dat bad hu-cane.

"Dem Brit tell em what to do n' take dey money fo de rice but don't wanna hep out none," said Ceasar, who'd been listening quietly.

---

[*] *Known globally as the Seven Years War, in the American Colonies as the French and Indian War, and in South Carolina as the Cherokee War.*

[†] *Georgia officially legalized slavery in 1751*

Silas added, "Bartholomew say he heah Massa Tuhna talk'n wid anudda white man dat he sick n tired o' de Brit bein all in hid biddness alla time."

News had circulated about tensions rising between the local South Carolina government and the British founders.

This became particularly evident after the Great Hurricane, when England failed to provide funding to the colony to cope with the devastation. In addition to funding repairs, the local government had to import food stocks from northern colonies at high prices in order to feed the population until their own agriculture rebounded. Local prices for just about everything had gone through the roof in the wake of the disaster.

Eventually, the South Carolina Commons House found its treasury without sufficient funds to pay its debts. Several wealthy plantation owners who'd stood security for the local treasury were forced to liquidate their entire estates to prevent default. South Carolina narrowly escaped total economic collapse, but the treasury's guarantors lost everything.

Disenchantment between plantation barons and the Crown grew substantially.

The fallout filtered through the local community and was echoed by the bosses on the plantation. The slaves, of course, overheard these conversations.

Although the details remained foggy, the message was the colonists, especially wealthy plantation owners, were growing tired of paying a good portion of their profits to the Crown while not receiving much in return.

The bottom line was the citizens of the British colonies were finding more and more reason to seek their independence from England.

This was all very confusing for the slaves, who'd always assumed South Carolina was the same as England. After all, it was the English who'd kidnapped them and brought them here in the first place.

But other seismic changes were taking place, further dividing the colonists and their British patrons.

News had been circulating about land routes connecting northern and southern colonies, in particular something called the Great Wagon Road.

Native American footpaths were eventually widened by horses then wagons as white settler populations grew in the colonies. Now, these footpaths had become major transportation routes where people could travel from north to south or vice versa without having to go to sea.

This facilitated easier trade over land, migration of colonial citizens, and the spread of ideologies.*

Preachers from the north were traveling these roads, bringing new ideas on how Christianity should be taught and practiced. This differed from what the Anglican Church prescribed, causing further dust-ups within the communities of South Carolina.

** Known as "the Great Wagon Road to Philadelphia," as listed on maps in 1753, it came to stretch over 800 mi. facilitating large shifts in population.*

It became a frequent topic of conversation among the slaves on Turner's plantation as a preacher named George Whitefield made himself well known in the area.*

One evening, while sitting around the fires after dinner, Silas brought this up for discussion.

"Y'all heah about dat preacha, call hissef Whitefield?

"Been comin' 'round Chas-ton stir'n all dem white folk up. He be tell'n em dat God be fo da nigga de same as de white folk, 'n dey ain't lik'n it none."

Betty, who was sitting nearby said, "I heah dat Silas.

"Dey say he be hav'n dem outdoe sermon what de nigga can go 'n heah de word o de Lawd."

"Ain't no good stir'n dem white folk up like dat," said Ceasar.

"Next ting dey be gitt'n tuffa on us, beat'n us down agin."

Betty retorted, "Well, Ceasa, he be tell'n 'm dat it no good ta be whupp'n on de slave.

"He tell'n de white man heah dat we all be human, just like de white folk, an d'serve betta."

The other men around the fire gave a few harrumphs as they contemplated this.

Old Ceasar mumbled, "Dat be de day, dat be de day."

Word had it Whitefield taught that African Americans were the spiritual equals of whites and slave owners shouldn't abuse their slaves, although he advocated for slavery and even owned slaves himself.

---

* *George Whitefield, one of the founders of Methodism and the evangelical movement*

But he caused quite a ruckus in South Carolina with his condemnation of South Carolinians' cruelty toward slaves and Blacks in general. He went so far as to declare Negros are human, which infuriated many citizens of South Carolina and got him barred from preaching on several occasions.

His view was God acted through the heart of each individual, and therefore was available to whomever opened their heart to him, white or black.

This was in stark contrast to standard Anglican doctrine which held God acted exclusively through the hierarchy of the church—starting with the pope, who then passed God onto the cardinals, who then passed God down to bishops, and so forth, until eventually reaching the priests, who could then pass God's gift on to the congregation. According to the Church of England, the only way to receive God's blessing was to attend a formal Anglican church—which was unavailable to non-whites.

But Father Whitefield's philosophy was gaining popularity among a growing number of white citizens. They started referring to themselves as the "New Lights," as opposed to the "Old Lights," who followed the Anglican version of Christianity.

Obviously, the word that Negros were human was enough to make Whitefield's teachings big news among the slaves. But it also worked to further divisions among white colonists.

There were citizens who continued to support the Crown, referring to themselves as Royalists.

However, many were becoming increasingly discontent with English rule and wanted their independence—a group soon to be known as Whigs and Patriots.

One thing was clear to both whites and Blacks alike—large changes were in the wind.

Some eight years had passed since the Great Hurricane of 1752. All during that time, undercurrents of social change were hard at work in the colonies.

For Jayvyn, however, he was still a slave, and would remain so for the rest of his life.

Now sixty-three, or so he thought, he was no longer the supple young man he'd once been. His back ached and he moved much slower, somewhat stooped. The years in slavery had taken their toll.

He'd seen many things over his time. Many, many slaves had come and gone. It had been fifty-one years since Jayvyn had been taken from his homeland. How he'd ever survived, he couldn't fathom. There were none who shared all this time with him, but he remembered quite a few who'd made strong impressions on him.

Jayvyn thought about Jacob often—of when they first met, chained together on the schooner, *Dorothy*. It was such a long, long time ago, and they were so young.

He remembered being auctioned off in Charles Town and how uncanny it was both of them wound up purchased by the same buyer. Fate was funny like that. You never knew whose lives would intersect yours and for how long.

Jayvyn thought about Hannah, too. The would-be queen among her people, forced into a life of slavery instead.

How unlikely that her and Jacob's lives would end up merging so beautifully—considering their tribes had been such bitter enemies in Africa. Everything seemed to fall into place so well when they finally had their family started, the gift of children bringing new dimensions of joy and happiness.

But, as Jayvyn had learned so many times over the years, nothing is ever certain in life. Fate turns in an instant. Theirs ended up being the saddest of the many sad stories he carried with him through life.

Jayvyn had never cried so long and hard as the night Hannah was buried. Sadness clung like a shroud of darkness, until finally he found peace imagining the family reunited—free and eternally happy in the afterlife.

And then there was Victor. He'd liked Victor quite a lot. He was fair and always took good care of everyone. Always finding a good balance between managing production and seeing to the slaves' welfare.

More than anything, Victor had modeled the kind of wisdom and discretion Jayvyn had so admired in both Andrew and his father.

Victor had lived a good life—such as any Ajamatau would be proud of. He never knew what Victor's tribe had been, but that was Victor's whole point—it simply didn't matter.

Victor had left them some eight or so years ago, taken by fever shortly after the hurricane. Jayvyn assumed he was about sixty-five.

Victor was laid to rest somewhere out in that big swampy graveyard, free now to join his ancestors in Sierra Leone.

Another who'd succumbed to fever was Old Margaret.

How he and everyone had loved Old Margaret! She was so full

of love and caring. She brought untold joy and happiness to the slaves at Turner's plantation throughout her years. Always there for their hardships and celebrations, through thick and thin. Jayvyn had often thought she was what Julia would have become—had she not been defiled by the white man and driven to suicide.

The sadness of so many wonderful lives lost for so little stayed with Jayvyn over the years.

But Old Margaret lived a long time. Old Margaret was wise indeed. As with others, Jayvyn warmed to the possibility her spirit, too, was free now, spreading love to all who passed her way.

And there were more—oh, so many more. It truly was a wonder to become one of the old hands at the plantation. It seemed the majority were short-timers, of five or ten years or less.

But there was the exception.

Take Bartholomew, for example. Jayvyn had almost forgotten about him. He was such a fixture around the place it seemed as if he were part of the very landscape. He just drifted around, mostly taking care of Master Turner's odd chores. He knew everything about the place, from the big white house to the barn and everything in between.

He lived in a room attached to the big white house and drove Master Turner's wagon on most occasions. Jayvyn remembered Bartholomew from his first day in Charles Town, the day they'd traveled from the auction to the plantation. It seemed impossible; it was *so* long ago! Bartholomew had been on Master Turner's plantation since the beginning. He'd seen it all.

If the slaves' wanted to know something, they asked Bartholomew.

He was never seen out in the paddies, however. That just wasn't his place. Besides, he walked with a pronounced limp and was just too old and worn out for that kind of work.

One time Jayvyn asked Bartholomew to tell him how he got his limp, and Bartholomew obliged.

Back when the plantation was in its early days, back in the late 1600's, he was working with a group of slaves to build Master Turner's barn. When they got to raising one of the bents, a rope parted, and the bent crashed down, pinning Bartholomew's leg underneath and breaking it badly.* The break never healed right, and he'd walked with that limp ever since. So, Master Turner put him to work on lighter tasks, and eventually he became his driver and personal servant.

Jayvyn, as well as the rest of the slaves, enjoyed the old man, who always had stories to offer, sometimes humorous, which were sorely needed around the plantation.

Jayvyn figured the old man must have been in his late eighties when he passed. He was found one morning lying in his bed, looking just like he was asleep. His life had reached the end of its earthly journey, just as naturally as one could ever want.

The slaves gave him a special burial, one with songs of hope, joy, and thanks for the blessing of a full life, as he, too, was laid to rest in the swampy ground.

There was no doubt about the significant role music had played throughout Jayvyn's life. He fondly recalled joyful occasions when songs broke out around the campfires at night with much clapping

---

** A bent is the term for an assembled, structural cross section in traditional timber frame construction*

and dancing. He remembered, as well, singing with slaves in the fields to take their minds off their pain and help the days go by easier. Just like Old Margaret, music was there like a salve to assist with joys and miseries alike.

Many songs contained lyrics of hope and salvation inspired by the Bible, as Christianity came to replace other religions the slaves might have brought from Africa.

Jayvyn noticed Christianity increasing as slaves arrived from other plantations. Many new slaves had spent time in their masters' houses as maids and butlers and heard their masters and families holding worship in their homes. Although services generally didn't include the slaves, they picked a lot up just by being around.

Jayvyn remembered Bartholomew telling the story of how he heard Master Turner reading aloud to himself one day and asked him what it was all about.

Master Turner had replied, "The good book is talking to me, Bartholomew."

Intrigued, Bartholomew inquired, "What it say, Massa Tuhna?"

To which Master Turner replied, "Many things, Bartholomew. It tells me how to live a good life so that I might reach salvation and receive the good Lord's blessing."

Of course, this interested Bartholomew greatly.

He told the other slaves when no one was around, he'd sneak up to the good book and hold it to his ear hoping he might hear it talking too. He wanted to listen to some of what Master Turner was telling him about.

Bartholomew said he never did hear the good book talk, but

from then on, he paid attention whenever the family read from its pages and shared what he heard with the other slaves.

They were stories of hope and salvation, which so many needed in their daily lives as they fought the ravages of slavery.

It would be a long time, though, before the white man allowed his religion to be formally shared with the slaves. So, they had to keep and grow this practice among themselves in the privacy of their quarters.

Ultimately, this changed when the preachers from the north, the New Lights, started bringing their new perspective to the practice of Christianity.*

Over time, Jayvyn began to pick up and appreciate much of what the slaves brought from the good book. He eventually came to equate God with Ata Emit—since God was considered the Creator of all things and Ata Emit to Whom belongs the universe.

For a long time, though, Jayvyn struggled to understand the difference. He envisioned God as an omnificent being existing outside the realm of the universe, serving only the interests of the white man. This, as opposed to Ata Emit, the force driving everything in the universe for the harmony and good of all things.

The biggest conundrum was what he understood to be the moral dictates of the Christian God.

---

* *Because slaves were considered to be sub-human and without souls that could be redeemed through religion, and also in order to keep them illiterate and without education, white people worked to deprive them of these institutions for quite some time, although a movement called the Great Awakening sought to change this as progressive, evangelistic preachers split from the Anglican church doctrine seeking to promote a more egalitarian God, a movement which created significant upheaval among the colonists*

According to the white man, God ascertained white superiority over all other races. Therefore, the white man had a moral obligation to exert his God-given dominance over other races for the good of all. It was the fundamental argument by which the white man justified and defended his duty to enslave Jayvyn's race.

This, however, was quite contrary to what he interpreted as the word of God.

For instance, Genesis 1:27 proclaims *God created man in his own image.*

Acts 17:26 further clarifies *he made from one man every nation of mankind to live on all the face of the earth.*

In Galatians 3:28, it is written *there is neither Jew nor Greek, there is neither slave nor free, there is no male and female, for you are all one in Christ Jesus.*

Nothing is mentioned distinguishing one race or class of humans as greater than another; rather, 'mankind' equates all men created under God. To claim or suggest otherwise would be to discredit the word of God and his creation.

From the teachings found in the good book, Jayvyn had heard the phrase—"*the peace of God, which passeth all understanding…*"

He substituted 'Ata Emit' to get "*the peace of Ata Emit, which passeth all understanding…*"

According to the teachings of his elders, Ata Emit is a great and provident force beyond the ability of mankind to understand. You just accepted it.

Jayvyn understood the Bible passage to mean—have faith in God's goodness and benevolence. The full passage in Philippians 4:7

states—*And the peace of God, which passeth all understanding, shall guard your hearts and your thoughts in Christ Jesus.*

He believed both the good book and his elders were making the same promise.

Some things would always remain just beyond the reach of mankind's understanding and simply had to be taken as an article of faith.

However, Jayvyn had always been struck by the use of the word "peace" in the passage and thought of it often.

'Peace,' in and of itself, seemed to be a concept that 'passeth' the understanding of mankind in general—the injustice of slavery being a prime example.

Mankind just didn't seem to have the capacity to understand and practice simple principles to create lasting peace in this world, any more than mankind could fully grasp 'to whom belongs the universe.'

Somehow, all other creatures of the world seemed much better equipped to live by these basic principles. Non-human creatures are more adept at accepting, working with, and abiding by the forces of nature in ways that ensure their species will thrive and survive alongside all other species. His people, the Ajamatau, believe these creatures, being of the natural world, hold greater status than men—as do all things of the natural world—the earth; the sky; its clouds and weather; even the passage of time itself.

Among all other creatures on Earth, mankind has the unique power of choice. It can be his strength or weakness, depending on how he decides to use it.

It harkened, for Jayvyn, the essence of wisdom, as Andrew had made clear so long ago when explaining the lessons learned from the futampaf. It was what the tribal elders strove to teach their young people—so they'd understand how to foster strength and peace in their tribe—in order to live and thrive—in harmony with nature—from the infinite benevolence of the universe.

At the root of things, Jayvyn believed this to be the intent of the teachings in the Bible as well.

Jayvyn had spent much time thinking back on his experiences, both on his ocean passages and on the plantations.

He never forgot the terrible day he was taken from his village and the nightmarish ocean voyage that followed. It was the time during which everything in his world had been shattered beyond recognition—the terror of being abducted and confronted with constant pain. The sorrow he felt at the loss of so many just like him—as he was sailed so far, far from his home, family, and everything he'd ever known.

He thought about his arrival in Barbados and the unspeakable acts of barbarity he saw there—how it just seemed to get worse and worse. He thought about his and the other slaves' confusion as they were kept in stockades and taught to work without any reward other than the avoidance of pain.

The images of ghastly torture inflicted on Jayvyn's fellow Africans never left his mind. He'd wondered, on more than one occasion, how the poor woman, whose front teeth had been permanently knocked out, had ever learned to cope and survive—or *if* she had—throughout her entire life.

So much suffering for merely eating a yam!

His experiences at the sugar plantation lived strongly in his memory.

He often thought about Andrew, drawing on the subtle but important things he'd taught him over time.

He wondered if Andrew knew how much his mentorship had meant to him. The lessons he'd learned taught him what he needed to know to survive. Without them, Jayvyn doubted he would have.

It would be hard for Jayvyn to explain how the experiences of he and Andrew's cruel punishments had taught him important lessons—things he'd benefit from for the rest of his life—but they did. He recalled how difficult it was to comprehend how any man's punishment and pain could result in good for another. But now he understood, in the great context of life, it can.

This came clear to him through the lessons he'd learned from the good book—as the man, Jesus, had suffered punishment and pain for the good of all men going forward.

Jayvyn considered how the bruises he'd suffered for not accepting his new name had strengthened the others in his hut. It affirmed to them the sacredness of their true selves—their unique spirit.

Andrew's sacrifice had inspired and strengthened the slaves' resolve to fend for themselves and care for each other.

In the same way, he wanted to think the scars he carried on his back would somehow contribute to freedom and salvation for his people—to be free at last!

Jayvyn thought many times of his old friend Baahir and everything they'd learned together. How they could find just the smallest amount of love and hope where none seemed to exist. How that could be shared—even without words—with someone you knew nothing about.

These lessons were made all the more powerful after he and Baahir had learned to communicate verbally and found out more about each other—revealing differences that in another place and time might have made them adversaries.

But that was not the time or place where they met.

Jayvyn marveled how the invisible and mysterious hand of the universe had somehow brought them back together after becoming estranged on the beach. It was then they discovered the magic of understanding and acceptance—of appreciating and respecting the differences between them. It was something that made each of them stronger rather than weaker.

It was one of the most significant lessons of his life, a memory that made his heart sing during his darkest hours. One he tried to share with others whenever he had the chance.

Jayvyn knew Baahir must be about his age and wondered what his life had been like. They'd shared so many experiences together and learned so much.

The last time he'd seen his friend, he noticed changes taking place in him. Baahir had been picking up on Andrew's lessons and opening his mind to new ways of seeing his world.

If there was anything he wished for Baahir, it was that his soul, too, had become as enriched as Jayvyn's by everything he'd learned in life. It was a richness that had given Jayvyn a sort of freedom. A freedom unbound by mortal constraints; a freedom he could know even though enslaved.

Jayvyn had indeed seen and experienced many things throughout his life and had grown to accept and learn from them as best he could.

He'd even reached a point where he no longer resented the white man for the things he did. In a way only he could understand, he'd come to forgive the white man. They were driven by powers and forces not even they could understand.

Jayvyn had often wondered if it could have been different—if somehow the Black man had been corrupt enough to take white men into slavery—in a world where the tables were reversed.

He wondered what this might have looked like. He wondered if he could have been coerced into such evil deeds had he been born into a different culture—one with influences of the type that had driven the white man to commit such acts.

But it was impossible. Jayvyn couldn't imagine himself acting that way. He hadn't been raised with those cultural influences. Thus, he was not that person—simple as that—he could not know what that would be like.

But it did cause him to wonder if these white men might have found themselves just as unable to comprehend the practice of slavery if they'd had the same cultural influences as he.

It was through this kind of empathy and reasoning that Jayvyn discovered his path to forgiveness.

When he'd finally reached this understanding—and was truly able to forgive—it was as if a great weight had been lifted from his soul.

His spirit soared, blossoming full and bright, filling his whole being in a way he hadn't experienced since the carefree days of his childhood in Africa.

One evening, as Jayvyn happily contemplated these thoughts, lying on his bunk in the house he'd lived for so long, he found himself, once again, standing amongst the ferns and mist in his beloved forest.

The incessant, calming sounds of the jungle cradled his spirit like an invisible blanket. Every cell in his body tingled with life. There was no fear—only the sensation of being one with Ata Emit.

Jayvyn found himself moving through the jungle in absolute silence, as if on a carpet of air. He glided past lush, dew-coated leaves, splashed with flowers in brilliant colors. Vines spilled gracefully from giant trees, dense canopies allowing intermittent bursts of sunlight to dapple the foliage. A cool breeze brushed his face. The familiar scents of tannin, sweet fruit, and floral nectar caressed his senses.

The image of Caksusa appeared out of the mist like a chimera, holding out his hand as one might if inviting another to pass this way.

Without effort or intention, Jayvyn easily progressed through the bush, coming to the trunk of a great kapok tree—its wide, flat roots extending outward.

His father stood there, naked and in perfect form. He held out his hand, saying, "Well, my son, you're here; let's get to work," as if it were the most natural thing in the world.

Jayvyn's spirit had returned home, free at last.

Afterword

Thank you for reading. I truly hope you found Jayvyn's story to be shocking, tragic, and horrible. At the same time, I hope you found it to be thought-provoking and enlightening. There's no pretty way to tell the story of the Trans-Atlantic Slave Trade, especially not from a slave's perspective. Although fiction, the story I crafted was carved from historical facts and records. After conducting all of my research, I have no doubt Jayvyn's story doesn't come close to telling the worst of it. There were over twelve and a half million Africans taken from their homes and families and forced into slavery during the Trans-Atlantic Slave Trade. As far as historians can tell, some two million Africans perished during the middle passage alone. This doesn't account for how many might have died before ever reaching the ships, and certainly many millions more died in slavery after reaching the shores of their destinations. Furthermore, these grim statistics do not consider the mortality of those born into slavery. It was difficult to decide how much of the horrors should be reflected in the pages of my book. Many times, as I was writing, I felt I might have gone too far, yet I also know the atrocities reached far greater depths—horrors that lie beyond the darkest regions of our imagination. On more than one occasion, when I closed my eyes at night, my mind fought against the reality that any human being could have the capacity for inflicting such high levels of pain and suffering on any living thing, let alone another human being. However sad and disturbing the truth is, it would be naïve to believe otherwise. Out of the twelve and a half million Africans who were taken, twelve and a half million stories remain untold.

As I'm sure anyone who has written any sort of book based on historical facts would agree, the task proved to be about two-thirds research to one-third writing. In researching the facts informing this narrative, I referenced innumerable sources from around the globe—far too many to list. I found many useful encyclopedic references from the National Archives of the U.K., the University of Oxford, the University of Cambridge, and the Royal Museums Greenwich. Many sources out of Africa informed my knowledge about various tribal origins, conflicts, migratory patterns, cultural habits, pre-colonial history, geography, ethnobotany, and much more—even just to list the categories here would be exhaustive. Suffice it to say, the study of Africa alone would be a fascinating but life-consuming endeavor. I found overwhelming volumes of information in the Library of Congress, Harvard, Brown, and other universities, historical associations, the National Archives, and more. Thankfully, most information in today's world doesn't know borders. Many of my references were global organizations dedicated to the remembrance and chronology of important history. Organizations such as AAIHS, UNESCO, ASWAD, the Colonial Williamsburg Foundation, the United Nations, and so many more. Most times my browser was so jammed with tabs it was hard to separate them.

Of course, none of this would be possible without the hard work of scholars and historians who have devoted their attention to studying and recording the events surrounding the Trans-Atlantic Slave Trade. To all of them I say thank-you!!

There is, however, one resource in particular I would like to draw your attention to: a massive body of work containing many volumes of invaluable first-person accounts with an interesting history of its own. In response to the Great Depression, our government embarked on developing programs to provide work for Americans under the umbrella of the New Deal. One branch of this initiative, thankfully, was dedicated to providing work for those engaged in the arts, including writers. Out of this came a program known as the Federal Writers' Project, which employed writers to interview and take down testimonial from Americans who lived at the turn of the century. Within these records are thousands of first-person stories from ex-slaves that otherwise would have been lost to history. I became fascinated with reading these accounts, which were most often recorded using phonetic transcriptions reflecting the vernacular of the person being interviewed.

In time, the program met with harsh criticism from some who felt it less valuable than other programs resulting in hard infrastructure. It was even accused of fostering communism. It only lasted from 1936–40, but within that time, over ten thousand writers worked to create more than three hundred thousand records containing over twenty-three hundred first-person accounts of former slaves. Today, the hard infrastructure, although having served its purpose well, has all but crumbled away. The history, however, remains to be carried with us forever.

In the preface to this book, I mentioned my inspiration arose out of the ill-conceived changes the Florida State Board of Education made to its curriculum requirements for teaching Black history as part of Governor Ron DeSantis' "Stop Woke Act."

In the span of writing this book, other high ranking public officials have joined this misguided initiative, including contenders for our nation's highest office, the presidency. One unabashedly proclaimed the causes of the Civil War were merely disagreements by states over how the government would run. Nothing was even mentioned about slavery, which any grade schooler should know was the primary issue. This was further topped off by declaring the United States has "never been a racist country."

As if the presidential race were some sort of competition for who could be the most ignorant of history, another candidate declared that that the whole Civil War could have simply been negotiated away, intimating that the fight to end slavery in the U.S. was ultimately unnecessary. One of these candidates is now president elect and will be in office by the time this book is available.

For some reason, the human race seems to have difficulty accepting certain realities. For instance, in the early 1600s, Galileo tried to tell the world that Earth and the other planets in our solar system orbited the sun—a handy bit of information for the time. What a mistake! In 1616, he was ordered by the Church "to abstain completely from teaching or defending this doctrine and opinion or from discussing it... to abandon completely... the opinion that the sun stands still at the center of the world and the earth moves, and henceforth not to hold, teach, or defend it in any way whatever, either orally or in writing." They were so averse to the idea that many wouldn't even look through a telescope to observe his findings.

Galileo was subsequently convicted of heresy and sentenced to spend the rest of his life under house arrest for his bold assertions. In fact, the Church only begrudgingly consented to drop its prohibition and charge of heresy for discussing the Earth orbiting the Sun in 1758. Even to this day, it hasn't completely conceded the point.

Think of the hotbed of controversy that must have subsumed the world for over one hundred fifty years as society fought amongst itself to sort out those educational standards! Think of all the scholars who were deprived this critical information; think of what they might have achieved! Why are we so afraid to open our hearts and minds to information that will only help us improve?

Today, the hot topic of critical race theory seems to share some of the same attributes. At its core, critical race theory is nothing more than recognizing that there are elements embedded within our culture that originated and grew out of our founding. It just so happens this country was founded from British colonies that embraced and relied on the widespread practice of slavery.

There's no disputing that many bad habits arising from slavery followed us out of the Civil War. How could they not? When the Civil War began, there were nearly four million enslaved Africans in the U.S., representing twelve and a half percent of our total population. After the war, all of these slaves suddenly became free and had rights under reconstruction amendments made to the U.S. Constitution. Not all of our white citizens were entirely comfortable with that. Out of this grew the so-called Jim Crow laws, laws enacted by state and local legislatures, which were really just extensions of the Black codes the British brought with them from Barbados in their initial founding.

Elements of Jim Crow persisted in our country until 1965. The specific laws referred to as Jim Crow included mandated racial segregation—prohibition of inter-racial marriage, inter-racial dating, inter-racial adoption, inter-racial social interactions of any sort. Voting rights were restricted—taxes and literacy tests were legally enacted to ascertain voter eligibility. Racially restrictive clauses were allowed in housing covenants—codes of ethics were developed for realtors to discourage introducing races that might devalue neighboring properties. Blacks were segregated and only allowed certain roles in the military, jails were segregated, and the list goes on. By some estimates, the total number of Jim Crow laws exceeded three thousand.

Because of segregation, public facilities and other public accommodations for Blacks were demonstrably inferior. Text books were different for Blacks. Schools and health care facilities in Black communities were underfunded. Blacks weren't afforded the same education or employment opportunities as whites.

Because communities of race reflected clear disadvantages, redlining became a justified and standard practice among corporations like banks, insurance companies, grocery chains, all seeking to establish themselves in prime communities promising the most favorable returns. Likewise, assessments of insurance and credit risks followed the same practice. These are facts. It's easy to make the case supporting critical race theory. Critical race theory is a byproduct of our history. But there's one thing critical race theory does not do. It does not demand shame or guilt. That's a personal choice, and a weak one at that. But it's become the crux of a social issue widening the divide between us. Critical race theory has been vilified and weaponized. It's become a source of anger and scorn instead of healing and reconciliation. We, in the present tense, didn't forge the foundation from which our country grew any more than we outlawed teaching the truth about planetary motion. I'll wager not too many of us would feel guilty about the latter, so why should we be so sensitive about understanding and correcting the wrongs of our forebears? Instead of embracing the opportunity to accept what is true, learn from the mistakes of our past, and become better people, we've chosen to turn the issue into a weapon to use against each other. Are these the lessons we learn in our churches? Is it what we want to teach our children? Is it what we truly want to believe?

Here's a strange fact about critical race theory: opposition to it today, along with "anti-Wokeness," has become the battle cry of the far right. The strange part is, Jim Crow laws and the resulting divisiveness were the work of democrats! That's right! Republicans made up the backbone of the abolitionists who provided civil rights protections under the Constitution. In fact, the term "Woke" originates from a group of militant young republicans in 1860 who called themselves the Wide Awakes in support of Lincoln's prerogative to abolish slavery. From there, the Black community adopted the term "Woke," as meaning "stay woke," or keep your eyes open to racially motivated threats in white America. But it was democrats who formed militant groups such as the Ku Klux Klan and others that violently overthrew Southern Republican legislatures. They ran republican office holders out of town so they could seize back power in the southern states and legislate Jim Crow laws. So, then, if we are going to assign blame to a political party, which party should bear the shame for perpetuating racism? The point is, straight party lines can't be drawn. That was then; this is now.

We know slavery and racism are wrong, and we know there are elements embedded in our societal norms that originated and grew out of our founding, e.g., critical race theory. Only if we recognize this truth will we be able to find and repair the flaws that continue to harm our society through racism.

We're better than that now. We know more. We're smarter. And if we can accept the truth and deal with the problem, we will live in a better world.

Discussion starters

- Does the book create a useful framework for understanding and accepting diversity? In what ways?
- Discuss the various stages of Jayvyn and Baahir's relationship and its influence on each of them.
- What role did the 'futampaf' play throughout the story? Can you make comparisons in today's society?
- Discuss Andrew and his role in the story.
- William's demise came to symbolize several things other than punishment. Discuss what they were and what it meant.
- How did Julia's short life impact the story?
- What were your impressions about the practice of slavery among some tribes in Africa?
- Discuss the price of family life for the enslaved, e.g. Silas and Clara's children.
- Discuss how Jacob, Hannah, and family impacted the story.
- Discuss the difference in historical perspective for the enslaved vs. the rest of the world.
- Do you think that retelling the horrors of slavery went too far? Do you think they went far enough? Why or why not?
- How did Jayvyn's spiritual beliefs differ from conventional religious doctrine? How were they similar?
- What is forgiveness? How does one achieve it? In what way was forgiveness essential to Jayvyn?
- Did Jayvyn die a poor man? In what way was his life good?
- Should our civic leaders and teachers be responsible for historical accuracy? Why is this important?

About The Author

Peter D. Brown is a Maine based author of historical fiction with a deep interest in social justice and a passion for preserving history. His writing relies on a deep commitment to historical accuracy while aiming to illuminate stories of the oppressed or misunderstood. Presented alongside proclivities typical of the human condition, he challenges his readers to confront uncomfortable truths and engage with the complexities of the human experience.

Retired now from formal enterprise, Peter lives in a quiet, pastoral township in Maine with his loving wife and two dogs, where he enjoys ample quietude and peace to gain inspiration, sort out his thoughts, and bring them to life.

Through his work, Peter hopes to promote thoughtful conversations about the enduring impact of history on contemporary society.

---

https://peter-d-brown.com

www.ingramcontent.com/pod-product-compliance
Lightning Source LLC
Chambersburg PA
CBHW030515130726
47901CB00014B/982